MW01493553

CRUELTY FREE

CRUELTY FREE

A NOVEL

CAROLINE GLENN

wm

WILLIAM MORROW
An Imprint of HarperCollins*Publishers*

HarperCollins books may be purchased for educational, business, or sales promotional use. For information, please email the Special Markets Department at SPsales@harpercollins.com.

hc.com

FIRST EDITION

Designed by Nancy Singer

Library of Congress Cataloging-in-Publication Data

Names: Glenn, Caroline author
Title: Cruelty free : a novel / Glenn Caroline.
Description: First edition. | New York : William Morrow, 2026.
Identifiers: LCCN 2025011644 | ISBN 9780063419193 hardcover | ISBN 9780063419209 paperback | ISBN 9780063419216 ebook
Subjects: LCGFT: Horror fiction | Novels
Classification: LCC PS3607.L445 .C78 2026 | DDC 813/.6—dc23/eng/20250402
LC record available at https://lccn.loc.gov/2025011644

ISBN 978-0-06-341919-3

Printed in the United States of America

25 26 27 28 29 LBC 5 4 3 2 1

To my family,
who suggested I write a love story.
This was the closest I got.

You don't need my autograph.
If you needed it, I'd give it to you.

—Bob Dylan, 1966

I know it's hard to see Britney Spears as a human being,
but trust me, she is. She's a person, she's like you or I.
And I don't know about you, but I know that I would be
pretty shaken up right now . . . All you people care about is
readers and making money off of her. She's a human!

—Cara Cunningham, "Leave Britney Alone"

CRUELTY FREE

PROLOGUE

Ten years ago, a senseless, horrific crime shocked the country. At the center of it was one of the most famous young actresses on the planet, Lila Devlin. In a world so desensitized to violence and tragedy, the staggering response hearkened back to the crime-of-the-century scandals of the 1920s and '30s, back when the country read the same newspaper and listened to the same radio reports. Here was a respected actress at the peak of her career who made a single, colossal mistake and triggered an irreparable sequence of events that rippled across social media, the press, and Los Angeles's elite. It was like watching a house of cards collapse in real time.

The tragedy of Lila Devlin has remained in the public consciousness for as long as it has not because she was a world-famous celebrity, not because of the salaciousness of the murder and the ensuing media circus, not even because she was a beautiful white woman. Her story flickers around us like a specter still because she was the encapsulation of an American dream come true. In this era of late capitalism, you don't get many of those anymore. She came from nothing and rose to the stratosphere on her own merit, without any help.

But, like every dream, eventually you wake up.

PART ONE

THE FALL

Excerpts taken from THE DEVLIN BABY: AN ORAL HISTORY, to be published by Sutton Books, spring 2024.

A decade after that fateful day in March 2014, many pieces to the Devlin baby puzzle are still missing. The following oral history has been compiled and edited over the last ten years from primary and secondary sources to piece together a background and timeline of the most infamous kidnapping of the twenty-first century. Though the aim was total comprehension, Lila Devlin and Aidan Reynolds declined to participate.

ONE

As she stepped onto the plane bound for Los Angeles, Lila Devlin was overcome with an acute sense of doom. It stopped her short in the walkway as it ripped the air from her lungs, burrowing through skin and bone until it settled deep within her chest. A piercing wrongness that howled for her to turn around and go home.

Lila had never liked to fly. She'd been twenty-two when she first set foot on a plane bound for Sundance, so nervous she'd vomited into her backpack the second the plane began to taxi on the runway. Susan Friedland had reached into her bag of "special pills" for something to calm her down, but it had never gotten easier. Lila hated the stale smell of the cabin that clung to her clothes, the seats so close together she'd bump her neighbor with too deep an inhale. Blithely placing her life in a stranger's hands and crossing her fingers she'd return to the ground.

It was just nerves, she told herself as she found her seat in coach. She used to trust those prickly feelings, her intuition warning her of what her conscious mind couldn't yet understand. But that intuition had become uncalibrated long ago and could no longer be trusted.

She did a cursory check of the people around her, as she always did in public spaces. A tall man sat in the aisle seat across from her, legs stretched out in the little room he could find. A middle-aged woman adjusted the TV on the seat back in front of her, her teenage daughter beside her tapping mindlessly on her phone. No one gave her a second glance.

The days she'd been incapable of going to the grocery store without being swarmed seemed like a distant dream. That girl didn't exist anymore—she had been replaced by younger, prettier girls who would eventually be replaced when they were no longer young and pretty.

Not to mention her hair. It had once been a radiant copper color— some red-carpet host had dubbed it her signature feature. So, Lila had chopped it to her shoulders and dyed it a limp, dirty blond. She preferred to be invisible. The world had expanded when she'd discovered wealth and celebrity before a cage shut around her. Now, it was open again.

She slept for the first few hours of the flight. She did not remember her dreams. When she woke, a familiar panic flashed as they rattled in her mind, but she had trained herself to forget them over the years. Wash them away before they could make a dent.

A sharp, ringing sound pierced the air, and Lila's body turned rigid.

That was what she hated most about flying.

A baby screamed at the top of its lungs. Its ears had popped with the altitude change, and it was afraid. Lila shifted in her seat, looking for the earplugs she had tucked into her purse for this express purpose. Lila could hear the frenzied *shh-shh*s of its mother, but the baby kept crying, starting and stopping in mouthy gasps of air. On the ground, she would have left the room. But here, there was nowhere to go. Even earplugs couldn't mask it.

It wasn't a sound you were supposed to block out.

Then how the hell had I slept through—

"Stop."

Had she said that out loud? Sometimes her mind raced so quickly that she chastised herself aloud, like her thoughts were sentient beings she had to scold into submission. She glanced over at her seat partner to see if he'd noticed, but he didn't look up from his book.

Lila unbuckled her seat belt and scooted past him to lock herself in the bathroom. It smelled like shit and there was barely room to stand, but she would have gladly spent the remaining hours of the flight inside if given the option. She stared at herself in the mirror under the fluorescent LED lighting, watching her chest rise and fall as she practiced slow breathing.

"I find peace in my life; in my life I make peace," Lila told herself. It was shocking how much of the healing process relied on picking a mantra and repeating it until it became a truth.

She'd been comfortable in her little house on the other side of the world. It was simple, quiet. No one paid her attention. Just another woman being swiftly outrun by middle age. Lila found she enjoyed being unremarkable. She'd planned to spend the rest of her life in anonymity. But after ten years, Lila awoke one night to three names rattling around in her mind.

Nico DeLuca, John Carmichael, and Nick Fox. She could see the specters of the three men hulking over her bedside. She'd screamed, yanked the blanket over her head like a child. They were gone when she'd woken in the morning, but she could feel their presences lingering around her: Fox sneering over her shoulder when she went to make her coffee, Nico cackling when she attempted to meditate.

Lila knew deep in her soul there was only one way to make them go away for good. For as long as she blamed, resented, and despised these men for their roles in her daughter's death, any healing she claimed to do was a joke. The only way Lila could ever truly move on was through forgiveness.

The idea felt revolting. Beyond impossible—an affront to the memory of Josie entirely. But the more Lila considered it, the more it made sense. Josie was gone, and Lila had to keep living. She knew Josie wouldn't want her to waste her life away.

Lila returned to her seat as the seat belt sign blinked on. She was settling in when she noticed the man beside her staring. He was tall and handsome, in his early twenties, with wavy golden hair and bright blue eyes. There might as well have been a blinking neon sign across his cheekbones that said ASPIRING ACTOR. He smiled at her politely and then looked at her again, brow furrowing.

For a panicked half second, Lila thought he recognized her and that she would have to go through the little dance she did during those rare circumstances. *Oh, that's so funny. No, I get that a lot.*

"Did you buy those earplugs from the flight attendant?" he asked.

Her chest deflated, and Lila returned his smile. "I brought them with me."

The young man buckled his seat belt and opened his dog-eared copy of *Play It as It Lays.* "Ah, bummer. You're really smart to bring them."

He returned to his book, and Lila leaned back in her seat. The baby was still crying, but it was less frantic now. Little whimpers of protest as its mother lulled it back to sleep. For the first year after Josie died, just seeing a child on the street sent her into a spiral. Babies in strollers, teenage girls in school uniforms. Everywhere she went, she found millions of clones that looked nothing like her. Lila had considered suicide, but it would have rendered Josie's death even more miserable and pointless than it was already.

The plane jostled, and the baby wailed. The man beside her noticed Lila's white knuckles as she gripped the armrest. "Not a big flier?"

"No."

"I learned this thing from my drama teacher in high school that helps me when I'm anxious. Start with finding four things you can see and three things you can touch," he said.

Lila searched his face for any sign of an agenda, but he appeared guileless.

"It really grounds you," he added. "I mean, we're on a plane, but still."

The plane shook again, and Lila supposed she had nothing better to do. The glowing seat belt sign, the ice in her cup shaking, a man snoring open-mouthed, a woman marathoning *The Real Housewives.* Then she focused on what she was feeling: the cheap fabric of her seat, the roughness of her blue jeans, the frigid air-conditioning coming out of the vent. Her attention had left the turbulence and the baby entirely.

"It works, right?" the guy said enthusiastically.

"Thanks," Lila replied, putting her earplugs back in.

The guy inhaled. "Wait."

Lila recognized his tone.

"I mean—I'm sorry, I don't normally do stuff like this. But are you Lila Devlin?" he asked, eyes bright and hopeful. What a story he'd be able to tell when he touched down.

Lila smiled tightly, preparing to drop her usual line, but he continued before she could say anything.

"I'm an actor; I just graduated from drama school. My professor showed us your monologue from *Too Many Mornings*, and we studied it as one of the best performances by a young actor, like, ever. You're a huge inspiration to me."

Lila hadn't expected that. She glanced across the aisle to see if anyone had heard, but no one was paying attention. "That's very kind, thank you."

He beamed at her. She waited for his eyes to turn downcast, or the inevitable apology, or the *It's unimaginable* . . . But instead, he just stuck out his hand. "I'm Peter."

Lila stared at it. Was he playing a game? She realized she had hesitated too long and shook it tentatively.

Peter continued: "I haven't seen you in much lately. Did you take a break from film?"

Lila was almost speechless. He was twenty-two—he had been a kid when it happened. Had he never heard? At the time, it had seemed inescapable. It was bizarre to think an entire generation of people didn't know.

"Yeah, I retired," Lila said, because she didn't know what else to say.

Peter nodded. "That sucks, you were really good. My professor said your performance was so natural he'd never want to train you formally. 'Cause that would ruin it."

Lila tried to remember herself on that set, performing in front of a camera for the first time, hanging out with the crew members in

Maine lobster shacks after shooting. But it was like imagining a different person entirely.

Lila changed the subject. "So, you're moving to Los Angeles?"

"Yup," Peter said. "We have a spring showcase for agents and managers we perform in, so, hopefully, I can get signed. I've only been to LA once—I don't know anyone out here. But I'm really excited. I feel like *Swingers* prepared me."

"*Swingers* prepared you?"

"You know, the movie?"

"Oh."

"I didn't mean actual swingers."

"Got it."

"Are you going home?" Peter asked.

"I'm moving back."

"From where?"

He didn't seem to be nosy, just curious. "I've been living all over. Asia, Europe."

"You were going *Eat Pray Love* mode," Peter said.

"Sure."

There was a voice in her head all the time, always. It screamed at her that she had failed to save Josie, just like she'd failed to save her father, just like she'd failed to save her marriage. Ten years ago, when the voice reached a fever pitch, she had driven to LAX and bought a ticket to the farthest place she saw on the departures board.

She wound up in India and discovered meditation. It didn't eliminate the voice, but it turned the volume down. On the good days, she could mute it entirely. As a teenager, she would have mocked herself as a privileged cliché, but she was so desperate for relief she could no longer afford to care.

"What do you do now?" Peter asked. "Since you left acting, I mean."

A couple of years after Josie died and the world had forgotten her, a small, rose-colored part of Lila thought she could return to her childhood dream of becoming a veterinarian. She enrolled in school and, to her surprise, the classes made her happy. For a while, Josie lived in a corner of her mind, distant enough to allow her to function but close enough to hold on to her memory. But as Lila grew more immersed in her studies, she found herself pushing Josie even further away. Some days she wouldn't think about her daughter at all. She couldn't do that. She would never allow herself to carry on as if nothing had happened. So, she dropped out, and Josie's corner of her mind remained.

"I'm starting a skincare business out here," Lila said, expecting him to lose interest.

He didn't. "Oh, sick! My ex-girlfriend took me to get a facial for the first time last year. It was amazing."

Part of Lila wondered if Peter had lived in a magical closet his entire life that warded off any trace of negativity and disappointment. The type of man who didn't just coast through life but floated. Aidan had been like that when she first met him. It didn't last.

"It's a little bigger than that," Lila said. It was going to be a tribute to her daughter. A way for Josie to live on by applying the principles of self-actualization and inner peace that she had learned in India. She wanted to help people heal just as she had.

"Thanks. For talking, I mean. When you sat down, I couldn't believe it. Yeah, your hair's different, but you look the same. I can't believe no one else recognized you. Sitting next to you on the plane out here feels like a good omen," Peter said.

"Good luck with everything," Lila said, and she meant it.

"You too!" Peter chirped. "I'm gonna buy your skin cream."

Lila chuckled as she put her earplugs back in, and Peter returned to his book.

THE SUN LICKED THE EDGE OF THE SKY BY THE TIME LILA REACHED HER new apartment in Studio City. It was a claustrophobic one-bedroom with a dubious-looking air-conditioning vent, but her savings had waned after a decade of traveling, and she could no longer afford to be picky. It reminded her of the apartment she'd moved to after her mother died. She told herself the familiarity was a comfort.

She hadn't had a chance to say goodbye to Peter. She hoped he'd realize the mistake he'd made in coming to LA to act sooner rather than later.

It didn't look much like one, but Los Angeles was a desert. It seduced you with hope and light, beckoned you in with sweet promises of the best version of yourself—until you were too close to escape. Close enough to see the empty smiles on everyone's faces. Close enough to realize it was just a candy-colored mirage and that you were only one of four million clawing over one another to survive.

Lila had suffocated under their weight the last time she'd been here. This time, she would not make the same mistake. She needed allies. She pulled out her phone and scrolled to her former publicist Cara Donaldson's name. They hadn't spoken in a decade. Cara was difficult, but she was more than capable. And if she resented Lila's sudden absence, she would still be too nosy to ignore the call.

"Lila Devlin, is it really you?" Cara's raspy voice came through the line.

"It really is," Lila said.

"I literally can't believe it. I'm literally in shock," Cara drawled in a vocal-fried monotone. "I don't even know how to start. How have you been? *Where* have you been?"

Lila laughed. "It's a lot to explain over the phone. Do you have any time this week?"

"My lunch tomorrow canceled, how's that?"

Lila smiled. "Perfect. We can text to find a spot. Talk soon."

She was about to hang up when Cara said, "Lila?"

"Yeah?" Lila said.

"You sound good."

Lila nodded, even though Cara couldn't see her. "I am."

THE DEVLIN BABY
An Oral History

Lila Devlin was born in 1985 in Chelsea, Massachusetts, the daughter of Denise, a nurse, and Mark, an electrician. Growing up in a small suburb of Boston, Lila never imagined she would be the biggest movie star in the world by age twenty-two.

ANALISE RHODES (*journalist*): To understand what truly made the Devlin baby scandal so captivating, you have to know Lila. After spending so many years studying this case, I don't believe it would have blown up the way it did had she not been in the center. It wasn't that she was beautiful or charismatic—she was, but so was every other actress in Hollywood. It was this fierce vulnerability she had that sucked you in. She made you want to root for her without even trying.

ANDREW SIMMONS (*childhood neighbor*): There's an aura around certain people—I don't really know how to explain it. It's just this blinding, intangible *thing* that some people have. I was eight when I moved to Chelsea, Mass., from Cincinnati. I remember when we were moving in, and I was so scared and so anxious—I didn't know a soul. And then there was a knock on the door, and Mom and Dad called me downstairs. There was a little girl with copper-red hair and the warmest brown eyes I had ever seen. "Hi, I'm Lila, I live next door!" From the moment I first met her, I knew she had that thing.

SIOBHAN DOHERTY (*babysitter*): Mark and Denise had a scheduled date night every other Saturday, so I'd come over. The Devlins were the sweetest people. Lila was an only child, but you'd never be able to tell. They kept her grounded. She had this deep empathy, this wisdom beyond her years. She loved animals so dearly that I think she was hellbent on becoming a veterinarian or marine biologist by the age of six. We went to the New England Aquarium so often the staff knew her by name.

ANDREW SIMMONS: We found a nest of baby squirrels once when we were out playing in the woods. The mom was nowhere to be found. Lila didn't want to leave them alone, of course, so she took them home and nursed them back to health. Literally bottle-fed them in her basement until they were well enough to go free.

MAEVE BRADY (*family friend*): Lila must have been nine, ten, when Denise passed. Breast cancer. It was very sudden, only a couple months after her diagnosis. It was devastating. Everything changed after that, the family was irrevocably broken. Lila worshipped the ground Denise walked on. And Mark, God bless him, Mark tried, but there was just a light in him that shut off. They moved to an apartment in nearby Jamaica Plain after. I know I couldn't have stayed in that house if I were them.

ANALISE RHODES: In an era of nepotism babies and rich kids strutting into the industry with no resistance, it's rare to find a story about an actress that comes from a working-class, a true blue-collar, background. That lack of judgment, that ability to converse with all walks of life, would end up taking her far in her career.

In 2003, Lila receives a full-ride scholarship to UMass Amherst to study veterinary medicine and marine biology.

VIV BAKER (*college roommate*): So many people ask me to tell this story and think I'm bitter. I'm not bitter. Frankly, I dodged a fucking bullet, considering . . . Don't put that in.

SUSAN FRIEDLAND (*film director*): *Too Many Mornings* was my third feature. I always think of it as my second, since no one saw the first one, but I digress. I was fascinated by cocaine trafficking in Maine at the time, so I wrote this little indie about a teenage girl trying to reconcile with her addict father on a lobster boat. As it turns out, casting an authentic working-class New England teenager from a pool of child actors from the Valley is slim pickings! After, like, five months of reading duds, I decided to do an open casting call in the area.

VIV BAKER: Lila and I were close in that freshman-year roommate kind of way. It was a big, intimidating campus, and it was nice to have someone you could rely on. I was a huge theater kid, and I loved that she wasn't. I had never met someone who was so into, like, *learning* before. I swear to God, she had a photographic memory. I used to make her run audition scenes with me 'cause she memorized them quicker than I could.

Right after spring break freshman year—I don't think she even went home; she just stayed on campus. I don't think her dad was super around. My friend emailed me a link to an open casting call for a new Susan Friedland movie in Boston the next weekend. The *queen* of Sundance. I asked Lila to come with me for moral support. She kept to herself so much, I always tried to invite her out to things. I felt sorry for her.

She sat with me in the waiting room, running lines. She's very cool under pressure. Whenever I started to get nervous, she just made me run lines with her again. She was always very, like, *You can't be anxious if you're too busy working toward a goal.* Like that type of vibe. It was exhausting, but sometimes, it was great. To be on that wavelength.

We waited for, like, six hours that day. There were still, like, twenty girls ahead of me by three p.m., so Lila asked if she could take a walk.

SUSAN FRIEDLAND: I think I saw two hundred girls that weekend? I was convinced the project was doomed. That Sunday, we'd been seeing girls for a day and a half by then. And when you're dealing with completely green talent, their first instinct is to try to impress you, to show off. But I didn't want someone showing off. I wanted someone playing a girl on a lobster boat. I couldn't take it anymore. I went outside on a smoke break, and then I saw her.

First, there was her hair. Gorgeous copper hair that sat on the edge of blond and red, depending on the way the sun caught it. She was wearing a T-shirt and jeans, no makeup. Just looked like a normal local kid sitting on a bench, but something was striking about her. Like a young Lauren Bacall.

"Are you auditioning?" I asked her.

She turned around and laughed, as though the question were preposterous. "I'm just here with my friend," she said.

I didn't want to go back inside, so I struck up a conversation. She didn't know who I was, must have assumed I was somebody's assistant. And thank God, 'cause I don't think she would've talked to me otherwise. I asked her what she did; she said she was studying veterinary medicine. I liked that. She said she helped her friend practice the audition scene but didn't think it was very good. I was hoping for an Oscar nomination for this script, so I obviously asked her why.

"Oh, I dunno. It didn't feel real, I guess. My mom died when I was younger, and my dad is kind of the same type of guy as the dad in the script, and he's not . . . we don't have that kind of relationship."

"So, you think the father character is too warm?"

"It's not that; it's that . . . he's succeeding too much with her, I guess? With my dad, he tries, but it never . . . goes anywhere."

And then there was this look, this gorgeous look in those big brown eyes, that made my heart stop. Just pure pain. I wish I had a camera. I had never seen grief captured so . . . plainly and beautifully. I knew in that moment I had found her. I didn't care if she could act or not, because it didn't matter—Lila didn't need to act. She *was* Eileen.

VIV BAKER: They cut auditions short that day, I never went in. Lila came back after ten minutes and was like, "I think I met the director in the parking lot?" I was furious she didn't come get me.

SUSAN FRIEDLAND: She did not want to accept the part, but I was persistent. I wasn't gonna make this movie without her. I think she finally came around when she saw the pay. She was saving for some research program in Australia. I don't remember. But it got to a point where she realized it would be stupid to turn it down.

Lila shot TOO MANY MORNINGS the summer after her freshman year of college.

SUSAN FRIEDLAND: She was so nervous that first day. She prepared and prepared; during the table read I caught her mouthing along to the other actors' lines. She had memorized every scene in the script, even the ones she wasn't in.

She pulled me aside before we shot the first take. She said, "I really don't think I can do this." She wasn't just talking about the movie. She was talking about inserting herself into the public eye. She was terrified. Which, well . . . in hindsight . . . Anyway, I said to her, "Do you remember what you told me about the script when you first read it? That you related to it, but it wasn't *right*. There are thousands of other girls just like you that want to be seen. You're the only person who can tell this story right."

And that was all she needed. There is something very noble in her nature—once she was persuaded this could help other girls, she was all-in. And she was a natural, immediately. The first day on set, the EPs were in the tent, like, fist-pumping 'cause we hit the fucking jackpot. And I still remember, when we wrapped day one, the crew applauded her. She was so embarrassed. I told her to get used to it.

JAN PIRELLI (*hairstylist*): In the hair chair every morning she'd be doing some kind of biology homework. It was like she was leading two completely different lives. She'd always talk to me about these big science internships she was applying for. She seemed to be the only person on set who was unaware that she was not going to be a scientist anymore.

TOO MANY MORNINGS debuts to rave reviews when Lila is twenty-one. Critics hail her performance as revelatory. She is immediately catapulted into movie stardom.

SUSAN FRIEDLAND: Her dad died around the time we were campaigning for a best actress nomination. When it came out it was liver failure from alcoholism, the press ate it up. She was a novelty to them. Lila was like this tragic Pre-Raphaelite heroine in a Masshole's body.

ANALISE RHODES: She was a portrait of a Cinderella story, a real-life twenty-first-century American dream unfolding right in front of you. She carried herself with such grace and intelligence, and both parents dead before she was twenty-two—that strength endeared her to people. People were riveted; her rise was meteorically fast.

SUSAN FRIEDLAND: Agents and managers and Hollywood descended on her like they do for everyone who shows promise. She called me after the SAG Awards that year. She was like, "I don't even know how I got nominated, I couldn't afford to join the union." And she was still in college, studying remotely. But she couldn't be a normal student anymore; she was too famous for that. She struggled, I know. She forced a normal life, but those days were over.

When she received a fucking Oscar nomination and was still talking about swimming with the beluga whales or whatever, I had to give her a reality check: she was too talented and too famous to go back to the way things were. And it was hard for her to accept. I told her she needed to take the time to grieve. In a way, she was losing the only life she had ever known.

But with her dad dying, the last thing she wanted to do was reflect. So instead, she just launched into her Hollywood career, full throttle. If she was going to be an actress, she was going to be the hardest-working actress on the planet.

Two

On her second day in Los Angeles, Lila realized she had aged. She'd had no reason to pay attention to her appearance when she'd been gone, but it was impossible not to here. The city was swathed in awareness, millions of eyes hungry for new faces to pick apart. Her rearview mirror reflected sunken and shadowed brown eyes, her cheeks flattened and fine-lined. For the first time in years, she felt ashamed she had allowed herself to get old.

Her phone rang—Aidan. He'd already called twice that morning. He would keep calling until she answered, and she had no good reason to avoid him. Their divorce had been quick and amicable. They loved each other too much to endure any more suffering than they already had. They tried to keep in touch—he called on her birthday every year, and she had met his wife on FaceTime. He never introduced her to his daughter. She never asked, and he never offered.

"Hello?" Lila answered.

Aidan breathed a sigh of relief on the other line. "Finally. Are you in LA?"

"Yeah, I just got in last night."

"Any reason I had to find out from Cara?"

Lila winced. She'd forgotten they were working together now. "I hadn't had the chance to call you."

"Come over, have dinner with us tomorrow," Aidan said.

Instinctively, she'd rather impale herself on the parking brake than make pleasantries with Aidan's perfect new family. The idea of going from Aidan's most intimate partner to a dinner guest made her nauseated.

She thought a decade would soften her feelings, but she'd never let anyone else replace him. She'd tried, but her insides were emptied and desolate; she had nothing left to give. A quick, annual FaceTime call was easy. She'd known living in the same city would be a challenge, but he was making it even goddamn harder by being so *nice*.

Maybe it was better to get it over with. Rip the Band-Aid off. Before she could second-guess herself, Lila said, "Okay."

"Amazing! I'm so excited to see you."

She recognized the forced casualness in his voice. The desperate need to stay positive around her. Like she was a landmine. If she listened closely enough, she could hear the faint crack of eggshells. He was a good actor, better than she'd ever been. Did he really want her there, or was he playing a part? She might have been able to tell ten years ago.

CARA SELECTED SOME TRENDY LUNCH SPOT ON FAIRFAX WHERE BOTTLED water cost ten dollars and the carb-heavy dishes on the menu were so detailed you could practically hear it whispering, *Are you sure you want to do that?* The host led Lila through a maze of crowded tables onto a quiet back patio. The diners wore hats and sunglasses to block the sun and any unwanted stares. She felt naked under their gaze.

Though she was in her late forties now, Cara Donaldson looked anywhere between thirty and fifty, depending on where the filler had set in her face that day. Her dark hair fell stick-straight in a flattering center part against her high forehead. It was the same haircut she'd had when Lila started working with her. She'd probably emerged from the womb with curtain bangs.

Lila swallowed and took a cautious step toward her. "Cara?"

Cara removed her sunglasses to get a good look. "Holy shit, you're really here."

"It's good to see you," Lila said, watching Cara appraise her, trying to hide the rows of goose bumps that leapt up on her forearms. Lila wondered if Cara could smell the death on her.

"Can I hug you? Is that okay?" Cara asked, her arms already out.

"Of course! You don't have to ask." Lila laughed.

Cara chuckled. "Girl, that's how I know you've been out of this industry for a long time."

Even as the waiter came over and took their drink orders, Cara didn't stop staring, eyes constantly flicking over Lila with tiny discoveries.

"I just can't believe it. You're a brunette now. I didn't even recognize you. I mean, you look amazing, but, like . . . you grew up," Cara said.

She devoured the softness of Lila's stomach, the flabbiness of her arms. Lila could feel her excitement that she had kept herself together where the movie star had let go.

"The red didn't fit me anymore," Lila said.

"Nooooo, it was so pretty," Cara whined. "I don't even know where to start. Where have you been? You went completely off the grid."

"Traveling all over Europe, Asia. I was pretty lost when I left," Lila admitted.

"Wow, I thought when you said you were going east, you were talking about Boston. I didn't realize you literally meant, like, another continent," Cara said in awe. "Did it . . . are you better?"

"I really am."

"That's amazing. You deserve that more than anyone," Cara said.

"Thanks. Lot of soul-searching. I wanted to apologize to you for how abruptly I left—"

Cara waved her hand. "In the moment, was it a little jarring? Sure. But it all worked out."

The server came and took their orders.

"Bet it's nice to be able to order a Cobb salad again," Cara said. "I mean, I like Asian food, but . . . *God*." All her teeth were the same, uncannily large length. Veneers.

When the server had gone, Cara took a big sip from her Arnold Palmer and clasped her hands together. "So, what made you come back?" she asked.

Lila took a deep breath. "I want to start a beauty brand."

"That's so random," Cara said.

It only felt random to Cara because she hadn't lived it. The press mocking Lila's acne breakouts and her pug nose. The studio execs encouraging her to drop two sizes. They'd given her a career for being beautiful only to claw her to pieces as ugly. At her lowest, she would have believed it had it not been for Josie. One afternoon Lila found her with lipstick smeared all over her face. *Beautiful like Mommy!* she'd said. Josie was untainted and genuine because she was too young to be any other way. And Lila had burst into tears because it had taken a toddler to put her back together.

"I want to create a beauty brand that stands on the sole ideal of self-compassion in my daughter's honor. I want to help people feel comfortable in their own skin," Lila said. And Josie's spirit would live through every dab of skin cream to make people feel less alone. "I took chemistry classes when I was away. It started as a way to just turn my brain off, but I learned a lot. I know how to make these products by hand."

"Oh yeah, I forgot you were a science nerd." Cara pursed her lips.

"It's not difficult; it's a lot like baking," Lila said. "Here."

She removed a small bottle of skin cream she'd made in her kitchen the night before. "Very simple, five ingredients, but it works great."

Cara nodded politely. "How can I help? Can I offer some advice, or . . ."

"I want to talk to you about becoming my partner. I don't think there's a better person for the job. It would be a fifty-fifty split; I would handle the product and you would take care of the publicity," Lila said.

Before Cara could respond, the server returned with their salads. "Ugh, I'm starved. One second," Cara said, and took a big bite.

Lila watched Cara chew on a piece of lettuce with her giant teeth. She looked like a horse grazing. "A lot of people try to launch these brands without knowing what they're doing. I know every recipe, every ingredient. There was this local university that had amazing seminars on cosmetic science."

Cara swallowed and pouted. "Lila, I *so* love the idea; it's *so* noble. And I'm *so* flattered you thought of me. But I just don't have the band-width right now for a project of that scope."

Until now, Lila hadn't realized she was expecting Cara to just say yes. "I'm sure we could come to a reasonable compromise."

Cara shook her head. "I don't think it's possible. A lot has changed since we worked together. I have my own firm now. Our clientele is A-list, so they'll notice if my attention isn't solely on them."

"I'm willing to use my image to market the product. I was at that level—"

"But you aren't. Anymore." Cara's smile dripped with pity. "And I mean, look at you! You're all the better for it! I love how passionate you are, but . . . it's just not a great idea to launch another beauty brand right now. Everyone's already done it. The market is oversaturated, and people are over it. To cut the noise, you have to really be, you know, *someone*."

Lila recognized the look on her face, though she hadn't seen it in a very long time. When Lila first was coming up as an actress, she saw it all the time. *Who did she think she was?* How did a poor kid from Boston with an addict father and no formal training get a starring role in a prestige movie? She wasn't pretty enough, wasn't thin enough, wasn't talented enough. She had to be special, but the special kind of special everyone else was.

"I'm sorry to hear that," Lila said, picking up her fork. She'd find someone else; she just hadn't described her vision well enough.

Cara tapped her chin. "*You know what?* I actually might know someone—she interned for me back in the day, and now she's started her own company. I've gotten drinks with her a few times, and she's hungry for work. Said she wants to model her career after mine, so it might just be the next best thing!"

"Thank you," Lila said.

Cara squeezed her hand. "Girl, I got your back!"

When she returned home, Lila googled the contact Cara had given her: Sylvie Lightly. The name did ring a tiny bell. Lila clicked through her professional website. Her work history was odd—high-profile celebrity firms in the late 2010s, and then after 2019, mostly dog food brands. What happened?

Lila went back to the Google search and scrolled through associated news articles. On the second page, as if buried, was a 2019 article from *The New York Times*: "Lightly Pleads Guilty in Crash That Injured 20 at Hollywood Nightclub."

"What the fuck?" Lila said out loud.

The article described Sylvie's blossoming career in PR before one October night when she got into an argument with a bouncer who wouldn't let her into a nightclub. Furious, she got into her Tesla and proceeded to back it over the crowd of people in line at the entrance. Allegedly, she could be heard screaming, "You're not the only one who can play God."

Sylvie was adamant that it was an accident and that she'd said no such thing. No one was killed, but ten people sustained injuries. She pleaded guilty to a felony charge of leaving the scene of a crash and a misdemeanor charge of criminally negligent assault. Further research revealed she served only thirty days.

She must have been blacklisted, Lila thought, fuming. It was an unmistakably Cara thing to suggest she attach herself to an insane person.

Lila would find a partner herself. Someone out there would take a chance on her. She still had her old phone full of industry contacts. If Lila had to go down it one by one, she would. Under no circumstances would she ever submit to the likes of someone like Sylvie Lightly.

THE DEVLIN BABY
An Oral History

In 2009, Lila meets Aidan Reynolds in New York City.

ANALISE RHODES: Aidan was only a few years out of drama school and had already landed a Tony nomination for the revival of *Streetcar*. Not many people outside the theater community knew his name, but he looked like Paul Newman and had a lightning-fast wit. His ascent was inevitable.

TIM WEBER (*friend of Aidan's*): We went to some after-party in New York when Aidan was doing a play on Broadway. He saw Lila, and I swear to God, there were little hearts in his eyes. Lila wasn't very impressed. Lots of men came up to her. But then he said his family was from Natick, and she lit up. People from Boston are fucking obsessed with Boston. They bonded over eating at Bertucci's or whatever. They disappeared. Like six hours later I finally found them on the roof, just talking.

JAN PIRELLI: I think she just wanted someone normal. Aidan came from the classic big upper-middle-class family in Massachusetts. Classic New England boy who liked to drink hard and watch the Sox. And she was tired of being alone.

SUSAN FRIEDLAND: I was surprised that her career went as mainstream as it did. YA franchises and popcorn movies weren't what I thought she'd want. To tell you the truth, it made me sad. I liked Aidan, he was a sweet guy. But I felt like she was dumbing herself down to be with him, to fit into this life. Well, not dumbing herself down. I mean, *making herself ordinary*.

TIM WEBER: Lila had this weird party trick she used to do if she was drunk enough. She'd make you play a whale call, like on YouTube, and then could tell you what species and gender of whale it was. It was dorky, but Aidan found it adorable. He was so patient.

ANALISE RHODES: There's an alternate, more cynical read on the relationship. Aidan was a "Hey, it's that guy!" Lila Devlin was Lila Devlin. And when he and Lila became inseparable, paparazzi were chasing them across Manhattan. A year later he's the lead in a Marvel movie.

TIM WEBER: It's not an evil thing to want to be famous. People act like you're a supervillain if you're openly ambitious about your career. But you can be a kind, good person and still want success. Aidan took acting very seriously as a craft, way more than Lila. He deserved to be known for it.

JAN PIRELLI: Aidan was good for her. She was afraid to go out in public after a while. She'd just get mobbed wherever she went. She was living like a little hermit between shoots and red carpets. But Aidan coaxed her out of her shell. When her anxiety was really bad, he'd bring disguises for them. They looked ridiculous, but no one ever imagined it was them. I had never seen Lila be silly before. Aidan brought that out of her.

GREER HOUSER (*host of the* Devlin Baby *podcast*): And she was good for him. He was a hard partier in his early twenties, and she helped him get it out of his system.

TIM WEBER: Nah, we still had fun together.

In 2011, Aidan and Lila marry after two years together and settle in a six-bedroom mansion in Bel Air, California.

TIM WEBER: I was shocked they got married so young. At twenty-six? You're only, like, eight years out of high school. She had baby fever.

CARA DONALDSON (*Lila's publicist*): *People* offered a cover story and full spread for the wedding as soon as we confirmed the proposal. Aidan and Lila waffled back and forth for a couple weeks—Aidan was open; he knew how to play ball. But Lila was a toughie. She said, "Do they want pictures of us at city hall? We're not going to have a wedding."

JAN PIRELLI: Her way of fighting the limelight was to make herself smaller.

TIM WEBER: Oh, Aidan was pissed for sure. His family wanted a big celebration. But Lila's way goes, I guess, like always.

ANALISE RHODES: So two of the biggest young stars in America stroll into Los Angeles City Hall one day for a marriage license. She isn't even wearing a dress, just jeans and a T-shirt. TMZ immediately finds out, and it makes national headlines.

SUSAN FRIEDLAND: She couldn't breathe without being accused of a publicity stunt.

TIM WEBER: She even wanted to move back to Massachusetts, but that's when Aidan had to put his foot down and be like, "No."

ANALISE RHODES: By that point, she was still more famous than him, but it was close. He was catching up. Her big YA series had ended, and Aidan's superhero thing was only just beginning.

CARA DONALDSON: She got pregnant almost immediately, and that pregnancy was hell. And after their first three or four months together, Aidan had to pick up and shoot a movie in Romania.

TIM WEBER: Aidan flew back as often as he could, but he was under contract. And someone needed to pay for the baby.

CARA DONALDSON: She wanted to stay in the States with her doctor. Her morning sickness was so bad, she got diagnosed with hyperemesis gravidarum. She was hospitalized, like, three times, she was so dehydrated.

JAN PIRELLI: She called me one night. She thought she was dying. She was scared the baby would grow up without a mom. She wasn't even born yet, and Josie was already the center of Lila's life.

CARA DONALDSON: Somehow she knew it was a girl. And she wanted to name her Josephine, her mom's middle name.

In October 2011, Josephine "Josie" Reynolds is born.

TIM WEBER: Seven months in, Lila goes into premature labor. Aidan was literally on his way back to her; he got off the plane and went straight to the hospital. He was terrified.

HOSPITAL NURSE (*anonymous*): She was in labor for twenty-three hours; it was brutal. Her body didn't want to let go. When Josie was born, she was three pounds eight ounces. She could fit inside a little shoebox. Lila didn't even get to hold her; we had to take her straight to the NICU. It was another month of waiting and not knowing . . . Lila would just sit in the hospital and watch her and wait. Aidan tried to get her to go home, but her only focus in the world was that little girl.

CARA DONALDSON: Everyone was calling me, trying to confirm reports about the baby. There was nothing to confirm. No one knew whether or not she would make it. We thought it was finally over when they brought her home, but that was only the beginning.

JAN PIRELLI: She withdrew. We stopped working together. She stopped calling for advice. After she took Josie home to Bel Air, I didn't hear from Lila again.

CARA DONALDSON: It became quickly apparent that something was very wrong with Lila.

TIM WEBER: Aidan said she was half dead. Wasn't sleeping, didn't eat. Didn't want to touch the baby. Aidan was doing it all on his own.

CARA DONALDSON: I'm close with all of my clients, but Lila and Aidan were different. I became a fixture in that house. I was their therapist, their life coach, their closest adviser—I was happy to do it, but it's a lot of pressure to put on someone. No one ever asked me if I was in the right headspace for this, you know?

LYDIA NOVAK (*nanny*): I was hired by Aidan first as a housekeeper and then to take care of Josie. She'd had a hard journey into the world, but she was a relatively easy baby. I suspect Lila had postpartum depression—people are more open about that now, and how common it is, but not then, and not with celebrities. I tried to get Lila to hold Josie more often, but she wouldn't pick her up. "I'll break her," she said.

JAN PIRELLI: It was devastating; she'd fought a war for that baby.

LYDIA NOVAK: Sometimes I'd hear wailing in the house—the house was so big, it would echo—and I'd run to Josie's room to find her sound asleep. It was Lila.

CARA DONALDSON: After six months, Aidan finally persuaded her to get help. And then things started to turn around.

TIM WEBER: Once she was, like, medicated, she was a great mom.

LYDIA NOVAK: It was like a storm had passed. I moved out of the house, only worked as a nanny. Aidan and Lila took me in as a fourth member of the family. I became their closest confidante. I've worked with many celebrities, and Lila was by far the most hands-on mother I'd ever met. It was like she was trying to make up for lost time.

You could tell just by the nursery—Lila painted this beautiful mural of sea creatures all over the walls. She was clear to me from the get-go that Josie would have the most grounded upbringing she could give her.

CARA DONALDSON: I started talking to her about maybe going back to work, but she had no interest. People would have started to forget her if it weren't for Aidan, who was fucking blowing up. He got cast as a new Avenger in the Marvel Cinematic Universe, back when that was still impressive.

TIM WEBER: Was the timing inconvenient? Probably. But he was grateful for his career and he was grateful for his kid. He was the sole breadwinner, so he couldn't be around as much. I don't like the implication he loved her any less.

When Josie is a year old, Lila goes public detailing her battle with post-partum depression.

CARA DONALDSON: She was very brave. She insisted on being open about it, to make other women suffering feel less alone.

LILA DEVLIN (*archival interview*): No one claims motherhood is an easy process, you hear God knows how many stories. But what happens when your experience deviates so far from that norm? It is so isolating. You feel like a ghost haunting your own child.

CARA DONALDSON: In a kind of extraordinary way, it revived her career. It brought her back into public consciousness. And the thing that made people root for her when she was coming up? There it was again. She was a born fighter. She tried so hard to shield Josie from all of it, but a pap caught them in a grocery store and that veil was lifted. The internet was enamored. America's sweetheart had a daughter.

ANALISE RHODES: I have a theory that part of the reason that the case became what it did was because of the way Josie looked. Even as a baby, she wasn't a face you'd forget.

CARA DONALDSON: She looked weird, but, like, beautiful weird. Very high fashion. Lily-white skin with a big forehead and these *huge* grey eyes—you couldn't see any white in them. She almost looked like an alien. It was haunting.

LYDIA NOVAK: She looked like—like a little fairy.

TIM WEBER: She looked like a really cute Gollum, if I'm being honest with you.

SUSAN FRIEDLAND: I reached out to congratulate Lila on the baby and commend her on how she handled the press. We hadn't spoken in a couple years; I missed her. She invited me over to meet Josie. She was just two years old, and I already saw Lila in her. We got to talking about what I had been up to, and I mentioned this script, *The Pugilists*,

I'd been working on. This sweeping period drama about female prize-fighters in the 1800s. I asked Lila for her thoughts and sent her the script. To my surprise, she called me the next day: "Have you cast it?" I said no. "Lizzie—I have to play her. I will do anything." I was thrilled.

Lila attaches herself to THE PUGILISTS, and that pushes it into prepro-duction to start filming in the summer.

CARA DONALDSON: It was a great fucking role. After overcoming severe depression, Lila Devlin reunites with Susan Friedland for a gritty feminist period piece. Lila would have been a frontrunner for best actress. She could've won this time.

SUSAN FRIEDLAND: She had worked it out with Aidan—he had a four-month break. They'd rent a house outside London, give Josie a normal life during the shoot. She was so excited. It felt like things were finally clicking into place.

She called me a month before we were gonna fly out. She said she wanted to shadow me on set, that she might want to transition into producing or something she could do while working a more regular nine-to-five with Josie. She was probably a little jealous that Aidan was becoming a movie star and she was home with the kid.

ANALISE RHODES: In all the press about Lila returning to film with *The Pugilists*, rumor spread that Lila and Aidan were fighting. He was gone all the time, and she . . . didn't get out much. She wanted them to share responsibility as hands-on parents. But stars like them typically have a team of nannies, support staff, et cetera.

On March 5, 2014, two weeks before Lila is supposed to fly to London with her family, the unimaginable happens.

THREE

The next day, Lila discovered she *would* have to go down her old contact list one by one, but it was not the success she had hoped for. She sat with a pad of paper sprawled out on the floor because she didn't yet have a desk. Quite a few of the numbers had changed, and many people didn't believe it was her calling. Once she had gotten over the hurdle of convincing them it was really her and she was really back in LA, the conversations were fragmented and awkward.

They were angry she'd refused to accept the order of things.

It was easy to be famous until you decided to make it hard for yourself. Be charming, but not cloying. Be smart, but not opinionated. It alienates people. God forbid you alienate people. Be pretty. Be so fucking pretty men lust over you, masturbate to your Google Image search, make fake pornography of you, hack into your personal computer because all that's not enough. And don't be offended, you have no right to be offended, because your image doesn't belong to you anymore, it belongs to them. You are *theirs*. You get money and adoration and fame, and they get you. Be intriguing, but make sure to stay relatable. Sure, you live in a mansion and fly private to movie premieres in France, you're the closest thing to royalty America has— but you're still a nice, normal girl next door who likes to eat cold pizza for breakfast and fangirls over her favorite celebrities in interviews. Because you still have to be a fan of someone else, even if they're now in your peer group. You think you're too good to have idols, that you have nothing left to aspire to? Everybody has room for aspiration—that's the foundation the country was built on. Give comfort to the thousands of strangers obsessing to meet you.

Be all these things loudly and publicly enough to stay in the spotlight, but if you upset the balance and lean too much into one, you risk overexposure. Overexposure is death. So smile wide and be grateful. You would be nowhere without your adoring public. And they do adore you, for now. But just remember—the higher you climb, the farther you fall.

She had fallen, and that yuckiness was blissfully pushed out of their minds. How dare she spoil things by coming back? When she reached the end of the list, Lila wondered if this whole endeavor had been a colossal mistake, if she'd been so blinded by her own goodwill she'd failed to see the writing on the wall. The world wanted her to lie down and take the beating; she wasn't supposed to get up after.

Her phone rang—a random 310 number. She answered on the off chance that someone important was returning her call.

"Hi, is this Lila Devlin?" asked a voice she didn't recognize.

"Who is this?"

"I'm Sylvie Lightly; it's so nice to meet you," the voice chirped.

FUCK, Lila mouthed. Lila desperately racked her brain for a polite way to hang up the phone, but Sylvie was too quick.

"I got a call from Cara Donaldson—*such* a sweetheart. She told me you were looking for someone with a background in business and PR. I'd love to hear more."

Lila bet she would. "Oh, Sylvie, I'm sorry, I think . . ." She stopped. It seemed silly to write Sylvie off when she had no other alternatives. She could hear Sylvie Lightly out for twenty minutes; she might even get a good idea. "Excuse me. Got a little confused with my schedule. Do you have any time today?"

OF COURSE SYLVIE HAD TIME TODAY. LILA WALKED DOWN THE CORRIDOR of a run-down office building on La Cienega between a gas station and a hookah lounge. Sylvie was desperate to be close to the hustle of West Hollywood, but her income relegated her to the outskirts.

When she reached the door at the end of the hallway, Lila hesitated. Was it really worth getting this woman's hopes up for nothing? Even if she'd almost committed manslaughter, Sylvie didn't deserve that. Lila started to turn back in the direction she'd come when the door swung open.

As though Sylvie had been waiting right on the other side.

"Hi there!"

Sylvie Lightly was a petite woman in her mid-thirties, no taller than five feet, but her six-inch heels split the difference. Her sense of style appeared to be "everything." Her floral blouse wasn't so much loud as it was screaming. She wore billowing seersucker pants cinched with a giant bow around the waist. She looked like a character from the children's books where you could mix and match heads and bodies.

"It's so great to meet you in person." She extended a hand. Her hair was an unnatural ink black that matched the color of her piercing eyes—a deep, inky blue.

When Lila took her hand, Sylvie clasped her second hand on top and squeezed. It was far too intimate, as though they were old friends reunited. Lila held her gaze, trying to mask her discomfort. Had Sylvie blinked since she'd opened the door?

"Thank you for squeezing me in," Lila said as Sylvie led her into the office.

Sylvie gestured for Lila to sit on a green velvet sofa next to the coffee table—a glass rectangle perched on the shoulders of a black ceramic panther in mid-roar. "Can I get you anything? Water, coffee?" Sylvie took a sip out of a giant reusable cup on her way to the kitchenette in the corner.

"I'm all right, thank you," Lila said.

"How about sparkling water? I just got a seltzer maker; it's amazing. It's so good with iced coffee," Sylvie said.

"What?"

"Something about me you'll learn—I love sparkling water. Can't drink it flat. And for the longest time, when I'd have my iced coffee in the morning, I'd be, like, where is the carbonation? So, I started putting my iced coffee in the seltzer maker, and it's delicious."

Lila glanced around the room for something to look at besides Sylvie chugging sparkling water. It was a shoebox of an office, the single window offering a sliver of a view of the telephone pole outside. She considered faking an emergency phone call as an out, but there was no one to call her.

Sylvie put on a pair of pastel-pink reading glasses and opened a Moleskine. "All right, tell me everything."

Lila sat back, a little surprised by the abruptness. But Sylvie just clicked her pen and waited. She had no choice but to start. "I have an idea for a beauty brand. The products would be high quality, inclusive to all genders and skin colors, and, crucially, *affordable* to working-class and lower-middle-class people. It would be built on a structure of self-love, to promote the idea that you're not ugly, you're just poor."

Sylvie finished writing and clicked her pen triumphantly. "I love it! The world *needs* this." She broke out into a huge smile.

Lila couldn't help it, she smiled back. After dozens of noes, the validation felt fantastic. Then she remembered who it was coming from. "That's very kind."

"No, I'm serious. I wish I'd had something like that growing up," Sylvie said. Her eyes were so dark a blue that Lila couldn't see her pupils. "I could never afford beauty stuff that actually worked."

That put Lila at ease. She felt a kinship with the people in the industry who didn't come from wealthy backgrounds. "Me neither."

Sylvie smiled again; she had a pretty smile. All the quirks Sylvie cloaked herself in softened, and she looked almost shy. Sylvie was odd, but she hardly resembled a psychopath who would plow down a crowd of innocent people.

"Listen," Sylvie said, shutting her book and clasping her hands together. "You're going to need someone to fight for you as a partner. It can so easily veer into 'I use Dove soap, which makes me a feminist'-type corporate pride bullshit. You have an actual agenda to change people's lives. Any investor will assume this is just silly lip service to sell more lotion. You deserve better than that.

"So, I'm gonna tell you a little about me. I started working in PR my sophomore year of college. I worked as an assistant while getting my MBA, and I also have a great deal of business knowledge. I've spent my entire adult working life—sixteen years—immersed in this world. No one knows it better than I do. I've worked for huge celebrity firms, but I went independent about five years ago and started my own boutique. I've really been interested in concentrating on small businesses. I wanted to explore a completely different world than Hollywood." It was impressive how she had spun being blacklisted. "But if you want someone who knows your mission and knows your target audience—it's me. I grew up poor. Even when I was an assistant at this giant A-list firm in my twenties, I babysat and walked dogs. If you want someone who can fight for you, it's me."

Frankly, Sylvie was perfect. But everything she said came with the unspoken parenthetical (*I mowed through twenty people dead sober*). The prosecution had tried to slap on a drunk driving charge, but Sylvie had proved she hadn't had a drop of alcohol. Inebriation might have been a better excuse rather than just "Oops!" What kind of a person could be so careless?

Lila sighed. There was no point in continuing the conversation; this would never work out. It was unfair to lead her on. "That's really nice to hear, but I forgot I have another meeting this afternoon and have to run. It was so great to meet you, and I'll be in touch . . ."

"At least acknowledge it." Sylvie stood up, a resigned amusement on her face. "If you couldn't even stay for a full fifteen minutes, then you owe it to me to just say it out loud."

"You seem great, but that accident is hard to get past. It speaks too much to character, for me. I'm sorry." Lila started for the door.

"As someone who's dealt with a lot of unfair speculation yourself, I'd hope you'd have some room for grace," Sylvie said, and Lila froze.

She opened her mouth, furious—to invoke her loss when the two were incomparable—but stopped short. Were they so incomparable? Sylvie had been turned into a laughingstock; her career dissolved into begging for Cara Donaldson's scraps.

"If you think you hate what I did, imagine how I feel. I live with the shame every day of my life. You make a horrible mistake, and then you have to look at yourself in the mirror. I got three years and served a month. All I can do is live my life to make up for it. And thank God every day that no one died."

For a moment, the eyes and the hair and the outfit faded away, and Lila saw an exhausted woman trying her best. She softened. "It was an accident? What about the person that heard you say . . . ?"

Sylvie blinked rapidly, winding herself up. "That guy was literally on meth; he took a drug test. The prosecution didn't hesitate to drop that from their case. My car's reverse camera broke, and I didn't turn fast enough to see I had gone too far back. I personally apologized to everyone I hurt and paid for it. Monetarily and personally," she added ruefully.

"I just don't think . . ." Lila started.

"Respectfully, I feel like neither of us is in a position to judge the other," Sylvie cut her off. "And, I mean, you were canceled too. That gross theory you murdered your own daughter? People turn evil when they start getting righteous; you know that better than anybody."

Lila couldn't argue with that. It didn't matter if that stupid theory had started as an online conspiracy; it had evolved beyond her into an urban legend. It was a question lingering in the back of people's minds whenever they spoke to her, no matter how outlandish it seemed. And she did see Sylvie's remorse—it was plain on her face. Now, Lila noticed the lines on her forehead, deep and cavernous. Lila had them too. It was strange to meet someone as lonely as she was. "You're right," Lila said. "I'm sorry."

Sylvie shook her head. "If I weren't me, I'd think the same thing."

"Has it been hard, trying to get back to how your career used to be?" Lila asked.

Sylvie laughed. "You have no idea. It's not as bad as it was five years ago, but right now, what I need most is a successful relaunch of myself, so to speak. Show people the past is the past. You understand?"

"Yeah," Lila said. "I guess I'm in the same boat."

"You want someone who can handle a crisis? There is no one better than me. I learned how to do it the hard way. But regardless of what I want, I like you." Sylvie stood close to Lila's face, unbothered by how intimate it was. "I'm gonna give you three pieces of advice, whether we end up working together or not. The first is not to let anybody turn this into something it's not. They get you to make concessions at the beginning, it'll snowball into this . . . mutation of itself. Number two, get a lawyer and loop them in now. It'll ease a lot of heartbreak down the line. And the last and most important thing: go back to red. Your hair is what made you *you*. And also, brown washes you out."

Lila touched her ponytail. She had been dyeing her hair with drug-store boxes for a decade; it was part of her routine. She couldn't even remember what she looked like with red hair, and it scared her. Her anonymity would be completely gone.

But Sylvie had been honest, and she respected that. Lila nodded her thanks and started to step away when Sylvie seized her shoulder: "I get it. It's easier to hide. But success means you're exceptional, and exceptional people don't cower."

THE DEVLIN BABY
An Oral History

GREER HOUSER: Here's an hour-by-hour timeline for the night of March 5. It starts normally: At five p.m., Aidan leaves to watch the Red Sox game with friends. Around seven p.m., Lila starts to get ready for a friend's bachelorette party. It's one of the first times she's gone out since Josie was born. She's nervous. She has two glasses of wine and then leaves Josie with the nanny, Lydia Novak.

LYDIA NOVAK: She was having second thoughts about going. She almost convinced herself to put her sweats back on and watch National Geographic with Josie. There was this one documentary on the Galápagos that Josie couldn't get enough of. She was such a cute toddler. She loved the turtles and the little fish, and it made Lila so excited . . . Anyway, I thought Lila needed a break. I told her she deserved to have some fun. Aidan was due back at nine anyway. I wish I'd . . .

GREER HOUSER: Lila goes out with some friends on the Sunset Strip for barhopping and karaoke. She's wearing this gorgeous teal dress, her hair is this gleaming red, she's lost the baby weight, she looks hot. If she was hoping to fly under the radar, the crowns and bachelorette sashes made it a little impossible. I think she was trying to blow off some steam and got carried away. Everyone has a crazy night once in a while, but Lila was on the world stage. They get swarmed, but at that point, Lila is too drunk to care.

TIM WEBER: Aidan came over to my place for the game. We had a couple beers, we smoked a little. I asked if he was good to drive home, he said yeah. He took his Mercedes and went on his merry way. I trust him. He wouldn't have driven if he wasn't all right.

ANALISE RHODES: At a shitty karaoke dive, Lila gets even drunker. In the bathroom, some friends offer her cocaine and she does it. It's on the TMZ home page within an hour.

CARA DONALDSON: Someone must've been in a stall taking pictures. She had been pretty squeaky clean with a father who died of substance abuse . . . so it did not look great.

GREER HOUSER: Aidan gets home at 9:14 p.m., and the nanny is sent home for the night.

LYDIA NOVAK: I put Josie to bed, but she started to stir when she heard her dad. I told him to go say good night. There was something in me—I shouldn't have left. I always heard of people talking about trusting your gut, and I always thought it was bullshit. But that night I felt deep in the pit of my stomach that something was wrong. I didn't listen.

According to phone records, Tim Weber receives a missed call from Aidan at 10:00 that night.

TIM WEBER: He butt-dialed me, relax.

GREER HOUSER: Aidan goes to bed, not wanting to wake Josie. At the bar, Lila feels sick and goes home early. She's back by eleven p.m. She walks in the door and realizes the alarm system isn't on, which is very weird. Aidan says he forgot to put it on. She goes upstairs to check on Josie, but Aidan stops her in the hall and tells her he just put her to bed and doesn't want her to wake up again.

TIM WEBER: She was strung out. Of course he didn't want her around the baby.

BILL THOMAS (*neighbor*): I remember my dogs were out of control that night. They were barking like hell. They must have heard something and were trying to warn me. I wish I had listened.

GREER HOUSER: Lila and Aidan are in bed by 11:30. At around five in the morning, Lila gets out of bed to check on Josie. We don't know what makes her get up. She couldn't sleep, maybe. Or maybe it was mother's intuition.

Lila goes to Josie's bedroom and finds Josie gone and her window wide open.

BILL THOMAS: Our houses weren't close together. I mean, it's Bel Air. But the scream was so loud, I could hear it like it was in the next room.

GREER HOUSER: Lila and Aidan find no trace of anything in the nursery. They go out into the yard and find impressions of a ladder in the dirt outside Josie's window. Lila finds a piece of Josie's blanket torn on a bush.

LYDIA NOVAK: I got a call at five in the morning telling me Josie had been . . . taken. I was in shock. They asked me if I had seen anything suspicious, but I hadn't. I wished I had. I have replayed that night over and over, racking my brain. But before I left, nothing seemed out of place.

The police arrive by 5:20 a.m., and the house is declared an active crime scene, headed by John Carmichael.

JOHN CARMICHAEL (*lead investigator*): We followed routine procedure, sectioned off the perimeter of the house. We only found family members' prints in the baby's room.

GREER HOUSER: The cops fucked the case. Josie never had a chance.

CARA DONALDSON: Somebody in the LAPD made a fuckton of money calling the *Daily Mail.* And then somebody at TMZ heard about it. And then suddenly the grounds were swarmed with reporters and paparazzi and fans within two hours.

LYDIA NOVAK: They were like *vultures*, just descending . . .

TOMMY OLSEN (*journalist*): Working the night beat is boring as fuck. They only make us do it in case there's, like, another 9/11 at four a.m. But that night I got a call from a source with the police. My guy's like, "I got something. I want five times the usual rate." I was like, "What the fuck, did someone get murdered?" And he said, *"Better."*

I didn't tell anybody about it, are you kidding? This was an exclusive. My footage is still used when people talk about the case. Because *I* got there first. TMZ and *Daily Mail* and the rest came after.

GREER HOUSER: It was raining on and off that night, so all the mud, combined with the foot traffic, ruined any chance the police had of getting a solid footprint. The officers in Josie's room didn't change gloves when handling evidence, which destroyed any usable fingerprints.

JOHN CARMICHAEL: There's a lot of hearsay about our investigation. I can say with certainty it was conducted with the utmost professionalism. I don't believe one of my officers leaked an active investigation to the media, no, I do not.

TOMMY OLSEN: Cops are fucking stupid; I snuck past the caution tape and hid in a tree. I saw everything up close. Aidan holding Lila. I expected her to be hysterical, like, this is a mother that just lost her kid. She'd made such a big deal about how important Josie was to her, but she was stone-faced. Not a single tear. Aidan Reynolds, this big, built guy, was sobbing, but she wasn't. Looked mildly inconvenienced at most. I thought it was bizarre. Of course I got pictures.

GREER HOUSER: The pictures were bad.

TOMMY OLSEN: Combined with the gonzo coke binge she did earlier that night—that mother-of-the-year stuff rang a little false.

JOHN CARMICHAEL: Despite the media circus, we were able to uncover crucial evidence.

NICK FOX (*detective on scene*): When I was scanning the yard, I found a small envelope tucked under a shrub by the window. It must have fallen off the windowsill. Inside was a typed ransom note addressed to Lila Devlin.

The ransom note read: "Dear Ms. Devlin, We have your baby. Prepare $5 million in cash. In two days we will provide further instructions. If you tell *the police, we will kill her. If any money is missing, we will kill her. If you value your child's life, act quickly."*

ANALISE RHODES: The note still baffles me. Why is it only addressed to Lila? Why does it use her maiden name? People wonder why Josie is known as the Devlin baby rather than what is technically correct—the *Reynolds* baby. The kidnapper put this in Lila's hands alone. They made it about her. No mention of Aidan—why? It makes you wonder how he felt.

TIM WEBER: He was upset, are you fucking kidding? He was a great dad. He loved that little girl more than anything. Lila got all this press for being God's gift to parenting, everyone figured he wasn't around much as a dad. And this just highlighted it.

JOHN CARMICHAEL: We thought it might be a stalker or an obsessive fan, though Lila was adamant she had never had any experience with one so far.

NICK FOX: I always thought it had to have been someone with knowledge of the house and the neighborhood. It was so quick and smooth, there was no room for error.

GREER HOUSER: I'm not saying—of course she didn't do it, but let's go O. J. mode—*if she did*—Lila gets home at 11:00 and the police arrive at 5:20. That's a six-hour window. Plenty of time to dispose of the body and come home. Picture this: Lila high on coke drops her kid and then panics and hides the body. Maybe Aidan gets brought into it, maybe not. She can't tell anyone; even if it's an accident she still now has a dead kid. So there's only one option: Fake a kidnapping. Type out the ransom note to be discovered when the police arrived.

TOMMY OLSEN: The cops took Lila and Aidan inside to show them the note. After a while, there was this commotion, and suddenly Lila comes storming out of the house. All of us in the yard are getting our cameras ready, 'cause we know something big is about to happen. She walks right to the edge of the crime scene tape. There's probably a hundred of us reporters or watchers or whatever. Her eyes are, like, wide and crazy. She plants her feet down and screams, *"Get the fuck off my property!"*

No one moved. I was taking video, so I couldn't. That pissed her off more. She started running back and forth across the lawn. *"Get the fuck out, fucking go!"* And right at that moment, some guy's camera flashed right in her face. And she looked him dead in the eye and, I swear, her eyes were empty. There was nothing behind them. She said, "I WILL FUCKING KILL YOU!" And then she *lunged*.

Aidan and some of the cops had to hold her back, she was fighting and kicking. She managed to swipe the guy's cheek with her fingernails, it was bleeding. It was a deep cut. She had this image as such a sweet girl; I never thought she was capable of that kind of violence.

CARA DONALDSON: Attacking a paparazzo, however justified—again, not a good look.

GREER HOUSER: That was the cover of every tabloid for weeks. There were already so many discrepancies in the case, the fact she wasn't behaving like a grieving mother was . . . problematic.

TOMMY OLSEN: If it were my mother, she'd be in the corner weeping. What kind of a person loses a child, and her first instinct is to viciously attack an innocent person? You could say it was the coke high, but then that begs another question: What kind of mother is out doing coke while her child is getting kidnapped?

One online publication in particular becomes the go-to source for updates on Lila and the case.

NICO DELUCA (*creator/editor in chief of* White Smiles, Bright Lights): *White Smiles, Bright Lights* was a fledgling little start-up I started after I left *US Weekly*. We were doing all right, but when my friend Tommy sold me the initial photos from that night and we broke the story, we skyrocketed. Suddenly, we were the American *Daily Mail*. We were a household name.

Lila was acting bizarre, but since when do celebrities act normal?

I couldn't fault her for that. Anything we publish—we do news, but ultimately, we're an entertainment website. I never pretended we were, like, *The New York Times*. It's not my fault if people treated it like that.

GREER HOUSER: And then, somehow, things get even worse. That morning, the ransom note leaks. It immediately becomes a Twitter meme.

QUEEFDIVA69 (*Twitter user, meme originator*): I don't know, I thought it'd be funny. The format was a picture of the cop holding up the ransom note and then a close-up of what it said.

GREER HOUSER: I saw a pretty brutal one where the note just said "For sale. Baby shoes. Never worn."

QUEEFDIVA69: I was young. You don't think of celebrities as actual people. But, like, we weren't sociopaths just mocking a tragedy. The note became bigger than the kidnapping. It just became a symbol of, like, bad news.

ANALISE RHODES: People would use the meme ironically to deliver bad news about mild inconveniences. The ransom note would just say "The train is running express." It was like people forgot what the actual source was.

GREER HOUSER: The internet was immediately suspicious of Lila. When a celebrity's persona doesn't perfectly match up with their private life and the public gets a whiff of that, they don't know how to make sense of it.

QUEEFDIVA69: I still kind of think she did it. Like she got super fucked up and dropped her toddler out the window, then tried to cover it up. Nothing else makes sense.

NICK FOX: There was a documented history of significant mental health problems. Andrea Yates, the one who drowned all her kids in the bathtub? It rang familiar.

TIM WEBER: The postpartum stuff was so bad I did kinda wonder . . . did she do something in the heat of the moment and then regret it? When you're that out of your mind—that doesn't just go away. You're the same person you were before, it's just dormant in you. And if you're not careful, it could snap back out.

TOMMY OLSEN: They are two huge celebrities who live on a gated property in *Bel Air*, and somehow no cameras caught a kidnapping?

TIM WEBER: Aidan wanted more cameras, even private security, but Lila wouldn't let him. She was caught up in this fantasy of being "normal." But you literally can't be.

CARA DONALDSON: I arrived at the house around eight the next morning. Neither of them had slept. Lila was still wearing last night's makeup. It had gotten cakey and runny, and her eyes were swollen. Aidan was pacing; he was distraught. But she just sat there, blank. It was like she completely dissociated.

LYDIA NOVAK: I was trying to get her to eat; she needed to eat. But she wouldn't move.

CARA DONALDSON: When she saw me, she snapped, "What are you doing here?" She was hostile, I understood. God knows what I'd be like in that situation if I saw my PR lady. I said, "Hon, we need to prepare a statement."

But she shook her head. *Viciously.* "*No.* I'm not doing it." There was no reasoning with her. Aidan was such a sweetheart. He treated her with kid gloves, always. "Lila, we have to." He was so gentle with her. Finally, he convinced her that a statement might help them get Josie back, in case anyone saw something. Aidan and I crafted the statement. Lila didn't say a word. I had to keep reminding myself that people grieve differently.

CNN runs the statement. It reads: "Last night, between the hours of 10:47 and 5:00 a.m., our beloved daughter, Josie, was abducted. We are devastated and want our daughter home. If you have any information, please come forward."

LYDIA NOVAK: I didn't know whether to keep coming or not, but they never told me to stop. They needed someone to lean on when they needed to give each other a break. They trusted me. The week passed so slowly. Outside, the house was mobbed with press just waiting. They couldn't leave the house. Lila lost ten pounds from the stress. It was like she aged ten years. She clung to Aidan like a baby blanket. I'd hear him crying in the bathroom. Never anywhere she could find him. He never wanted to upset her.

TOMMY OLSEN: My days consisted of coke, wait outside their gate, more coke, piss in the bushes, more coke—just kidding—*benzos*, then sleep for two hours in the back seat of my car. I was an animal. The sole focus of my life became getting a picture of Aidan and Lila Reynolds. They had to be going stir-crazy in there.

NICO DELUCA: After the initial posts on my site, people were . . . *eager* for updates. Very eager. It was a number one trending topic nonstop for days.

ANALISE RHODES: It goes without saying that it's highly doubtful that this case would have reached the notoriety it did if the Reynolds family wasn't white.

GREER HOUSER: "Evil Kidnapper Steals Away Baby Girl in the Night from Beautiful Caucasians." It was like a fairy tale.

ANALISE RHODES: And as badly as Lila ended up being treated, she still had a great deal of privilege, especially in her interactions with the police. A woman of color would never have scraped by the way she did, with the way she conducted herself.

NICK FOX: The case being so high profile, tips started coming in immediately.

JOHN CARMICHAEL: Lila wanted to know all of them. She was terrified we would overlook something.

NICK FOX: We were patient, explained we'd do our due diligence. "Oh, like at the crime scene?" she said. The contamination of the crime scene is a strong exaggeration.

GREER HOUSER: Forensic scientists show it as an example of what *not to do* at a crime scene, actually.

JOHN CARMICHAEL: After the first twenty-four hours without finding her, Lila got antsy. After the first forty-eight hours, she was petrified. It was a tough case—no prints, the ransom note was typed, no DNA. Some cloth fibers, but they were a dead end. She thought we were hopeless. There was no reasoning with her. She wanted to investigate it herself.

NICK FOX: We couldn't get through a conversation without her lashing out at us. You need some level of trust in order to work together. We wanted Josie home just as much as Lila did.

JOHN CARMICHAEL: Lila wanted to know why the kidnapper hadn't sent a follow-up note. I explained there's no negotiating in these situations, because the abductor will just ask for more or escalate the situation. Aidan swore to me they wouldn't do it; she was livid. We were afraid she'd attempt to follow the instructions in the ransom note as soon as they gave her an address.

GREER HOUSER: At this point in the case, armchair detectives on Reddit started to investigate Lila's possible guilt. The cops were blinded by her celebrity and ignoring the possibility that was staring them in the face. The theory was she picked up Josie while high on coke and dropped her. The total absence of evidence, combined with her explosion at the crime scene and the letter being bizarrely addressed to Lila alone, made her the prime suspect.

NICO DELUCA: *White Smiles, Bright Lights* got a tip from a legitimate source that the cops weren't ruling her out behind the scenes.

Four days after Josie's abduction, with no updates from the cops or a follow-up note from the abductor, Lila is seen by the public for the first time.

JOHN CARMICHAEL: We decided to bring Lila, Aidan, and Lydia Novak in for questioning. Standard procedure for everyone that close to a crime. We snuck them out in our car so the reporters wouldn't see. Aidan and Lydia understood we had to cover all our bases, but Lila threw a tantrum.

NICK FOX: When I took her into a private room, she was ranting that we were wasting our time when we should have been focusing on the fact there was no follow-up note. "Does that mean Josie's dead?" she asked, but her voice was flat. It struck me as odd. "That's where your mind jumps to?" I said.

JOHN CARMICHAEL: Fox was green as hell. This was his first big case as a detective, and he wanted to prove himself. He and his wife had also just had a baby, so little Josie hit close to home. He went harder on Lila than I'd thought he was even capable. He wanted to be thorough. Me, I didn't . . . I didn't know. Sometimes I believed her, but she was also an actress . . .

NICK FOX: She just said, "You're a fucking moron."

JOHN CARMICHAEL: She said, "I watched my mother die. My father's dead. If you think I'd wish this on myself again, you're a fucking moron."

NICK FOX: "It may not have been intentional," I said. I asked her if she'd been doing cocaine the night Josie was abducted. She knew she couldn't lie; she said yes. I asked her when she'd last ingested it. "Ten fifteen, probably," she said. "If you think I got high and killed my daughter, the effects only last fifteen minutes. I didn't get home until after eleven."

"Usually," I said, "it lasts fifteen minutes. Do you use cocaine regularly?" "Absolutely not," she said, like I expected her to. I said, "Some users, especially if they're inexperienced and take too much, can experience severe side effects that last up to four hours. Cocaine psychosis is a real condition that can cause violent thoughts. And violent thoughts can become violent actions."

She was speechless. She was a rich, famous actress. This was probably the first time in her life someone had dared to question her. "Is this an interrogation?" she asked. I was honest. I said, "Everyone in this house is a potential suspect. We haven't ruled out anyone."

JOHN CARMICHAEL: But Lydia's alibi was airtight, and we had no reason to suspect Aidan. You do enough of these and you learn to trust your gut. Lila was the only one who set off alarm bells. Fox was thrilled. He'd riled her up. He thought if she was scared, she'd start to slip. I wasn't as convinced, but circumstantially, it wasn't great. There was this thing I kept catching myself doing—I'd only ever seen them in movies, it's like my brain didn't register them as real people. That she was a real woman with feelings. Fox did it too.

LYDIA NOVAK: When we got home, Lila was in a daze. She didn't speak to anyone, just paced back and forth across the living room, following the patterns in the carpet. "They think I did it," she kept whispering to herself. Then suddenly she turned to Aidan and me. "Do you know what they're saying about me on the internet?"

Aidan couldn't talk her down. He just said, "They're saying stuff about both of us." Lila looked ill. "No, it's me. They're targeting me. What the hell did I do to deserve this?" She grabbed the car keys off the hall table and walked out the front door. Aidan and I tried to physically block her. "Lila, hang on, don't go out there right now when you're like this—"

"I can't be in this house anymore."

TOMMY OLSEN: I was doing coke in my car when suddenly all the guys around me started jumping up and angling their cameras toward the driveway. Someone screamed, *"She's coming out!"* We all rushed to our positions as the gate opened, and she drove out in her Mercedes. There was a big dent on the front bumper; rich people are fucking awful drivers.

LYDIA NOVAK: It was terrible. They stopped being people, they were just . . . one mass that ran into the road and consumed her car.

TOMMY OLSEN: She couldn't move, there were too many people around her, screaming at her. She tried to inch her car forward, but no one was gonna budge. Finally, she sat back and put her head in her hands. She gave up. It was like a light went out in her. She just sat there for five minutes with the light bulbs flashing down on her, shielding her eyes.

LYDIA NOVAK: It was like a dog lying with its stomach in the air. Aidan and I ran out through the swarm and helped her back into the house. She was exhausted and dehydrated; she collapsed right as we came through the front door.

TOMMY OLSEN: Those pictures of each of them with an arm around her walking her back to the house sold for $500,000 to the *National Enquirer.*

NICO DELUCA: The photos are sadly iconic. This amazing artist in Bushwick, Saffron Hagen, made an installation with them called *Woman in Peril* and started touring it around the country.

FOUR

Up, up, up, Lila drove, watching the houses grow scarcer and the properties grow larger. Aidan lived at the very top of the winding hills overlooking Hollywood. It was a far cry from Bel Air. Farther to the east, closer to the real world. It made the Westside look stuffy and dull. He wasn't like *those* millionaires; he was a new, enlightened breed. Above the traffic and the encampments and the smog and the petty troubles of the less fortunate—there was still a distance, there *had* to be some distance—onto the doorstep of Mount Olympus.

While the road was technically open for all to drive on, it grew narrower and steeper the higher it went. There was no room even to pull over until it reached the top—an unmistakable warning for those who didn't belong to turn back.

The air tasted crisper, sweeter. The hillside was dotted with lavender penstemon basking in the sunlight and billowing manzanitas with red trunks. Bougainvillea so vibrant and rich she wanted to reach out and taste it. It felt unfair that this natural glory was walled off from the rest of the world. Or maybe that was what kept it standing.

At the end of the cul-de-sac stood a wrought-iron gate. A security camera blinked at Lila's car, and in a few seconds, the gate parted. Lila made her way down the long, paved driveway shrouded in bushy eucalyptus trees. Did she miss this life? She didn't miss acting. She didn't miss those stupid YA franchise movies she did. But she'd liked the financial security, after growing up with so little. She'd liked the adoration, after a childhood of being ignored. She enjoyed it for a little while, at least.

The driveway opened to a stunning two-story Spanish Colonial Revival house with white stucco walls and a red-tiled roof. Bright beds of yellow and blue flowers snaked up the brick path to the front door.

Lila noticed another camera hidden beside a vintage lantern above the door as she knocked. A few moments later, the door opened. A statuesque woman in her early thirties stood beaming on the other side. "Lila! It's so nice to meet you in person."

So this was Sonnet. The brief meetings on FaceTime didn't do her justice. She was beautiful, but that was to be expected. What surprised Lila about her beauty was how warm, how open it was. Her hazel eyes were round and curious, betraying no sign of unease. She was so secure it almost put Lila on edge.

The foyer was gorgeous. Glossy quarry-stone floors with a winding staircase and blue mosaic steps. It was palatial but decorated casually with folk art on the walls and racks of shoes by the door. It felt like a real home. Lila's house with Aidan hadn't been a home. She had never been good at being rich; she didn't wear it right. She'd never owned a house before, let alone a mansion, so she'd hired a designer to decorate it for her. She'd figured that's what wealthy people were supposed to do. Even before Josie was kidnapped, it had felt hollow and frigid. A stranger's house. A mausoleum for the living.

Lila glanced at the fancy alarm system beside the door. Aidan took security seriously now. "You have a beautiful home," she said.

"Thank you so much," Sonnet said. "It's my pride and joy. Aidan and I joke it's our second kid."

She padded across a spacious living room out into the backyard. From the house's perch on the hill, there was a full panoramic view of Los Angeles, tiny and insignificant before them. It was magnificent, breathtaking, and Sonnet didn't even cast a glance.

A barefoot man stood at the barbecue beside the infinity pool with his back to them, pouring charcoal onto a grill. Lila smiled softly—all these years later, and he still refused to wear shoes.

"Aidan!" Sonnet called.

Aidan turned to face them, and Lila's breath caught in her throat. He'd grown up. He had always had boyish features, but now they'd settled. It suited him.

For a moment, they stared at each other, unmoving. Taking in how the other had changed, trying to recognize the person they knew. Lila felt thirteen again, standing in front of the boy she liked at her seventh grade dance. A gaping chasm formed before the words *Hi, how are you?* Aidan's lips parted when he met her eyes, quirking into a small smile.

"Lila!"

Then the moment broke, and Aidan reached forward to pull her into a hug. Lila held him tightly, tears pricking her eyes. She hastily wiped them away before they parted.

"It's good to see you," he said.

"It's good to see you too," she said. "I was just telling Sonnet how much I love your house."

"Oh yeah? She tell you we call it my second child?" He laughed.

Lila smiled tightly.

"Yep, we need new bits, babe," Sonnet said. Lila had forgotten she was there. "I'm gonna grab some beers from the kitchen. I'll be right back."

Her hips swung as she disappeared inside. Lila watched Aidan watch her go, trying to remember if he had ever looked at her like that.

"You look great." Aidan nudged her elbow when they were alone, his voice soft. He always tried to be gentle with her. "You look healthy."

She knew he didn't mean it as a dig, but it still stung. Healthy compared to when she'd been forcibly committed? Healthy compared to when she'd scattered her child's ashes into the ocean? "Healthy. You know how to compliment a woman." She forced a laugh.

"You just—you seem a lot better. It's nice to see," Aidan said.

Something about his expression, how sincere it was, made her deeply embarrassed. "Thanks. You seem better and healthy too."

Aidan chuckled, igniting the charcoal with a lighter. A flame burst out of the grill. "It's the years of preventative Botox."

"You're kidding," Lila said. Aidan only grinned. "Aidan. You didn't."

"As it turns out, losing a child at twenty-nine really ages you," Aidan said, his voice dry. That dryness had made him famous. It's what he always hid behind.

"When we were together, you never cared about how you looked," Lila said.

"Everyone does it," Aidan said, a little defensive. "Even the guys that I thought were completely natural. If Botox keeps me good-looking enough to stay in the movies, I don't mind it."

She noticed it now, how his expressions were muted, how his smile was slightly shallow. He could still go through the motions of feeling, but his spirit was missing. She wondered what he looked like when he cried.

They chatted until he'd finished grilling the burgers and then sat down on the deck. The sunset washed a light purple across the sky, the city's glittering lights stretched out before them. They ate dinner every night with the world at their feet.

"So, Lila, I've been trying to think of an organic way to ask you, but I'm coming up short. What brought you back out here?" Aidan asked, his gaze fixed on her.

Lila had become very good at giving a succinct answer after pitching her entire contact list. She told them about her healing journey and then briefly introduced her idea for an affordable, self-empowering skincare company. She didn't mention Josie; it felt too strange in front of Sonnet.

"Damn. I was not expecting that," Aidan said when she had finished. "I didn't think you'd ever want to go back into the public eye again."

Lila didn't like how judgmental he sounded. "You managed just fine," she said lightly. The table went silent. Aidan took a long swig of beer.

Sonnet pretended the quiet was because they were chewing. "You know, if you're looking for investors or a business partner, I have a bunch of contacts in that general sphere. I would be happy to give them a call if you'd like."

"That's so generous of you, but I have some people in mind," Lila said.

Aidan put his arm around Sonnet's chair. "Seriously, Li. It's nice to use all . . . this"—he gestured to the wealth around him—"for good. I would gladly invest even just to help you get off the ground—"

"Thank you, Aidan, but I can't accept it," Lila said. She resented that he felt the urge to look after her. That after all this time, he still did not trust her with her own well-being.

"Then let us at least invite you to some events," Aidan started.

Sonnet put her hand on his knee. "Babe, it's her company."

"I'm sorry, I just want to help," Aidan said.

For a second, his eyes met hers. They were stricken with unspoken grief. Lila softened; he was better at hiding than she was, but it always peeked through.

"Who knows?" Aidan smiled. "Maybe your stuff can substitute for Botox."

Lila rolled her eyes. "No one's figured out how to make collagen cream *that* good."

Aidan changed the subject, gesturing to her burger. "What do you think? It's good, right?"

"It's delicious," Lila said.

Aidan watched as she took a bite, pink lips tearing through the patty. He licked his lips, long eyelashes blinking. "Well, I mean, yeah, this grill I just got, it fucking rocks."

"I bought it for him last month—it's now his prized possession," Sonnet cut in. "Burger night is now three times a week."

"Veggie burgers, otherwise, I'd go into cardiac arrest," Aidan said.

"Mom? Dad? I'm hooome!" A little voice soared through the house.

Aidan turned away from Lila toward the glass patio doors. "We're out here, honey!"

Out skipped a little girl in a plaid school uniform and bright red high-top Converse. She didn't look precisely like Josie—she had her mother's button nose, tan skin, and dark hair. But her eyes, her eyes were Aidan's grey like Josie's had been. The air left Lila's lungs as the girl walked up to the table with a gap-toothed smile.

"How was Ashley's?" Sonnet asked.

"Good! We did gymnastics," the little girl said. She looked at Lila curiously. "I'm Talia." She stuck out her hand.

Lila reached out to take it, blushing when she realized her hand was shaking. "I'm Lila," she said.

"Talia, this is your aunt Lila. She's an old friend of mine," Aidan said, his voice soft. "Lila, this is our daughter, Talia."

She was a beautiful little girl. Judging by the scrapes on her knees, she was active and curious. Lila thought about her birthday parties— without a doubt, there had to be a puppy playpen, maybe a bouncy castle. She wondered what kind of subjects she liked in school, whether she'd inherited Aidan's love of theater or if she preferred science. She thought about where this little girl would go to college and the type of person she'd marry. And she thought about Sonnet and Aidan getting to experience all of it at her side, and then Lila realized she'd dug her nails so deeply into her palms that they were bleeding.

"How old are you, Talia?" Lila asked.

"I'm six and a half," Talia said proudly. "How old are you?"

"Don't answer that," Aidan said to Lila before turning to Talia. "We talked about this; you can't ask people that."

"Why not? People ask me all the time," Talia said. Lila tried not to laugh. "See? She's okay with it; she's smiling."

Sonnet looked at Lila apologetically, then lifted Talia onto her lap. "Once you get to our age, it becomes impolite to ask."

"But why? I want to get old. I can't wait to be, like, an old witch. An old crone." Talia wriggled in her mom's lap.

"You don't get magical powers as you age," Aidan said, laughing.

Talia shrugged. "Can I have a burger?"

"Go wash your hands first," Sonnet said. "Excuse us." She followed Talia into the kitchen.

Aidan watched Lila watch them go. "I can't tell you how nervous I was for that," he said quietly.

"She seems like a great kid." Lila reached out and squeezed his hand. "You have a beautiful family."

She pulled back quickly, nervous she had overstepped. Aidan smiled and gently took her hand. He brushed his thumb over her fingers. "You can have one too, you know. You're back home. You can meet someone and settle down."

Lila withdrew her hand with a curt nod. If he thought that was something she was capable of, he didn't know her at all. "We'll see."

Sonnet came back out before Aidan could question her further. "Are we ready for dessert?"

As Lila helped Aidan and Sonnet clear the table, she wondered what she would have been like as a mother to a girl this age. Josie had only just started talking.

"I said Talia could watch her iPad while she was eating dinner," Sonnet told Aidan.

"Can you imagine having an iPad at age six?" Aidan asked Lila.

At the end of the night, Sonnet put Talia to bed, and Aidan walked her to the door. They stood outside the front of the house, staring at each other, neither knowing what to say. It was difficult to remember there was a time in her life when they were inseparable.

"I'm sorry," Aidan said finally. "This is still so surreal."

"I know," Lila said.

Had they run out of things to say, or things they were allowed to talk about? Aidan cleared his throat. "Good luck with, uh, everything."

Sonnet came to stand beside him in the doorway, and he put an arm around her. Lila thanked them again for dinner and wished them good night, and then the great door shut.

She might as well have been at the base of that mountain, staring up at the people on top. She told herself, in that moment, that she would never allow herself to feel like that again. She wouldn't let anyone condescend to her or pity her. She would be no one's charity case.

And one day, she would be at the very top, laughing in their faces.

THE DEVLIN BABY
An Oral History

A week later, Lila and Aidan receive a second note from the kidnapper reading "Dear Lila, You deserve better than how they're treating you in the press. I feel for you. Josie is in safe hands and will be back to you provided you deliver $10 million cash to my associate tomorrow at 5:00 a.m. at 1319 N. Altadena Dr. Tell the police and Josie is dead."

LYDIA NOVAK: Aidan went to call the police, but Lila stopped him. She didn't trust them. She wanted to do it. Didn't have that kind of money just lying around, but she thought she could find a way to get it by the end of the day. Aidan was scared it wasn't even from the actual guy, that it was just a copycat. The notes weren't signed or anything. "Aidan, *please*. They're bungling this. I won't let them kill our daughter," she said.

"Do you hear yourself? What if the police are the only ones who can save her?" Aidan said.

"They just want money," Lila said, "and I can give them that."

I stepped in at that point. I said, "Lila, I don't think you want to mess around with this. It's too dangerous." She told me to mind my own damn business. It hurt, like I couldn't have opinions of my own or care about Josie.

"Every day they don't find her is another day where this guy gets impatient," Lila said.

"I'm not happy with the police either," Aidan said, "but we have to let them know. They should be there in case—"

"It's too risky." Lila's eyes got all big and sweet. "Aidan, I am asking you to trust me."

And he must have really loved her, because he said okay.

GREER HOUSER: Lila and Aidan immediately make the decision not to show this note to the police.

ANALISE RHODES: It's one of the greatest what-ifs of modern crime. It haunts me.

TOMMY OLSEN: That morning, a bunch of us were playing poker on the side of the street. It had become a little like camping, except with more stimulants. Then someone starts yelling that Lila's car is pulling down the driveway again. So, we hurry to get into position as the gate opens and she pulls out.

She didn't cower this time; we surrounded her car to get a picture, and she just held down her horn. It was blaring, and she kept moving forward. I got right in front of her, but she kept going, and I realized she was just gonna mow me down if I didn't move. She didn't give a shit.

LYDIA NOVAK: She drove off somewhere to get the money. I tried to talk to Aidan, tried to reason with him. "Call the police," I said. "They need to know what she's going to do."

"I can't," he said. He would never ever admit it, but I think Aidan was a little afraid of her. She came back a few hours later with two duffel bags full of cash. To this day, I have no idea where she went or what she did to get them. Nothing would stop her; she was determined to see this through.

And then I knew I didn't have another choice. Detective Fox had left his card; it was pinned to the refrigerator. I went home that night—it took me a couple hours to work up the courage to call. I knew Lila would see it as a betrayal. I knew I was sacrificing my livelihood and my friendship. Ultimately I had to look at the bigger picture. Josie didn't deserve to die because her mother was being stubborn.

NICK FOX: I joined the police force to protect the innocent. We are public servants. When people say they hate the police, they don't trust us, it really rubs me the wrong way. The sole purpose of my job is to keep you safe. Assuming my bad intentions is just, like, *projection.*

We got a call from the nanny late that night. One, two in the morning. Lila was going to fuck us because she was so goddamn paranoid. The housekeeper sent a picture of the second note. She said, "Please don't let that little girl die."

JOHN CARMICHAEL: We were shocked. It was so impulsive, so ill-advised.

NICK FOX: So stupid.

JOHN CARMICHAEL: We had to stop it. We drove out to the house in the middle of the night to talk to them, I knew there would be no reasoning with her on the phone.

TOMMY OLSEN: I recognized the detectives when they pulled in at two a.m. I knew something was up.

JOHN CARMICHAEL: Aidan answered the door. He thought we had an update on the case. I told him to get his wife. She came out, she wasn't in her pajamas. She was dressed in jeans and boots, fully ready to leave the house.

"Lydia Novak called us about the second note," I said. Lila kept her face neutral. She was a rock. "You do realize hiding evidence is obstruction."

"We were scared earlier, but we weren't actually going to go through with it." Aidan tried to speak for them, but she cut him off.

"I will do *whatever it takes* to bring Josie back. Every day that goes by with no lead and no update, I get less convinced that you will."

Aidan, rightly, didn't think it was a good idea for his wife to be talking to the police this way. I felt for her, to be honest. I said, "Lila, I'm a father. If my daughter went missing, and I couldn't see instant results, I would be scared too."

"It's not the lack of results," she argued. "It's the lack of *anything*."

Police work is a methodical and slow process. If civilians are frustrated by it, imagine how we feel doing it every day. Interviewing every single person in the neighborhood, in a two-mile vicinity; tracking every lead from every random person that gets called in; leaving no stone unturned and then turning over the stones a second time to make sure we didn't miss anything.

NICK FOX: "I got the money, I'm making the trade-off," she said. Obviously, that was unacceptable. And yeah, I raised my voice. A little. "You don't know if it's even a real note. The ransom leaked, someone could just be swindling you." But she was willing to take that risk. It was like she had this deep desire to blow up her life even more. I said, "You know the second we got that note, we sent guys out to that address in Pasadena."

Her face fell. "You fucking idiots. You fucking *boneheaded*, incompetent, fucking—" She had to put her hands on the couch to physically steady herself. She was boiling over.

"Careful," I said. I was running out of patience.

I knew she was smart. I had a thought that she was doing all this intentionally to confuse us. That this was all a big distraction, and behind the scenes, she was laughing at us. Either she did it or Aidan did it and she was protecting him.

JOHN CARMICHAEL: She said, "Fine. Now you know. I'm still gonna go. If you want to stop me, you need to physically restrain me."

Poor Aidan, who had tried so hard to be the mediator, finally snapped. "No, you're not. You're going to fucking do what the police tell you. I'm sick of this shit."

"It's all right," I said. "We decided she can make the exchange. We'll be there with her."

Fox cut her off. "If you want to do this, we do it my way. You talk about wasting time—if you leave me out of the loop on anything again, you're going to make things a hell of a lot more difficult for your child."

She said okay; she knew she didn't have a choice.

NICK FOX: We got her ready, wired her up. The drop-off spot in Pasadena was a 7-Eleven parking lot. We got there around 3:30, plainclothes in an unmarked car. We were careful in case the person was scoping out the area, but we didn't see anybody.

LYDIA NOVAK: My phone rang around three a.m. I wasn't sleeping; I couldn't. I answered it on the first ring. It was Lila. I knew she would be mad; I was expecting her to be mad. But she was ice cold. "The police came," she said. "They said you called them." I said, "I'm sorry, Lila. It was too dangerous to let you do this by yourself. For you and Josie."

Her voice was so quiet, it was like she was whispering. "If my daughter dies, that death is on your hands now. I will never, ever forgive you." And she fired me.

I was devastated. Aidan and Lila had become my family over the past two years. And I had given them so much, you have to understand. I stood by Lila through her entire bout of postpartum. Who took care of Josie when Aidan was working and Lila couldn't be bothered? I did. To claim I was trying to kill Josie was deeply hurtful. I was doing what my job had been since day one—keeping her safe.

All I could say before she hung up was "I will pray for you." I never spoke to her or Aidan again.

TOMMY OLSEN: We were on high alert outside, waiting. And when Lila's car pulled out of the house, police blocked us so the car could get through. Something was happening. I jumped in my car to follow.

GREER HOUSER: Aidan and Lila should have been in hiding. The police weren't used to the press interfering in a case at this level. So much of the case was already available to the public through leaks and on-scene reporting, the police should have been more careful. Watching it unfold, it made me think how *lucky* the Lindberghs had been when it happened to them.

ANALISE RHODES: There are videos of the car chase. It was like Princess Diana in the Paris tunnel. The roads up in those mountains are narrow, with a lot of blind turns. The paparazzi are right on their tail. At one point, they nearly get run off the road.

NICO DELUCA: I would never encourage something so unethical for the sake of my publication.

TOMMY OLSEN: I am a journalist. People might not like the kind of journalism I do, but they all consume it anyway. They were public figures, which made this a matter of public interest.

JOHN CARMICHAEL: Lila and Aidan called from the car. There were paparazzi following them, and they were driving through the hills at night. There was nowhere to hide to shake them off. We managed to get a car waiting for them in an underground parking lot in North Hollywood. They drove in and made it look like they were going in to some meeting with us. But in reality, they came out in another car through the back.

It worked, but it cost us a lot of time. Lila and Aidan were supposed to get to the handoff point early, but now they would be lucky to get there in the nick of time.

Lila and Aidan arrive at the 7-Eleven at 4:57 a.m.

JOHN CARMICHAEL: We had guys inside the 7-Eleven, inside the laundromat next door. We had guys in a van down the street, in the trunk of a car in the parking lot. We had a guy dressed as a homeless person panhandling outside. If *anything* happened, we were ready.

Lila and Aidan turned up one minute before the exchange was supposed to happen. They pulled up, waited in the parking lot. Aidan was drumming his fingers on the steering wheel. Lila had the money sitting in her lap.

My alarm went off, which marked five a.m. The street was dead quiet, and the sky was dark. It was—there was something eerie about it. Like you knew disaster was about to strike, but all you could do was wait for it to happen.

But nothing happened. Five came and went, then 5:01. Then 5:05. I texted Lila and Aidan to sit tight, that the person was likely nervous. Lila texted: *I'm gonna wait on the curb.*

That was a bad idea, but Fox and I couldn't risk calling her. If the kidnapper saw her on the phone, they'd get suspicious. But before I texted her to wait, she was getting out of the car with the duffel bags.

She went to a mailbox on the curb, dropped the duffel bags, and sat. I will give her this, that woman was fearless. She didn't even hesitate. I'll never forget that image. This tiny woman under a streetlamp, facing out into blackness, all alone.

NICK FOX: Then it was 5:15, and still no one had come. I knew it was fake the whole time. This was a charade; this was a waste of our money and our time and our resources to appease a woman who had a documented history of mental illness.

JOHN CARMICHAEL: Around 5:17, an unmarked van came speeding down the road. The windows were tinted; we couldn't see the driver. It saw Lila and slowed. I thought, *Holy shit, she was right.* Lila started heading toward the van.

NICK FOX: The door started to open, and it was dark and it happened so fast... One of our guys, dressed as a homeless person, he thought he saw someone with a gun inside. So, he ran out and raised his weapon to protect Lila.

JOHN CARMICHAEL: Lila claimed someone was holding a—a bundle inside, but we were too far away to see. The officer fired, and the van drove off.

ANALISE RHODES: What a surprise, a cop was trigger-happy and some-one wound up dead. This has never happened in the history of police work.

NICK FOX: I trust our force. If he saw something, he saw something. No matter what she said.

JOHN CARMICHAEL: Lila sprinted after the van, screaming, chasing it down the road. She almost caught up, but it ran the light and was gone in a second. She crumpled in the middle of the street on her knees, hyperventilating. Aidan ran to grab her. She couldn't walk.

I asked her if she was all right. She didn't answer, she made a bee-line for the officer who had fired his weapon and punched him in the face.

NICK FOX: She broke his fucking nose. We had to physically restrain her. She was screaming that we were intentionally sabotaging the case. I held her back, but she kept fighting, kicking and screaming. She was feral. And then it was like everything caught up to her and she fainted.

She thought her daughter disappearing meant she could live with no consequences. She assaulted an officer. I told him he should press charges, but Carmichael talked him down.

At 6:00 a.m. on March 17, Lila is admitted to Cedars-Sinai Medical Center for dehydration and exhaustion.

NICO DELUCA: We all thought the big secret of them driving out of the house in the middle of the night was her getting hospitalized. The real story didn't leak until much later.

ANALISE RHODES: The level of public scrutiny, of people starving for details of her hospital stay . . . it was disgusting.

GREER HOUSER: At the time, I was working a desk job, which just meant I spent all my free time on the subreddit. I was obsessed. It was inspiring, honestly, that all these strangers from all over the world had come together to find this little girl and bring her home.

Someone found an old interview with Lila after her dad had died. She was talking about drug and alcohol addiction and how dangerous it could be. Combined with everything else we knew, or didn't know, I guess, it looked damning. It went viral.

LILA DEVLIN (*interview*): For most people drugs and alcohol aren't something you have to think about. You just do it and have fun, and that's it. But with an addict, or someone with addiction in their family, it's something you're hyperaware of. After my mom died, my dad wasn't the same. The drinking stole the last familiar pieces of him. He was angry on the best nights, and on the worst nights he was violent. Never with me, but it terrified me that he even got close.

GREER HOUSER: She literally admitted drug and alcohol abuse ran in her family and caused dangerous behavior. She was high the night it happened. People thought the police were missing a red flag that was waving right in their faces.

I even thought she did it, and I'm a seasoned true crime expert. I *believe women.* I started the podcast because many of these theories were peddled so widely that we misremember certain details as facts.

NICO DELUCA: I think people were drawn to the case, and continue to be all these years later, because we naturally gravitate to tragedy. I mean look at, like, Shakespeare. He wrote some gnarly shit, and those are his most popular plays. To assume everyone prefers happy endings is a cliché, and it's not even right. Lila had been America's sweetheart for seven years. That's a long time to celebrate someone for just existing. People were hungry to see her fall.

After twenty-four hours in the hospital, Lila is released and returns home.

TIM WEBER: I stopped by to bring them dinner. I didn't see Lila, but Aidan looked like shit. Dark circles under his eyes, hadn't shaved in a week. You don't know how to talk to someone in that situation. You can't say *I'm sorry,* because that's what everyone says. You end up just not speaking at all. Aidan looked like he didn't want to be alone, so I sat with him, and we ate California Pizza Kitchen in dead silence.

I asked how Lila was doing. Aidan just shook his head. He was down bad. She wasn't speaking to him, or anyone. When Josie went missing, it was like someone put a magnifying glass on all the issues in their relationship. He was an extrovert. He liked to talk things out and lean on other people for support, just like people could lean on him. But she kept to herself. And when she came back from the hospital, she stopped speaking to everyone completely.

Aidan was like, "It's fucked to even think this when my daughter is missing, but I'm really fucking lonely."

FIVE

By the time Lila turned seventeen, her dad had let go of the remaining threads of fatherhood he'd been holding with a limp wrist. She rarely saw him, and when she did, they did not speak. It wasn't intentional; they'd just run out of things to say. She tried to remember the person he'd been before her mother had died, but she found it was easier to accept that that person had died with her and a stranger had taken over his skin.

He drank a lot. He never touched her but would grow mercurial if a coat was hung on the wrong hook. Most nights after work, he'd head to the pub down the street and watch whatever mindless game happened to be on. Once every few weeks, she'd get a call from the bartender to pick him up—he'd started a fight, threw up, pissed himself, or some combination of the three. They kept her number taped under the bar for easy reference.

Sometimes, if he was drunk enough on the car rides home, he would tell an old story about her mom she'd never heard before. He'd even make Lila laugh with tales of his high school exploits, like the senior prank her mother had masterminded where they'd put a live cow in the middle of the library and he had taken the fall for it like a gentleman. But usually, he stared blankly out the window in a pool of his own vomit.

The night before her AP exams junior year, the bar called around 12:30 a.m. She considered leaving him to figure out the way home himself, but she chastised herself for her cruelty and got out of bed.

As she pulled into the parking lot, the bartenders were forcing him out the door. They pointed to her car and let him go. He took one step toward her, spun around, and took off running into the dense forest behind the bar. She had to get out of the car and go after him on foot.

Mark was out of shape with a weakening heart; it didn't take long before she found him sprawled out on his back in the middle of a clearing. He was staring up at the night sky, green eyes glazed over, whatever light that was once inside of him snuffed out. He didn't say a word as she pulled him to his feet, nor when she wrapped his arm around her shoulders and helped him limp back to the car.

Finally, on the drive home, he turned to her and said, "This isn't fair to you."

They hadn't had an honest conversation in seven or eight years. Lila sat rigid in her seat, unsure of what to say. He seemed sober enough. Maybe he'd hit a breaking point; maybe he'd finally decided to turn around.

He continued: "We got bad genes in this family. We sink our teeth into something, and we don't know how to let go. I was hoping you'd take after your mom, but you're like me."

Lila recoiled, the rage she'd contained for years threatening to creep through. "I'm nothing like you," she said quietly.

But Mark just shook his head and leaned against the window. "Might not be drinking, but it'll be something. One day you'll find it and the shadow will cross through you and you won't notice till it's swallowed you whole."

Lila felt his spirit pulling her toward that descent when she lost Josie. But he hadn't had an outlet like she did. Her mother had died, and he'd carried her with him alone. Channeling that pain into something meaningful was the only tool she had to overpower it. Maybe a cosmetic company was silly, but it was tangible and possible and real. As long as she didn't dwell. If she dwelled, she'd sink.

WHEN LILA RETURNED TO SYLVIE'S OFFICE A FEW DAYS LATER, HER HAIR had returned to its old copper. Sylvie looked up from her desk and whistled. "Oh, thank God," she said. "Now you're not starting from total scratch."

It was shocking how much of a difference a change of hair color could make. The glow came back to Lila's cheeks, the life back in her eyes. People treated her differently too, regardless of whether they recognized her. She was pretty now; therefore she was worthwhile. She was insecure with the new attention—it was like a muscle that had gone unused so long it had atrophied. But she appreciated it. It made her feel human again.

"I have to say I'm pleasantly surprised you came back," Sylvie said. "You think over my offer?"

Lila nodded. "I realized I need to work with people I trust. And I think you have the potential to be someone I could trust."

"With your life." Sylvie put a hand to her heart. A little intense, but Lila was tired of noncommitment. She needed a partner who would pour her soul into their work.

"Then let's do it. Sixty-forty split." Lila offered her hand. Sylvie shook.

"Hell yeah." Sylvie spun around in her chair for emphasis. Suddenly, she grabbed her desk, stopping her chair. "Wait, you never mentioned, does the business have a name?"

"Glob," Lila said. She didn't elaborate.

"I love it." Sylvie chewed on her pencil. "We're gonna bring glob to the globe."

Sylvie poured a glass of seltzer into her mouth. Then she picked up a small bottle of flavoring and put a few drops in, swallowing. Lila must have been staring, because Sylvie smiled cheerfully. "I do this whenever I can't decide what kind of soda I want. I have four of them." She gestured to four little bottles with flavors like lemon/lime and cola.

"Couldn't you just pour multiple glasses?" Lila asked.

"That's a waste of so much water. This is just way easier." Sylvie was interrupted by her iPhone vibrating beside her. She glanced at the caller with a frown. "I have to take this," she said, holding a finger up.

"Sylvie Lightly's office," Sylvie announced with her voice raised three octaves. "Let me see if I can get her." She muted the phone and unmuted it a beat later. "This is Sylvie," she said.

"*The shoot is a disaster.*" The volume was so loud that Lila could hear the voice on the other end. "The fucking dog jumped on the woman playing its owner. It's so fucked—the dog is, like, gonna maul her, and then it turns into a complete sweetheart the minute she leaves the room. The dog's a racist."

"Now hang on a second, Tyler, it could just hate women—" Sylvie interjected.

"The video is already on Twitter, and people are going fucking insane. The company mascot is a fucking incel dog. Purina is gonna have a field day—"

"First of all, take a breath. In through your nose, out through the mouth, okay?" Sylvie twirled a fidget spinner between her fingers. "Okay, take the dog off set. I'll find an identical decoy. If anyone tries to talk to you about it, say you were rehabbing a rescue," she said. "No one can cancel a rescue."

The man on the other end hesitated. "What about Twitter?"

"Who gives a fuck about Twitter? In ten minutes something else is going to happen, and they'll move on," Sylvie said. No matter how outlandish the case was, Sylvie shone as she gave instructions.

When she hung up, she took a long sip of sparkling water. "Incel dog. Fucking incel dog. Do you know how exhausting it is to deal with idiots all day? Like, I'm not asking you to be a genius. I'm keeping it strictly in the realm of possibility—just be competent. I know you can do it if you put your mind to it."

"That sounds frustrating," Lila said.

"I deserve better than this," Sylvie said. "Dog food commercials are the glass ceiling for some people, but not for me. I won't put up with this shit anymore. Incel dog. I'm gonna get started on investor lists this afternoon." Sylvie's face grew serious. "Lila, I'm honored that you picked me to work with you. I won't let you down."

THE DEVLIN BABY
An Oral History

A week after Josie's disappearance, the police receive an interesting tip.

JOHN CARMICHAEL: The failed trade-off was an internal disaster. Small details slipped through the cracks to the press, but what had happened needed to be steel-trap shut. If the public heard that a cop had potentially doomed this little girl to die, we were afraid there would be riots.

NICK FOX: We worked overtime after that; we interviewed all the neighbors, all the people that worked for the neighbors—hell, if you walked dogs in the neighborhood *once*, we interviewed you.

GREER HOUSER: They should have done that immediately. Their scope was too limited when they canvassed the neighborhood the first time.

JOHN CARMICHAEL: And then, finally, we talked to the gardeners who worked on the Reynoldses' property. There was a new guy who had started working for them three months prior. That man went by the name David Lewis, but fingerprints revealed his real name was actually Arthur Allen. Arthur Allen was previously convicted twice for sexual assault and child pornography in Arizona.

GREG JONES (*gardener*): We came once a week, every Monday. Most of us had been working there a few years. Arthur comes in and is obsessed with Lila and Aidan, wants to know everything we know. One time we passed by an upstairs window, and he asked if it was the baby's window. At the time, I thought he was just starstruck and curious, but a few days after Josie was taken I started to get a sick feeling in the pit of my stomach.

LYDIA NOVAK: Arthur Allen and I were friendly. We both were fond of wisteria; we'd chat whenever he was working. He'd ask how the family was, and the baby girl. He was so shy and sensitive it never occurred to me that he'd be capable of . . .

NICK FOX: After hearing the window story, we brought him in for questioning. He was an odd guy. Quiet, meticulous. He was six-five but the smallest person in the room. Very soft-spoken and polite. He tried to make himself invisible. He wasn't prepared for this.

JOHN CARMICHAEL: I asked him if he was a fan of Lila Devlin and Aidan Reynolds. He said he didn't know who they were before working for them. "Four of your coworkers can vouch that you asked about them on six separate occasions." He was scared: "I mean, I didn't know them; I just knew they were famous. I was curious."

Fox was ready. Guy was a pit bull. He took out a couple pages from his folder. They were printouts of Arthur Allen's Twitter likes.

NICK FOX: A lot of deepfake Lila porn. He put his own face as his profile picture, so there was no way to deny it.

JOHN CARMICHAEL: He was white as a ghost. "Where were you between eleven and five a.m. on March 5?" I asked. "I was asleep in bed by ten p.m.," he said. "Can anyone verify that?" I asked. Arthur looked between Fox and me, and then he just said, "I want a lawyer."

NICK FOX: We got a warrant to go through his apartment almost immediately. The more time that passed, the more nervous the DA got that we wouldn't solve this. Think about it: we had the press, the public, and two of the biggest movie stars in the country breathing down our necks. If we failed, the optics would be a nightmare.

ANALISE RHODES: There was mounting pressure for them to find a suspect, whether or not they did it. There was too much pressure to let it go cold.

JOHN CARMICHAEL: I called Aidan and Lila to let them know we had a suspect. Aidan was thrilled. Even Lila was hopeful. Arthur Allen was the guy; even Fox, who had been so skeptical, knew it. Allen knew the house, knew their schedules. He was friendly with the nanny, no doubt heard details about their private lives. He was a gardener, for God's sakes; he had easy access to a ladder. The prior convictions for child porn and sexual assault . . . Lila and Aidan were scared.

I'm not a perfect man, but I try to be a good one. I became a detective to help families like theirs. Lila and I had had our misgivings, but we'd come to an understanding, and we were going to work together to get Josie back. I respected her strength.

This was going to be my last case before my retirement, and I swore to them and to myself that we'd bring her back, no matter what. The hostage exchange had been a failure, no matter how much I refused to admit it at the time. I could not fail them again. I wouldn't be able to live with myself.

The police search Arthur Allen's apartment and find no evidence.

JOHN CARMICHAEL: There was nothing. Arthur had learned from his last charge. Josie wasn't there, any trace of anything had been wiped. I thought he had to have hidden Josie somewhere else, if she was still alive. We had nothing tying him to the case but circumstantial evidence. There wasn't enough to charge him on, and he was refusing to talk.

When I had to tell Lila and Aidan, it shattered me. Bad news got worse. I told myself we'd catch him, that this was only a small setback.

ANALISE RHODES: As the weeks went by with no updates from the case and no sign of Josie, the Reynoldses' marriage fully deteriorated.

TIM WEBER: Aidan started asking me to come over more often or would come over to my place when he needed space. He said the house was suffocating. I knew they weren't gonna make it, even though neither of them would admit it.

NICO DELUCA: We had a lot of sources coming to us with stories about the two of them not getting along. A pity. You want times like this to unite people, but it never works out that way.

SUSAN FRIEDLAND: We tried to get through to her, but eventually she just started blocking people whenever they reached out. It was like she was trying to cut herself off from the world.

TIM WEBER: One day Aidan admitted to me that he thought Josie was dead. He said he saw it in a dream, and it had felt so real he woke up in tears. Aidan always thought psychic woo-woo stuff was bullshit, but he was shaken. He and Lila weren't sleeping in the same bed anymore, she slept on the floor of Josie's room every night.

GREER HOUSER: About six weeks after Josie was abducted, two huge stories dropped in quick succession: the first was an anonymous source recounting the failed hostage exchange to *White Smiles, Bright Lights*, and the second was a tell-all interview with their housekeeper for the *LA Times*.

NICO DELUCA: We got the story of the fucking century. The prestige papers can claim whatever they want, but we were the ones who broke the hostage exchange story. One of the most insane failures of modern police work. That was *us*.

LYDIA NOVAK: I felt like my side of the story deserved to be heard, so yes, I went to the press. My unfair termination affected my home and my livelihood.

ANALISE RHODES: My interview with Lydia Novak was my first involvement with the case. It was quite salacious, though I didn't intend it to be. She painted a dark picture of their marriage and Lila's mental state.

GREER HOUSER: Even though Arthur Allen was a named suspect, Lila was still getting hate online. Lot of men's rights guys thought Arthur was being framed. It seemed like half the internet despised Lila for the totally botched hostage exchange, and the other half wanted to nuke the LAPD.

CARA DONALDSON: Lila's agent contacted me after the articles broke. Lila's public image was in dire shape, and she needed to be rehabilitated.

In the worst-case scenario, the pedophile gardener would be cleared and the police would likely arrest Lila due to public pressure. That obviously couldn't happen. I had to coordinate with Aidan in secret, because I knew she wouldn't answer the door if I came. It was like a fucking intervention.

Aidan let me in and called Lila downstairs. "Lila, I want to schedule a televised interview with Diane Sawyer," I said. Lila started gearing up for battle. "Cara, I don't have the energy for PR stuff," she told me. She didn't understand how dangerous this was. "Listen to me," I said. "This situation is atrophying. If you don't do something, you won't be able to come back from this." She said she didn't care about being an actress.

I stopped being gentle. I told her, "I have worked with you for six years. Like it or not, you are a public figure. Not just a public figure, *the public's figure. They own you.* They feel entitled to judge you. People think you are mentally unstable and heartless. We need to take back the narrative. You need to trust me when I say this isn't about acting." I almost shook her. "This is you for the rest of your life. People will *hate* you. They need someone to hate when tragedy happens, and you're rich and beautiful and you're a woman. It will be easy."

Aidan cut in. I had expected him to say something earlier, but he didn't back me up. He barely spoke at all, except to say, "If you don't do it for you, do it for Josie. Set things right," before leaving the room. And I think Lila felt so bad she said, "Okay."

Lila accepts a televised interview with Diane Sawyer airing that Sunday night.

CARA DONALDSON: That morning of, we were getting ready and she started having second thoughts. She didn't think she could do it. I said, "You are an actress. If you can't do it, be someone else."

LILA DEVLIN (*interview*): The public scrutiny is unavoidable, I guess, as a celebrity. But the way I have been derided and mocked for trying to cope with the loss of the person I love most in the world is beyond cruel—it's inhumane. I feel like I'm in a fish tank sometimes and people won't stop knocking on the glass.

CARA DONALDSON: There was only one moment—I wanted to cut it, but ABC insisted—that was a bit . . . divisive.

DIANE SAWYER (*interview*): What would you say to the person who took your daughter, if they're watching this?

LILA DEVLIN (*interview*): I have your money. Give me a time and a place and I will be there. I will never let anything or anyone get in the way of my daughter again. I swear on my life.

CARA DONALDSON: It was a little . . . intense. And we were worried it might be interpreted as a threat.

The interview premieres to a stunning 17 million live viewers and is talked about for weeks.

ANALISE RHODES: It's a special kind of interview that manages to break into wider pop culture.

GREER HOUSER: People were talking about it like it was a live sporting event. The ads were everywhere. When it aired, it was the number one trending topic in the world. There were, like, seventeen million people watching live, which is fucking unheard of.

To be honest, it convinced me she was innocent. Truly innocent. They should have done it way sooner. There'll always be the people that she can't convince no matter what, that say she's an actress, but it was way too raw.

DIANE SAWYER (*interview*): What would you say to those who think this tragedy happened due to your parental neglect?

LILA DEVLIN (*interview*): There is no such thing as a perfect mother. I think a lot of people expect motherhood to turn you into this enlightened figure, and it just doesn't. You're the same person as before. I'm twenty-nine, I did something stupid with my friends. And now part of my soul has been ripped out and she's just out there somewhere. I would give up everything to bring her back to me.

CARA DONALDSON: The rest of Lila's team and I were relieved. It felt like now, at the very least, her life could be salvaged, even if the police couldn't . . . you know.

NICO DELUCA: Yes, it's fair to say we softened our coverage after that. *Softened* isn't the right word—we weren't being hard on her in the first place. We were just being accurate to the story as it unfolded, and it turned out she wasn't as guilty as she might have seemed in the beginning. The tide turned in her favor with that interview.

ANALISE RHODES: When the scale shifted in Lila's favor, Arthur became the target.

GREER HOUSER: Everyone was determined to catch him and bring him to justice. Internet sleuths hacked his email, went through his trash, desperate to find Josie.

NICK FOX: While all of that was happening, the police were staking out Arthur's apartment and following him everywhere. For weeks. But we couldn't find anything. And then the internet people started trying to "help." That *White Smiles* website had a daily "Arthur Update." He started complaining about people stalking him. There was no way he was going to lead us to her with the entire world watching.

JOHN CARMICHAEL: And all of us watching gave him the perfect alibi when . . .

On April 27, a third note is discovered.

JOHN CARMICHAEL: Lila got another note, a week after the interview. Aidan called me, told me to come over. I found him and Lila on the couch. She was still as a statue, but I could see her hands shaking in her pockets. I looked at the note, it said, "Dear Lila, I regret to inform you that Josie is dead. I saw your interview. I am sorry for your loss."

"It's not real, it doesn't mean anything," Aidan kept saying. But Lila wouldn't listen to him anymore. "It's real," she said quietly. And I hated to admit I agreed with her. The kidnapper wrote in this weirdly sympathetic voice, it fit.

"Are there any updates on Arthur Allen?" Aidan asked me. I told him no. He shook his head. "You have him, you know it's him. Arrest him." I told him I wanted to, more than anything, but couldn't. "He killed my daughter right under your nose," Aidan said. "This can't be right. This isn't right."

Fox agreed with Aidan, the note could have been a fake. And maybe it was. We would keep working. But in my gut, I knew Arthur Allen had sent it. I left them in their big house that day, and the failure that I had been running from the last two months caught up to me.

Six

Nick Fox was smug; that's what Lila hated most. During the ugliest moments of Josie's investigation, he'd meet her with a cruel, dismissive smile. Ten years later, as he sat across from her at the desk in his office, his gaze was amused. Maybe he was right to be. He'd ruined any chance of finding her daughter, and now he sat in the corner office Detective Carmichael had once held.

Lila felt talons in the pit of her stomach, clawing up its walls. She forced them down. *I find peace in my life; in my life I make peace.* Josie wouldn't want her mother to be a bitter old woman. If Fox wanted an apology, she would give it to him. A small price if he let her close this chapter of her life for good.

"Thank you so much for finding time to see me," she said.

Fox took a sip of his coffee. "You could imagine my surprise when you called."

He still took great care with his grooming—his black hair was slicked back, and his bushy mustache was neatly trimmed. His putrid cologne brought Lila back to the night they'd first met, when he'd interrogated her like a suspect. It made her nauseated.

"I spent the last ten years learning how to manage my grief, and a big missing piece of the puzzle is making amends. I hoped getting to talk to you again would help me move on," Lila said.

Fox inhaled through his nose. Lila knew that expression—he was summoning his patience. He thought this was bullshit. "Of course," he said.

His office was sparsely decorated. It lacked any personal touches except for a Dodger ball and a photo of his family on his desk. His daughter was Josie's age, or Josie would have been her age.

"I was at the lowest point of my life when my daughter went missing. I'm deeply sorry for how I treated you. I just wanted her back," Lila said.

Fox's eyes twinkled, but he nodded. "I appreciate the apology, Ms. Devlin. If anything happened to my girl, I'd be a shell."

"She's beautiful," Lila said.

They sat in silence for a moment. She waited for him to give his apology in turn, but he said nothing.

Disdain soaked into Lila. She tried to stop it, to remind herself that an apology from him wasn't why she'd come, but she couldn't help it. He was a cruel man. There was no reason he wasn't as suspicious of Aidan as he was of her other than petty dislike and sexism. And after ten years, with that smug, serene smile, he still delighted in making her squirm.

"I wanted Josie's killer arrested more than anyone. The fact that they got away with it is an abomination of justice," Fox said.

"Have there been any updates?" Lila asked.

Fox shook his head sadly. "It went cold. Killer fled, went into hiding somewhere."

"You mean Arthur Allen?" Lila said softly. She never said his name out loud, as though it would conjure him beside her.

Fox took another sip of coffee. "Mm. I won't give up."

And then Lila realized he wasn't talking about Arthur Allen at all. He was talking about her. She started to clench her jaw reflexively but stopped, knowing he was watching closely for any proof of guilt. She wanted to yank that mustache off him—

No. That's not who she wanted to be. Josie wouldn't want her to live as a bitter, spite-fueled woman. Fox had worked hard, she told herself. He had been so passionate because he cared, she screamed at herself. She exhaled the frustration out with a deep sigh.

Sometimes she wondered where all that anger that lived inside her went. If a sigh was truly enough to get it out. It felt like it was gone. She told herself it was gone.

"My kid died ten years ago, Detective Fox. It would be nice to close this case for good. Let us all have some peace," Lila said.

Fox let out what almost sounded like a laugh and quickly took a swig of coffee.

"Something funny?" Lila said.

"Sorry, just some indigestion," he said.

The only thing he'd apologize for was pretend indigestion. He hadn't treated her with respect when she was the most famous actress in the country, and now he cared even less.

"You getting any harassment online? We've gotten some reports about the 'Devil Baby' stuff on TikTok," Fox said.

"What?" Lila said.

"It's a QAnon thing. *Devlin* sounds like *Devil*; they think you sacrificed her to Satan," Fox said. She could have sworn he sounded eager.

"Oh," Lila said. "No, I don't know anything about that."

Fox nodded. "Well, keep an eye out. Lot of people out there don't like you," he said.

Appreciate the reminder.

"I should probably get going," Lila said.

Fox did not stand up from his desk to say goodbye. "Take care." He smiled that omniscient smile as Lila walked out the door.

She felt the clawing in her abdomen again and put a hand to her stomach, willing it to go away. There was something small and dark that lived just under her heart. She first felt it when she attacked the swarm of reporters on the night Josie was taken. She could mostly ignore it. Gaunt, deformed, and silent, it had turned dormant during her decade away, and she'd assumed it was gone for good. But coming back to LA had shaken it awake. Maybe it was the nearness to where Josie's spirit had been taken. Some days, she could feel it pacing back and forth, steps vibrating through her body, reminding her it was there waiting—and that it was losing patience.

Lila didn't like how hungry it was. And no matter how hard she tried, she couldn't exorcise it. It stayed tucked safely inside, demanding to be let out. Maybe it had always been in her, silent and unassuming, waiting to wake up.

"I find peace in my life; in my life I make peace," Lila whispered to herself as she got into her car. "I find peace in my life; in my life I make peace."

The only way to get rid of the thing inside her was to let go of that rage and move on. She was only hurting herself. Fox had been too big of a swing. She had to start smaller: Nico DeLuca. The reporter who broke the story and ballooned it into a nightmare.

That night, Lila found him on Instagram. Her cursor hovered over the direct message button. She closed the page, then opened it again. Then closed it again. She must have sat there for ten minutes, just toggling the window. *Hey, can we talk about my dead kid?* she typed. Delete. *Been a while, did you use the money you made on the back of my daughter's corpse for hair plugs?* Delete.

She wasn't doing this for him, she reminded herself. *Hi Nico, I'm back in LA and would love to find a time to talk.* Before she could hesitate, she hit send.

THE DEVLIN BABY
An Oral History

On May 30, almost three months after Josie's disappearance, an infant's body is found in Lake Gregory, right outside of Los Angeles.

WALTON MORRIS (*witness*): I drive up from Los Feliz on the weekends to fish sometimes. I was out early in the morning, and my line caught on something heavy. I thought it was a shoe until . . . until it surfaced.

JOHN CARMICHAEL: My friend out there called me. When he said he had bad news, I knew they'd found her. He said they'd identified the body as a female toddler, but beyond that, the skeletal tissue was too badly burned for an actual DNA sample. But the size and length of decay matched the profile of Josie Reynolds.

GREER HOUSER: Again—NOT SAYING SHE DID IT! *But*—Lake Gregory is a ninety-minute drive from Bel Air with no traffic. Three-hour round trip.

NICK FOX: Carmichael was a good guy; he was the heart of the department. Everyone looked to him to guide them. And that morning, I saw him take the call in his office. We worked ugly cases, terrible cases. He never broke once. People called him "the Rock." I saw him cry for the first time in my life, and I knew it was over.

JOHN CARMICHAEL: I drove up to go see the body in person—I couldn't tell the family without having seen her with my own eyes. I never believed in God much, but I prayed that I'd get there and find out there'd been some horrible mistake. But I got there, and they took me to see her. The note had been real like Lila had known it was. Looking at Josie in person—the cruelty of it was horrifying.

All I could hope was that whoever did it had the mercy to give her an easy death. It still haunts me to this day, thinking about what her last moments must have been like.

I ordered the body brought to Los Angeles, and then I went to report to the family. I drove to their house, and Lila was waiting at the door. I didn't even have to say the words, she already knew. She turned around before I could see the tears start to fall and yelled for Aidan to come downstairs.

He came out to meet me, and I couldn't meet his eyes, and his face fell. I told him her body had almost certainly been recovered in a lake this morning. He let out this scream of pure anguish, and Lila took him into her arms. And she held him as he wept into her chest.

All I could say was how sorry I was. Not just for their loss of Josie. Sorry for the way my men handled the crime scene. Sorry for not protecting them from the press. Sorry for Fox hounding her. Sorry for that buffoon firing that fucking shot that fucked us for good.

This case was a catastrophic failure on my part. I know I've said otherwise in these pages, but . . . The LAPD would never admit it. I expedited my retirement.

After Aidan calmed down enough to speak, he asked how I knew it was Josie's body for certain. "Without DNA, there's still a chance—" Lila cut him off. "Give yourself the gift of knowing." She was right. Not knowing, that was even worse.

That afternoon at an LAPD press conference, Carmichael makes the announcement that Josie's body was discovered that morning.

JOHN CARMICHAEL: I'm no good at public speaking. I could barely get the statement out.

NICO DELUCA: It was terrible. Every parent's worst nightmare. We dedicated that week's online issue in Lila's honor.

ANALISE RHODES: The whole world mourned that little girl. It was horribly ironic—the public scrutiny on the case destroyed any chance the police had of bringing Josie back to her family alive and the culprit to justice. Yet they felt entitled to mourn.

GREER HOUSER: No one could believe it. A lot of people straight up didn't. Without confirmed DNA evidence, people thought it was a decoy or a coincidence. Josie became the modern Princess Anastasia. There would always be a question of whether it was really her, no matter how likely it was.

Josie's funeral was held in Cape Cod, Massachusetts, one week after her body was discovered. Her ashes were scattered in the Atlantic Ocean. The funeral was closed to the public and attended only by Lila, Aidan, and his family.

TIM WEBER: Lila and Aidan's marriage was hanging by the single thread of Josie coming back and them getting to be a family again. But when Josie died, that thread broke. They tried after the funeral. But, like, when you're in a relationship, there can only be a certain amount of pain. You can only carry so much until you collapse, right? And between them both, there was just too much. It could never go back to the way it was before.

Two months after Josie's funeral, Aidan moved out. Two months after that, they were done for good.

ANALISE RHODES: Lila and Aidan announced their divorce six months after Josie's disappearance, and the whole incident began to fade from the public eye. The case wasn't splashy and sordid anymore. Now, it was just gawking at two people who had lost everything. There's no fun in that.

NICK FOX: I stayed with the LAPD. I'm a detective inspector now. That was my first case as a detective, and it was trial by fire. But it taught me a lot, taught all of us a lot as officers of the law. I wouldn't say we made mistakes at all. We did the best we could, under the circumstances.

CARA DONALDSON: Lila quit acting and didn't need me anymore, but Aidan hired me as his publicist. I've been on his team for ten years now. Going through that with him—we understand each other.

ANALISE RHODES: Aidan went back to work about a year after Josie was kidnapped. He threw himself into his acting career with full force. All the publicity and public sympathy gave him a huge boost. The world was rooting for him. Lila fell off the map. There were sightings of her occasionally for another year or so, but then they grew rarer and rarer until they stopped altogether.

NICO DELUCA: *White Smiles, Bright Lights* scoured the globe for years. But she disappeared without a trace. I think she had a full-face makeover. Or maybe people didn't care enough to say anything. Since Lila's case, we've flourished as a website. As the new trendy gossip blogs come and go, we're always there. And we know everything. Fuck you, Deuxmoi.

ANALISE RHODES: I covered this case for the *LA Times* until Josie was laid to rest. I've written a couple of long-form retrospectives as the years have passed. I don't think enough will ever be said about it. It's a kaleidoscope of a thing; everyone's perspective is different depending on how you see the woman at the center. Lila Devlin and the Devlin baby case have earned a permanent spot in the annals of pop culture. The only thing people like more than a movie star is watching them get snuffed out.

GREER HOUSER: Aidan Reynolds is now one of the most successful actors in Hollywood. The millennial Tom Hanks. No one has ever attempted to cancel him. No one would even consider it. He's too good of a guy. Everyone who meets him says he's the kindest, most positive person. He's done so much work for victims of abuse and violence. People see him as an inspiration.

Nearly four years after Josie died, Aidan Reynolds remarried, to model Sonnet Montgomery. Today, they have a six-year-old daughter named Talia.

ANALISE RHODES: When Sonnet gave birth to Talia, everyone was thrilled. Of course, she could never replace Josie, but it felt like Aidan, after having been through so much, was getting a happy ending. Or a hopeful ending, at the very least.

It makes you wonder, ten years later, what's become of Lila.

GREER HOUSER: All you can do is hope that she's found some semblance of peace, wherever she is now.

SEVEN

What if Lila called it off? Fifteen minutes, there was still time. She hadn't expected him to return the Instagram DM within three minutes. She hadn't expected him to clear his schedule to find a time that worked. She hadn't expected the meeting to take place within a week. There had been no time to prepare.

She wasn't ready. She wasn't ready, and Nico would see. She'd sweat long, languid drips down her forehead, and he'd see, but she wouldn't notice until they splashed on her cheek. And then he'd write an article, maybe even a think piece, asking why was she sweating, why was she so nervous, does she have something to be nervous about? And that sweat was proof she'd descended into the deep pit of hysteria and was out of control—

"I find peace in my life; in my life I make peace," Lila hissed, digging her nails into her palms.

Nico knew her face like a painter. He had studied every twitch of the lips, every eyebrow raise, every shade of expression when she was upset. Under no circumstances would he make her cry. If she cried of her own volition talking about Josie, fine. It would probably even make her sympathetic. But Nico would not pull her triggers today.

Think of it as an acting job; she was a good actor. Wasn't she? Lila Devlin in the role of: the best version of herself. Confident and even-keeled, with an impressive budding company and a heart fully healed.

"Starting now." She closed her eyes and opened them again. She tilted her head slightly in the mirror, better to look down than up. But she looked the same as before.

She caught her hands fidgeting. The best version of herself didn't scratch at her hands until they spouted blood. The best version of herself didn't pick at the crevices in her skin until they split. Lila closed her eyes again.

"Starting now."

SYLVIE WAS GRACIOUS ENOUGH TO LET LILA HAVE THE OFFICE FOR THE afternoon. Lila sat on the couch, her posture rigid. Sylvie put a gentle hand on her shoulder. "Hey, you're gonna be great. Remember, this is for you, not him."

Lila nodded. Sylvie took a swig of seltzer and opened the door. "Call me when you're done!"

And then Lila was alone. She stared down at the panther carrying the coffee table on its shoulders. It looked like it was screaming. She was struck by how shabby the office looked—the half-finished starter kits, box cutters, and craft supplies strewn about; the dull grey walls. Nico would judge all of it.

The second the clock struck four p.m., there was a knock at the door.

Nico was a tiny man, around forty years old, no taller than five feet four inches, and had dedicated his life to compensating for it. His compact body was poreless and toned; his arms so muscular little veins poked out. In his Instagram bio, he ironically described himself as a "power twink." Lila had expected him to look more like an extremely online Gollum, but he took better care of himself than she did.

"Lila! You look gorgeous." His eyes flashed to the thickness of her thighs and then up to the folds around her mouth with a little smirk.

"Thank you," Lila said. "Can I get you water, coffee?"

"Sparkling water would be great," Nico said, following her inside. Lila vaguely remembered the rule that vampires had to be invited in.

Lila headed over to Sylvie's seltzer maker and poured Nico a glass. Sylvie had left her little flavor bottles out on the counter. Lila covertly swiped them into a drawer.

Nico had made himself comfortable on the couch. Lila set the glass down and took the chair across from him. The creature in her chest was quiet today. Or maybe she'd gotten better at drowning it out.

"I appreciate you finding the time," Lila said, once he'd taken a sip. "I know it's an unusual DM to get—"

Nico cut in. "No, are you kidding? I was thrilled. I feel like we're fire forged in this incredibly traumatic event, so we understand each other. It altered the course of our lives."

Lila held her tongue. She'd gotten so used to the feeling that she might as well have swallowed it. "Has your website been doing well?"

"We're not just a website anymore—we're a brand. I like to say we're gen TMZ," Nico replied.

"Isn't Gen Z into the Deuxmoi person?" Lila asked.

Nico soured. "No. Deuxmoi is a try-hard and—God bless her—a janky bitch. I have the reputation that I do because I don't publish everything I hear. Three-quarters of the stuff she posts ends up being wrong."

He failed to see the irony. There was no point in putting the energy into hating him because his insides had been hollowed out.

"That sounds frustrating."

"It's just an eternal hustle. You have to keep innovating," said Nico. "Ten years ago, I didn't know what a podcast was. Now, I have a deal with Spotify. It's wild. But enough about me. How are you? I heard you're starting a company?"

"We're taking our time to get it on its feet. I'm a little impatient, if I'm completely honest, but it's more important to launch the right way with all our ducks in a row."

"Totally," Nico said. The mole below his left eye looked like a tear. "When I heard you came back to LA for this, I thought it was a joke. But here you are!"

"Here I am." Lila laughed along as though he were familiar enough with her to joke like that. He probably thought he was. His home page had a full tab that said *DEVLIN BABY* for the first two years after Josie's disappearance. He knew deeply intimate details about her marriage and her private life. *I find peace in my life; in my life I make peace.*

"Um, you're bleeding."

Lila glanced down and saw blood pouring from the fresh cut on her thumb. "Shit," she said, grabbing a napkin off the table to put pressure on it. "My skin gets dry," she explained, and then kicked herself because she didn't owe him an explanation.

Nico watched her wrap the napkin around her finger. "Lila, we were always on the same side. I cared more than anyone about bringing Josie home. I stepped up because the police were doing such a shit job."

Lila's lips quirked up, and she squeezed the napkin around her finger until the knuckle turned white. Wasn't forgiveness supposed to make her feel better? It felt more like suicide.

"Also, I know you were in India or whatever, so you probably didn't get much time on the internet, but I want you to know that I dedicated the website relaunch in Josie's honor. We love you. It's so fun to finally see you get a win," Nico added.

"A win," Lila echoed.

Nico nodded. He opened his shoulder pack and rummaged around before removing a foldable metal straw. He put it in his seltzer and sucked. "I never thought you did it."

Lila could feel hot blood pumping in her chest, her heartbeat slamming against her skin.

Nico didn't notice. "We had a pool in the office for whether you did it. And all the people who didn't suck thought you were innocent."

"I appreciate your support."

"Could I grab some more water?" Nico asked.

"Of course." Lila grabbed the glass off the table, eager for a small reprieve. There was a soft static ringing in her ears. She tried to blink it away, but it was stuck.

"Can you make it extra bubbly?" Nico asked. "I like it spicy."

The room was silent except for the seltzer machine's periodic roars. Lila stared at it, counting the seconds in her head. The ringing was piercing now, at a frequency so high she held on to the counter to steady herself.

I find peace in my life; in my life I make peace.

She set the glass down in front of Nico. It was damp from the sweat of her palm.

"Amazing, thank you," he said, not looking up from his phone.

Only when Lila sat back down in her chair did he make eye contact.

"Work thing." Nico stuck out his tongue. "How are you and Aidan?"

Lila bristled at the personal question but remained polite. "He's great. I see him and his family every now and then."

"They're so cute," Nico said.

"So cute."

Lila glanced out the window. The world went on outside, shining and oblivious. *Three things you can see* . . . A woman pleaded with a meter maid. A cyclist sped through traffic. A beleaguered assistant hurried down the crosswalk juggling two giant bags of take-out lunches.

"Look, I invited you here to clear the air. This . . . thing . . . has defined my life, and I don't want to live like that anymore. Josie wouldn't want that either," Lila said.

Before Lila could continue, Nico cut her off. "I appreciate the invitation. Otherwise, I never would have known how to reach out to you. I want to apologize for how my site wrote about you ten years ago. There's nothing I can say to excuse it. I know it sounds nuts to say it was nothing personal, but it literally wasn't. Take comfort that it was never about you. People just wanted more of your story."

She should have been happy she'd gotten an apology at all, but . . .

"But all of it was a lie," Lila said.

Nico put a finger up. "We hire fact-checkers to verify—"

"You spread conjecture. Your 'reporting' started a hate movement against me." The little grey creature peeked out of its nest. *No.* Lila shut her eyes for a moment, collecting herself.

Nico hung his head. "2011 through 2016 were my dark years. I was a grizzly little ketamine troll who wore flip-flops to work because my sole focus in life was getting *WSBL* off the ground. Honestly, Trump getting elected was a huge wake-up call for me." He paused, searching her face for a mutual understanding she couldn't give him, and then continued. "That's not, like, a justification for me being nosy, but it is an explanation. I wasn't trying to ruin your life, of course not. It just became a public story, so I had to cover it to the best of my abilities."

At least he was the one to bring it up. She supposed that had to count for something. "I appreciate your apology."

"2014 doesn't seem that long ago, but we've come a long way in how women are treated in the press. Cards on the table, like, reporting on such a horrifying, brutal crime day in and day out really affected my mental health."

"I'm sorry to hear that," Lila said.

"Do you ever think Josie might be alive?" Nico asked. "I rewatched *Anastasia* the other day, and I was like, *Wait a second.* 'Cause the body they found in Lake Gregory was too badly burned."

"No, I don't," she replied quietly.

Nico tried to recalibrate. "I mean, obviously it's, like, a tiny chance it's not her. But what if? Have you ever tried to—"

"I spread my daughter's ashes ten years ago," Lila snapped.

Shit. She wasn't supposed to snap. She was supposed to give him grace.

"I'm sorry."

"I get it. I'm the same way when people ask me about it," Nico said.

Silence. Lila had given up on the urge to fill the room, to make him comfortable. Frankly, she enjoyed watching him squirm. His eyes flicked, he pretended to admire the panther table, he took a long sip of water. Finally, when the quiet became excruciating, he cleared his throat.

"God, that feels better. Ugh, I love a new leaf!" Nico said. "Okay, new topic—I feel like you're trying to launch this business thing, and I think I might be able to help you."

"How?" Lila said.

"I host one of the biggest podcasts in the country. Twenty million listeners a week. My reach is essentially the stretchy guy from the Fantastic Four. Every season I do a series of interviews with different celebrities around a single theme. Like, I've been nominated for awards. I want you as a guest."

Thank God. They were finally through the hard part. She'd guest on his dumb podcast, promote glob, and then she'd never have to deal with him again. Lila nodded politely. "What's the theme you want me for?"

"Motherhood."

A pigeon was sitting on the telephone wire outside the window. It was fat, almost fully spherical, with little grey feet poking out underneath. The wire was thin, maybe an inch or two. Lila was concerned it would tip over and fall; it hardly had the balance to perch for long. And yet it sat there, unwavering.

"Every episode, I interview a different kind of famous mother. So, like, last week we did an episode on stepmoms, and this week we did an episode on working moms, moms who don't stay at home."

The pigeon turned its head and looked right at her. There were tiny yellow rings around its eyes. She wanted to warn it. To tell the fat, stupid pigeon to fly away, far away; if it had the wings to go anywhere, why was it wasting its time on that wire?

"And when you reached out, I thought—wouldn't it be so amazing and inspiring if you guested on an episode where we talk about moms who, you know, don't have any children?"

The piercing sound in her ears was deafening; Lila could only make sputtering noises. This time, when the heat in her chest rose and rose until it reached her throat, she was too weak to fight it. Lila weak, the little grey creature finally gained the power to burst out of her chest. It tarred her soul and its hands became hers and it sewed her mouth shut.

Lila picked up the box cutter she'd been using for glob's starter kits, reached across the coffee table, and slit Nico's throat.

HE TOUCHED HIS THROAT AND STARED AT THE TRICKLE OF BLOOD. HE looked more confused than afraid. It was faint at first, just a few drops, and then it grew into a downpour. Lila watched as a flood of maroon washed over him. He opened his mouth to speak but only managed a muffled moan. His hand suddenly reached out toward her, straining to grab her—

And then he fell to the floor.

Suddenly, Lila was back inside herself, frantically clasping his throat to save him, but the force of blood was impossible to stop. She sat on her knees with his head in her lap. He grunted as the color drained from his face, staring up at Lila with wide and terrified eyes. Almost childlike.

"It's okay," Lila said quietly, sucking back the panic. There was nothing she could do except cradle him in her arms. Had he always looked so young? "Everything's okay." She rocked him back and forth, humming softly as Nico's hands gripped her shirt collar, making sure she wouldn't leave him. She would never. "I'm right here," Lila assured him. And then his grip eased, and he leaned back, and Lila stroked his face as his eyes fluttered shut.

She wasn't sure how much time had passed as she sat covered in his blood. She didn't like his limp weight on her, but she couldn't bring herself to move.

Nico was dead, he was fucking dead. She thought her life had been cut off when Josie died. But she had been wrong. She came back from that. In pieces, put together the wrong way, but she came back.

There was no coming back from this.

There had to be some mistake. Yes, a cosmic mistake. The world had . . . malfunctioned somehow, and Nico had ended up on the rug. She tried to remember what had happened—how it had happened—but her mind was empty. Purely blank, no recollection of anything beyond this present moment. Maybe someone else had done it. A violent criminal had snuck in, slit his throat, and fled. Maybe Arthur Allen had snuck in to frame her. He was always lurking, wasn't he? Nico was a vile person, but he didn't deserve this. What made her any different from Arthur Allen?

"Think," she told herself. "Think."

But she had no idea what she was supposed to be thinking about.

The elevator went straight down to the underground parking lot. She could load him in and stuff him in the trunk, that would be simple. So simple. And the rug was soaked in a dark burgundy—it looked like just a wine stain. Yes, a merlot. Lila would tell the cops she got out some wine for the two of them (at four p.m.? for a work interview?) and spilled the bottle, and then Nico left, but she didn't know where he went.

She sounded insane. But then, sane people typically didn't commit random acts of fucking murder.

Nico's absurdly muscular corpse felt like granite on top of her. His body was starting to cool now. She pushed him off as gently as she could. Was there even a point in trying to cover it up?

A better question—could she live with herself if she did?

The doorknob began to turn, and Lila froze.

It was over before it had begun.

"I'm sorry, I'm sorry, I just forgot my soda flavors—" Sylvie stopped when she saw Lila standing over Nico's lifeless body.

She looked from Nico's body to the blood on Lila's chest to the red claw marks on her neck, and finally met Lila's gaze.

But her eyes weren't afraid. They were sparkling.

And then Lila knew she was safe. The little grey creature was in Sylvie too.

Her car accident had not been an accident.

Sylvie shut the door and locked it before turning back to Lila. "What happened?"

"I killed him," Lila whispered.

"Self-defense?" Sylvie asked, crouching on the floor beside him to get a closer look.

"Do you want me to lie to you?"

Sylvie shook her head. "Fucker deserved it. Good riddance. Are you okay?"

Lila stared at the diagonal slash across his throat. "His throat was so thin. I never knew how easy it would be . . ." She trailed off, staring at the blood on her cuticles. For once, it wasn't her own. She knew something in her had changed; whatever remaining innocence was in her had flown out. "I'm so sorry," Lila said to no one in particular. She tucked her head into her knees and sobbed.

A hand came to rest on her shoulder. She opened her eyes and saw Sylvie looking down at her. Sylvie knelt to her level, wiping her tears away. Her hands were gentle against Lila's cheeks. "Lila, I'm not going anywhere."

"You're not going to turn me in?" Lila needed to hear her say it; she couldn't believe it.

Sylvie rolled her eyes. "He was jabbing you with a thousand tiny knives for a decade. It's not your fault you didn't want to get stabbed anymore. Where's his phone?"

Lila found it on the floor under the table and handed it to her. Sylvie pulled Nico's eyelids open, and the phone unlocked. "What are you doing?" Lila asked.

"Well, first of all, he was recording your conversation, so I'm pausing and deleting it," she said. "And now I'm going to find out what people know." Sylvie scrolled through his texts. "Okay, he texted multiple people he was meeting you today at four . . . obviously, that's not the most convenient for us. But it's fine; we'll keep his phone active to prove he left your place. And you will need a rock-solid alibi for the rest of the day. We may have to push the actual body disposal back a couple of days. I can keep him in my garage."

"Body disposal." Lila put a hand on the table to steady herself. Bile rose in her throat. "Have you done this before?"

"No, but I listen to a fuckton of true crime podcasts. We'll need to pull out his teeth and cut off his hands so they can't identify him. Then we'll dump it somewhere." Sylvie paced, tapping her chin.

For a moment, Lila was alarmed by her readiness to accept the situation and problem-solve. But only one of them was a murderer, and it wasn't Sylvie. Wasn't this why Lila had hired her in the first place? Because she could get shit done?

"Help me move the table. We're gonna roll him up in the rug," Sylvie said, but Lila didn't move.

She couldn't. She just sat on the floor, dumbly staring at Nico's corpse. She felt as though she were watching the entire situation play out through a window, like she was a third-party spectator in her own life.

"Look at me, Lila, I'm serious." Sylvie dropped to her knees in front of Lila and tilted her chin to her eye level. "He's gone. There's nothing you can do to change that. But you're still here. And if you decide to shatter, you've ended two lives today. You have been through too much to give up now, do you hear me?"

Lila nodded, and Sylvie helped her onto her hands and knees. Together, they rolled the rug forward until Nico was wrapped tightly.

"We have all those gifting supplies in the closet." Sylvie leapt to her feet. "We can wrap him in plastic and duct-tape it."

But Lila had frozen again, eyes fixed on the rug burrito.

"It's okay to be scared," Sylvie said, "but you gotta keep going. Like a shark. If you stop moving, you die."

"That's not why I'm scared," Lila whispered. She couldn't bring herself to look Sylvie in the eyes. "I'm scared because I feel relieved."

Once the initial horror and disgust subsided, Lila realized Nico was gone. Forever. He couldn't smear her, stalk her, or hurt her anymore.

She was safe. And most important, Josie's memory was protected. Her breath came easier, her shoulders felt lighter. She could tell herself all she wanted about how the meditation and the positive affirmations and the trauma therapy had fixed something inside her, but none of them even fractionally compared to this.

"I'm not a murderer," Lila said.

"I know," said Sylvie.

"I never wanted to hurt anybody."

Sylvie clasped Lila's hands in hers and squeezed. "I know."

They got to work.

PART TWO

The Rise

EIGHT

It took the cops a week to show up to the office. Nico had been dead for four days before a missing person report was filed. Apparently, it was not unusual for him to descend into a partying binge with no contact for days.

There was no outpouring of thoughts and prayers on social media; barely any missing person posters were shared. *White Smiles, Bright Lights* continued blithely posting celebrity dirt as usual without a single mention of his name. As it turned out, conducting his life as a parasite had not earned Nico many friends.

"Ms. Devlin, can you walk me through your meeting with Nico DeLuca last Friday afternoon?" one of the detectives asked. Two of them had showed up, Lila didn't bother to learn their names. This one had taken on the role of the "nice guy." Amiable, relaxed, just wanted to get to the bottom of things. Lila had dealt with cops long enough to know better.

She had practiced with Sylvie over and over. It was like the big monologue she'd had at the end of her first movie, the one they'd used in her Oscar reel. *Keep it brief; don't offer more than exactly what they've asked for. And no overwrought bullshit,* Sylvie had told her. *And then this'll be over, and you can move on, and you'll never see them again.*

"Nico and I were discussing a potential collaboration. I reached out to him on Instagram," Lila said.

The detective looked at his partner, who raised an eyebrow. Their faces were dull and plain. Long, featureless faces that Lila would forget the second they left her field of vision. She wondered if that was why they'd become cops. The world didn't give a shit about them, so they'd make it by force.

"But you two have a history, don't you? He reported pretty extensively on the abduction of your daughter," the other cop spoke up. This was the tough guy who would call her on her bullshit.

"I wanted to clear the air," Lila said.

Out-of-touch white woman, white woman on a healing journey. Become a parody of yourself. Sylvie's words echoed in her mind. The easiest way to get the cops off her back, they'd decided, would be to annoy the cops out of the building. *Mention you traveled abroad as many times as possible.*

"After my daughter died, I looked inward and didn't like what I saw. In India—I lived there for a year—I learned to practice holistic healing. And I discovered forgiveness is the best balm for a fractured soul. Nico and I were in a good place. He even agreed to promote my new company, glob. It's designed to take that holistic way of healing I learned in India and put it in a—"

"Got it."

They had nothing. Lila wasn't even the last known person to see Nico alive. As his phone records showed, he texted his dealer (marked in his phone as *Adam Drugs*) asking for a hookup, and then went on a messaging spree on Grindr. He'd wound up in some shitty club in East Hollywood, where a witness had seen him high out of his mind stumbling into the night.

Between the swamped crowd, the party drugs, and the dim lighting, it was impossible to know that Sylvie had hired a look-alike off an escort website. There were a lot of muscled twinks living in Los Angeles.

"Did he mention any plans he had, people he was meeting?" the nice cop said. It was sweet that they were taking turns.

"No, we just made plans to record next week," Lila said. That was backed up by the text Nico's producer had received that night.

The disposal of his body had been the hardest part. Having to saw off his hands and remove his teeth made Lila reconsider the prospect of turning herself in. At one point, Lila had fallen to the ground and sobbed. It wasn't supposed to be this way. None of it was supposed to be this way. But eventually, concealing a murder stopped being looming and impossible and just became a series of banal tasks. When she got through it, she could rest. When she got through it, she could return to focusing on glob. When she got through it, she could cry.

Lila had made an unspeakable mistake. She wasn't denying it, not even to herself. She accepted the gravity of what she had done and the lengths she'd have to go to get away with it. She felt sorry for Nico's family; she understood the unique pain of not knowing whether a person was alive or dead, of having to wait for news—any news—only to be continually beaten down and forgotten as the world left you behind.

But there was a small, flickering part of her that didn't care.

Lila was ashamed of it; it wasn't who she was. But it had its positives—her mind's relentless rush of anxiety had quieted. Even for a fleeting while, she found herself enjoying moments of calm.

Maybe it was because the threat of Nico was finally gone, maybe it was because she had refused to sit there and take it, once and for all. Lila didn't know why, but the grey thing was satiated. It was over. A bad thing had been done to her, and she had done a very bad thing in turn, and now that ugliness was settled and it was time for good.

The nice cop pulled a card from his wallet and handed it to her. "If you think of anything else, here's my number."

"Let me know if there's anything else I can do."

SYLVIE PUSHED HER AHEAD, REFUSED TO LET HER DWELL. THEY PLUNGED into building out the business. It frightened her a little how much Sylvie believed in her, wanted to protect her. She wasn't used to people taking her side. Weeks passed as Sylvie courted potential investors to no avail. Lila's name was mired in controversy, there was no proven track record with their products, and neither Lila nor Sylvie had any experience in cosmetics. Lila tried to occupy herself adding color tints to the moisturizer or experimenting with new scents, but it felt fruitless without someone to buy them. This was purgatory. Most nights when she couldn't sleep, she drove the length of the 110, trying to remember the time in her life when she had somewhere to go.

Finally, Sylvie got a bite. Atlas Capital called itself a "consumeronly" venture fund, priding itself in investing in early-stage startups and growing them into household names. It was located on the forty-second story of the north tower of the Century Plaza Towers in Century City, so tall it blocked out the sun. This was where LA's masters of the universe worked, skipping through the labyrinth of reflective skyscrapers like children in a hedge maze. Lila's ears popped on the elevator ride up.

An assistant led Lila and Sylvie into a sleek lobby where they were offered twelve different flavors of sparkling water. They waited fifteen minutes for three men in their forties to call them into the conference room like dogs. Robert, John, and John. They wore their Brooks Brothers sleeves rolled up to their elbows. They were clean-shaven to show off their strong jaws.

Robert's canine teeth sparkled, so pointed they looked like fangs. "It's great, probably the best true crime series I've ever seen. It was about this family in Cheshire, Connecticut. The mom and the kids were murdered by this rando while the—"

He stopped then, as he noticed Lila walk into the room. The room went silent. She could feel every pair of eyes waiting to see what she would do, almost eager. So, she smiled pleasantly—she was good at making herself pleasant.

"Lila." One of the Johns clasped her hand in his. "So great to meet you. Thanks so much for taking the time," though they all knew Lila was not the one "taking the time" in this situation.

"Thank you for having us," Lila said.

The pitch was fine. Lila could do the pitch in her sleep. Perhaps it was because she knew the pitch so thoroughly that her mind could fixate on how Robert, John, and John didn't seem to be paying any attention at all.

The Johns would glance in her direction, nod, and then return to their phones. Robert watched her with a stupid smirk, eyes running up and down her body so thoroughly Lila had to fight the urge to double-check she was wearing a shirt.

Sylvie passed out the eye cream Lila had made, and the men nodded at it politely like she was a child showing off a macaroni necklace. They were so blatantly uninterested that Lila wondered why she'd even been invited in the first place.

And then she got her answer. Every phone in the room buzzed as a John abruptly looked up from whatever he was doing on his phone, face red, and excused himself to go to the bathroom. He was halfway out the door before Lila had a chance to check: it was a photo of Lila in lingerie from an old photoshoot. John had accidentally AirDropped it to everyone in the room with the caption, *Who is hotter—prime Lila Devlin or Casey Anthony?*

"FUCK 'EM, WE DON'T NEED FUNDING," SYLVIE SAID AS SHE FOLLOWED Lila into the elevator afterward. "We'll do it guerrilla style. Distribute eye creams like the Vietcong. Drum up interest through the press, grassroots it into blowing up. The investors will come knocking on our door."

But no one was interested. Sylvie managed to get a beauty supply store on Larchmont to carry their products, but aside from a couple of missing bottles, the skin cream sat in the back untouched.

Still, they pushed on. Lila continued to try new recipes, and Sylvie became a willing lab rat to test on. Sylvie would sit at the small table in Lila's kitchen as she melted coconut oil in a pan on the stovetop. Sylvie would remark how she found it soothing to watch Lila combine everything: the vitamin E oil, the aloe vera, and, finally, the collagen powder.

Lila found it soothing too—it kept her mind at bay. It reminded her of being in her kitchen in India, when all of this was the distant dream she would flee to when the pain of Josie's memory grew too unbearable. Lila tried not to think about Nico, tried to keep the space in her brain where he lived dark and muted, but he always climbed out to stand right on her shoulder, to laugh at her. Every day, she half expected the cops to appear at her door because Sylvie confessed, but they never did. Lila didn't know what to make of her. She lived in her own little Technicolor world, blissfully compartmentalizing the murder as if it had never happened.

Sylvie would chatter away about her ever-depressing dating life like they were old girlfriends catching up. "We went to, like, this random Thai restaurant that he's obsessed with, and I was totally cool with that. I like food from other cultures. Like, I love Italian food. But yeah, so I ordered the chicken plate, and I didn't see it on the menu so asked if I could have a side of mayo. And the waiter looked at me with this, like, misogynistic, condescending glare and was like, 'We don't have mayo.' And Max was judging me too. Like, sorry, I like to enjoy food?

"But it was fine, because we were right next to a gas station, and I knew they would have packets of mayo. So, I pretended to go to the bathroom, went to the gas station, and got the mayo—they didn't have packets, so I had to buy a miniature bottle, which obviously wasn't as subtle as I was hoping for, but it still fit in my purse, so it was whatever. When I came back, I realized Max must have thought I was pooping, so I was like, 'Sorry, my skirt split in the bathroom, and I had to sew it.' He said no worries, and we chatted for a bit, and then the waiter brought our food out.

"And I swear, I tried it without the mayo. But the only stuff to dip it in was this weird spicy peanut thing, and I'm not good with hot stuff. I just, you know, casually squirted a little bit of the mayo on my plate. No big deal. But Max is like, 'What the fuck is that. Is that mayo?' I was like, 'Dude, chill.' I mean, seriously. This is why dating women is so much better. He was like, 'Where the fuck did you get that?' I was like, 'I forgot I had it in my purse.' He said, 'You forgot you had a miniature bottle of mayonnaise in your purse?'

"One thing about me, Lila—I don't like being interrogated. Like, show some respect. I was like, 'No need for your concern.' But when the waiter came by and saw the mayonnaise, he looked legit over my head to my boyfriend, and it was all such patriarchal bullshit.

"But whatever, I don't believe in passive-aggressive conflict. I apologized to Max after we left, and he said it was fine. When I got home, yeah, I left a Yelp review for the restaurant. I don't care if you're a small business, women have to take a stand. So, I gave them half a star. And then I get a call from Max, who I guess is friends with the manager there, and he's like, 'What the fuck, they're a family-owned business, they didn't do anything.' It's just so typical male, right? To not even try to empathize? And then he ended things. I was really mopey and sad at first, but I'm starting to realize just, like, how much I dodged a bullet, right?"

Lila chose not to judge. Sylvie had remained steadfast and loyal no matter what obstacles were hurled at them, and Lila sincerely appreciated her for that. She even began to respect, if not like, Sylvie's outfits. Her style, Sylvie had explained after catching Lila staring, was maximalist. Clashing enough patterns turned harmonious. Her outfits held a person captive and made Sylvie impossible to forget. As the weeks passed with little movement forward, and Sylvie continued to show up to work in rhinestoned go-go boots or crocheted duck sweaters, Lila saw them as a symbol of hope. At least one of them refused to let the rejection get to her.

Sometimes, on her breaks, when she was feeling especially self-pitying, Lila opened her iCloud and scrolled through the photos taken from 2011 to 2014. She'd never deleted them, not even the ones of Aidan. Her sole indulgence.

It shattered her that the first six months of Josie's life were hardly documented, back when her depression had failed her. But from then on, the camera roll contained hundreds of photos of Aidan, Lila, and Josie smiling big on walks, playing in the park, at Josie's first birthday party—it was painful but good. It reminded her that Josie had been real.

She scrolled through the makeshift slideshow until she reached February 2014. There weren't many photos from that month—she'd been busy trying to throw herself back into regular life outside the little bubble of her home and her daughter. How little she'd known.

And then she hit March 5. There was a photo she'd taken of Josie that afternoon, her tiny face scrunched up as Aidan tried to feed her a piece of broccoli with lemon sauce. What was it Aidan had said? He had wanted her to have a sophisticated palate.

ONE AFTERNOON, A SOUTH ASIAN WOMAN IN HER EARLY TWENTIES STRODE through Sylvie's office door. She was tall with beautiful brown eyes and long black hair that had streaked in the sun. She wore a USC crewneck and a shy smile. "Hi, I'm Maya. I'm an intern for glob?"

Sylvie squealed and rushed to meet her. "Maya! So great to meet you in person, welcome!" Sylvie gestured to Lila, who was staring at her in confusion. "This is Lila Devlin, our founder and queen. She is over there *slaying* some gift wrap."

Maya smiled awkwardly.

"It's nice to meet you," Lila told Maya. "Could you excuse us for a moment?"

Sylvie turned to Maya behind her. "We're making gift boxes. If you want to start folding the box templates, that would be mucho appreciato."

Lila shut the door behind them. "Sylvie, what the hell? I can't afford an intern," Lila said.

"I *know* that." Sylvie rolled her eyes. "That's why she's unpaid. She's getting paid in life experience or whatever."

"Where did you even find her?" Lila asked.

"I put a posting on the USC job board. And I went through a lot of people. Maya can write sentences well enough not to make me blow my brains out, so I picked her," Sylvie said. "And besides, we do need an extra hand. Our momentum is slowing down just making sample kits all day."

Lila hesitated. It seemed like a bad idea to welcome someone in before they'd even gotten their feet off the ground. But maybe Sylvie was right. Maybe an extra hand would free up some time to focus on the bigger-picture stuff.

"We're paying her as soon as we can afford to," Lila said, compromising. She sighed. "And until then, she gets free lunch."

"But I can't expense that," Sylvie whined.

"Don't make her drive anywhere. We can't pay for mileage either," Lila added.

Sylvie mimed a knife to her heart as she opened the door, and Lila followed her back inside. "Sylvie said you're a student at USC?" Lila asked.

"Yeah, I'm just wrapping up my senior year," Maya said.

"What do you study?" Lila asked.

"Chemistry, I want to do lab work for cosmetics," Maya said. "I'd love to start my own brand focused on products specifically for brown girls one day. The opportunity to learn from you guys is invaluable."

Lila's hesitation thawed a little. She liked the girl's drive. "That's really great. I'll do my best to teach you as much as I can, though fair warning—you are getting in on the ground floor here. It may not always be pretty."

"Nothing is," Maya replied, and laughed. *It was her eyes.* They were just like Josie's: large and wide-set and upturned at the ends. Not the same color—Maya's were a rich russet brown—but the same curiosity, the same hopefulness. Lila had never met someone with eyes like her daughter's before.

"Where are you from?" Lila asked.

"Cape Cod," Maya said.

The hair on Lila's arms stood up. Cape Cod was where she'd spread Josie's ashes. It was a bizarre coincidence. It almost felt fated. "No way, I'm from Boston."

Maya lit up. Massachusetts people were forever bonded by their deep and profound love of Massachusetts. "Oh my god, really? I can't hear your accent at all."

"It comes out when I'm angry," Lila said.

"Do you miss Dunkin'?" Maya asked. "I know there's one in, like, Encino, but I can't justify driving all the way over there."

"Oh my god, so much. My body actually went through withdrawals when I first moved out here." Lila laughed. It was like something had jolted awake inside of her.

"Have you ever tried carbonated iced coffee?" Sylvie cut in.

They started Maya off easy, organizing the inventory of skin and eye creams Lila was tooling with. "Why did you name your company *glob*?" Maya asked.

"It was—it was this word my daughter used to say," Lila said softly. "She liked to sit and watch me do my makeup and skincare, but she didn't know what it was. She'd just point and say 'glob!' So, I'm making glob."

"That's so sweet," Maya said. "I like that a lot." She didn't offer anything else to hint whether she knew Josie's story. Lila appreciated that.

A FEW WEEKS AFTER MAYA'S INTERNSHIP BEGAN, GLOB RECEIVED ITS first glowing review. It wasn't much—just an inclusion on a list of underrated brands on the Skincare Addiction subreddit. Someone had picked up a bottle at the Larchmont store on a whim and was pleasantly surprised. But within a day, they received fifty new orders. Maya, Sylvie, and Lila jumped around the office, hollering. People liked the product; they just had to make it easier to find.

Maya looked at Lila the same way Josie looked at her, full of hope and admiration. Lila gave her a high five. "I think you might be our good luck charm."

NINE

Lila hardly ever thought about Nico anymore. The way his body hit the rug, the way she'd rocked him to sleep. How *good* it felt to finally have that voice finally shut the fuck up. As the weeks passed, she found she didn't feel as guilty as she thought she would. In fact, she felt settled. Centered. The little dark part of her brain was at peace.

Besides, there were bigger things to worry about. The decade without a steady income was nipping at Lila's heels. The few dozen orders from the occasional Reddit recommendation could hardly sustain glob as a company. Months slipped by without success, yet Lila and Sylvie pressed on. Lila wasn't sure whether it was because they believed in themselves or because they were living in denial.

MAYA HAD FAR EXCEEDED LILA'S EXPECTATIONS AS AN INTERN. SHE WAS an inventive, thoughtful young woman. On the two days a week she didn't come into the office, Lila found herself missing her. Lila had never been a mentor before, but she imagined it not unlike being a parent. A work parent. Maya was full of potential, but glob could hardly consider itself a success. It was humiliating.

Sylvie kept a massive list of all the major publications (online and print) and relevant influencers who could promote glob. They had soft-launched their website and were technically accepting orders, but no one knew they existed. Press would be vital. Every day, they sent out gift boxes to get glob into the right hands.

Each box contained a starter kit with skincare serums and Lila's collagen face cream. Sylvie wrote a handwritten note of thanks with each box containing their social handles. Once they were shipped off, all there was left to do was wait.

Lila took great pains to keep the worry away from Maya. She was an empathetic kid; Lila knew she'd internalize any concerns about the company. The failure loomed quietly over her head each day until Maya left the office on her lunch break. Today, Lila stared down at the explosion of gifting supplies around her. Being so close, she hadn't realized just how many packages they were stuffing. Hundreds of products sprawled out on the floor before her, misfit toys that no one asked for. She was drowning in them.

For a break from the stress, Lila liked to google John Carmichael at night before bed. The lead on Josie's case. It hadn't been a conscious decision when she'd started; it was a distraction. The last time she'd seen him, he'd taken her to the morgue to see Josie's body.

He'd been gruff but also the most empathetic of the policemen she was subjected to work with. He treated her with a fraction of kindness, despite never actually listening to her. That almost made it worse. He'd ignore and dismiss her with a smile. Some part of him reminded Lila of her dad. He'd failed her too.

According to the internet, he retired a year after Josie's murder. He was eight years divorced with three grown daughters. No social media except for a photo of him on a boat holding up a bass. The post was tagged in Lake Arrowhead. Lila searched his name in combination with Lake Arrowhead; she found an online registry with his public records.

And then she had his address.

It was only ninety minutes away. She could make it in eighty without traffic.

The grey creature perked up; the voice returned. If she was honest with herself, the relief from Nico's death had been a high like nothing she'd ever felt before. Maybe when Josie was born, maybe her wedding day. It was a jolt to her core that had zapped awake some part of her she didn't even know was asleep. And then a month passed, and that high faded, and she wanted more.

"No." Lila shut the laptop, scratching at the skin under her thumb. She was not a murderer. What had all that mindfulness training taught her? Her mind went blank—nothing. Literally nothing. Mindfulness was for impatient people in rush-hour traffic, not parents who had watched their child be failed over and over again by—

Lila's first few months in India had been hell. Her life alternated between forty-eight-hour manic benders and weeks on end refusing to leave her bedroom. She kept a journal attempting to track the grief cycle—denial, anger, bargaining, depression, acceptance—to see how much more she had to suffer. But she'd realized that the stages weren't linear at all; they were a wheel. Every time Josie appeared in her mind, she spun the wheel, and it was impossible to know where it would land. As the months wore on, the strength of those feelings never subsided. She just learned to spin the wheel less. Lila wondered how often Carmichael spun the wheel.

"Stop," Lila whispered, her head splintering. No, she had a choice. She had to see forgiveness as her choice. Forgiveness would bring her relief. She had come back to forgive. Josie wouldn't want to see her like this. Josie would want her to move on.

Wouldn't she?

Why did Carmichael deserve compassion? After everything he'd done, after everything he'd *refused* to do? Why was the onus on her, when he'd run away like a coward? There was no doubt in her mind that Josie wasn't the only victim he'd failed, before retiring on a comfy pension with his reputation plated in gold. Life had bent over backward for him. Someone had to even the scale.

With Nico, she'd been clumsy. If she was going to do this again, she couldn't leave any room for mistakes. And then Lila knew she would need some help.

THAT NIGHT, LILA POUNDED ON THE DOOR OF SYLVIE'S BUNGALOW IN West Adams. It was a neat two-bedroom cottage snugly tucked among other neat two-bedroom cottages in a rapidly gentrifying neighborhood just south of the 10. After a few seconds, Sylvie appeared at the door in pink sweats.

"Lila? What's going on?" she said.

"Can I come in?

Sylvie led Lila to a purple monochrome living room. Long velvet drapes ran down to the purple shag carpet on the floor. It looked like the inside of a psychic's lair.

Questionable fashion sense aside, Sylvie had helped her, and there hadn't been a word from the cops like she'd promised. *They were the same.* Something inside of Lila knew instinctively that Sylvie would help. She understood.

"I want to kill Carmichael," Lila said.

"*What?*" Sylvie's eyes bugged out of her head.

"Since Nico died—it's the first time I've felt *okay* again. I've spent the last decade of my life chasing that feeling, denying and pretending, but I can't do it anymore. I don't owe these people forgiveness, I don't owe them *anything.* And they're just gonna continue living their pleasant little lives in a vacuum like none of this happened. Josie deserves better than that. I can't kill Fox; he's too high profile. But Carmichael's already isolated."

Sylvie took a moment to collect herself. "I mean—Lila, we just got away with one murder. Maybe we should quit while we're ahead."

Lila shook her head. "One of us would have noticed a tail by now if the cops were concerned about me, but they're not."

"He's an ex-cop. He could kill you."

"I'll buy a gun. I'm a decent shot. My dad used to take me to the range with him," Lila said. She'd hated it, but as a fourteen-year-old it was one of the only ways she could spend time with him. "I know I can't do this by myself. I need your help. Will you help me, Sylvie?"

"You want me to come with you?" Sylvie asked.

"No, I'm going by myself. But when I come back with him, can I store him in your garage?"

"Whoa, alone? That's not a good idea. We should—"

"No, it has to be me," Lila said.

"If something goes wrong 'cause you were impatient, I'd never forgive myself—"

"I can't ask you to do that. I'm making this choice; I have to see it through."

"I am your biggest fan." Sylvie put her hand on Lila's cheek. "Don't ever forget that."

Lila cleared her throat and took a gentle step away. "Good. I'll go tomorrow night."

She spun the wheel again.

TEN

That morning, Lila's nerves were vibrating out of her skin. The arrangements were made; the plan was done. All that was left was to carry on with work as usual. She tried to focus on shipping out packages, but her mind kept drifting to Carmichael. Because if Nico and Carmichael were dead and Fox unattainable, then there would be only one person left on the list, the one person even her most naive self could never forgive.

Arthur Allen.

She'd searched for him online, but there was nothing. He was a ghost. Changed his name and crawled under some rock where no one could find him. Coward. It didn't matter, she'd find him. She knew how to hide too.

A distant whimper yanked her from her thoughts. Was someone crying? Lila got up from her desk and went out into the hallway. It was coming from the fire escape. Lila opened the door and found Maya sitting on the stairs with her head in her hands. She glanced up at Lila and flushed, scrambling to wipe her tears. "Shit, I'm sorry—"

"Are you all right?" Lila asked. There was no way she could possibly know.

"I'm just PMSing, I'm fine. Sorry about this," Maya said, standing up. Mascara was smeared under her eyes.

Lila hesitated; she had no idea how to go about consoling a crying employee. She offered a gentle smile. "Don't apologize. I'm happy to talk if you need a shoulder."

Now, Maya hesitated. Her eyes searched Lila's face, debating whether it was a good idea. Finally, she sighed. "Did your parents have any problem when you told them what you wanted to do?"

"For work?" Lila said.

"Yeah."

She hadn't told her dad at all. She just didn't come home the summer after freshman year because they were shooting, and then there hadn't been any reason to come home again. She'd talk to him on the phone sometimes, but he never asked about her life. He either didn't want to know or didn't care. At a certain point, it had been more painful to keep trying. And then he was dead.

"You having some trouble?" Lila asked, sitting down beside her.

Maya sighed. "When I said I was studying biochemistry, they pictured me as a cancer researcher. They're mortified that I want to go into beauty. They think it's shallow."

She looked at Lila then, worried she'd offended. Lila nodded for her to keep going.

"And no matter how many ways I explain it to them—it's like, yeah, of course it's shallow, that's the point. I want to go in and change that. But they won't even try to listen."

Lila shook her head in disappointment. Any half-decent parent should've been over the moon to have Maya as a kid. Her big aspirations made her special. She deserved better than to be browbeaten and mocked.

"That's tough, I'm sorry," Lila said.

"I mean, on some level, I get it. The beauty industry is racist and sexist as hell—they want to protect me. And maybe it'll suck and I'll give up. But I want to at least try."

"That's very admirable," Lila said. "I don't think the beauty industry can survive without people like you pulling it into the future."

"Thank you. I really needed someone to tell me I'm not crazy," Maya said, tears subsided. She laughed a little, wiping mascara on her shirt. "I promise this is the first and last time I've cried in front of a boss."

"You can cry in front of me any time." Lila smiled.

"Can I give you a hug?" Maya asked.

For some reason, Lila's breath caught in her throat. "Of course."

She pulled Maya into a quick hug. She hadn't hugged anyone in a long time. It was nice. Lila led her back to the office, a gentle arm around her shoulders. Lila didn't have a family anymore, but she had discovered she could make one. Carve it out of collagen and skin cream. Sylvie and Maya, her little work family, her second chance. She wouldn't let anyone get in between them this time.

ELEVEN

The drive up into the mountains outside of Los Angeles was winding and unyielding. The road was dark and empty; Lila's insides twisted when she caught glimpses of the edge of the cliff that dropped hundreds of feet below. It reminded her of the drive with Aidan to exchange the ransom money, when the paparazzi had tried to run her off the road.

She drove in silence—after changing the radio a hundred times, Lila had given up and shut it off. Instead, she replayed her plan for Carmichael's death over and over in her mind. Break into his house, do not engage, fire quickly while he was still off guard. He may have been retired, but he had still been a cop for thirty years. Any fragment of hesitation and she could be dead.

The towering pine trees that dotted the mountain looked a little like New England. They weren't the same; none of this was the same, but it was enough of an approximation that if she concentrated hard enough, she could still see herself playing tag in the woods with the boy who lived next door.

Sometimes, on the blue moon when her mom wasn't working, she would race out to find them and play "monster." Denise would curl her hands into claws and skulk after them as they ran, giggling. But Denise was a high school cross-country champion—the monster always ate them in the end.

A deer shot into the middle of the road, pausing a few paces ahead of the car. Its coat was a pure white, so bright against the headlights it was almost blinding. It was small with gangly legs, probably just a fawn. For a fraction of a second, it looked straight through the windshield, and its pink eyes locked with hers and the words TURN AROUND boomed through Lila's mind. She screamed.

"*Jesus!*" Lila slammed her foot on the brake, narrowly swinging around it. She felt a thud as the car skidded across the road, coming right up to the canyon's edge.

Lila sat wheezing for air, refusing to look down off the precipice. Bile rose in her throat as that thud played over and over in her head. She could have driven on, but something propelled her to open the door and step outside to check for its little body. Something inside her pleaded to turn around, turn everything around, and go home.

The moon cast a long, solemn shadow under Lila as she walked around the car. The mountains were silent; a smattering of storm clouds was just starting to clear. Outside the pollution of Los Angeles, Lila could make out a few stars dotting the night sky.

"What the hell?" Lila said when she reached the front of the car.

The gangly fawn was gone.

She'd hit it, hadn't she? She'd felt it. There was no way it could have run away so quickly; she would have seen it. And had she ever seen an albino deer before? Did they exist? She checked under her car, tried to look down the road, but there was no trace.

LAKE ARROWHEAD WAS THE HOLLYWOOD EQUIVALENT OF LAKES IN MAINE or Vermont—a man-made, paltry copy. It was claustrophobic by design, built as a reservoir, with lakeside homes stacked practically on top of one another in long columns and rows with neighbors on all sides. In California, everyone wanted their own little piece of the wilderness created for them.

Carmichael's listed address belonged to a small grey cabin tucked between two renovated mansions. It was closer to the upper road than the lake itself. He didn't have the money for prime real estate. Lila would have to be careful not to attract attention.

As she drove closer, she realized that the house wasn't grey at all. The paint on the wood was so degraded that the color had turned pallid, like the cabin had succumbed to an illness.

Lila exited the car, removing the revolver and silencer she had purchased from her glove compartment. She retied her hair in an austere bun, pulling until it was so tight it hurt. So tight she could only focus on the pain, so there was no room for distractions.

Lila peeked into the window of the house. A slouching figure sat illuminated by an old television set. She stepped back and walked around the perimeter of the house. On the back end beside some fallen shingles, the bathroom window was open a crack.

The audacity to retreat to a little cocoon in the woods to retire. As though he deserved rest.

Lila pushed the window open and crawled through.

She landed on the bathroom floor louder than she would have liked. She paused and waited for Carmichael to burst in, but he didn't come. She let out a shaky breath—she allowed herself just one—and then stepped over the soggy bathmat to twist the doorknob.

The door swung open. She could hear *Midnight Run* blaring in the next room, could hear his recliner creaking as he shifted in it. She wondered if he was asleep. She wondered if she would prefer him to be asleep.

She began to walk. Careful, deliberate steps on the balls of her feet, refusing to falter when the floor creaked. Adrenaline ricocheted through her bloodstream, sinking into her marrow, lighting it aflame. Charles Grodin made a joke, and she could hear Carmichael exhale a soft laugh through his nose.

All she had to do was round the corner now. Lila raised her gun, readying it, and entered the living room—

Where John Carmichael was waiting with a shotgun. He was about to fire when he recognized who he was aiming at. His face turned ashen; his fingers shook so violently the gun fell to the floor. "You came back," he whispered.

John Carmichael was not the man Lila remembered. His hair had greyed in uneven patches. His teeth ground down and yellowed. He was in threadbare pajamas: a Deadhead T-shirt and plaid boxers. Her memory of him loomed behind him—an imposing, gruff figure with the capacity to ruin lives. He looked like a husk, a shadow of himself.

Fire quickly, she told herself. *Don't hesitate.* But Lila was struck still.

"I knew you would," Carmichael said. He didn't seem at all fazed by her gun, made no move to pick up his own. Instead, he inched toward his worn armchair. Lila tracked him with the gun as he sat back down, but her hands wouldn't fire. "I always knew. A person can't go through that and not . . ."

For all her hatred and rage, for all the times she had replayed these moments in her head, all Lila could think to say was "You killed my daughter."

"I know," he said softly.

"You know?" Lila lowered the gun a fraction.

Carmichael hung his head. "We didn't pursue Allen quick enough because we were too tied up with you. We were too tied up with you because there was so little evidence pointing to an intruder. There was so little evidence pointing to an intruder because we fucked the crime scene."

Lila's eyes pricked with tears at the sheer relief of hearing someone else say it out loud. She blinked them away. "What changed your mind?"

"I see her in my dreams sometimes," he said faintly. "She's older, though. Looks like you. We're out in my boat on the lake, fishing. And then this storm comes, and the boat gets tipped over. And I lose track of her, trying to stay up. And I manage to get back in the boat, but by then, I realize I left her . . ." He stopped.

A stone lodged in Lila's throat. The floor creaked behind her, and Lila jerked her head back. "You live alone here?"

"Nine years now," Carmichael said. "I wish it were quieter."

Lake Arrowhead at night was almost entirely devoid of sound, but Lila knew what he meant. The real noise lived in his head, and it would follow wherever he went. Scream when he tried to drown it out.

"Are you gonna kill me?" Carmichael asked.

"Yes," Lila said.

"About time."

"I don't understand," Lila whispered.

"I'm sorry I failed you," he responded.

A little whimper escaped Lila, and her hand flew to her mouth to keep anything else in. This wasn't right, Lila told herself. He was trying to make amends so he could die in peace. She saw through it. "If you were sorry, you would have kept fighting."

Fire the gun, fire the fucking gun—

"I found Arthur Allen."

The grey creature roared.

Lila kept her gaze level, hiding her surprise. He was retired, he didn't have any of the resources he used to. It wasn't possible. Not when—"The LAPD couldn't even find him."

"They can't find a lot of things," Carmichael said.

He stood up from the chair, and Lila took a step closer. "What are you doing?"

"Writing it down," Carmichael said. "It's my gift to you."

Lila tracked him with the gun as he grabbed a pad of paper off the TV stand. "Took me ten years. He lives in Slab City under the name James Smith." Carmichael scribbled in a frenzy. "I was going to go, but . . ." He glanced at her gun and held the pad out to her. "You'll find him."

Arthur Allen is alive, Arthur Allen is alive, the creature sung. If Carmichael was right and she found him, all the pain and guilt she had suffered, it all would have been worth it.

"Everything I did was to save her. I thought I was doing right," Carmichael said, and Lila believed him. She pitied him, this old man in Grateful Dead pajamas who liked fishing and '80s action comedies.

Maybe, if he existed in a vacuum, she would have been able to let him go. To let it go.

"But you were wrong," Lila said. "And you were leading an army."

She couldn't stand to look at his watery moon eyes anymore. She raised the gun to fire, to actually fire, and then paused. There was a better way to do this.

"Follow me," she said, ushering him with the gun.

Carmichael let her herd him to the front door. "Where are we going?"

"I'm going to shoot you in the trunk of my car, so I don't have to worry about bloodstains in the house."

Carmichael laughed a little at that. "Fair enough."

He wasn't taking her seriously. "I know where your wife and daughters live," Lila added. She didn't mean it, wouldn't hurt them, could never hurt them. But he didn't know that. Carmichael's body tensed. "If you try anything, I'll kill them too."

"You have my word I won't—just don't hurt them, please," Carmichael said. That was all she wanted. To be taken seriously.

They walked up the hill in silence. It shocked her how easy it was, how little he resisted. How his will had already given out, and his body seemed a foregone conclusion. When they reached Lila's car, she popped open the trunk. It was lined with the plastic tarp she would roll his body in. "Get in," Lila said. Waiting for him to fight. Daring for him to fight.

Pleading with him to fight.

Carmichael crawled in and lay on his back, his hands up like a dog surrendering to an alpha. "I hope this brings you what you're looking for."

Lila fired one shot into his head. She didn't want to talk anymore.

The kick of the gun threw her onto the ground. She waited for a moment, waited for the rush of relief she'd felt after Nico. It didn't come. There was only a deep hollowness. For a moment she lay there, depleted, wondering what would happen if she didn't get up. She pressed the back of her head to the gravel, the tiny rocks denting her skin. It wasn't fair. Once again, Carmichael had been wrong—his death hadn't brought her anything.

The grey thing nipped at her insides, and suddenly she felt the scrap of paper burning in her pocket. She yanked it out and read Arthur Allen's new name. Nico and Carmichael were stepping stones leading her to him. Lila picked herself up off the ground and slammed the trunk shut. It was too early to give up, there was too much to be done.

LILA PULLED INTO SYLVIE'S DRIVEWAY AND CALLED HER CELL. "I'M OUT-side," Lila said, and the white garage door slowly rolled open. Lila drove inside, waiting in the car until the door had swallowed her whole.

Sylvie appeared in the doorway in pink athleisure. "Did it go all right?" she asked as Lila got out to join her.

Lila opened the trunk and revealed Carmichael's dead body wrapped in the tarp. "Yep."

"How did you get him in your trunk by yourself?" Sylvie asked.

"He walked," Lila said.

"Damn," Sylvie murmured, her eyes slightly darkening.

Together, they pulled Carmichael's body out of the trunk and heaved him onto the collapsible table Sylvie had set up in the corner. He was bigger than Nico and probably two hundred pounds. Once they'd stopped and collected their breath, Lila pulled out the electric saw from the closet where Sylvie's landlord kept his power tools. Sylvie handed her a plastic rain poncho. "For the blood."

Lila stared down at the body, still in the Grateful Dead T-shirt. Carmichael wasn't in there anymore; he was about as sentient as her electric saw. It would just be slicing through matter. That's all he was, matter. And once this was done, she could make him disappear.

Sylvie set a plastic bucket beside Lila and patted it. "In case you vomit again."

She'd vomited when they'd done this to Nico.

A lot.

"Thank you."

"Wait!" Sylvie said as the saw hummed to life. She pulled out her phone, and her musical theater playlist blasted through portable speakers. "I hate the sound."

Sylvie sang along to "The Wizard and I" as they got to work. Lila had read somewhere once that a human finger was as easy to bite off as a carrot, but the brain put up a psychological barrier to protect it. Cutting into Carmichael's hand, she discovered that the barrier was true for other people's fingers as well.

It took hours as they went piece by piece until John Carmichael ceased to exist. Their last step was removing his teeth with pliers; Sylvie was very concerned about dental records making a positive ID. It was somehow even worse than the dismemberment.

Just looking at his face, it was easy to forget he was dead. His eyes were closed, thick black eyelashes curling at the ends. He had nice eyelashes. If Lila didn't look down past his neck, he could be mistaken for sleeping.

Once he was just gums, they removed their ponchos, both drenched in gore, and wrapped everything up in the tarp in the trunk. Sylvie turned off "Defying Gravity" and led Lila into her living room. Without a task to occupy them, Lila noticed how badly her hands were shaking. The feeling of righteousness was gone and the catharsis was missing. She observed that from a bird's-eye view without context, you would think she was a psychopath who had brutally dismembered a human corpse while listening to the *Wicked* soundtrack.

Lila shoved her hands in her pockets so she wouldn't have to look at them anymore, then felt the scrap of paper. "He gave me the address."

"What?" Sylvie said.

"He told me where Arthur Allen is," Lila said.

Sylvie's jaw dropped. "Arthur Allen? As in . . ."

Lila nodded.

"Holy shit."

She did not ask Lila what she was planning to do, because even after struggling to dismember their second corpse, that was a foregone conclusion.

"He's in Slab City. I'm going next weekend."

Sylvie put a hand up. "Whoa whoa whoa, Lila, can we pause for a second? I understand your pain, you are seen and heard, but at a certain point everyone's luck runs out. Nico and Carmichael were one thing, but this man is a *murderer*. I can't let you go; he could *kill you—*"

"*I don't care.*"

Arthur Allen could mutilate and burn her corpse, it didn't matter. The worst-case scenario had already happened. And if he killed her, maybe she'd get to see Josie again.

"There is something inside of me that is gnawing at me and it won't leave me alone, and this is the only thing that will make it stop. *I just need it to stop,*" Lila said.

"Josie wouldn't want—"

"Don't *ever* tell me what my daughter would want."

Sylvie's eyes widened, and she shut her mouth. Lila sighed, running a hand through her hair. Even after killing two people, Sylvie still didn't take her seriously.

"Do you know what Slab City is?" Sylvie asked. "It's where people go who want to disappear. It's dangerous, especially for someone like you. There are bad people there. Like, *murderers*," Sylvie said, a speck of John Carmichael's blood dripping down her forehead. "I'm coming with you."

Lila shook her head. "Absolutely not."

"It's a bunch of people living in campers in close quarters. It's gonna be a fuckton harder with all those eyes on you," Sylvie said. "I'm coming."

Lila sighed. Sylvie was right, it would be stupid to go alone not knowing what she was up against. "Okay," she said, finally.

"Do you . . . feel better?" Sylvie asked.

Lila yanked a flap of skin around her pointer finger until blood started to pool. "Once Arthur's gone, I will."

TWELVE

In the office the next morning, Maya sat at her desk looking morose when Lila came in. "The editor at *The Cut* responded. She said the product is good but lacks a wow factor to make it stand out," Maya said.

"At least she responded at all." Lila forced a smile. In the face of defeat, it was best to be grateful.

But Lila was tired of gratitude. Who were these magazine editors who titled themselves tastemakers? What gave them the right to break someone's dreams? Without millions of dollars of funding, it was difficult to reinvent the wheel, especially if Lila wanted to keep her products at an accessible price. Glob was good; she knew it in her bones. It was right on the horizon, just peeking through—it was the editor's loss she couldn't see it yet.

Maya shook her head. "They're not the authority. We know the product is good. That's what matters. No one gets to tell you what you think of yourself." Then she brightened. "There was this TikTok influencer in my Spanish class junior year; she still follows me. I'm going to ask if she'll check out our stuff."

Lila was impressed. Maya was just an intern, but she was intuitive and clever. She had a knack for this. It was almost a bit embarrassing— Lila was supposed to be helping her, not the other way around. It meant a lot, to have someone looking out for her. "Thank you, that would be great," Lila said.

"*The Cut* is a flop." Maya closed the laptop. "They're behind on everything; they're too old. You need people my age to champion you. That's how you pull this industry into the future. Everyone dismissed TikTok until it became a tastemaker. It's just a matter of getting the product into the right hands."

"Smart. You graduate soon, don't you?" Lila said.

"In about a month," Maya said.

"Are you excited?"

"Excited and scared," Maya said. "A lot of my friends already have jobs or grad school lined up, and I'm still figuring things out. My parents are stressed."

Those damn parents. Maya was twenty-two. She had her entire life ahead of her. It seemed that every opportunity they had to support her, her family chose to beat her down instead. It broke Lila's heart.

"You have nothing to worry about, trust me. You're going to be fine," Lila said. Something seized her then before she could use her better judgment. Maya was an invaluable worker—intelligent, resourceful, and empathetic. Lila didn't want to lose her in a month. She didn't want to lose her at all. "I'd like to offer you a position as my assistant after you graduate."

Glob was running on borrowed time, but she knew it would fail without Maya at her side. There were plenty of other unpaid interns, but none of them would be able to fill her shoes. Lila would find a way to scrape together a weekly salary for her.

"I—really?" Maya's eyes lit up. "You want me?"

"You are so gifted, Maya. I want to help you however I can." Lila smiled. And seeing the joy spread across Maya's radiant face made all the fear and stress melt away. Maya needed someone to believe in her to blossom.

"Thank you." Maya's eyes welled up with tears. "Thank you so much, Lila. I've loved working for you. You're the best boss I've ever had."

Lila grinned as she watched Maya put her hands over her mouth, trying to contain her excitement. "If you're gonna run your own skincare company one day, you need practice, right?"

They were interrupted by a knock on the door.

"Did you order something?" Lila asked Sylvie in the kitchenette.

"No." Sylvie looked at Maya, who shrugged.

Sylvie went to open the door, and Peter stood on the other side.

"Yooooooo!" he said when he saw Lila.

California suited him, to no one's surprise. His skin had darkened into a glowing tan; his blond hair was shaggy at the ends. He looked like a Greek god of the sea.

"Peter, oh my god." Lila laughed. "I never thought I'd see you again."

"I got a Google Alert about glob, and I found this address, and you're here!"

Lila turned to introduce Peter to Sylvie, who was fluffing herself up like a bird: "I met Peter on the plane ride home," Lila said.

"She told me everything about the skincare brand, and I promised I would be her first customer," Peter said, ignoring the saucer eyes Sylvie was giving him.

"How are you? How's acting?" Lila asked.

"Oh, I quit acting. It wasn't vibing with me on, like, a spiritual level," Peter said.

Lila smiled ruefully. "I remember that feeling. What are you doing now?"

"I'm a model," Peter said. "And a magician, but I don't get paid for that yet."

"A magician?" Maya said.

Peter glanced over at Maya, noticing her for the first time, and went still. His lips parted in wonder, stretching into a dimpled smile. Maya blushed and looked down at her feet.

"Yeah, I started learning card tricks for fun and I got hooked." Peter's eyes glittered in the harsh ceiling light.

"This is Maya, our intern," Lila said.

Sylvie stuck out a hand. "I'm Sylvie, her business partner."

Peter shook Sylvie's hand limply, but his eyes sparkled as he turned back to Maya. "I always thought Maya was such a dope name," he said.

"Thank you." Maya smirked. He amused her. His innate goofiness offset his chiseled features—the kid was charming.

Peter flipped his golden hair, trying to play it cool. "So, can I buy one of your skin creams, Lila?"

"Don't be ridiculous. I'll give it to you for free," Lila said, grabbing a collagen eye cream from the gifting pile.

"No, you don't have to do that—" Peter objected.

"Use the thirty bucks to work on your magic tricks," Lila said.

Peter flushed, then grinned. "I'll send you an invite to my first show. I can't wait to try it."

"Do you know where it goes?" Lila asked. Maya bit the inside of her cheek to keep from laughing. Peter smiled at her; he liked to make her laugh.

He glanced at the container. "It's eye cream. So, on your eyelids?"

"No no no no no," Lila, Sylvie, and Maya chorused at once in concern.

"Under eyes only," Lila said.

"Copy that." Peter saluted.

"Take care, Peter," Lila said.

Peter stole one last glance at Maya. "For sure. Have a good one!"

He walked out of the office. Maya tried to hide that she was watching him go.

As soon as the door closed, Sylvie turned to Lila. "Lila, why did you never mention you knew a handsome twenty-three-year-old magician? That's, like, exactly my type."

Before Lila could reply, the door opened, and Peter strode back in, focusing solely on Maya. "Are you doing anything tonight, Maya?" he asked without a trace of shame.

Maya held his gaze for a moment, then smiled. "I'm off at five."

Peter nodded, unable to keep from smiling. "Great, I'll pick you up."

He played it cool as he walked out of the office, taking extreme care not to turn around to take another look at her.

The instinct rose to tease Maya, the way Lila might have gently ribbed Josie if she'd seen her with an adorable crush, but Maya was her employee, and she would never want to make her feel uncomfortable or unsafe. Instead, she quietly applauded her. At least one of them was having a good time.

Thirteen

Because Lila had never met Arthur Allen, or the gardener named David Lewis, only seen his ghoulish mug shot in the news, she had no idea what kind of person he was. She used to think of him as a boogeyman, a hulking, silent figure who appeared out of clouds of smoke and ash. She had not considered him human. Humans couldn't do what he did, to other children and then to Josie.

But now, Lila could admit he was a person, just broken beyond repair. He did not offer one single worthwhile thing to the world. Lila would be doing him a favor.

She was diligent in preparing for the trip. Carmichael's death had been clumsy; she would learn from those mistakes. She paid $500 in cash for a 2004 Toyota van from Rent-A-Wreck. So innocuous you'd forget what it looked like the second it drove past. She and Sylvie wore disguises they'd purchased from a Salvation Army: old jeans, weathered T-shirts. They stripped their faces of makeup and donned ratty wigs. Lila doubted anyone in Slab City was likely to recognize her, but she still wanted to blend in.

The car ride out of Los Angeles was never-ending. The car was a lemon—the radio and air-conditioning were broken, so they sat in silence and their own sweat as the bubble of LA burst into outlet malls and gas stations. Sylvie glanced at the map as they reached the Inland Empire.

"You're gonna be here for a while, so you can get into the carpool lane," she directed. Her wig was a light blond probably close to her natural color. It softened her features. For the first time since Lila had known her, she looked like a normal woman in her mid-thirties. "Have I ever told you about when I lived in New York?" Before Lila could blow her off, she added, "I'm trying to distract myself because I get carsick."

Lila sighed. "No, you haven't."

Sylvie looked at her sneakers. Lila couldn't remember if she'd ever seen Sylvie shy before. Or in sneakers.

"When I first started working for a big firm as an assistant, I moved from LA to New York. I wanted experience there because I knew I'd end up in LA for good. I didn't know anybody. I moved into a studio in the West Village that cost way more than I could afford on my salary. It was so cute, Lila. It was on the second floor of an old walk-up." Sylvie liked to paint a picture, and Lila could see it past the cars in front of her. "It had a fireplace—this beautiful old brick fireplace. It was sealed over; I couldn't light it, but just the outline was so striking. And when I got there, the walls were this awful turquoise, so I repainted them a pale, pale pink—I don't like dark rooms.

"My window looked out onto the side of another building, but if I went onto the fire escape, I could watch people on the sidewalk. And I bought a whole new wardrobe—I refused to be an outfit repeater. I was going to have my Carrie Bradshaw moment," she said ruefully. "But that didn't happen like I thought it would. People were cliquey, and I struggled to make friends. You have to know people socially for work, of course, but beyond that—no one was interested. Like, at work, they loved me. I'm great, I'm a wunderkind, but the minute we went on our lunch break, I turned into . . . a fly buzzing in their ears." Her eyes fluttered as she was pulled deeper into the story. "You ever felt like that? Like you only exist to please other people?"

Lila nodded, eyes on the road. "Yeah."

"Yeah. I felt like I was at the end of my rope. And then one night, I went out to this bar, and there was a live band there doing kinda jazzy stuff. I'd never been into jazz, but it actually sounded good. And there was a guy behind everybody who was playing piano. We made eye contact—he had the nicest eyes I'd ever seen. I flirted with him after the show, and he invited me out for a drink, and that was that. I was in love with David.

"We were attached at the hip from then on. He had a day job waiting tables and was with his band most nights, so we had to work to find time together. But we did. You would have liked him, I think. I'm not just saying that. He was kind. I needed someone softer like him to . . . balance me out. He loved with his whole heart. I thought I'd experienced love before, but I had no idea. He made me feel safe. So, we got married."

"Married?" Lila cut in, shocked. Sylvie spoke constantly of her dalliances with people, but she had never mentioned a marriage before.

Sylvie laughed. "Oh my god, that was such an insane day. We'd been together for two years; he'd moved in. I'd assumed we'd get married one day, but I wasn't putting any pressure on it. You know me, I'm chill. And then, one day, he told me his mom was diagnosed with cancer and he was going to move back home to Azusa to be with her. I told him I'd come with him. He didn't want me to abandon my career, but I knew I'd come back to LA inevitably. This is where everything important is. So I started searching for a one-bedroom for us, and he was like, 'Would you elope with me?'

"He didn't want to do a big wedding with friends and family, not when his family was so stressed. And, I mean, I'd love a big wedding, of course, but my family—I'm not close with them. I realized none of that stuff was important as long as I had him. So, we went to the courthouse with two of his bandmates as our witnesses. We got there at, like, eleven a.m., and there was already a huge line. People from all different walks of life. Pregnant girls, cowering guys in formal suits. A lot of girls that I thought couldn't have been older than sixteen, but they were, like, twenty-one. I couldn't believe it—kids just look younger and younger. David and his bandmates and I started doing rock-paper-scissors tournaments, we were so bored. It was so humid—we went in July. Can you imagine how stupid that was? I was wearing this really pretty white lace shift, but it stuck to my skin. David was wearing shorts, I think. I didn't blame him, it was too hot.

"I was watching all these people who were tired and stupid and thinking how lucky I was not to be them. It made me wonder if someone was watching thinking the same thing about me.

"Three hours later, when it was finally our turn, the four of us filed into the clerk's office, and we had our little ceremony. I think I have a picture somewhere, on an old phone. David said as soon as his mom was better, we'd throw a real wedding to celebrate with everyone. Afterward we went to Margaritaville in Times Square and got drunk. I think it was the best day of my life.

"When we moved to LA, I met his family—we didn't tell them we were married because we didn't want to throw another thing on the fire, you know? They were great; we were happy. We kept the marriage license at the bottom of our sock drawer, to keep it safe." The cheerfulness in Sylvie's voice faltered. "And we were together . . . about two years, probably, before we ended it. I ended up being glad we never went through with the big wedding!" She forced a laugh.

"What happened?" Lila asked gently. *No wonder Sylvie is so lonely.*

Sylvie shook her head. "Oh . . . his mom's cancer got worse, and the only treatment the doctors said might cure her was something insurance wouldn't pay for. I tried to help pay, but I . . . overreached. David said I was a control freak and that he couldn't be around me anymore. We . . . divorced."

For a second, Lila thought she saw a tear in Sylvie's eye, but it was gone before she could even register. "I'm sorry," Lila said softly.

"It worked out for the best, of course. I moved closer to the city, found a job with a bigger PR firm, and then got promoted, a couple big clients. You make mistakes when you're young, you have time to learn from them." Sylvie smiled, but Lila could see it flickering. There was more to the story, it was etched across Sylvie's pale face, but she didn't want to pry. Instead, Lila did the only thing she could—she reached out and took Sylvie's hand in hers.

Sylvie looked at her in surprise, and Lila did not respond because she was surprised too. Where the instinct had come from to comfort Sylvie, she didn't know. But Lila was sure Sylvie didn't deserve that kind of pain. Sylvie was weird and annoying, and she was also brilliant and fearless. Lila had met plenty of people who claimed to be extraordinary, but it wasn't until she knew Sylvie that she understood what it looked like in practice. She thought, *This person beside me is different than anyone I will ever meet and she is remarkable.* But Lila couldn't find any of those words to say. She hoped her hand said enough: *I'm here, I understand, I've lost someone I loved too.*

Sylvie rested her head against the window, staring out at the desert. "We did have some fun times together, though. We really did."

IT WAS NEARLY 100 DEGREES BY THE TIME LILA PULLED ONTO A DIRT ROAD toward a cluster of run-down, Technicolored structures in the middle of the Sonoran Desert. Slab City wasn't a city at all; it wasn't even a town. It was a tiny grid of rusted RVs and campsites. Desert trees dotted the arid landscape, providing the illusion of shade. Locals wandered around in shorts and ratty T-shirts. According to the Wikipedia entry Sylvie had recited on the way there, the locals called it "the last free place in America." This was where society pushed the outcasts so it wouldn't have to look at them.

"Holy shit," Sylvie yelped as they passed a pickup truck covered in baby doll heads. "These people are fucking *Mad Max*."

Lila looked around at the dunes surrounding them. An old man drew in a sketchbook under an umbrella. A couple of people lounged on La-Z-Boys in the sun, their skin frying on the worn black leather. Lila parked the car on the side of the road.

"Wait, hang on, how are we going to find him?" Sylvie asked.

"By asking around."

Lila walked across the dirt road, Sylvie hurrying to catch up. A middle-aged woman with a deep tan glared at them before murmuring something to the heavyset man with a grey beard sitting next to her. He looked up from his book straight at them. "Can I help you?"

"We're looking for James Smith," Lila said. "Told me he came out here but didn't say where to find him."

The woman hovered behind the man, her arms folded. She could have been anywhere between fifty and eighty, her skin ravaged and scarred by the sun. She watched Lila with pointed, wary eyes.

The man cocked his head, inspecting the new arrivals up and down. "Don't know him," he said. "As a matter of principle, folks don't come here to be found."

"Don't loiter, we don't like gawkers," the woman sniffed. She sat back down, signaling the conversation was over.

"Bitch," Sylvie scoffed.

They wandered farther down the road, past rows of homes. Lila was struck by the sheer amount of art everywhere. The Wikipedia page hadn't mentioned how oddly beautiful it was. There was a giant wall of dozens of old televisions, all vandalized with phrases like "BOW BEFORE YOUR GODS." A rusted car was impaled with disembodied mannequin legs. Piles of old junk had been repurposed into intricate sculptures. Slab City seemed more like a colony of eccentrics than true outlaws.

Lila found herself envying its citizens. The outer world dismissed them, but that was only because they had discovered a secret that could collapse the order of things if it got out: the utter bliss of being left alone.

"Let's try her." Lila pointed to a woman in her early thirties sitting in an inflatable pool outside a roadside trailer. She wore pink heart-shaped sunglasses and a bikini covered in flamingos. Lila approached her carefully, determined not to scare her off. "Excuse me?"

The woman's head snapped forward, and she ripped off her sunglasses. "Who are you?"

Lila wondered how someone so young wound up in a place like this. The older people, she understood. But this woman still had her life ahead of her.

"Friends of James Smith. He around here?" Lila asked.

The woman sneered. "I must know a different guy. James I know don't have friends."

Lila's heart leapt. He was here. "Where can I find him?"

"Who are you?" the woman said.

Lila took a step toward her; the woman had to crane her neck upward from the kiddie pool to see her. "I'd prefer we keep our business to ourselves."

"Who you are is my business," the woman said. "'Cause you're sure as hell not whoever you're pretending to be."

Lila froze. They had been so careful.

"Your teeth." The woman grinned, tapping her canine. It was murky and crooked.

Fuck. Keeping her teeth blindingly white was basically part of her job description.

"You have a problem with dental hygiene?" Sylvie said. Lila shot her a look.

"Are you cops?" the woman asked.

"No," Lila said.

"I'm not gonna believe you, no matter what you say," the woman said, waving her arms back and forth in the foot of water. She seemed to be enjoying her new role as gatekeeper.

"Then what do you want us to do, solve a fucking riddle?" Sylvie rolled her eyes. "Can we pay you?"

The woman spat on the ground, narrowly missing Sylvie's foot. "We come here to get away from that stuff."

"We respect that. You tell us where he is, and we won't bother you anymore," Lila said.

"Course you won't, 'cause you'll have got what you wanted," the woman snapped. "Either tell me who you are or get the fuck out of my sight."

Lila thought fast. "His ex-wife," she said. "This is my sister. We just . . . want him to come home."

The woman squinted, regarding Lila closely for a terrible moment. If she knew the real identity of "James Smith," she would know Lila's cover was a lie.

Finally, the woman barked out a laugh. "How the fuck'd he bag you?"

Lila and Sylvie laughed uneasily along with her. She must have known something was off, but she was amused enough to point east. "Follow the road to the left. He's the last house before East Jesus."

"Thank you," Lila said.

The woman raised her beer can high in the air. "Good luck to the love birds!" she snorted, then slid into the pool, cackling.

The mid-day sun pressed them with waves of dry heat, the wind stirring dust off the ground. The desert swallowed the sounds of the town except for the faint clanging of metal. It felt like the apocalypse had come and gone.

Lila and Sylvie followed the road until they saw a handmade sign that read "East Jesus" pointing left. Across the road was a small, yellowed RV distanced apart from the rest of the community. It was plain and neatly kept. There was no furniture or decorations outside. In a community of nomads, Arthur Allen was a true hermit.

Sylvie seized Lila's wrist. "It's too risky to shoot him. They're close by."

Lila nodded. "I have a box cutter."

The grey creature hummed within her, stirring awake.

"I'll keep watch outside," Sylvie said. "If someone comes."

This would fit their marriage lie too. This moment with Arthur was for her alone. Her, Josie, and the grey creature who was awake and clicking its teeth. Sylvie kept watch as Lila walked up the step to the door. She rapped three times, her heartbeat tolling in her ears like a church bell.

The trailer gently shook as she heard footsteps come toward her. A hand opened and shut the front curtain before Lila could catch a glimpse of him. "No visitors," he said from behind the door. His voice was soft and higher pitched than Lila had imagined.

She knocked harder, pounding as loudly as she could against the hot metal.

Arthur yanked open the door. "Jesus Christ, what the fuck is going on—"

Lila put the box cutter to his throat and shoved him into the trailer, shutting the door behind them. Caught off guard, Arthur fell backward onto the floor. She had her first close look at him now. He had lost quite a bit of weight since his mug shot. He was so meager, Lila could wrap her arms around his rib cage. His face was gaunt and lined. His dark hair was prematurely streaked with silver. He was so pale he looked almost blue. Lila straddled his chest, knife pointed to his throat.

She used all her concentration to keep her hands steady as her body, something beyond her conscious mind, registered where and who she was. She could feel his hot, panicked breaths on her face, his watery brown eyes blinking rapidly like a rabbit caught in a snare. She wanted to recoil in revulsion, but she kept herself still.

"Please don't hurt me, please don't hurt me," he whimpered, tears gushing from his eyes. "I swear, you got the wrong guy. I swear—"

"Really, Arthur?" Lila said.

When he heard his name, his pupils became saucers. "No, that's not me, please—"

He was a piss-poor boogeyman. Lila would have honestly preferred it if he gloated. At least he'd acknowledge what he had done. He wriggled underneath her, and Lila pressed the blade to his throat. "Look me in the eye," she said.

Arthur squeezed his eyes shut, willing her away.

"Open your fucking eyes."

His gaze met hers.

"Do you know who I am?" she said.

"No, I don't. I'm not who you're looking for." He shook his head rapidly. His limbs flopped underneath her like a dead fish.

She grabbed his cheeks and forced him to stop and look at her. "Think," she hissed, her face so close to his that their noses were nearly touching.

Round, stupid tears rolled down his hollow cheeks. "Please . . ."

Lila used her free hand to yank her wig off. Unmistakable red hair tumbled out. Arthur paled.

"*No.* No, listen, it wasn't me. I swear to God, I swear on my life, it wasn't me. I came out here to get away—I'm not hurting anyone here."

"What about my daughter?" Lila leaned over him. "You hurt her quite a bit."

Arthur lowered his voice as though he were unsure of how to address her by name. "Lila, I swear, I was set up. I never—they let me go because there was no proof. I swear I didn't touch her."

It was offensive he was even attempting this to her face. Even the man who murdered her little girl didn't take her seriously. Lila drove her knife through his hand. She could feel it cut through bone. This time, there was no psychological barrier. Lila shoved her hand over his mouth to cover his scream. The trailer shook as he thrashed under her.

"Try again." She yanked the blade out and returned it to his neck. He grabbed his wounded hand, wailing.

He blinked up at her with wet cow eyes and spoke clearly, despite the fear in his voice. "I'm sorry for what happened to you, but it wasn't me," he said.

The directness took Lila aback. No. *No.* "You were convicted for child porn twice. You made deepfakes of my body. You stalked my family until you knew our lives inside and out—"

"I didn't take her. I didn't take her, *I swear.*"

She looked away. This wasn't right. She needed to hear him say it. None of this was worth anything if he didn't say it. She slammed her right fist into his face. "*Stop lying to me,*" she shrieked. And hit him again.

With her attention away from the knife, he grabbed her hand and hurled the knife across the trailer. She heard it land with a clang but didn't know where. "I don't wanna hurt you," Arthur said. "Go home."

Go home? Like she was a child who had been disciplined? No one ever believed her pain. They'd made her rich and successful, and she was expected to keep her mouth shut and be satisfied. She wasn't satisfied; she needed to hear him confess. But the grey creature didn't care about confession, forgiveness: it wanted his head. Lila slammed the heel of her palm up Arthur's nose. It broke instantly.

He let out an ear-splitting scream as a flash flood of red gushed from his nose. He looked up at her, his eyes narrowing. He grabbed her by the shoulder and threw her off him. She landed against the table, and it broke under her weight. She groaned, forcing herself to get up before Arthur did.

"Please don't make me hurt you," Arthur said as she came to stand over him.

She slammed her boot into his trachea. He let out a strangled wheeze and grabbed her leg, pulling her down to the floor beside him. Lila tried to wriggle away, but his grip was too tight.

"I don't want to be this; you make me this. *Do you understand?* I just wanted to be left alone."

He was yanking her toward him, his nails digging into her skin. The lips of Lila's fingers brushed a whiskey bottle on the floor just as Arthur gave her another tug, and she gripped it just in time to smash it in his face.

Glass flew everywhere, into his mouth, his eyes. Little cuts formed on his lips and cheeks. He howled in pain, rolling onto his back. "*Say it,*" Lila said, shaking the glass out of her hair. He only moaned, bloody tears streaming down his face. She slammed her fist into his face. "*SAY IT!*" He said nothing. She hit him again.

Arthur's nose had swollen to the size of a golf ball. His right eye couldn't fully open. He weakly tried to fight her off, but the effort was gone. He knew he had lost. Still, Lila kept going. There was a rhythm in her punches; she matched them to her heartbeat.

And then he lay there, his face a bloody pulp, just taking it. She shoved his shoulders, trying to wake him up. "COME ON!" she screamed, shaking him to do something, anything. But he only looked at her in a daze. She grabbed his collar and pulled him toward her face. "PLEASE!" She felt wetness on her cheek—she thought it was his blood. She didn't realize she was crying.

Lila peeled herself off him and walked across the room to get the box cutter. It had fallen behind a stockpile of *Cat Fancy* magazines. Arthur sputtered short, labored breaths as she walked back to him, his one eye fluttering to look at her. "Admit it," Lila said.

Arthur closed his eye, then slowly opened it again. And just barely, with the remaining strength he could muster, he shook his head from side to side.

The grey creature screamed from the depths of Lila's gut as she slit his throat. He barely reacted; his single eye continued to blink at her until it finally shut. Lila waited for the wave of satisfaction to wash over her, to whisper gently and tend to her wounds. But she felt no closure at all. Lila sat back in the bloody mess and sobbed.

A moment later, Sylvie burst through the door. "Is he—" She stopped when she saw Arthur's faceless body beside her. "Goddamn."

Lila touched her finger to the gash on his neck. It was a lovely crimson—it reminded Lila of the Old Hollywood lip look she'd worn to the Oscars. She brushed his blood across her cheek. It almost felt like her skin cream.

She glanced back at Sylvie, who was trying not to stare. Sylvie put a hand on the doorknob. "I'll get the tarp."

They did not speak while they wrapped Arthur up and scrubbed the crime scene of any prints. They left without incident. By the time they had finished, it was dark, and the residents of Slab City were quietly in their homes. On the way back to their car, Sylvie grabbed a lamp to make it look like the jilted wife was taking her things back. She didn't ask a single question when they loaded Arthur into the trunk or on the entire ride home. Lila sat in the passenger seat, rereading Arthur's case files on her phone over and over again. The proof was all there. She had killed the right man. He was a good liar. He thought he could sway her.

But the feeling of satisfaction she'd been waiting for never came. She could still feel the grey thing inside of her, biting and clawing. *Not enough*, it whispered. Three men were dead, what more could she do?

Not enough, not enough.

Fourteen

Finally, when they'd laid Arthur's body out in Sylvie's garage, Sylvie spoke. "Before we start, how about you take a shower?" She was gentle, careful, like Lila was a wild animal. "It'll make you feel better, nice and clean."

Lila glanced down and realized her body was caked in Arthur's dry, crusted blood. She hadn't even noticed. She let Sylvie herd her to the bathroom.

"Take your time," Sylvie said before shutting the door behind her.

Then Lila was alone. She ran the water and waited for it to steam. She stepped out of her jeans with a shiver as flecks of blood smeared against the floor tile. Her skin itched and burned from the sun; plum bruises ripened across her chest and forearms. When the air was so muggy she felt faint, she stepped inside the cascade of water.

She should have been happy Arthur was dead. He had banked on the world moving on to newer and shinier acts of violence, but Lila hadn't forgotten. It took ten long years, but he had finally seen justice. Instead, a deep sorrow seized Lila the second his body went limp on the floor of that trailer. The grey thing was right—he wasn't enough. Arthur was only the scapegoat.

Lila watched as swirls of Arthur's blood melted down the drain. She was tired of being on her feet and crouched to sit on the tub floor, letting the water beat down on her back.

The terrible, undeniable truth was that the entire world had killed Josie. Everyone who read the story and treated it like a spectacle, a delicious case of schadenfreude. Josie had died by billions of their cuts. Arthur and Nico and Carmichael didn't heal her because they were Band-Aids on a gaping wound.

They all deserved to die. Every one of them. The people at the very top had made an astounding profit exploiting her story, and the people at the very bottom had eagerly lapped it up. Either way, they lived miserable, empty lives consuming other people.

A golden, shimmering path appeared before Lila, and all the confusion, frustration, and anguish crystalized in her mind, and she knew exactly what to do. Lila got to her feet, touched by the light of something far greater than she. Power surged through her—she had power now. There was no reason to be afraid of death. Death was a gift; it was consistent, familiar.

Lila hadn't realized how much of her soul had died with Josie; when it came flooding back, she was floored by the sheer weight of it. The grey creature—she could never admit it to herself, but she knew in the depths of her soul that it was Josie's spirit and it was whispering to her, and she'd tried to drown it out because it was like stepping on glass, but for the first time she stopped. And she listened. And she opened her heart to her daughter and cried.

Josie's spirit lived inside her skin, vibrated in her bones with every breath she took. Lila had tried to escape her, fled Los Angeles to remake herself, but there was no way to outrun a ghost.

And that was all right. It was a good kind of torment, she understood now. She'd tried to tuck the grey thing away just like she'd done with Josie. Because the world expected her to move on. She was robbed of everything in her life, and the world had told her to move on. Why had she been so desperate to start over? What did she owe these people to appease them? If the world wanted to keep turning, it was her duty to dig her heels into the ground and hold it back.

And for once, since the day Josie died, she felt like she had done something right. She could feel the warmth in her abdomen—it was Josie saying thank you. Finally, she had done right by her child. She had been a failure when Josie was alive, but she could make up for it now.

"Whoa, you good?" Sylvie said when Lila emerged from the bathroom with wild eyes.

Lila only smiled. "I used to be so scared of what was inside of me, but I never realized it was trying to do *good*."

Sylvie sat up a little, noticing the shift in Lila's demcanor. "Lila, what's going on?"

"Nico and Carmichael and Arthur Allen were never going to be enough. Not when they're only three out of *billions*," Lila said. "I want all of them to pay. The whole world killed her. *They all deserve to die*."

Sylvie tried to hide her alarm as she watched Lila stalk back and forth across the room. "I think you gotta start a little smaller than exterminating the human race."

Lila rolled her eyes, drying her hair. "You want to know something, Sylvie? Aidan and I used to have this theory. At every party we went to, there were always three types of people. The people who spoke, the people who listened, and the people who weren't in the conversation at all. And I've realized that that applies to everyone in general. The people who talk are the decision-makers—they're corrupt. The world needs to be rid of them. The people who listen follow orders—they're weak sycophants; we don't need them either. And for the people who just consume—if you don't get a say in anything, what's the point of being alive?"

And then a shadow passed across Lila's face, and she fell and she let out a cry and she crumpled into herself and she wept open-mouthed. "I'll never hug her again, I'll never hold her . . ."

Sylvie knelt on the ground beside her, desperate to ease her pain. "Hush, hush—it's okay. You're okay." But Lila wasn't listening, and Sylvie wanted her to listen. She took a deep breath and stood. "I know where you can start."

She disappeared into the hall and returned with a hardcover book. The back was covered in five-star reviews that Lila couldn't make out.

"For inspo." Sylvie handed it to her.

Lila took it from her and looked at the title.

The book fell out of her hands.

"Why the fuck do you have this?"

Sylvie put her hands up, showing she meant no harm. "It came out yesterday, and I wanted to read it so I could warn you if someone asked . . ."

Lila picked the book off the ground—it was heavy, at least three hundred pages. The fact that they squeezed out that much unsanctioned bullshit about her family made her nauseated. The fact that people had reviewed it and lauded it as anything other than muckraking made her want to self-immolate.

Lila turned to the first page. It was a disclaimer that she and Aidan had not agreed to participate. She snorted and then turned to the next page. It was a fifty-person list of everyone interviewed for the book titled "Cast of Characters."

Cast of Characters. It was a stage play to them.

"Did you read it?" she asked quietly, not looking up.

"Yeah," Sylvie said.

"Is it bad?" Lila whispered, though she already knew the answer.

Sylvie shifted awkwardly on her feet. "You get the feeling that it's a little biased toward Aidan—"

Lila ripped the "Cast of Characters" page out of the book. "This is the list," she said. Sylvie nodded vigorously.

Lila scanned the names for anyone she recognized. She saw a couple of people from her childhood in Boston. She wondered if they'd been paid or if they just wanted to stake a claim in a tragedy.

"Cara?" she said quietly. A wave of sadness sank into the pit of her stomach. The first person in LA she'd sought out for help. *She knew this whole time about the oral history and never told me.* Cara could be jealous and callous and petty, but she had also almost singlehandedly kept Lila together during the media circus. For some naive reason, Lila had expected a little bit of loyalty. But there, right on paper, showed just how little Cara thought of her.

"Lydia Novak? Of course she'd jump to sink her little claws into this again. And Tim Weber? You're fucking kidding me, that asshole? He hated me because I took Aidan away from whoring around with him. I'm sure he gave a lovely interview. This is trash!"

Open up, everyone had told her. *The people want to know you! Open yourself up to the world.* Well, here she was, and it was too late to change their minds. Lila let out a scream that rattled her rib cage. Out poured the most calamitous parts of her soul, and now they would live with the consequences.

Something big and impossible to understand laid its hands on Lila's shoulders and told her to quiet down. It massaged deep into her spine, and ripples of calm shot through her synapses. She had been so tired of being alone for so long it brought tears to her eyes to realize Josie had been watching over her all this time. She was overwhelmed with reverence toward her daughter. Josie would live through her now. Josie would be free.

Lila folded the page and put it in her pocket. The book was actually a *blessing.* It was a map to start her off on her journey. She understood now that she had divine, unfathomable purpose. Others might see her mission as wrong, but that was only because they didn't *understand.*

When she and Aidan had gone to see Josie's body, her first instinct was horror. She didn't want to remember her daughter like that; it was unbearable. Carmichael had tried to herd her out, and she'd almost gone with him, but she didn't. Lila didn't deserve the privilege of turning her head away. She owed it to Josie to see what had been done to her. Nothing, she'd learned, is truly impossible to bear. You take some on, and then a little more, and then you learned to carry it.

Lila wouldn't turn away from this either.

"Lila?" Sylvie said in a small voice. Lila didn't know how long she'd been quiet.

"We need to get rid of Arthur Allen," Lila said.

Energy hummed at Lila's fingertips, leaving golden prints on the door as she returned to Arthur Allen's body in the garage. Sylvie followed at a cautious distance.

The bruising across his face had turned into a gorgeous blend of blues and purples. It was like looking at the brushstrokes of an impressionist painting. He was an ugly man with an unremarkable face. It was a shame he had had to die to become beautiful. His cheeks were nearly black and caked in blood, but they were rather prominent. "His cheekbones weren't bad," Lila said thoughtfully, tracing their outline.

Sylvie glanced down with a shrug. "For a pedophile murderer that lived in trash land."

Lila picked up the electric saw. All this time she'd felt ashamed, guilty. Could barely handle the sound of the blade colliding with bone. She wouldn't vomit this time. *She wouldn't turn away.* And to think she'd feared it was inhumane—how absurd! It was *completely* humane. To use *humanity* as a word for mercy was the greatest lie ever told.

Lila was about to turn the saw on when she noticed Sylvie shake her head. "What?"

Sylvie shook her head again. "It's just such a waste."

"A waste?" Lila looked at her oddly.

Sylvie clucked her tongue. "We pay boatloads for collagen to put in the skin cream, and it's not like he's using his anymore . . ."

Sylvie and Lila looked at each other, eyes wide.

LILA HAD BEEN SO DETERMINED TO DEFY THEIR OPINIONS ABOUT GLOB that she had never considered Cara Donaldson and the venture capitalists and the reporter at *The Cut* were *right*. Glob hadn't become a trend because they had failed to deliver a once-in-a-lifetime product. There was nothing extraordinary about lotion made from the same bovine collagen everyone else used. It was only now, when the answer had fallen into her lap, that she understood the *difference*. *This* was their wow factor. Lila knew deep within her soul that a hundred years from now, people would look back on this moment as the beginning of something *extraordinary*.

"We couldn't," Lila said, forcing herself back to earth. "It's too dangerous. And we don't even know if it would work."

"I read an article about it once." Sylvie's eyes widened. "The Chinese government was selling executed prisoners to the Europeans to use their collagen. And say what you will about the Chinese government, but you gotta admit they know what they're doing."

"What about Maya?" Lila asked. It was too much, *too* crazy, too many obstacles. Maya was her greatest concern and needed to be protected.

"Maya would have no idea. We'll extract it ourselves. She wouldn't know where the collagen is from. It's like horses being used for glue," Sylvie said, smile broadening. "It's not as impossible as you think."

Lila had never wanted this. She had wanted to be no one, but they had ripped anonymity away and forced immortality upon her. They had stripped her naked and taken and taken until she was just ashes of herself. They had consumed her, and now it was their turn to be consumed.

"They did say we needed something to set us apart," Lila said.

This is insane, this is insane, this is insane, a soft, urgent voice in Lila's head whispered. And Lila knew the voice was right, but the world was finally clicking into place.

This is insane, Lila agreed, *and I don't care.*

"Sylvie Lightly, you have a breathtaking mind."

Sylvie's lips curled into a Cheshire cat grin, thrilled at the compliment. Lila started to giggle, and Sylvie joined in, and suddenly everything was so hysterical that Lila nearly pissed her pants. The world opened its jaws wide before them, inviting them to leap in.

Sylvie's eyes lit up, and she cleared her throat, holding an imaginary microphone. "I'd like to announce glob's new line of products—Chinless Virgin," she said, gesturing to Arthur's body.

Lila burst out laughing. She pulled out an imaginary notepad and pretended to scribble, raising her hand. "Can you give us any details, Ms. Lightly?"

Sylvie nodded. "The scent has notes of antisocial personality disorder and an inability to talk to women."

Lila furrowed her brow with faux concern. "How do you explain the facial hair in the serum?"

"*What* facial hair?" Sylvie jumped in the air, clicking her heels together.

Lila pulled out the "Cast of Characters" sheet and showed it to Sylvie, pointing to Lydia Novak's name. "This is a prototype I'm still working on, it's called Starfucker. Contrary to most beauty products, it actually works to physically repel family and friends."

Sylvie snickered. "But you'll look great for any TV appearances you commandeer."

"Of course! If your loved ones hate you, it's time to sic yourself on the public!" Lila howled.

Sylvie took the "Cast of Characters" list and pointed to Fox's name. "Ladies and gentlemen, that's not all. This is way, way out in development, but I'm thrilled to share with you . . . Roasted Pig!"

Lila exploded, laughter pouring over her body in waves.

"W-w-w-w-w-wait." Sylvie held a finger up, wheezing. "Interestingly enough, it's the first known lotion in history that turns you racist."

"It really is amazing. You put it on at night, and the next morning, you wake up with a buzz cut and Oakley sunglasses," Lila shrieked, and Sylvie grabbed her hands and they twirled around the room, cackling. Lila couldn't remember the last time she had this much fun. It occurred to her that maybe she never had.

Only then did Lila realize how close Sylvie's face was to hers. Her pupils were so big; they nearly swallowed her irises. Lila felt struck by her beauty. She had never noticed it before, never looked past Sylvie's eyeliner and bangs to see the soul underneath. Sylvie pressed her lips to Lila's, and then their mouths were hungrily moving against each other, hands scrambling to touch every inch of each other's bodies.

The dam that had prevented Lila from enjoying life burst open, and the world was on fire.

Sylvie broke away, leaving Lila's chest heaving. "Can we go into the other room?"

"What? Why?" Lila panted, confused. Sylvie nodded toward the festering corpse a few feet away from them. "Oh."

THEY MADE LOVE FRANTICALLY. LILA HAD NEVER BEEN WITH A WOMAN before, and it was better than she could have imagined. Sylvie knew how to anticipate and answer her body before she even posed a question. Lila reveled in learning every corner of Sylvie's body, each discovery new and wonderful beneath her fingertips.

When they lay in bed afterward, Sylvie watched Lila with adoring blue eyes. They seemed lighter than usual, two gently rocking oceans. "Lila, I . . . that was amazing. That was earth-shattering." Sylvie rested her head on Lila's breast, fingers ghosting across her stomach. She gave Lila's belly button a friendly poke. "I love that you're an outie."

Lila felt the weight of her gaze but couldn't meet it. It was too intimate. "Thank you."

"I've wanted to do that from the moment I first saw you," Sylvie said, reaching out to trace Lila's breast. "I've never told anyone about David before. No one ever compared. But you . . . you helped me heal."

Her vulnerability was unnerving. Lila was beginning to think she'd made a mistake. The sex was a great release of energy, but it wasn't worth telling her now. Not when they still had to dismember a body.

"Do you believe in fate?" Sylvie dragged her hand in lazy circles up and down Lila's arm. "I didn't used to. I thought life was random and some people just got lucky, but then I met you."

Lila smiled politely. "That's nice."

Sylvie rested her head on Lila's shoulder, molding her body into hers. "You're brilliant, Lila, you know that? You're a genius. You're an innovator. I feel like I'm in the passenger seat to a revolution."

Lila turned her head and kissed Sylvie hard. Their teeth scraped against each other as their tongues fought. Lila let her mind go blank, forcing all her energy into Sylvie's mouth. They broke apart, panting, and Lila moved her lips down Sylvie's throat. She could feel her heartbeat.

She could feel Nico's heartbeat when she slit his throat.

"We should get back to Arthur," Lila said.

Sylvie nodded and pulled her close for another lazy kiss. Lila couldn't look at her anymore. She got out of bed and hurriedly picked up her clothes scattered across the floor. Lila recognized the look on her face—for the first time since she'd met her, Sylvie was at peace.

They would begin with an exclusive limited supply trial. As they learned from Google, collagen accounted for about 30 percent of the protein in the human body, and those manufactured serums contained barely any. They could make Arthur last a long time.

They found a YouTube tutorial on how bovine collagen was extracted and figured it was close enough. There was even a helpful infographic. They tore through skin, smooth muscle, and vein until they reached hard bone and rejoiced like they'd been digging a well and hit water.

The video told Lila to put the stripped bone in a large pot of cold water on Sylvie's stove to boil for ten hours, then to place everything in an ice bath. This was called blanching, to get rid of any excess blood, dirt, hair, and nasty bits. There were a lot of nasty bits.

Arthur might have even been pleased to know that his body was going to a good cause. That in the end, he wasn't all worthless. It was selfless on Lila's part, actually, to offer him the redemption he didn't deserve. It was like he had donated his body, contributing to Lila's scientific breakthrough. She was grabbing the skincare industry by the neck and yanking it into the future.

They worked through the night into the following morning—sawing, skinning, blanching, and cooking. Lila's mind and body soared in perfect cohesion. As the hours passed and she neared her goal, she gained enthusiasm. While Sylvie was sickened by the smell or needed water every couple of hours, Lila feared any loss of momentum would make the feeling of wholeness inside of her go away. She'd never felt more connected to Josie in her life; she couldn't let her slip away again.

By the next evening, Arthur was a sack of burned organs thrown into a lake, and Lila and Sylvie had dehydrated the broth into tubs of fresh collagen powder. By the time they sat down to rest, it had just struck eight p.m. Sparks flew out of Lila's fingers, eager for more.

"We need to send out updated press kits."

PART THREE

Arrival

FIFTEEN

"If you want to get rid of wrinkles but don't want to use Botox, I found your holy grail. It's glob's brightening eye cream. It has all the goodies you want, like green tea and vitamin C, but the secret ingredient is their collagen, which is formulated *without* bovine collagen, so great news for us animal lovers who want results. It is said to remove eighty-five percent of wrinkles. The results are truly incredible. You have to try it," a TikToker said into her camera. Her face was poreless and dewy, lit by a bleach-colored ring light.

A new TikTok played. "This is the glob liquid collagen serum. It's a science-backed cruelty-free serum that has literally changed my life. You know me, I'm a skeptic. When everybody started talking about this, I was like, *No other collagen-based products work*. Glob is changing the game by formulating a collagen that actually absorbs through the skin barrier," another girl said as she spread it all over her face.

Another TikTok: "Glob is so good and so cheap—Lila Devlin, you are mother to us all."

Lauren Hunt and Rob Hayes, the hosts of *Wake Up, America*, the biggest morning show in the country, laughed as the clip show ended and turned to face the camera. "Those are just a few clips from the new beauty company sweeping the nation, glob. We're sitting down today with Lila Devlin, founder and CEO. Thank you so much for being here, Lila," Lauren said.

After months of floundering and false starts, it really took only one product and a thirty-second TikTok from Maya's college friend. A week later, the video was viral, and Lila was rich again. Suddenly, they were racing to meet the demand. They started with an exclusive, limited run. Arhtur wasn't going to last long. They hired a warehouse full of employees who manufactured Lila's recipe with the collagen powder that arrived in nondescript boxes every week, and no one was the wiser.

Within weeks of glob trending on TikTok, news organizations began to reach out for interviews, mouthy for a new teat to suck. Lila and Sylvie happily obliged, setting up a whirlwind New York publicity tour a mere day before it began.

And now Lauren Hunt, the ice-blond queen of morning news, sat across from her as an excited fan.

"Thanks so much for having me," Lila said, smiling brightly to the crowded audience. She hadn't seen this many people smiling at her in a long time. Male boomers dragged there by their wives, Midwestern women on New York vacations. A sea of ordinary faces lapping up the celebrities whoring themselves. She had made glob to appeal to the masses, but . . . was this it? Were the masses so dead-eyed and slow? Passively accepting life with dull-eyed wonder like they'd accepted her as a child murderer?

"And your hair, my *gosh*," Lauren said. "That is the prettiest color red I've ever seen."

Lila only wore her hair up now. In the past, she'd kept it down past her shoulders, wearing it as a shield. But she was a redhead with beautiful bone structure, and the world was going to look at her. Sylvie decided her standard uniform should be a tailored cream turtleneck suit. She needed to be seen as regal.

Rob nodded appreciatively beside her. He was in his mid-forties and trim, with a smile that swallowed his face. Lila noticed that Lauren's dress matched his tie. "It's been two months, and glob has skyrocketed into a national phenomenon. How does it feel?"

"Exhilarating," Lila said. "We poured blood, sweat, and tears into this company. To see our goal of making good quality cosmetics accessible to everyone is the greatest reward I could imagine."

She was happy the success had not come earlier. She hadn't been ready before; her footsteps were shaky, and glob had been meaningless. The universe had needed Arthur to die first.

Behind the desk, Lila noticed Rob's hand brush against Lauren's knee. Lauren gave him an extra big smile, then turned to Lila. "I had a chance to try your eye cream. I couldn't believe it! It's magic, and at that price! What is your secret?"

"The highest-quality collagen."

"Talk to us about the genesis of your company," Rob said.

"Have you ever been haunted by something?" Lila asked.

Rob and Lauren blinked at her in confusion. "Like a ghost?"

"By a memory of something that never happened. By this idea of what your life could have been, or maybe what it *is* in some parallel universe, but you're trapped in this one," Lila said. "Life would be so much easier if ghosts were just people."

Rob looked uncomfortable. The audience shifted in their seats. She used to worry about making people uncomfortable. She didn't anymore.

"Ten years ago, my daughter was kidnapped and murdered. I did everything in my power to leave her behind, but after ten years I finally realized I couldn't. I carry her with me. Everything I have done and will do is in service of her. This company is my tribute to her. I want the world to carry her with them too."

The rapturous applause came like a clap of thunder. Lauren blinked back tears. Lila listened to the audience and felt the studio lights shining down on her like brilliant stars.

"Lila, I want to say something from the bottom of my heart. It is impossible to imagine what you've been through," Rob said, face growing earnest. The crowd quieted. "I don't know what I'd do if I lost my family. But the grace with which you've carried yourself over the last decade is one of the most extraordinary things I've ever seen. And to take something so awful and make something so empowering like glob is amazing. You are a real-life superhero."

One woman started crying. Lila put a hand to her heart in appreciation. "I would not be where I am without every single one of you," Lila said.

Rob turned in his chair to encourage the audience's applause, his breath brushing Lauren's cheek. He chuckled bashfully and turned away.

"Now I understand you have a little tutorial for us?" Lauren said.

Lila set a tube on the desk. Lauren inspected it and held it up for the camera. "This is glob's eye-brightening cream. It combines collagen with vitamin C to lessen fine lines and dark circles."

It did not frighten Lila to wipe off her makeup and bare her face to millions on national television. It was a privilege for them to see her bare face, to see beauty they could only emulate with face-tuning apps.

"The dark circles and wrinkles under my eyes were what I hated most. I tried everything to get rid of them, but they were permanent. I had a choice: go the route that made sense for Hollywood, get a blepharoplasty and filler and Botox, or accept them," Lila said. "The principles of glob helped me realize that they are the greatest representation of who I am. I earned those dark circles. I wear the lines under my eyes as badges of honor because they show the world I'm alive. Glob isn't trying to erase the parts we're insecure about—it's helping us realize they're beautiful."

Lila squeezed some of the eye cream out of the tube and gently dabbed it under her eyes. She always loved the rush of cold when it touched her skin, soft like a first snow. She patted until it had soaked into her skin.

She smiled and held it out to Rob. "Wanna try some?"

"Right now?" he said uneasily. The audience whistled and cheered for him to put it on, because watching a man try skincare was apparently unbelievable.

Lauren grinned and seized the tube from Lila. "Yes, he does."

She brushed her finger on his upper cheeks, looking out at the audience like they were in on a big secret together. "It feels nice," Rob said. "The eye cream, I mean."

The audience laughed heartily. "Try it every other night; it'll make your eyes pop," Lila said.

"I've never had a skincare routine before," Rob said.

"Lauren, you can remind him before bed," Lila said.

Lauren and Rob glanced at each other, then at the audience, then back at each other, then burst out laughing. "Oh, no, we're not married!" Lauren said.

"Well, I do call you my work wife." Rob chortled.

Lila looked out at the audience that laughed along. All adoring her. It was uncanny.

But they weren't actually smiling at her. She wasn't a person to them; she was someone from "the TV" they got to stare at in real life. They'd go home and tell their friends they saw her in person. *She looks great now*, they'd say. *She's so brave, going through all that.* Everyone loved a comeback, even when they were the ones who'd brought about the downfall in the first place.

"TWITTER IS *LOVING* YOU ON THE SHOW," SYLVIE SAID AS SHE GUIDED LILA out of the mob of fans to the waiting SUV. Since glob's success, Sylvie had upgraded her wardrobe. Today, she wore an emerald-green trench coat and fedora. Her style was as terrible as before, but now, each piece of her outfit cost at least a thousand dollars.

"I thought no one watches these morning shows outside of housewives in Middle America," Lila said.

"True, but one of your stans posted the clip of you taking your makeup off for the demonstration, and it's going viral for your courage," Sylvie said. "They're saying you're serving cunt and being mother."

The New York summer humidity beat down on them as Sylvie opened the car door. Once Lila was seated, Sylvie turned to the driver. "Central Park South."

Overall, Lila had enjoyed the press tour in Manhattan. During the day, she did a morning show. Then lunch or sightseeing, then a late-night show, which left the night free for whatever she and Sylvie wanted. She had loathed doing talk shows when she was in her twenties, but now watching Jimmy Fallon laugh at every word of her unfunny stories made her feel like a god. Millions of people were actually taking minutes out of their lives to tune in to her playing Simon Says with some kid from Netflix. Of course it was stupid, but at least she wasn't the person watching it.

The response to Lila and glob had been overall positive. There would always be the people who wished her dead on Twitter and her hate subreddit and those Facebook groups, but aside from them, the tide was generally in her favor. The only thing more fun than a downfall was a comeback.

Even Lila's relationship with Sylvie was great. As soon as they were away from prying eyes, they could not keep their hands off each other. Sylvie was determined to impress and excite Lila. Her New York sex goal was to fuck on every baby-changing table in every bathroom they went to. "Being a little gross is what makes it fun!"

Sylvie was an eager, adventurous lover, but more than Lila's outlet for pent-up stress, she knew every aspect of Lila's public and private life. Sylvie—sweet, bizarre Sylvie—had become her greatest champion. If Lila couldn't love her, she could appreciate her.

Sylvie rolled up the partition. Once it had sealed the driver off, she turned to Lila with a mischievous grin. "This isn't a changing table, but I think it should suffice."

She sprung forward and sealed her lips to Lila's jaw, but Lila wasn't paying much attention. Her thoughts were occupied elsewhere. "Two months is a long enough wait, don't you think?"

Sylvie hummed in agreement against Lila's neck. "You're so patient, babe, so patient," she said between kisses. "We'll start as soon as we're back in town. We have enough collagen left for a little—"

"Why wait until then?" Lila asked.

Sylvie slowly pulled away to look Lila in the eye. "What?"

"Greer Houser's podcasting studio is based in Williamsburg," Lila said. "I don't have any more interviews today. We could go get her."

Greer Houser, the cockroach who hosted the *Devlin Baby* podcast, had created a true crime empire on top of her daughter's ashes. She hosted *Devlin Baby* live shows—touring the country, drawing crowds of hundreds. She had franchised a dozen spin-offs about other murdered children. She had the audacity to speak in the oral history like Lila should be grateful to her for recontextualizing her life through an intersectional feminist lens. Greer refused to acknowledge that the greatest gift she could've given Lila would have been to leave her alone.

Sylvie frowned, then tried to smile, then frowned again. "Lila, I love your enthusiasm, but we go home tomorrow. We should wait till we're back in LA." She ducked her head back to Lila's neck, hands moving to untuck her sweater.

"It'll barely take any time at all," Lila snapped.

"We don't have any of our tools here. We can't dismantle her body in a hotel room," whined Sylvie to Lila's left nipple.

Lila pushed away from her. "Then we'll take her with us."

"What?" Sylvie looked up at her, disoriented.

"We'll fly private. I can get a discount—"

"Lila, we can't traffic a dead body across the country," Sylvie said.

"Why? If we put her in a chest and cover her in ice, she'd be fine for a six-hour flight," Lila said. "We'll wrap it in plastic and duct tape, pretend she's some antique I bought."

Sylvie sputtered, genuinely at a loss for words. "What about—"

"We kill Greer this afternoon; by tomorrow, the decay won't be terrible. I don't think we'll have to worry about the smell," Lila said.

"But . . . today was supposed to be our fun couple day. I got front mezz seats to *Wicked*." Sylvie pouted.

Lila smiled at her cheerily. The easiest way to win Sylvie over was to appeal to her inner romantic. "Sylvie, you're the only person who can help me. I *need* you."

Sylvie tucked a strand of hair behind her ear, a little bashful. "My love language is acts of service . . ."

Lila sat back, knowing she had won. She pressed the button, and the partition rolled back down. "Actually, can you take us to the nearest Target? I need to run a few errands."

SIXTEEN

Since Williamsburg had been seized by trust-fund kids and upper-middle-class hipsters, it looked more like Downtown Disney than Brooklyn. It had become a grid of perfect, dull streets boasting architectural feats like Whole Foods and an Apple Store. The waterfront was manicured parks and glass high-rise condos where the rich had expansive views of Manhattan and the Brooklyn neighborhoods they'd never visit. Greer had opted instead for a town house on a quiet street. It must have cost at least $3 million. As Sylvie drove around the block in a rented SUV, Lila looked for security cameras or Ring doorbells, but there were none.

Sylvie parked a block away, and they silently walked to Greer's house. They wore black turtlenecks and jeans and carried the supplies they had purchased at Target earlier that day. "Be ready," Lila said.

Sylvie stopped at the base of the front stoop while Lila approached the door. "I'll be right out here."

After two months of waiting, the familiar jolt of anticipation shot through Lila's body. But she felt different this time, more relaxed. Prepared. The first three times, she'd been clumsy and overeager. Now, she stood with quiet confidence. She wasn't an amateur anymore.

Lila knocked. A few moments later, a petite white woman with light brown hair opened the door. She was in her early thirties, pretty, but desperately wanting to present as bookish. She wore a slouchy sweater and a necklace that said *Anxiety* in gold cursive.

"Can I—*oh my god.*" Greer Houser's jaw dropped to the sidewalk when she recognized Lila on her doorstep. She did her best to collect herself and stuck out a hand. "I mean—it is so nice to meet you, Lila."

Lila smiled warmly. "I'm sorry, this is a little out of nowhere, but I wanted to find time while I was in town to see you."

"Oh my gosh, are you kidding? This is a dream come true, come in!" Greer ushered Lila inside, shutting the door behind them. She let out an awkward giggle. "I'm sorry, I'm fangirling so hard right now. You are an icon. I have to tell—"

Before she could pull out her phone, Lila cleared her throat. "Could I trouble you for a glass of water?"

"Of course." Greer led her down the hallway. The house had to be at least a hundred years old. Lila could just make out the original art deco crown molding on the walls peeking out from underneath shelves of Hufflepuff memorabilia.

The hallway led into an open kitchen with marble countertops and a full bar. The stove and oven looked completely untouched, while the steel trash can overflowed with empty take-out containers. The fridge was covered in an assortment of ironic serial killer magnets and vague girl power quotes. On the breakfast table, Lila could see Greer's laptop opened to Twitter, Discord, Instagram, TikTok, and Reddit.

"Thank you," Lila said when Greer handed her a glass of ice water. "Your house is beautiful."

"Oh my god, thank you so much. I'm a homebody at heart; that's one of the best things about working in audio. I never have to leave my house." Greer laughed.

"I listened to your podcast," Lila said.

Greer's cheeks reddened. "Oh my god, you have no idea how badly I've wanted to hear that. I have tried to get in touch with you for years."

"It's very well researched."

"One hundred percent accuracy is, like, my ride-or-die thing with reporting. Integrity in podcasting is so important," Greer said.

"You thought I killed Josie at first," Lila commented, and smiled.

"Wh—oh, wow, you really did listen." Greer blushed, hands curling in the oversized sleeves of her sweater. It was strange to watch a grown woman act like a preteen. "I did, but only for, like, a month. I started the podcast to help correct the theories I fell for myself."

"Like what?" Lila enjoyed making her squirm.

"Well, I guess the main reason I thought you'd done it was because I thought Arthur Allen was innocent."

Lila stilled. "I'm sorry?"

Greer rubbed her arm awkwardly. "I—yeah. No doubt he's a bad guy, but I felt like all the evidence they had against him was circumstantial."

Despite her best efforts, the seed of doubt that Arthur had planted in Lila's mind had only grown with time. No. If he didn't do it, if he had told the truth, then that would mean she had killed an innocent man. And that wasn't possible. Josie had *told her* she was right. Lila tried to push it away as glob's business grew, but the question lingered. And if Greer Houser, who had made this trauma her career, believed Arthur's innocence—

No. Now was not the time for weakness and uncertainty.

Lila pressed on. "And the podcast has been going for how long?"

"Five years in a few months," Greer said. "It started as a retrospective miniseries, and then it just kept going."

"Wow," Lila said. "Congratulations."

"Thank you so much." Greer smiled. "I remember when I was starting out, I had no idea what I was doing. I had the worst impostor syndrome. And now it's an entire network."

"I'm very impressed you're still finding things to say after all this time," Lila said.

"I feel like it's my duty to keep the case alive," Greer said. "As time passes, it's fascinating to recontextualize it in the modern era. There is so much to be examined through this lens now."

She talked about it like it was a war in the eighteenth century. "What is there to recontextualize?" Lila asked.

Greer puffed with pride. "Okay, a couple years ago, during the Black Lives Matter protests, I drew a parallel that you were kind of the first big ACAB moment of the 2010s."

"Wow."

"I got, like, mini-canceled for that, but it blew over. And I'm not afraid to say risky things. 'Cause you are a feminist folk hero queen, and it is my job to tell your story to the world," Greer continued. "I want your voice to be heard—"

"What makes me a feminist folk hero queen?" Lila interrupted her.

Greer paused. "What?"

"What have I done to become a feminist folk hero queen?"

Greer shifted onto the balls of her feet. "You started glob, which is already, like, the greatest skincare brand in the country."

Lila was stone-faced. "No, you started the *Devlin Baby* podcast before I did that. You only knew me as an actress whose child died."

Greer laughed, her hands fidgeting. Lila's eye contact seared through her. "Well . . . essentially, your case was a crime-of-the-century thing. And seeing you go through what you went through was super inspiring."

"But I didn't do anything," Lila said. "It happened to me. I was a victim."

Greer shook her head furiously. "No. *Never* call yourself a victim. You were a *survivor*. You're an inspiration."

"I had multiple public meltdowns. I was hospitalized. I was mocked, derided, outcast. I didn't survive anything." Lila's face darkened. "How does that make me an inspiration? What did I inspire you to do?"

"You—you inspired me to be strong. And—"

"Fight for the people you love?" Lila made a jerk-off motion with her hand. "The only thing I inspired you to do was make a podcast. You're not pedestalizing me because I've done something to deserve it; you're pedestalizing me because you feel guilty."

Greer clearly understood now that something was very wrong. She smiled uneasily, taking a small step backward. "I can totally understand why it might feel like that, but I promise that's not it at all. People love you and the podcast because—"

Lila held a finger up. "Let me ask you a question. When I didn't respond to your requests to do the podcast, and you were told that I had refused to participate in the oral history, did it ever occur to you that I didn't condone you peddling my life?"

Greer swallowed. Lila could see the gears in her head turning, trying to figure a way out of an impossible question. Either way, she was evil or a moron. "I—I didn't think you were outright rejecting anything. I assumed you were traveling, and they couldn't find you for comment."

Lila stalked closer to Greer until she was nearly backed up against the wall. "Then why, do you think, I would go to a place where I couldn't be found?"

"Coming from that perspective, I totally understand. But I promise you, it was never my intention to hurt you." Tears welled in Greer's eyes.

Lila took a step back, giving her space. "You're right. I'm sorry," she said softly. "I'm sorry. I'm just wary of my story in other people's hands."

"No, I totally get it." Greer looked relieved. "But you can trust it in mine."

"It's kind of funny, when you think about it—it's my life, but in the end, it boils down to another story on a podcast." Lila chuckled lightly.

A second later, the doorbell rang again.

"Don't tell me it's Detective Fox," Greer joked as she walked down the hall to the door. She did not notice Lila pick up a hardcover Hogwarts cookbook from the kitchen counter behind her. Greer grabbed the doorknob, but before she could turn the handle, Lila slammed the book on the back of her head with all the strength Greer had told her she had. Greer collapsed to the ground, out cold. Lila stepped over her and ushered Sylvie inside before anyone saw her.

Sylvie glanced down at Greer and shook her head, clucking her tongue. "Not everyone can pull off bangs."

"Grab her arms; I'll get her legs," Lila said.

From the old floor plan of the house they'd found on Zillow, Lila knew her first-floor guest bath was just on their left. They carried Greer inside and laid her in the bathtub. Greer started to stir as Sylvie ran the faucet. Lila hit her again with the book, and her head slackened against the tile wall.

They waited in silence as the tub filled with water. As soon as it was up to Greer's neck, Lila put her hands on her shoulders and Sylvie held her legs down, and they pushed her under the water.

Within a few seconds of being submerged, Greer woke up. There was a brief moment of stillness; her eyes opened and she failed to process why the world was so blurry. And then she realized she couldn't breathe. Lila and Sylvie held on as Greer thrashed in the water, crying out for air. She dug her nails into Lila's arms, bit down on her wrists. Lila shrieked and nearly let go.

"Hang on!" Sylvie yelled as Greer's hand burst out of the water, clawing for air.

Lila threw her entire body weight onto Greer's chest until she let out a final, hopeless bubble of air. Her arms slackened and she went still.

They waited a few moments just to be sure, and then Sylvie turned the faucet off. Greer's eyes were closed under the water, brown hair swirled around her, black eyelashes curled at the ends, lips slightly parted. She looked like a millennial Ophelia, and Lila now understood that people were either born beautiful or died beautiful.

It was a generous way to kill her. Greer's hypoxia in her final moments would have meant she left the earth on a wave of pleasant hallucinations. Lila hoped she met her Patreon subscriber goal in heaven.

Lila and Sylvie turned to each other, sopping wet. "The car's out in front. We gotta hurry," Sylvie said.

Lila left Greer in the tub as it drained and followed Sylvie out the front door to the SUV. The street was empty, a few scattered cars going through an intersection in the distance. Sylvie opened the trunk, and together they lifted out a massive antique chest. Sylvie had found it at some junk shop near Greenpoint. To Sylvie's credit, her initial hesitation was long gone, and she had fully risen to the challenge.

They carried the chest into the house and left it by the door, returning to Greer. Her drenched clothes made her twice as heavy as they struggled to move her. "Fuck it," Sylvie said, and slung Greer over her shoulder. Lila opened the chest wide, and Sylvie dumped Greer inside.

They locked it, added a padlock and a third digital lock, then wrapped it in bubble wrap and duct tape, obscuring the chest altogether. Lila went around the kitchen and wiped down all the surfaces she had touched.

An orange tabby sat in the corner on the windowsill. She hadn't seen him before. His big green eyes blinked at her, watching. For a small, odd moment, Lila felt the need to apologize. She hurried on.

By the time Lila and Sylvie left the house and put the chest in the SUV's trunk, it was dark. Sylvie drove the SUV onto the highway back toward the Manhattan skyline. "Holy fucking bananas," Sylvie said. "We fucking did it!"

Lila opened her arms to the warm, gentle hug of success. She was finally out of the downward spiral. The world was rewarding her for her patience, and fate was encouraging her to thrive. She screamed and then Sylvie screamed, and Lila pressed a long, wet kiss to her cheek. Without warning, Sylvie pulled off at the next exit and parked. She unbuckled her seat belt, climbing on top of Lila. "Sylvie, here?" Lila was laughing.

Sylvie didn't respond, she didn't need to. They didn't talk for a long time after.

SEVENTEEN

When Maya looked back at her life, there was a distinct before and after glob. Five months ago, she'd been a broke intern desperate for any work she could scrounge up. Now, she was in the passenger seat on one woman's single-minded journey to build an empire with her bare hands.

And she was succeeding. Lila had started in a tiny office in Mid City, and today glob had its own industrial chic office. Maya had immediately liked Lila, but how many famous white women decide to start their own beauty company because they think they're special?

But Lila *was* special. She actually cared. Not just about the product but about the people beneath her. Maya had worked with plenty of bosses whose promises of equity and fairness for the assistants beneath them were lip service. Lila asked for Maya's opinion and cared. She let Maya accompany her into the little testing lab off her office that she used to tinker with new ideas. That's what Maya liked about her most: she still wanted to be involved, even when she could just let other people handle it.

That wasn't to say Lila was a perfect boss. She was always kind to Maya, but Maya saw the difference between her and the other executive assistants. The coolness, the remove. Was it a requirement for visionaries to be so mercurial? How could someone so welcoming and open toward her be so shut off to the world?

Maya supposed it was trauma. Lila had been through literal hell.

She had decided she could trust Maya, but others were unproven. She had been through so much; she probably wasn't particularly eager to let a bunch of strangers into her life.

Maya felt special, chosen. She often felt like an alien, like she didn't belong. Her anxiety was so bad, Maya had the tendency to replay every social interaction in her head on a loop and chastise herself when they went wrong. She wasn't a statuesque white woman like many brands clearly favored. She dealt with a galling amount of condescension and racism in even trying to get an internship.

Still, Lila saw her. It had been a bit alarming at first to have that kind of undivided respect from someone like her—what had Maya done to deserve it? But gradually Maya began to see Lila's ambition and Lila's loneliness and came to think of her as a kindred spirit.

Her parents thought she was a joke for pursuing this as a career, that no one was ever going to take her seriously, but Lila understood. Lila was going to change the industry for the better.

"Maya, you wanna help me with some new recipes?" Lila leaned against the doorframe of her office.

Maya sat in the assistant bullpen just outside. "Sure!"

This was the best part of her job. She'd studied biochemistry, and her hands itched to be back in a lab. It amazed and impressed her that someone of Lila's stature had taken the time to learn how to make cosmetics by hand.

Maya followed Lila into her office and through a locked side door on the left wall. They entered a small lab space with a stovetop and a fridge. Lila slipped on an apron and handed Maya one.

"Oh, just so you know, the investor call is at one now—"

Lila groaned. "Let me enjoy this."

Maya laughed, tying her apron. "Don't shoot the messenger."

"Do you think we can find someone else to do it?" Lila asked.

"Sure. I'll try." But Maya knew she wouldn't. Lila often pretended that she didn't like the total power that came with the job, that it was unimportant and a necessary evil, but Maya knew she was no egalitarian. If there was someone who could go on that call in her stead, Maya doubted she'd even want them to. Lila wanted to know everything at all times.

"Can you heat the oil for me?" Lila handed Maya a pan. Maya poured the oil in and lit the stovetop.

Lila poured aloe vera, vitamin E, and hyaluronic acid into a bowl and began to mix. She was careful, precise. There was something graceful in the way her hands took fluid, lithe swirls. Maya wondered how many times she'd done this same thing with the wrong recipe or the wrong ingredients. How many times she'd nearly given up and failed. Hundreds, if not thousands.

Maya watched as Lila removed a small package of collagen powder from the cupboard and poured the fine white powder into the mix. *The highest possible quality,* Lila liked to tout. On some level, Maya recognized that this was a little bullshit, that even the best skin cream couldn't change your skin's genetic predisposition. But what was wrong in trying? It was true that whatever was in this stuff worked better to hydrate and brighten than any skin cream she'd ever tried.

"Your parents must be proud."

"What?" Maya snapped back to attention.

"They must be proud of you. They must have seen glob on the news. You got in at the ground floor of this and you were behind the TikTok that blew us up. You've more than proven yourself."

They weren't proud. They wouldn't be proud even if this made her millions of dollars. They thought it was vain and shallow. She loved her mom and dad more than anything, but they could be so bullheaded. Maya had learned not to bring it up to them anymore, even to share good news.

"Yeah, they came around. They're really excited," Maya lied. There was no point in bothering Lila with this.

But Lila's hands stopped mixing, and she turned to look Maya in the eye. Fuck. *She knew.*

Maya blushed and looked down at the stove. "I mean, it's a work in progress."

"You can talk about this stuff with me, you know. I've—I've had my fair share of parent issues," Lila said, pouring the melted oil into the mixture.

"They must be proud of you, of this," Maya said.

"They're dead now," Lila said.

"Oh, I'm so sorry," Maya said.

Lila shrugged. "On my journey in India, I realized the importance of the family you build on your own. You find it with a few special people, and you don't let them go."

"Are you proud?" Maya asked. "Of glob? Is this everything you imagined it would be?"

Lila smiled softly, her eyes flickering to something distant inside of her. "I can't say it is. But it's turned into something *better.*"

The mix in the bowl was growing into a heavy cream. Lila poured it into a glass container and put it in the fridge to cool. "Can I give you some advice?" she said.

Maya nodded.

Lila leaned against the fridge. "By virtue of being a young woman, a lot of people aren't going to take you seriously, whether it's personally or professionally. And what I wish someone had told me—what would have changed everything if I'd heard—is *fuck them.* You're smart. Trust your gut. It's lonely, believing in something that no one else seems to understand. But I understand. And if there's two of us, you're not delusional."

"Sometimes I feel like they're ashamed of me because I'm ambitious," Maya said.

"That perseverance and drive make you *you.* Don't let anyone stamp that out," Lila said.

"There you guys are, I couldn't find you anywhere," said a voice behind them. Maya turned to see Sylvie strolling in, her bangs so long they brushed her eyelashes.

It was frankly astonishing to Maya that Lila kept her around. It had to be because they'd come up together, because otherwise Maya found their relationship baffling. Sylvie was obnoxious and bullish, willfully unaware of other people's thoughts and feelings. She seemed to encourage the cold and distant parts of Lila. But she was loyal, that was clear. Maybe loyal to a disturbing extent. Did Lila just want a sycophant as her partner?

"What are we cooking up in here?" Sylvie stuck her finger in the mixing bowl and tapped a bit of the remaining cream on her cheek.

"Careful, Sylvie, that's hot—"

"Fuck!" Sylvie said, wiping it off.

Lila wet a paper towel and handed it to her. "It's okay, you're fine."

"Can you hold it for me? I feel faint."

Maya watched in bemusement as Lila touched the paper towel to Sylvie's cheek. Even in the office, Sylvie brazenly flirted with Lila, but then again, she flirted with *everyone* with a modicum of wealth and power. If you put a top hat and a monocle on a rock, Sylvie would walk up to it and ask for its name and phone number.

"Maya, did you reorganize the FileMaker Pro?" Sylvie asked.

Sylvie had her own assistant. Her name was Kaitlyn, and she was good at her job and fully capable of doing what Sylvie told her to do. Yet, Sylvie went out of her way to ask Maya for help. It felt targeted, like she was punishing Maya with menial labor, but Maya had no idea what she had done.

"Yep, it's updated in the Dropbox," Maya said.

"Slay queen," Sylvie said, looking between Maya and Lila. "Well, Lila, I know you're very busy, so let's get out of your hair. Can you help Kaitlyn with the opening party invites next? There's an Excel."

"That's all right, Maya's helping me in here," Lila said.

For a split second, Maya could have sworn Sylvie's eye twitched. "For sure, for sure, for sure, right on. Do you need another hand? I'm happy to help. I can bring my portable speaker in if you want some tunes—"

"We're good." Lila nodded. "Thanks."

Sylvie smiled tightly. "Okay! Sounds good! Don't forget, we have that call at one."

"Copy that," Lila said.

Sylvie waved and left. Lila turned back to Maya, a little embarrassed. "I'm sorry. She gets very . . . intense."

"No worries!" was all Maya said. She knew better than to engage on the topic of Sylvie. It was isolating being a woman at Lila's level. And for all of Sylvie's faults, she got shit done. She was like Lila's personal attack dog. It was probably comforting to have someone like that on her side.

Lila's phone buzzed and she glanced down at a text. "Fuck, I gotta take this. But remember what I said, okay? There are a lot of people who don't understand people like us, but you let it roll off your shoulders. That's their problem. Remember that, okay?"

Maya nodded. "Okay."

Eighteen

Over the summer, Lila had left her one-bedroom shoebox for a two-story modern farmhouse in Encino. She opted to rent it furnished—bland Restoration Hardware catalog. She liked the light greys, beiges, and creams. The house had five bedrooms and was built for a family; the people who owned it had moved to Texas for the mother's work. There was a basement with a playroom, a gym, and a wine cellar. It reminded her of an empty display case.

The only challenge had been to figure out what to do with the four kids' bedrooms. While the toys and the stuffed animals and the clear markers of childhood had been removed, it was easy to tell which ones they were. One was a soft purple with two floral-patterned twin beds, another a forest green with a rug with Dalmatians on it. She picked the least offensively painted one—the walls were a nice, *normal* eggshell—to redecorate as an office and a yellow light-filled one as a guest room.

She hated going inside those little rooms. It felt as though at any moment, tiny footsteps would come barreling up the stairs and an equally tiny voice would demand to know where all their stuff had gone. But she wouldn't be spending much time upstairs anyway. What had appealed to her most about the house was the wine cellar.

It was a huge, windowless space tucked in the corner of the basement. The former owners had taken the wine, leaving tall, empty racks. The insulation and cement made hearing anything from the first floor impossible. After she made a few adjustments to the decor—added an industrial-sized stove and a metal operating table—it was perfect. The garage had been a cute stepping stone, but now was time to move forward.

Except she couldn't progress because there was too much fucking heat on Greer. Her traceless disappearance had caught the media's attention, even without a suspect. Sylvie feared someone might put the pieces together with them in New York at the same time, so she'd insisted they lay low for a few months. They didn't want the police to come around again with questions. Lila found it all absurd. Greer's literal job was profiting off the stories of dead children, and she was hardly the only person with a grudge. She grew more frustrated every day the new workspace sat still and unused.

And then there was the loneliness. It struck her in odd moments, when she was lecturing at the office, when she attended industry cocktail parties. All those people would go home to families. Every night she returned to piercing silence. She remembered attending those stupid parties with Aidan, the thrill they got from making a sneaky early exit to get back to Josie. Because they were happiest as a unit. Any moment without the two of them, Lila felt incomplete.

Lila had been incomplete for a very long time.

That wasn't to say she was unhappy. Of course she was happy— glob was a smash hit. She liked watching people experience it for the first time, questioning, demanding to know, how the quality was possible.

The sheer stress was difficult to bear, but she had developed a diligent nighttime routine to manage. Before bed, she'd draw a bath and soak in jojoba and laurel leaf. She'd emerge naked and air-dry, letting the cold invigorate her. Then she'd dress in silk pajamas and sit at the vanity in her closet. Remove a small tube of her highly concentrated special formula marked *AA* and apply it to her tear troughs and forehead wrinkles. Then smear another tube marked *GH* across her lips.

Her skin had never been better; she looked a decade younger, at the very least. And without a drop of plastic surgery. She'd pushed that suggestion away with a principled hand. She didn't need it—she could reverse the clock herself.

LILA ARRIVED AT THE GLOB OFFICE EVERY DAY AT NINE A.M. SHE HAD actual employees, young and impossibly hot employees, doing the work she had toiled over for months by herself. Executives swirled around her—getting her feedback, giving her feedback—whose sole purpose was to bring glob to the globe.

The office's design was viciously modern. Lila liked the stark white, how sterile it felt. Clinical, serious. Like the color of her collagen powder after she'd bleached the dullness out. Just past the receptionist's desk was a bullpen of assistant working spaces. Lila knew none of their names and didn't bother to learn. In her defense, it wasn't like she'd bothered learning the executives' names either.

Maya's desk was a few feet away from the central group, in front of Lila's office. With glob's success, Maya finally began to flourish. She carried herself with a newfound confidence. Lila was proud to see her creep out of her shell a little more every day.

"The new ad campaign just came in," Maya said as Lila passed her desk, ushering her to watch her computer.

On screen, an edit of a commercial played: An anxious model flees an award show, and a magical stage door transports her to an open field of lilies. The sky is crisp and clear, and the grass is verdant and spotless. She twirls around and laughs in wonder. Then a title across the screen: *glob. Return to the spring of your life.*

"It looks great," Lila said.

Maya nodded. She looked out of place among her statuesque coworkers. Her dark hair was piled high up on her head in a butterfly clip. She wore an oversized grey sweater and dark jeans. Glob didn't have a uniform, but Maya dressed to fade into the background.

Lila appreciated her style, she did. Maya was a beautiful girl, she looked nice in anything, but she was still dressing like glob was a fledgling start-up. It was difficult not to feel a shock of disrespect. Glob wasn't an average office job—it was a lifestyle. Wasn't Maya taking this opportunity seriously? Did she need money for better clothes? Lila made a mental note to find some excuse for a bonus and write her a check.

Lila held her to that standard only because of her potential. This was just a minor quibble. This was why she needed her outlet back; since Greer died, she'd wound herself up too tight. She was ready to come undone.

Maya's eyes widened, and for a split second Lila feared she'd said something aloud. But she wasn't looking at Lila, she was looking just over her shoulder. Lila glanced around and saw Peter bounding toward them, holding a sweatshirt. Maya looked mortified.

"Hey! Here's your sweatshirt," Peter said. Maya took it, barely making eye contact. Peter glanced at Lila and smiled. "Hey, Lila! Long time!"

They're still together?

Lila was shocked. It had to be a casual hookup. Five months was too substantial an amount of time given how bizarre their pairing was. He was too soft, too content with the world, for someone like her. Lila didn't know what common ground they even found.

"It's nice to see you, Peter. How's modeling going?" Lila asked.

"Good! I booked a national campaign," Peter said with the nonchalance of someone describing what he'd had for lunch. "And I got hired to do magic at my first kid's birthday tonight!"

It was clear which he was more excited about. "Congratulations," Lila said.

Maya was beet red, and Peter was looking at her like she was the sun.

"I, um, don't want to hold you guys up. I was just dropping this off." Peter turned to go, waving goodbye. "Love you!"

Maya glanced at Lila, then gave Peter an awkward thumbs-up in reply.

Love you? Lila watched Maya smile to herself. As embarrassed as she was, she couldn't really be all that annoyed with him. She clearly loved him too. Sure, he was handsome—but that wouldn't last long—and charming, in a third grader sort of way. She'd known plenty of boys like him—sweet until they had to step up, and they always failed in the end. Just like Aidan did when he left. Maya deserved better than someone like that.

Lila walked into Sylvie's office without knocking, nodding at her assistant (Gretchen? Matilda?) as she shut the door. Sylvie arrived at the office every morning at six a.m. and stayed until the cleaning crew vacuumed at night. Lila found her pacing at her treadmill desk on a Bluetooth headset.

Sylvie was born to be bourgeois. The flush of cash finally allowed her to achieve her dream of dressing as a jewel-toned Cruella de Vil. She'd zipped right up the property ladder, ditching the West Adams cottage for a gaudy Bel Air mansion. Today, she kept her attire casual: a baby-blue velour sweatsuit with silver trim. Even while exercising, her eyes were coated in black eyeliner—her war paint.

"Yeah, we open in two weeks!" She held up a finger at Lila and pointed to the phone. "As many plus-ones as you want. No, we don't allow emotional support animals inside. Sorry to hear about your PTSD." Sylvie mimed putting a rifle in her mouth and blowing her brains out before returning to the caller. "Okay, thanks so much. Bye!"

When she hung up, Sylvie pretended to collapse in exhaustion but forgot she was on a moving treadmill, so slammed back against the wall. As she collected herself and turned off the machine, she continued. "Did you see the commercial? It looks incredible—"

"I want to take another name off the list. It's been nearly three months. We need more collagen."

"I thought this was a social visit," Sylvie said with a sigh.

"I've been patient enough. I want to kill Cara."

Lila first started working with Cara Donaldson during the terrible dystopian teen movie. It had been her first studio movie, and Cara smoothed out her rough edges for the press tour. Lila hadn't liked Cara per se—they had nothing in common and disagreed constantly—but she had respected her. She had trusted her. Cara hadn't bullshit her the way everyone else had. They worked well together for six years and became friends. She said it was her job to stand with Lila no matter what.

But reading through the oral history, it was clear that applied only to paying clients. The chance to be a part of Hollywood history had come knocking, and Cara had lifted her skirt and wiggled her bare ass. It was sickening to see just how little she cared. Lila had let Cara into her home during the worst moment of her life, and Cara had used it for a game of telephone.

Cara had realized she'd fucked up since she rejected Lila's pitch for glob—she'd sent multiple texts inquiring about their PR strategy and was waiting on Maya to get Lila's avails for dinner. And that was satisfying revenge for a little while, but it was weak. A little nip. Lila wanted to clamp down on her flesh and rip it off.

Sylvie groaned. "Not the goddamn list again. Lila, we have an actual, reputable *business* now! I have . . . *connections* to source more collagen; there's a black market for cadavers. We don't have to keep going back to that, erm, well." Then, a little quieter: "Aren't you happy?"

She wasn't. The grey thing was as mouthy as ever, gnawing at her insides. She couldn't let up, waste time enjoying her success, when Josie was sitting on her shoulder watching. She had the keen sense something was missing, that there was a hole somewhere inside of her, but she had no idea how to find it.

"Lila?" Sylvie looked at her, wounded.

Lila didn't know how to make it clearer that before Sylvie as her business partner, before Sylvie as her lover, Josie would always take precedence. The list was the only thing that mattered.

"Next week," Lila said.

"We're getting ready for the store's opening," Sylvie said.

"The week after."

"It *is* the store's opening."

That was the problem with success—they no longer had time for anything else. Sylvie loved the busywork; she loved yelling at people on the phone and signing her name on things. She loved being flamboyantly wealthy and would do anything to get wealthier. And while the business had occupied Lila for a time, the longer she went without the list, the more tedious it all became. Everything she did, every choice she made, was just in service of passing time until she could return to those names. Glob meant nothing without her purpose.

"C'mere." Sylvie grabbed Lila by the waist and pulled her over. Lila swatted her away, looking back through the glass doors. "No one can see, relax."

"I'm not in the mood," Lila snapped.

"Hey, hey," Sylvie said. "I haven't forgotten about the list. We just need to put it on the back burner for a little while until things have calmed down. We don't want to get caught now and jeopardize the rest, hmm?"

She didn't need Sylvie. It would be difficult, but she could do it without an assistant. The only problem was she didn't have Sylvie's mind. Sylvie was almost preternaturally observant. She picked up on things Lila would have missed entirely. One slip-up without Sylvie to catch her, and she'd be fucked. And there was a part of Lila—a tiny, shameful part—that had grown attached to her. She was like a bedazzled security blanket. Not comfortable, extremely flashy, but steady, reliable, protective. And she had grown to care about her. It was impossible not to feel for Sylvie. The bitch had made herself indispensable.

Lila let Sylvie take her into a hug, tracing circles on her back. "I don't want you ever to think I don't care, because I do. More than you'll ever know." Sylvie pulled back to look Lila in the eye, clasping her hands in hers. "I love you, Lila."

Lila would have preferred she kept this to herself. She racked her brain to think of something to say. Something that would make Sylvie drop it but was still nice enough for them to continue having sex.

But before she could speak, Sylvie shook her head. "You don't have to say anything. I know you're not ready. I just want you to keep that in your back pocket."

Lila tried to smile, but it felt more like a grimace.

"Do you know what I love about you most?" Sylvie asked. "There's a part of you that's mean."

Lila's mouth fell open to protest, but Sylvie cut her off. "You dress it up, you perform little tricks to hide it, but I see it. I always have. Please don't be ashamed. It's there because you think you're superior to everyone else, *and you are.*"

By the grace of God, Lila's phone rang, and she excused herself to answer it.

"Hello?" Lila said, stepping out into the hall.

"Hi," Aidan said on the other end. "I saw you on *Kimmel*." They'd been in touch sporadically since she'd visited his house eight months ago, but nothing beyond a few polite texts. Her heart leapt when she heard his voice.

"How'd I do?"

"Solid A-minus, there's always room for improvement," Aidan teased. "So, listen, Sonnet insisted on throwing me a birthday party this year. It'll be at our place the week after next, the ninth."

"I know when your birthday is." Lila felt herself smiling.

Aidan laughed too. "I'd—we'd love for you to come."

When Lila was with Aidan, he'd hated his birthday so much he would only allow them a small dinner date. "I'll be there," Lila said. "That's very sweet to think of me."

"Lila, just because we're not—doesn't mean I . . ." Aidan sighed. "I still want you to be in my life. It's not me being sweet. I'm inviting you because you will always be my family."

The universe had dropped a gift into her lap. Lila couldn't heal the past until she mended the relationship that had been severed at the very center of everything. Now that glob was a success, they were back on even terms. They'd be able to connect as people again. This was their chance to start over.

Aidan was hers; he always had been. She had tried to deny it, pushed him away, fallen for Sylvie, but she would always be bound to Aidan. He was her family. The only family she had left. He could remarry, have another kid, play make-believe in another life, but deep down, they both knew that she was his and he was hers and Josie was theirs. Nothing could ever change that. There was a piece of her missing that he had taken with him, and now she had a chance to get it back. She could feel Josie's spirit smiling down on her. She was going to get her life back.

"I'll be there," she repeated.

"Bring whoever," Aidan said. "Can't wait to see you!"

"You too," Lila said, her voice soft.

It was what Josie would have wanted.

NINETEEN

The empty storefront in the Brentwood Country Mart stood barren and cold among the upscale shops and restaurants, its winged-ankle logo poorly scrubbed off, the faux gold fading. Then, one day, a woman with raven-black hair made her way through the barnlike labyrinth and pressed her face to the glass, eyes wide. The next, contractors were coming in for a fresh paint job.

From the dejected remains of a luxury sandal store rose a behemoth. The headquarters for a newly crowned titan of the beauty industry. The space was large and airy, the windows casting light that seemed to come from the grace of God himself.

Sylvie insisted that they had been so focused on glob appealing to all kinds of women that they had left out an entire subsection: rich ones. Wasn't Lila contradicting herself by ignoring them? It was a demographic that deserved to heal just as much as anybody else. To get Sylvie off her back, Lila decided to throw her a bone. So, Sylvie pursued that bougie Westside storefront she had bookmarked all those months ago to give their skincare products a real home.

Photos of beautiful people with sultry nymph eyes and rose petal lips covered in glob lined the walls. Lila questioned whether you were meant to fuck them or become them. Sylvie had been insistent when hiring models. "I want to make something very clear: We do not discriminate. We want all shapes, sizes, colors, genders, abilities, disabilities, whatever—as long as they're hot."

Lila stared at herself in the bathroom mirror and reapplied her red lipstick. Her skin was the palest shade of white. Makeup artists used to always put her in an orangey-red lip because of her hair. She preferred a red so blue it looked frigid.

"I find peace in my life; in my life I make peace," Lila said. It had taken years, but she was finally starting to believe it.

Long ago, her mother had instilled in her the belief that a place was only as good as its bathroom. Glob's bathroom was lavender scented and pale pink, with an antique dressing room light bulb mirror. The sounds of the store outside were muffled by relaxing instrumental music.

"*Lila! Come out here!*" Sylvie yelled over the music. "*I wanna show you something!*"

Since her love confession, Sylvie's neediness had grown suffocating. Her new income afforded her to spend money with the flippancy of a nineteenth-century robber baron. She showered Lila with flowers and gifts, desperate to buy the one thing Lila couldn't provide.

In honor of the grand opening of their store, Sylvie wore a glittering black beret with a purple sequined sweetheart dress, which cost $5,000.

Lila found Sylvie right outside the door. Sylvie's voice softened. "Sorry, I didn't mean to rush you if you were pooping."

"I wasn't," said Lila.

"Can I show you something?"

"We need to make sure everything's ready for the party—"

"It'll be two seconds," Sylvie said.

Lila sighed. "Okay."

Sylvie put her palms over Lila's eyes. "Keep them closed, okay? Don't open them until I say."

"Okay," said Lila.

Sylvie moved back slowly, making sure Lila didn't peek. Then she scurried away. Lila could hear her heels scratching the sidewalk. A few moments later, she heard, "*Okay, open!*"

Lila opened her eyes and saw Sylvie seated in a bright red Tesla convertible. She honked the horn a playful but annoying number of times. Pedestrians covered their ears.

"Wow," said Lila.

"Do you like it? I can't be a CEO and drive a basic car," Sylvie said. "Also, for the record, they don't explode that much. And when they do—that's just part of the process."

"Congratulations," Lila said.

Sylvie fluffed her hair in the rearview mirror, then looked at Lila. "There's just something about women who drive red cars, right?"

"Sure," Lila said, checking her phone. The more Sylvie pushed, the more Lila withdrew.

Sylvie pressed her breasts against the steering wheel, trying to get Lila's attention back. "Wanna come over tomorrow night?"

"I can't. I have to go to Aidan's birthday party," Lila said.

Sylvie lit up and scurried out of the convertible to Lila's side. "I'd love to come! I love birthday parties! Is there a theme?"

"The forties. 'Cause he's turning forty."

"I love that," Sylvie said. "Oh my god, I hardly have any time to plan. Don't worry, I'll figure out something fabulous."

"Sylvie . . ." Lila racked her brain for an excuse. "I don't know if I can bring a guest." *Weak. Wouldn't deter her in a thousand years.*

"His house is, like, huge. He can fit me. And it's not like you're already bringing another date, right?"

Their relationship was weird and impossible to define, but Sylvie would become unbearable if she thought Lila was seeing other people. Lila figured the best point of action was to let her come and keep her distance. "No, of course, please come. You can drive us there in your new car."

They walked back inside the glob store, and Lila beckoned Maya from where she was talking with a salesgirl. Lila was overjoyed they could celebrate their success together. She clasped Maya's and Sylvie's hands. "I just want to say how grateful I am for the two of you and how proud I am that we've built this together. I couldn't have done this without you," she said.

"Let's fucking *dominate!*" Sylvie slapped them both on the backs.

"Uh, I'm here for *gloob*?" The DJ stood in the doorway with his gear. Sylvie went off to help him set up his station.

Maya turned to Lila. "I'm so happy for you. You deserve everything that's coming."

Lila pulled her into a hug. "None of this would have happened without you."

When they broke apart, Maya applied a glob collagen lip balm from her pocket. "You—you're using glob products?" Lila asked.

Maya's brow furrowed. "Of course. Seems wrong to not use the stuff we're making."

Lila tried to mask her concern. Maya couldn't put that on her *face*. These products weren't for *her*. Lila racked her brain for a reason to tell her to stop, but allowing Maya into the lab had made her just as big an expert on the product as Lila was.

All Lila could muster was a weak "Well, I'm honored." She would buy Maya a basket of the most expensive, high-quality skincare products. Anything to get her to stop. She wasn't like the rest of them. She was pure.

"Maya," Lila said suddenly, "I want to take you under my wing."

Maya was the future. It was time to show her how much she was valued. Maya didn't understand that she and Lila were a cut above everyone else, didn't realize how special she was. Lila would have to teach her.

Maya beamed. "Really?

"Glob is finally expanding, and I want you to shadow me. I want to teach you everything I know so you can build your generation's glob," Lila said.

Maya shook her head, speechless. "I'm . . . so touched, Lila. I don't know what to say."

Lila gave her another hug. "We're gonna change the world, kiddo."

AN HOUR LATER, THE OPENING PARTY WAS IN FULL SWING. A SLEW OF celebrities and their handlers flocked through the store. The DJ played chill synths as guests browsed the cosmetics and chatted. A photographer took pictures in the corner. Sylvie buzzed around the floor, shaking hands and offering compliments that were too nice. Lila dutifully thanked the guests for coming, though they should have thanked her for being invited.

Though it was marvelous to see glob open its doors as a physical space, and so inspiring to create a space for people of all different races and genders and ethnicities and body types and *blah blah blah*, it was hard to sit there and smile at people buying skin cream when Lila could be doing far more vital things with her time. She missed her list, she missed it more than anything.

Once Aidan's party was done, she could return to it. She just needed to keep it together for a few more days. There was a tentative tap on her shoulder, and Lila nearly leapt out of her skin. She turned to see one of the shopgirls Sylvie had hired smiling bashfully.

"I'm sorry to bother you, Ms. Devlin. I just wanted to say how honored I am to work here. Glob is the only thing that doesn't make my face break out," she gushed. She was blond and thin, beautiful in any other part of the country. For LA, she looked rather plain.

What this girl didn't realize was that she wasn't really a fan of Lila—she was hopping on a bandwagon because the world told her it was right to like Lila now. Ten years ago, if this girl recognized her in public, she would have spat in her face.

"Thank you," Lila said. The girl smiled at her awkwardly and then hurried off. Lila made a mental note for Sylvie to replace her with someone less mousy.

"Hi, Lila!" Peter's towhead materialized out of a group of chatting women. Of course he had weaseled his way here. "Congratulations, the store looks great!"

"Hi there," Lila said. It irritated her, how good-natured he was. Like he had challenged himself to play a character to his absolute limit and never broke. "Nice of you to come."

"I saw you on *Jimmy Fallon* playing Simon Says! That was so sick!" Peter said.

Lila exhaled through her nostrils. "Thank you."

"I told some of my model friends I knew you; they all really wanted your new campaign," Peter said.

"Not you?" Lila asked.

"Nah. I mean, I'd be honored to shoot for you, but I think I'm retired," Peter said, brushing back his floppy blond hair.

He had gone from actor to model to magician in the span of nine months. "Already?" Lila asked.

Peter shrugged. "I'm twenty-three, I got time to figure stuff out as long as I can pay my rent. I've been making solid money doing magic stuff. I think I'm going to start my own party company. 'Cause I love entertaining people, and weirdly, when you're in entertainment you kind of forget that's what you're supposed to be doing in the first place."

"Hmm," Lila said. She wondered what was underneath the hair and the smile at his core. She wondered if he was really broken down, what he could become.

Peter's smile wavered. He could tell something was wrong but didn't know what it was. "Listen, hearing you tell your story, about everything you went through—I had no idea. I couldn't believe—you're just a person. I want to, like, scream at everyone that you're just a person."

Lila was flushed with a wave of discomfort so overpowering she thought it was premature menopause. Her throat went dry, and she found herself at a genuine loss for words.

Peter seemed to understand. He changed the subject. "Maya speaks so highly of you. I said to her the other day, you kind of made girlboss culture cool again. Bringing back eighties power-suit-core. I met Maya's family on FaceTime last week and told them how much of a badass you are."

He'd met her *family*? When had they gotten so serious? And his audacity to talk about her with them! He was a children's birthday party magician. He had no idea who she was or what she did.

Before she could reply, Sylvie clapped her hands together from the corner of the room. "Lila, come here!"

"Excuse me," Lila said, and hurried over.

"Attention, attention, everybody!" Sylvie yelled. It took a moment for the room to get the message to quiet down, but Sylvie wouldn't continue until there was silence. "I'll wait," she said. And kept repeating "I'll wait" until she had quiet. When she had everyone's attention, she smiled big. "I just wanted to thank everybody for coming out today. Glob has been the greatest passion project for Lila and me—it's changed my life, and I hope it changes yours too. We appreciate your support!"

Peter led the applause. Lila hated how plainly he wore his goodness. He didn't brag about it or flex with it. He kept his heart open and without shame. She was so distracted by her irritation that it took her an extra second to realize the room was waiting for her to speak.

"It's wonderful to see you all here." Lila smiled. "I was inspired to start glob because I wanted to use my trauma as a force for change. The thing about pain is you can either sit in it and let it paralyze you, or you can channel it into good. So when you use our eye cream, I hope you find that strength in you. You might not even realize it's there! Thank you so much for all your support. We're so thrilled to share this with you."

Suddenly, there were hands everywhere, extending to shake, flagging her down, offering her drinks—realizing how much money she had made and was going to make and trying to pitch themselves before their last opportunity was squandered. Trying to get as close as possible for her beauty, her money, her success, to rub off on them.

What they were too stupid to realize was that they all had the capacity for success. Lila wasn't particularly lucky or intelligent; she just understood that when an opportunity presented itself, she had to take it without question.

Peter found Maya sitting on a bench outside the Country Mart beside the overpriced ice cream shop. She'd made a break for it as soon as Lila got mobbed by well-wishers after her speech. The party was too crowded, too loud; she couldn't hear herself think.

"What are you thinking about?" Peter asked, taking a seat beside her.

Maya shook her head. This was supposed to be everything she had ever wanted, and now, when everything was finally coming to fruition, she felt paralyzed.

"I have to watch Lila's interviews and stuff to check social media reactions for the company," Maya said. "And listening to her talk about glob and her mission made me realize how *corny* this all is."

Peter laughed. "Everybody sounds corny when they talk about stuff they care about. Lila seems to really want to help people."

Maya shook her head. "Look at the people who were invited to this party. No one here has a yearly income under three hundred thousand except for us. How is that accessible?

"I mean, I'm sure she cares. Of course she does," she continued, wincing. "And I know she doesn't come from money, but . . . I feel like once you're famous, it changes you. You can't go back. Lila talks about these big ideas to help people, and I used to find them so inspiring, but now I just keep thinking . . . fancy skin cream isn't going to save anyone's life. And then I start asking myself *what the fuck have I been doing* the last eight months, what was I expecting to happen? Did I get caught up in the glamour of it all? Was I so desperate for a job that I ignored it?"

And she'd had a lot to ignore. Every time Lila waxed poetic about her magical trip to Southeast Asia, Maya locked into a full-body cringe. She couldn't say anything, of course; Lila was her fucking boss. Well meaning and nice enough, but completely tone-deaf. She wasn't naive enough to think Lila might appreciate a heads-up when she misspoke.

And then Maya felt guilty, because Lila's infant child had literally been murdered and dumped in a lake, and she couldn't even fathom what that did to a person, and maybe living in India and immersing herself in a culture that wasn't Lila's own had genuinely helped her. But it wasn't fair to excuse her behavior either—just because something shitty happened to her didn't give her a pass for her own shitty behavior. Maya had been spiraling for the last three months.

"Maya, hey, hey." Peter put his hand on her shoulder to stop her spiral. "Don't put that kind of pressure on yourself. You don't have to be a superhero."

"I don't want to be," Maya said. "But I don't want to spend my life just talking about helping people . . . I want to actually do it."

"Damn." Peter was quiet for a moment. "What are you gonna do?"

Maya shrugged. "I have a biochemistry degree, there are a lot of options. I just know from watching Lila—that's not me."

The Lila that Maya had met months ago, that Maya was inspired to work for, had dissipated into the same bland beauty guru she'd been trying to run away from. Ironically, Maya had idolized Lila's courage and her perseverance *until* glob became a hit. With the tiniest bit of success, all of Lila's grit and authenticity had melted into bland, palatable slush. Maya would never allow herself to become like that. It didn't matter how much money Lila's promotion offered for someone her age—she refused to sell her soul to accept it.

"I am with you through anything. You know that." Peter kissed her on the cheek. Maya rested her head on his shoulder. If nothing else came from her job at glob, at least she'd found Peter. When she first met him, she'd found him intimidatingly good-looking, nearly writing him off as just another handsome, vapid bro frolicking around this city. But every day in tiny, soft ways, he showed her how wrong she was. Peter didn't announce his goodwill to the world like Lila did; he didn't have to. He offered himself to people and didn't expect anything in return. He was impossible not to love.

Peter sat up, removing a tiny box from his pocket. "I got you a congrats-on-opening gift."

"Oh, Peter, you really didn't have to." She knew how little he made as a party entertainer. Peter just smiled and nudged her to open the box.

Maya pulled the top off and found it was empty. She looked at him in confusion. He cocked his head, brow furrowing. "Oh no, that's not . . . wait a second."

He brushed his hand against her cheek. Maya thought he was leaning in to kiss her, then realized he was reaching behind her ear. He pulled out a small turquoise ring.

"I wonder how that got there," Peter said, and grinned.

Maya rolled her eyes, laughing. "You're such a dork!"

"Considering my main clientele is children, it would be weirder if I was, like, suave," Peter said. He gently slid the ring on Maya's pointer finger. "Do you like it?"

Tears welled up in Maya's eyes. She didn't know why she was crying. "It's beautiful."

Peter burst into his big, goofy smile. That was her favorite part about him, his slightly crooked smile. The only flaw on his face. She never wanted him to get his teeth fixed. They were so human it took her breath away.

Maya knew in that moment everything was going to be okay. It didn't matter how weird Lila was or how stupid her job was, because she had Peter. A rush of excitement seized her as she wiped her tears away. "You mentioned wanting to live in New York in your twenties. Let's go."

Peter's eyes widened. "What?"

"You already travel there for modeling. Sublet your apartment and let's get an Airbnb. I could find a fellowship in the city, maybe apply to grad school," Maya continued. The more she thought about it, the more exciting it sounded. She'd be on the East Coast, closer to her family. She'd explore a new city; she'd get out of Los Angeles. She hated it here.

"You're going to quit?" Peter asked.

"Yeah," Maya said, shocked by her words. "My boss just offered to put me on the executive track, and I'm going to quit and move and leave all the connections I made in LA. Is that crazy? You don't have to come with me if you don't want to, I know it's sudden."

Peter pressed his forehead against hers and laced their fingers together. "Maya, I'd follow you anywhere."

TWENTY

Lila often dreamed of what Josie would have been like grown up. She'd had vague conceptions before, but the picture that had developed in Lila's mind in recent months was so clear and so perfect that the memory that this person would never see the world brought her to tears.

She had red hair—darker than Lila's and crossed with Aidan's brunette, a deep, rich auburn color. It hung just past her shoulders in waves. Her eyes were steel grey and wide-set, like Aidan's. She had Lila's snub nose—when people would pass them together, there was no doubt that Lila was her mother. When Josie was a baby, Lila had been embarrassed to see she had inherited her worst feature. But adult Josie loved their nose. She said it gave their faces character.

Josie never had any interest in Hollywood, never followed the nepotistic instinct that plagued most celebrity children. Aidan had secretly hoped that she would become an actor like him, but she wanted to be a scientist as soon as she learned to say the words.

She was a straight-A student, took all AP courses. In her junior and senior years of high school, she interned at a UCLA research lab. Somehow, on top of that, she found time to serve as student body president and volunteer at local homeless shelters. Because, even more important than her intelligence, Josie was kind. The most crucial thing Lila did as a parent was instill humility and gratitude, so she carried those values into adulthood.

Josie grew into a radiant, selfless young woman. Often, Lila even had to remind her to take care of herself; she was so intent on putting others first.

Josie attended Harvard University on a scholarship. She was the first kid in her tax bracket to be offered a full ride, they were so desperate to have her. Her college advisers remarked that she'd be a brilliant politician if she hadn't been so committed to environmental science. And not in the manipulative, cunning way—Josie was purely idealistic and forward-thinking in the way that resembled history's greatest leaders. She might even be the very first scientist turned president.

Everyone who met her fell in love with her, platonically or romantically; Josie was impossible to hate. There was never an ulterior motive, never a sideways glance. Lila had made many mistakes in her life, like her father before her and his father before him. But if there was one positive that Lila contributed to the world, one single thing that she could look to and be proud of, it was Josie.

The only thing—and it was tiny, it was so minuscule it shouldn't have even bothered her—was Lila couldn't hear Josie's voice. She tried to imagine what she would've sounded like, how she would've spoken, but Josie was always mute. When Lila met Josie in her dreams, she was met with a cavernous silence.

But Lila would never stop trying. Lila would listen for Josie until the day she died.

THERE WAS A CRACK IN AIDAN'S DRIVEWAY. A LONG, JAGGED CRACK THAT cut through the pristine pavement like the world was splitting in two. The property was old—the house built in the '20s by some big-shot director whose name no one knew anymore. Under the ebony sky, it was easy to be swept up in the glamour of what it might have been like. Aidan and Sonnet had made some renovations—the standing lanterns that lined the drive to the house had once been gas, the wrought-iron gate had been electrified and given a key code—but the bones of the house were still standing. Lila wondered what they had seen.

"This is such a nice house," Sylvie said, teetering in six-inch heels behind her.

For the 1940s theme, Lila tried to look immaculate. Her hair curled in red layers down the nape of her neck; her eyes pierced through smoky charcoal lines. She wore a green off-the-shoulder cocktail dress that clung to every curve and fold of her skin. She looked like she'd just stepped out of a golden age movie.

Sylvie, of course, saw the dress code as a goalpost to vault over. She wore a black tea-length strapless gown and a glamorous golden cape. Written in glitter on the back was *LORDY LORDY, LOOK WHO'S 40!*

Lila stopped a short distance from the front door. "I want to be clear—you are here with me as a friend, do you understand?"

Sylvie nodded enthusiastically. "Of course. We don't want to fuck glob's reputation right now." She lowered her voice. "But can I just tell you how hot you look?"

"I platonically thank you." Lila jumped away from Sylvie's wandering hands.

Lila was not trying to conceal their relationship to protect glob; she was trying to remind Sylvie that there was no romantic relationship between them in the first place. It was purely convenient sex. She should have ended it months ago, but Sylvie was a great lover. She knew the most intimate parts of Lila, both physically and emotionally—the idea of having to do it all over again with someone else was exhausting.

Fortunately, there was a happy medium between Sylvie and someone new: Aidan.

He still loved her. He could mask it with generosity and goodwill and "looking out for her," but she recognized the affection lurking. Of course, he loved Sonnet too, but in a different way. She was Lila's replacement and would never measure up. Lila just had to remind him.

The first to greet Lila at the door was the red blinking camera. An angry little cyclops perched in the corner above a decorative lantern, doomed to meet all guests but never come inside. Lila knocked. From the front steps, she could hear big band music in full swing and the rapturous partygoers inside. At the beginning of the year, she'd felt trapped at the bottom of the hill, desperately trying to attract the attention of the people on top. Now, she walked with the confidence she belonged.

A burly security guard greeted them with a clipboard. "Name?" he said, not looking up at her.

That didn't deserve a response. Lila waited until he met her eyes. They widened, a slight pink appearing on his cheeks. "Welcome, Ms. Devlin," he corrected, holding the door open for her.

"I'm her plus-one," Sylvie said, racing to catch up to Lila inside.

The night was glittery and purple. They walked through the house out into the backyard, which had been reconstructed as an authentic '40s dance hall. The grass was covered with a wood floor, where guests tangled together as a Benny Goodman–style orchestra played on a platformed stage. On the sides, unbothered men and women sipped vintage cocktails and nibbled on seafood hors d'oeuvres. The opulence was breathtaking.

A waiter in a World War II sailor outfit handed Lila and Sylvie glasses of champagne. Sylvie gulped hers down. "I haven't been to a party like this in *forever*," she said, then turned to the waiter. "Do you have anything more carbonated?"

Underneath an uprooted vintage streetlamp, Aidan stood happily chatting with guests. He looked so handsome in his white tux he was almost a caricature. His eyes shone in the twinkling lights. Every time he smiled, the world lit up around him. Lila could feel Josie nudging her toward him. When his gaze landed on Lila, he stilled. He raised a hand and gave a small wave, smiling as though there were a secret they shared.

The couples on the dance floor seemed to part as she glided to meet him. He grinned at her, capturing her hand and kissing it. "You look beautiful."

Yep, she was going to fuck him. It may not be tonight, but it would be soon.

"Happy birthday, love." Lila pulled him into a hug. "This is an incredible party. You're even wearing shoes."

Aidan burst out laughing, grinning down at her. "I'm glad you made it."

"I missed a decade's worth of birthdays. I have a lot of catching up to do."

His gaze softened. His eyes flicked to her lips. Lila was wearing Arthur Allen tonight, and she wanted Aidan to lick him off her. "Lila, I—"

"Happy birthday, Aidaaaan," Sylvie yelled over the music as she pushed through a dancing couple to reach them.

Lila grimaced as Sylvie put a hand on the small of her back. She arched away, but Aidan had already seen it. His brow furrowed. "Hi—Sylvie, right? Huge congratulations on glob."

"Thank you, doll! I couldn't ask for a better partner." Sylvie elbowed Lila.

Lila could sense Sylvie's eyes running between her and Aidan, trying to get to the bottom of the chemistry sizzling between them. She wasn't going to let Lila out of her fucking sight.

Lila finally cleared her throat. "How does it feel to be forty?"

"Same way I did at eighteen, my body's just way ahead of me," he replied, and chuckled.

"You're lucky you look so good for your age." Sylvie took a swig of champagne. "It'll catch up to you eventually."

Aidan just stared at her.

Before Lila could grab Sylvie by the cape and chuck her into the canyon beneath them, Sonnet appeared. "Oh my god, Lila! You look gorgeous!"

Now, the moment was ruined and it was Sylvie's fault. "Sonnet! So good to see you." Lila gave her a hug, if only to get her hands off Aidan.

It bothered Lila how relentlessly nice Sonnet was, like she had something to prove. Sonnet was fine with Aidan having a relationship with his ex-wife; she was fine with being his second choice.

Sonnet must have known on some level that he was slipping away right through her fingers. She must have known that the minute Lila returned to Los Angeles, their relationship was in jeopardy. There was a wolf at her door, and Sonnet had unlatched it with open arms.

"Thanks," Lila said, not paying her a compliment back. It would have been a lie, and Lila believed in honesty. Her black feathered dress and long legs made her look like an ostrich. She stared down at Lila with that dim, pleasant smile. Aidan would never have chosen to be with someone so dull in normal circumstances, the grey thing assured her. Sonnet was just a placeholder until she came back. Deep down, he wanted her home with him.

The band blasted a new song, and Sonnet gasped, tugging Aidan's hand like a bratty child. "Come dance with me!"

Aidan murmured something about talking later and then followed her off to the dance floor. Lila watched them disappear into the mass of partiers.

"May I have this dance?" Sylvie said, extending a hand.

Lila pretended not to hear her and took off in the opposite direction, creating as great a distance between herself and Sylvie as possible. She weaved through the crowd of famous faces, all stopping to greet her with big smiles, not daring to see if Sylvie had followed.

She stopped at the bar to order a tonic water. Alcohol dulled her senses too much. A balding blond man in a dark suit leaned against the counter beside her. "There's a line—" he said, then stopped when he recognized her. "Lila?"

It was Tim Weber. Of course he was still friends with Aidan.

"Tim!" Lila pulled him into a hug, smiling.

He hugged her back, a little tentative. Like he was afraid. "I didn't think you and Aidan were still in touch. You look amazing."

Lila squeezed his shoulder affectionately. "You do too. I assumed you would have lost your hair now."

She had been afraid to cross him when she and Aidan were married. Tim saw her as a scold and a nag. She had always wanted Aidan to think she was down to hang. Now he was tired and gaunt; the alcohol had aged him, and he was the one who should be afraid.

"So, what's this I hear about an oral history?" Lila asked him.

Tim was puffy and red in his white shirt, the vodka sweat clinging to his armpits. He scratched at his collar, avoiding eye contact. "Uh, yeah, they reached out, and I wasn't gonna do it, but I figured you guys needed someone who, like, knows you to set the record straight, right?"

"I appreciate that," Lila said, keeping her voice light. "What was it you called me? 'A strung-out Jekyll and Hyde'?"

She smiled at him like it was an inside joke between them. Tim swallowed and looked away, turning to the bartender. "Yo, can I get that vodka soda, please?"

Lila watched and waited. She liked the way his eyes surveyed the party, desperate to crawl out of this hole. But he was trapped. "Is that what you think of me?" Lila asked, her voice completely neutral.

Tim laughed, avoiding looking directly at her like she was the sun. "I didn't—that was taken out of context."

"What was the context?" Lila said, emotionless.

Tim tugged at the collar of his shirt. The sweat was starting to pool around his neck like a chunky wet choker. "Well, I mean . . ."

Lila slapped him on the shoulder. "I'm just fucking with you."

Tim forced himself to laugh along with her. "I love you guys. I'd never say anything to hurt you."

"I know that." Lila put a hand to her heart. "Of course you didn't do it to hurt me; you did it to stay relevant, because you're washed up."

He stared at her open-mouthed. The bartender handed Lila her tonic water. Tim was still empty-handed. "Cheers!" Lila raised it in the air and walked away.

Even outside, the air was hot and muggy with the push of bodies against one another. "Lila? Lila!" She could hear Sylvie's voice getting closer. Lila needed space; she walked into the house and shut the door.

The foyer was empty, the music muffled. Lila checked the corridor to ensure she was alone, then folded her dress beneath her and perched on the staircase. She took a long sip of tonic water, letting the bubbles burn her throat. As long as Sylvie attached herself to her, any chances at Aidan were dashed.

"Hello," came a little voice from behind her.

Lila spun around and saw Aidan's daughter Talia peering down from the top of the staircase. She wore dachshund pajamas—little wiener dogs like polka dots. She held the banister shyly.

"Hello," Lila said.

Talia's face was open and sweet in a way that reminded Lila of Aidan when he was young.

"Couldn't sleep?" Lila asked. It occurred to her that she had no idea how to talk to a child. She thought about how she would have wanted to be spoken to at that age. Gentle, but with respect.

Talia shook her head, clutching the banister tighter. "I had a bad dream."

"Those aren't fun."

"Do you know where my mom is?"

"Outside," Lila said. "Do you have someone watching you?"

"She went home after I went to bed," Talia said. She studied Lila closely, swinging down to peek through the gaps in the winding banister. "Are you my dad's . . ."

Lila bowed her head. "Yes."

". . . friend?" Talia asked.

Lila frowned. They had never told Talia the truth of who Lila was? That she had a goddamn sister? Aidan's life had been hidden away from her. What a snake Sonnet was. Sugary sweet to Lila's face and undermining her behind her back. Rage stirred inside Lila, and she took a step up the banister.

Talia saw her come forward and took a step back.

"It's okay," Lila said softly. "Your mom's busy drinking with her friends, but I'm here."

Talia glanced at Lila and then at the door to the back patio, hesitating.

"I like dachshunds too," Lila said, and Talia's hand relaxed on the banister. She had such small hands.

"They're my favorite," Talia said. "But we can't get one 'cause my mom doesn't like dogs."

Lila pouted. "That's no fair. You should have a dog; they're the best."

"Could you talk to her?" Talia asked eagerly.

Lila laughed a little. "I can try, but some rotten people just don't appreciate animals the way they should."

Talia looked one more time at the back door in a last fleeting hope that her parents would abandon the party to put her back to bed. No one came. Talia considered Lila for a moment, then asked, "Could you check my room for monsters?"

Lila hesitated, but there was no reason to hesitate. There was nothing wrong in putting a little girl to sleep. "Sure."

Lila took a tentative step up the winding staircase just to make sure Talia didn't change her mind. Then she took another one, and another, all the way up until she was at Talia's level. She was tiny, even for her age. Her grey eyes were wide and searching as Lila towered above her.

She followed Talia down the hallway. For a house as lavish as it was, the upstairs was decorated simply with family photos of Aidan, Sonnet, and Talia. In the snow outside his parents' house in Natick, swimming with dolphins in Mexico, wearing mouse ears at Disneyland. They looked so normal. Lila dug her nail under her thumb until it hurt.

Talia's room was the second door on the left. It was bigger than a kid's room had any right to be, bigger than her old Studio City apartment. The walls were a soft canary yellow with a canopy twin bed centered against the wall. A large bay window with a little bench looked out over the pergola in the backyard. Dog plushies of all shapes and sizes lined the walls. Talia climbed into bed, cuddling a stuffed dachshund close. Lila took exaggerated pains to check the closet, then under her bed, then the window, for any sign of boogeymen.

"You think the monster's out the window?" Talia asked nervously.

"You never know," Lila said.

Heavy footsteps came down the hall, and Aidan appeared in the doorway.

"Daddy!" Talia leapt out of bed to hug him.

He held her tightly and looked at Lila in confusion. "What are you doing up here?"

Lila smiled. "I stepped away from the party, and Talia asked me to check for monsters."

Aidan's expression softened. "Monsters, huh?"

"I had a bad dream, and Katie left," Talia said.

"Could you give us a second? I'll be right out," Aidan told Lila.

"Of course," she said. "Good night, Talia."

"Good night, Lila!" Talia chirped.

Lila stepped back into the hall, listening to Aidan soothe her. He was a good father, even in the middle of his own birthday party. More hands-on than he'd ever been with Josie. He'd been working far too much back then. But they both knew better now; things could be different.

A few minutes later, he emerged with a guilty smile. "I'm sorry about that. I hope she didn't bother you too much."

Lila waved him off. "She's a gem. I'm sorry if I overstepped. She just asked me, and I—"

Aidan put a gentle hand on her shoulder. "You're fine."

Sparks danced from Aidan's hand to her bare skin. They both stared down, Aidan quickly letting his hand fall as if he'd been burned. "We should get back to the party."

She followed him to the top of the staircase and reached for his arm before he could descend. She liked this little back-and-forth game. Couldn't touch too much, couldn't do it at the same time. They took turns extending little intimacies.

"How have you been, Aidan?" Lila asked softly.

He forced a laugh. "The party's great. I'm having a great time."

"That's not what I meant."

His expression fell, and he scratched the back of his neck. "I'm fine."

Lila sat down at the top of the stairs and made room for him. Aidan hesitated for a moment, then sank down beside her. She closed her eyes, luxuriating in the brief second she could pretend they were in the Bel Air house and Josie was sitting between them.

"You didn't tell Talia about her?" Lila asked, but it was a statement.

Aidan shook his head. "She's too young."

"Don't you think she should know she has a sister?"

Aidan rubbed the back of his neck. She could feel the exhaustion radiating off him. "Of course, Lila, I'm not trying to—" His voice caught. "I see her everywhere, in every girl I pass on the street. I feel like I'm betraying her, but I want to preserve Talia's innocence for as long as I can."

Tears formed in his eyes, and he hastily wiped them away, refusing to let them interrupt.

"I thank God every day that she comes home from school and some kid hasn't told her the story about me he heard from his parents."

Lila put a hand on his back, gently rubbing it as the tiredness and the denial and the alcohol hit Aidan full force, and he could no longer tuck Josie away.

"I miss her," Aidan whispered.

"Me too," Lila said softly, resting her head on his shoulder.

They sat there for a long while in silence, feeling the rise and fall of the other's chest. At the house in Bel Air, they used to sit like this every night on the balcony outside their bedroom. His heat, his smell, enveloped her. Lila gently lifted her head from his shoulder. Coming out of a daze, Aidan turned as he felt the weight disappear. They locked eyes, and something dropped in Lila's stomach.

She didn't know who kissed who. It was sudden and urgent—one second, they were still, and the next, their lips were moving together.

Lila sighed into his kiss, and he pulled her closer. If she could make him understand, maybe they could love each other again. She wanted him to gorge himself until there was nothing left of her, until the world disappeared and they could start over.

They broke apart, panting. She pressed her forehead against his, putting a hand to his cheek. They sat there for a while, breathing each other's air, imagining they were somewhere else. Lila watched his face, lips slightly parted, eyes shut, a freckle below his eyelashes. She could see Josie in him, smiling at her. But when Aidan opened his eyes, he did not smile.

He pulled away from her and stood up, the warmth and the solace ripping away. He cleared his throat. "I'm sorry . . . I'm drunk."

"Aidan . . ." Lila started.

He was already hurrying down the stairs. "We should get back to the party."

"Aidan, wait." Lila ran after him, her heels desperately clip clopping on the hardwood.

Aidan stopped and turned to face her a few steps below. "That was a huge mistake. I . . . I'm sorry."

"You feel the same way I do. You never stopped," Lila said.

He looked down at his feet in shame. "I can't do that to my family."

"What about our family?" Lila said.

Aidan couldn't look her in the eye. He just turned around and hurried across the foyer, leaving her alone.

Lila had lost him all over again.

TWENTY-ONE

Lila did not stay for cake. She called a car as soon as Aidan walked out the door, afraid she would shatter if she took a moment to pause. Sylvie was buried deep in the moving crowd, swaying back and forth as one Technicolor mass. Lila did not bother waiting for her. Within minutes, Lila was walking back down the long, winding driveway.

He didn't care, or he was too afraid to let himself care. Either way, he wasn't worth her time. She had let him distract her from far more critical things. Pathetic. Her shoe wedged in the crack, and she yelped. Lila tried to yank her heel out, but it was stuck. "Fuck it." Lila took her foot out of the shoe.

The gravel was sharp against her bare toes, but she didn't care. She yanked the shoe out of the ground and stumbled back on her other heeled foot. Instead of putting the shoe back on, she removed the other one, held her heels in her hand, and ran.

HER SLEEP WAS SHALLOW THAT NIGHT. SHE ROLLED BACK AND FORTH IN fits, desperate to fall deeper, to descend for just a few hours, but her brain was wide-awake. When her phone rang around three a.m., it did not startle her. She flipped it over on her nightstand and saw Sylvie calling. Most likely drunk and hoping to come over. Lila declined the call and rolled back over in bed.

But the phone rang again.

Sylvie was persistent when she was horny. Lila ignored it again.

It rang again.

The woman is relentless. Lila snatched the phone off the table and answered. "I'm sleeping, stop call—"

"Come to my house now, it's an emergency." Sylvie sounded frightened on the other end.

"What's going on?" Lila asked.

But Sylvie had already hung up.

Lila sat up in bed; her blood went cold. What if it was about the collagen, and she couldn't say it over the phone? Had someone discovered them?

"Impossible," Lila told herself. They had been too careful. Still, she swung the covers back and got out of bed to dress. Whatever it was, it wasn't worth the risk of ignoring.

SYLVIE LIVED OFF MULHOLLAND DRIVE IN THE HILLS BETWEEN BEL AIR and Sherman Oaks. She had rented the most garish (*How else will people know it's expensive?*) Tudor mansion available and referred to it as her "starter house" while she looked for a permanent space to buy. Lila had avoided driving through these hills since Josie died. They had seen too much. She instinctively wanted to hold her breath as she passed through, the way she used to when she passed cemeteries as a child.

Lila parked beside Sylvie's car in the cobblestone driveway. The house looked like something out of a storybook. A picturesque English cottage that had ballooned into a giant eight times its size. The shuttered windows were quiet, like the house was asleep.

Lila used the lion-shaped doorknocker, and the sound boomed through the stillness. She readied the handgun she had brought in her jacket pocket for the worst-case scenario. She did not know what to expect. Sylvie was the most capable person she knew, and if she was panicking, then they were truly in danger.

A few moments later, Sylvie appeared in the window, her pale face luminescent in the dark. Her black liner and eyeshadow were badly smudged across her eyes, almost like a mask. She opened the door and ushered Lila inside. She was still dressed in her outfit from the party with the cape missing.

"What the fuck is going on?" Lila demanded.

Sylvie put her hand over Lila's mouth. "Follow me."

She moved silently and swiftly, opening a hidden door leading from the kitchen to a staircase. Sylvie ascended into the dark, then paused when she didn't hear steps behind her.

"Come on," she said.

The secret room off the kitchen was small and cramped. If the house was as old as it looked, Lila assumed it had been the servant's quarters once upon a time. Sylvie flipped the lights on, and Lila gasped.

"Who the fuck is that?"

In the center of the room, atop a long bureau that had been turned on its side, lay an unconscious man.

He was short with a trim black beard. He wore plaid boxers and no shirt, like Sylvie had just gotten him out of bed. Up close, Lila noticed a rapidly purpling bruise on his forehead.

"I saw you at the party," Sylvie said behind her.

Lila turned back to her in confusion. Sylvie's eyes were deep pools of black.

"With Aidan," she continued, on the verge of tears.

Oh no. Those were angry tears, the worst kind. Lila tried to quickly think of a way to de-escalate, but Sylvie had caught her off guard.

"Am I just your Ghislaine?" Sylvie spat.

"What?" Lila said.

"You keep me close to help with your little schemes and then ditch me as soon as I become an inconvenience." Sylvie put her hands on Lila's shoulders and shoved her backward. "Am I your Ghislaine?" she cried. "I thought we were both Epstein."

"Neither of us is Epstein," Lila hissed, then pointed to the man on the table. "Who is *he*?"

Sylvie glanced at the man on the table and smiled. *"Poor, pathetic Sylvie,"* she said. "So unlucky in love. Can't keep a man. Can't keep a woman. No matter how hard she tries. You thought you were so sneaky when I told you about my personal life. Laughing about me behind my back. And yeah, you hid your judgment well enough. You were nominated for a fucking Oscar. But I could *feel* it coming off you. My life was just a source of entertainment, you never cared."

"Sylvie, that's not true . . ." Lila started.

"I'm not done," Sylvie growled. "It didn't bother me, though, that I had to prove myself to you. Because I would do anything for you, Lila. You and me, we are the only people who matter in the whole world. And I won you over like I knew I would. No one will ever love you like I do. No one will ever fuck you like I do. But it turns out I was just . . . just a placeholder."

She stalked back and forth in front of the man, her petite legs growing long and lithe like a panther. "Who is he?" Lila repeated, quieter.

"You didn't hire me to be your assistant. You hired me to be your partner. You would be nowhere without me. And yet it never occurred to you that I might want a say in things," Sylvie said, stopping before her. They stood inches apart. Lila could feel Sylvie's breath on her lips. "Not anymore, babe. You have a list; I have a list too. *All the people who didn't love me back."*

Sylvie removed a small bottle from her pocket, and Lila saw it was a travel-sized bottle of mayonnaise. She unscrewed the cap and dipped a finger in, tracing the white sauce on the man's lips. "Would've been so much easier just to let me order mayo on the side, huh?" she cooed in his ear, then turned back to Lila. "You're going to help me harvest him just like I do with yours."

"No," Lila snapped. "Absolutely not."

"I'm used to being underestimated, doll. It's how I thrive. But if after all this time together you still don't understand how serious I am, you're not half as bright as I thought you were."

"Pull yourself together," Lila snarled. Usually, Sylvie would bow to her and cower, but she didn't move. "This isn't what we do. This is a joke."

"You came to me, and you said you wanted to rake down the entire world. Think of it as two birds with one stone." Sylvie smiled.

It was a pathetic bastardization of her life's work, but deep down, Lila was touched. Just hours after Aidan skulked away from the feelings that didn't fit with his perfect new life, Sylvie leapt to prove how much she cared.

"I never underestimated you, Sylvie. You're the miserable little bitch I always knew you were," Lila said, not without affection. Sylvie recoiled like she'd been struck. Lila spun on her heel and started for the door.

"I don't think you realize you don't have a choice," Sylvie said. "You walk out the door, I will tell everyone what really goes into glob's products."

Lila froze. Sylvie crept up behind her, her breath tickling her ear. "You'd out yourself as an accomplice?" Lila said.

"If only you had just let me love you." Sylvie rested her chin on Lila's shoulder.

Lila's shoulders sank.

"See?" Sylvie licked her lips. "I fucked you better than Aidan Reynolds ever could."

Lila spun around to face her, and Sylvie stepped back in surprise. Lila grabbed hold of Sylvie's throat and squeezed tightly. Sylvie sputtered and twisted in her arms, but Lila did not let go. Her eyes bulged and twitched, and only when she saw that defiant spark flag out did Lila release her.

Sylvie collapsed on the ground, hungrily gasping for air. Lila watched with a faint smile. When Sylvie picked herself up to look back at Lila, their eyes locked, and they grabbed each other.

Sylvie pushed Lila against the wall as their mouths mashed together, trying to get the other to submit. Lila tore Sylvie's dress as

Sylvie hurriedly unbuttoned Lila's jeans, while the man lay dead on the table with mayo still on his lips. Sylvie was everywhere: on her neck, on her chest, kissing a trail down Lila's stomach. "I'm going to make you scream," Sylvie whispered in her ear.

Lila dug her nails into Sylvie's back until she drew blood.

LILA AWOKE IN SYLVIE'S BED AS THE SUN SET THE NEXT EVENING. THEY had worked on dismembering and cooking her ex-boyfriend until late that morning. Every time the gravity of the situation hit Lila, and she grew angry with Sylvie all over again, she realized how impressed she was with Sylvie. Sylvie was right—Lila had underestimated her. Sylvie had made her pay for it, and it was sexy as hell.

Sylvie's side of the bed was empty and made. Even after a night of binge drinking and dismembering someone, she kept to her schedule. Lila peeled the covers off and emerged naked, going into Sylvie's closet for the most low-key outfit she could find.

Deep in the recesses of Sylvie's junk drawer, Lila found an old grey dog-walking shirt and threw it on. She turned around to look at herself in the full-length mirror and gasped in horror. Her under eyes were dented and dry, the contour in her cheeks so deep that she looked ill. Her temples were hollowed like tree trunks. Her skin—that luscious, creamy white skin—looked washed out and dull. Even her hair had lost its gleam. She looked like an old Renaissance portrait left out in the sun. She examined herself in terror, tilting her head from left to right in search of an angle that made her look like less of a monster.

But no matter what, her face remained the same.

"Hey there, Sleeping Beauty." Sylvie poked her head in the door.

Lila turned to face her, waiting for Sylvie's face to change when she saw, but Sylvie's expression remained pleasant. She was blinded by love, Lila realized in disgust. She couldn't be objective if she tried.

"I had this thought last night." Sylvie wrapped her arms around Lila's waist. "When was the last time you had a vacation?"

Lila raised an eyebrow. "I had one for about ten years."

"No, not like that," Sylvie said. "A real one that's just about relaxation and rejuvenation. We have the money now. We could go somewhere really luxurious. Take a break from things. You deserve a break. Doesn't that sound nice?"

Lila shrugged. A vacation only seemed like a pretty distraction. But Sylvie didn't give up.

"I want to take you to this fantastic beach I know. It's, like, one of the best in the world. The water is so warm and clear. There are these little sharks—they're not actual sharks, they don't have teeth—but they swim around you. And the sand is softer than the beaches here. You'd love it. We could snorkel in the morning and go to dinners on the boardwalk."

"Where is it?" asked Lila.

"*San Diego,*" Sylvie said.

Lila turned back to the mirror to hide her laughter. "My cheeks are getting flat. Topicals can only do so much," Lila said. "I need filler."

Sylvie eyed her, confused about where this was coming from. "Okay, I mean, for what it's worth, I don't think you need it. And fillers can give your skin a bad reaction."

"Not if they're collagen based." Lila pointed to the fresh jars of collagen powder outside the door. "We'll use his."

TWENTY-TWO

A transcript of Lila Devlin's speech at the 2024 Unsung Heroines: Women in Hollywood Awards.

The gala applauds as Lila takes the stage and accepts the award. She is visibly overwhelmed by the warm reception.

LILA DEVLIN: Thank you, Jennifer, for that beautiful introduction. It is truly surreal to be standing up here. To my fellow honorees, I will forever be in awe of your courage and grace. Being a woman in this industry can be hell, but your strength reminds me that I do not walk alone.

I've been thinking a lot about the concept of karma lately. In the darkest moments of my life, I used to ask what I had done to deserve the hand I'd been dealt. If karma was real, when would it get justice for me? The truth is it didn't. I waited a very long time for karma to rescue me, and it never came. It took me a very long time to realize karma doesn't exist. That what happened to me was horrible and random. I wasn't being punished for anything, and no one would be punished for me. Because I held that power myself. I could make my own karma.

· · ·

Cara Donaldson returned to her red Mini Cooper with a reusable grocery bag filled with fresh fruit. It was mid-December in LA, but the weather was still a pleasant, sunny 70 degrees. She'd spent an hour browsing stalls at the farmers market, her Sunday ritual, scrutinizing every piece of produce until she found the ripest, juiciest option. She didn't eat processed sugar, hadn't for fifteen years, but allowed herself a piece of fruit at the end of the day to enjoy with her bedtime decaf espresso—

"Shit," Cara said. Her back tire had a flat. "Goddamn it."

Sunday afternoons were designated for self-care, to veg out and watch old *Vanderpump Rules* episodes from before they fired the racists. It was eleven a.m. and the day was already circling the drain.

A car pulled up beside her as she riffled through her purse to get her phone. *"Ohmygosh, Cara?"*

Lila Devlin waved from the front seat of her . . . Prius? She was on the cover of *Forbes* this month, and she was driving a fucking Prius? Cara vaguely remembered reading something about how the richest people often choose to live modestly and wrinkled her nose. She understood not wanting to be tacky, but did it have to be so practical?

That was Lila. A celebrity shooting back onto the A-list and still digging her heels in to be a shrinking violet.

"Lila?"

They hadn't spoken in several weeks—their lunch date kept falling through because of Lila's schedule, and Cara didn't want to look desperate. But every day, Cara internally bashed her head in with a golf club, because Lila had offered the world to her on a platter, and she'd spat on it.

She should have been at Lila's side, not the pint-sized psycho Sylvie Lightly. Cara hadn't expected Lila to actually sign with her. It was a joke—a mean joke, but a joke. She thought Lila would come out of the meeting with a good story for parties. The woman had plowed through a crowd of people! She dressed like a toddler's idea of a grown-up! And yet, somehow, they were the new dynamic duo of the beauty industry.

Cara assumed Lila was still mad at her and that was why it had been so hard to schedule lunch. But Lila would have just driven past if she didn't want Cara's company. Maybe Cara was wrong.

"Did you go to the farmers market?" Lila smiled. "I was just there."

"Oh, really? Can't believe I didn't see you!" Cara said.

Lila glanced at her phone and then at the road ahead of her and then back at Cara. "This is extremely short notice, but I was going home for tea. I know we've been meaning to catch up—would you want to join?"

Of course. Lila Devlin finally extended an olive branch, and it was on a day like today. Cara sighed. "I would, but I just got a flat."

"Oh, damn," Lila said. "And on a Sunday too."

"What's wrong with Sundays?" Cara asked.

"AAA takes forever on Sundays. Someone told me it's their busiest day," Lila said.

Cara had never heard that before, but then, she knew fuck all about cars. She groaned, leaning against the hood. "Great. Amazing."

"I could give you a ride?" Lila said. "You could wait over at my place, Uber back here to meet AAA?"

Cara smiled. Maybe today wasn't going to be so bad after all.

LILA LIVED IN ENCINO, BECAUSE THE PRIUS WASN'T DULL ENOUGH. THE only reason anyone went to Encino was for therapy or if they had a sudden hankering for mid-tier chain restaurants.

Her house was a two-story modern farmhouse—white with a black roof and furnishings—off a spacious tree-lined street with rolling hedges of ivy. It was a little cliché, but cute enough. Nothing like the Bel Air house—that had been one of the most elegant houses Cara had ever stepped foot in. Lila had often complained that the house felt too ostentatious; she never let herself enjoy her good fortune.

It drove Cara crazy then, how ungrateful she'd been. So dismissive of her money and her beauty and her celebrity, never considering how that felt to the handlers flocking around her. She was millions of people's dream, and she didn't take any of it seriously. One of the highest-paid rising actresses in the world, and she'd wished she was a veterinarian. It was infuriating.

That was why Cara had talked to the book people. Lila didn't take any of it seriously; Cara didn't expect her to care. She'd probably been a little too forthcoming, but it was all for Aidan. He'd gotten the short end of the stick in that case. Everyone remembered only Lila's part of the story. As his publicist, it was Cara's job to protect him (and remind the world he existed).

Lila led her into an open-plan chef's kitchen with glossy marble countertops and forest-green cupboards. The light from the bay window cast a yellow sheen on Lila's lustrous hair. She was nothing without that hair. When she'd met Cara for lunch almost a year ago, it had been the color of dishwater. Cara hadn't even recognized her, she had looked so plain. Maybe if she'd been a redhead then, maybe Cara would have seen her star power. Maybe she would have signed on to glob.

"Have a seat." Lila gestured to the tall stools in front of the kitchen island. "I'll put the kettle on."

"Congratulations, by the way, on all the success with the new store," Cara said as Lila removed two mugs from a cabinet. They were shaped like snowmen for Christmas. *How cute.*

"Oh, thank you," Lila said, igniting a flame on the stove with a faint ticking sound. "Yeah, there was such an uproar we're already expanding."

Knife me in the tit. "That's amazing!"

Lila was rich enough to expand out of Encino. She could buy the Sherman Oaks Galleria if she wanted to, own a personal Cheesecake Factory. She could have the SkinnyLicious avocado tacos whenever she wanted.

"Yeah, manifest destiny and all that." Lila smiled. "I can't thank you enough for putting me and Sylvie together. She's incredible. No one could do her job better."

Lila's skin had improved too, Cara noticed. Earlier this year, it had been so dry, her forehead wrinkles gaped. She could credit glob all she wanted, but Cara knew she'd had some kind of work done. Super subtle, but Cara knew how to spot it. Her cheekbones were sharper, her lips were just a bit more bee-stung. Filler or fat grafting? Filler, even in trace amounts, always left an airbrushed unnaturalness, but fat transfers never held in the lips, they were too mobile. Was her surgeon a fucking wizard?

"Yeah, after I gave you her info, I remembered her accident. I was scared I'd set you up with a maniac! But I'm glad it all worked out," Cara said.

Lila laughed, pouring the tea into two mugs. "Who was I to judge?"

So, they'd bonded over their mutual criminal investigations? *Ugh.*

Lila set the snowman in the red scarf before Cara and clanged her green snowman against it. "Cheers."

The tea was rooibos, a dark amber color. Cara didn't recognize the smell, but her allergies were also acting up with the December Santa Anas. Those fucking winds ravaged her sinuses. She took a sip and tried to mask her wince. It was bitter, worse than black coffee, and salty.

She looked over at Lila, who was watching her, sipping without issue. "What is this?" Cara asked.

"Blood," Lila said.

"What?" Cara said, thinking she'd misheard.

"Hot water and blood. Pretty diluted, otherwise it'd be too thick to swallow. But, blood," Lila repeated.

So, she was still bitter about that lunch. This was her stupid revenge for Cara rejecting her glob proposal. Cara laughed nervously. "Is this a joke?"

"It's Arthur Allen's."

Cara coughed so hard the liquid flew out of her nose. She could see how red it was, splattered on the counter in front of her. "You have a sick sense of humor."

She refused to let it faze her. The first assistant desk she'd worked was Mel Gibson's publicist—Cara had heard way worse.

"I killed him," Lila said, "and skinned him, and then I cut him into pieces and boiled his bones and saved the blood in a Brita pitcher."

Cara felt the goose bumps on her neck she usually only got when a guy was getting too close. "What?" was all she could think to say.

"I wanted you to taste it, so you'd know you're going to be used for *good*."

Cara stood up, a little shakier than she'd hoped, and took a step away from the kitchen island. Lila was taking the joke way too far. "I gotta head back to my car in case AAA gets . . ."

"What did the oral history give you?" Lila asked. "At first I thought money, but you make more than enough with your business. Sympathy for Aidan? The world was already sympathetic; he didn't need it. No, it's far more valuable than either of those—attention."

Cara could feel her heartbeat in her big toe. Lila kept her tone playful, but as she licked the rim of red around her lips, she looked like a wild cat. A silky predator readying itself to pounce. "Lila, that's ridiculous . . ." Cara started.

"You couldn't stand that I was more successful than you. You resented me because I was in front of the cameras, and you weren't. Don't blame me, Cara, blame your parents. They're the ones who gave you a strong jaw."

Cara's hand flew to her chin, and she flushed. *Stop it*, Cara told herself. Lila was bitter and hurling barbs to see what stuck. "So that's why you invited me here? To mock me?"

Gold flecks danced in her big brown eyes. "No, I invited you here because carrying your dead body into my basement is way easier from my house than from a secondary location."

Lila was crazy. Cara knew that. She'd lost it the second her kid died. She had hoped the last ten years had given Lila a handle on her mental health, but the woman was clearly still delusional. She needed a 5150. *Again.*

Cara took a slow step back, and then another, and then wondered why she was trying to be polite when this woman was fucking crazy and spun around and ran. Or tried to. Lila grabbed her ponytail and yanked.

Cara's head whipped backward and Lila slammed it against the countertop. When Cara opened her eyes, she saw a trickle of red flowing onto the marble. *Where had that come from?* Her hand flew to her nose. *Oh.* This nosebleed was way worse than the Santa Anas, Cara thought faintly. Tic Tacs swam in her mouth and she spat them out: eight white little flecks.

"My veneers," Cara whimpered. She caught a glimpse of herself in the reflection of the wine rack beside her. Without her veneers, her front teeth showed, shorn down to tiny nubs.

And then she noticed the knife pressing against her neck.

"Again, credit where it's due." Lila smiled. "I couldn't have done any of this without you."

And then Cara saw black.

• • •

LILA DEVLIN (*cont.*): I have lost count of the number of times I've been told glob is a stupid name for a company. No one knows what it means or why it matters. It's not sexy or sophisticated enough. But it stayed.

Over the last ten years, I've learned a great deal about the value of names and how powerful they can be. My name, for example, became synonymous with death. My name cost me my personhood; I became another tragedy.

I've found that I don't like being a tragedy.

I tried accepting it. I sat, stewed, and brooded for years because it was easier, because it made everyone more comfortable. No one likes to watch the aftermath, not when the good bit is the original tragedy. It took over a decade, but ultimately, I refused to let the sum of my life be the death of my little girl . . .

Her voice breaks, and she pauses. An encouraging soul in the audience starts to clap, which grows into an uproar. Hundreds cheering her on.

LILA DEVLIN: It wasn't an easy choice. I could accept that my name wasn't my own, or I could piece together the shards of myself and take it back. But it wasn't about what would be easiest for me, because it wasn't just me who became a tragedy. It was about Josie too.

Everyone has room for aspiration. Every day I wake up and I decide to change myself for the better. And every member of the glob family makes that decision too. We built this movement hand in hand; we challenge the world to change.

• • •

Tommy Olsen looked pretty damn good for fifty years old. He had all his hair (thanks, Propecia) and made daily use of the Peloton his daughter had gifted him a couple of years ago when they were still talking. His Tinder profile photos were handsome, carefully picked by one of the ladies in the office. So, it wasn't surprising that a twenty-four-year-old with daddy issues had super-liked him, asking to meet up that night.

Her name was Chloe. She was a D cup. It was a no-brainer, even when she'd picked the Motel 6 in bumfuck Van Nuys to meet up because she didn't want her boyfriend to find out. At first, he'd hesitated—she was so close to Naomi's age—but Naomi had sided with her mother and hung him out to dry, so fuck it! He was fucking a twenty-four-year-old.

Naomi used to complain all the time about how embarrassed she was by his chosen profession. He was ruining people's lives, she said. He stalked people. Sure, Tommy had been away a lot, with the night shoots and the long hours, but his photos had paid for three-quarters of her tuition at Oberlin.

Fucking Oberlin. Sixty thousand dollars a year to experiment with purple-haired lesbians.

He parked in the Motel 6 lot at 9:56 p.m. and waited in his 2015 Saab. He didn't want to get there first. He was the suave older man; he wanted to keep her waiting. He wanted her pussy to be hot and aching when he walked into the room.

At 10:07, he emerged from the car. The parking lot was dark and empty, lit by only a couple of streetlamps. Tommy could see flashing lights underneath the motel room doors, the residents settling down with cable before bed. He shivered—despite the Valley's brutal heat in the summer, its winter nights were the coldest in LA County.

The room was 206, she'd said. He looked around until he located it on the second floor, a narrow row of doors that looked out over the asphalt. Tommy started toward the stairs when he heard a door open behind him, and something cold hit the back of his head.

"HOW ARE YOU FEELING, HONEY?"

His first thought was Evelyn. They were in their apartment in Palms in 2000, and she was pregnant with Naomi and she didn't know about the drugs yet.

But as he came to, he realized the voice wasn't hers. It was too cold. Evelyn's was soft. He did recognize it, though; he had followed that voice for six months like it was the Pied Piper. Tommy's eyes snapped open, and he saw Lila Devlin staring down at him.

"Jesus!" He tried to push away from her but found he was strapped to a surgical table, cold metal a shock against his skin. If she was trying to scare him, he wouldn't give her the satisfaction. "What the hell is going on?"

Lila disappeared from his line of sight, and when he blinked again, there was a picture in his face. When his eyes adjusted, he saw the famous photo he'd taken of her the night she went crazy outside her house. She's half collapsed, Aidan Reynolds with one arm around her, the nanny on the other side.

Then it was gone, and Lila was back. "You said you made half a million from that. You didn't deserve it. The lighting's shit, and the angle's off."

"What do you want?" Tommy said. Had the bindings on his wrists gotten tighter?

"To show you how to take a real photo." Lila shrugged.

It was only then that Tommy realized he'd been stripped naked. He fumbled to cover himself, but his hands were too far away. "Let me go," he said. "You do not wanna fuck with me."

A woman with bangs appeared beside her. Lila's new business partner, he vaguely remembered. Sandy? Sasha? "Holy shit, he has a clown dick," she said.

Tommy squeezed his eyes shut, willing a way out of this situation. Bangs reached a French manicured hand out and gave him a long stroke.

"It's so . . . sad. And floppy."

"Get the hell off," Tommy snapped.

"How is that any different than what you did to me?" Lila said, pulling a camera strap over her neck.

"I didn't touch your—"

"You exposed me at my most vulnerable," she said. "Sold the most private parts of me."

Bangs's hand squeezed like she was trying to pop him, and Tommy let out a sharp cry of pain.

"Look up at me, Tommy." Lila wiggled her fingers, and with Tommy's attention on her, Bangs reached down and sliced his dick off with a butcher's knife.

Tommy screamed.

It was an impossible amount of pain, so blunt and excruciating he nearly lost consciousness on the spot. Unfortunately, he didn't. He felt warm waves of blood pooling beneath his legs; he could hear the women fidgeting with his penis beside him.

"Put it on the table, Sylvie. Yes, there. Tilt the light like . . . there! Don't touch it," he heard Lila say, and then the camera snapped.

Tommy wondered if he would go to heaven or hell. He didn't think he deserved either. Somewhere in the middle seemed fair. He hoped he'd have a chance to argue his case, wherever he went.

Lila appeared again a few minutes later. Tommy tensed against the table, trying to edge away from her, but she held a printed photo in front of his face. Frankly, it was a masterful shot of his dismembered member against a white tablecloth, drenched in syrupy blood.

"That's how you frame a photo," Lila said.

He thought of Naomi and Evelyn and everything he never said.

"Please just kill me," he whispered.

"If you insist."

. . .

LILA DEVLIN (*cont.*): As women, we're told to be afraid of aging. That we'll grow frail and weak, that we'll lose our desirability, that we'll be forgotten. But as I get older, I find myself appreciating life more than I ever did when I was young. I feel like with every passing day, I become more and more myself.

I started glob as a vessel for my daughter's legacy. Her spirit shines through our products and our mission. The truth is I don't give a fuck if you think the name *glob* is stupid. Because it's not yours, it's *hers*.

. . .

On Saturday nights, Taylor Park worked the late shift at the Gower Gulch Denny's. She'd been there for just over two years. It was no one's childhood dream to work in a cowboy-themed strip mall sandwiched between a homeless encampment and a Sweetgreen, but she made do. She had to pay for grad school somehow.

It wasn't so bad, really. The customers were typically packs of drunk partiers kicked to the curb after No Vacancy closed at two a.m. Women dolled up in tight dresses and heels and men who looked like they'd just rolled out of bed, congregating at the cheapest watering hole in Hollywood. They were bleary-eyed and rowdy but rarely unkind. An old ex-girlfriend had even been one of them; that's how they met.

The tips were meager but survivable. It was just a stepping stone, Taylor told herself as she wiped the shreds of lettuce from the cracks in a vinyl booth. She watched the line of Ubers gather on Sunset to collect crowds of twenty-somethings, like elementary school pickup. This was the Hollywood glamour she'd heard so much about.

There was a glob billboard across the street. Lila Devlin with smoky eyes tilted so far upward she looked half cat. Taylor had read about glob on skincare Reddit and TikTok, but she hadn't tried any of the products. It was too awkward knowing Sylvie was involved. Their breakup hadn't been bad, exactly, just weird. Sylvie was weird.

But Sylvie's weird veered away from quirky and straight toward *off*. When Taylor had ended things between them—she'd gotten busy with school and didn't want a big commitment—Sylvie had been devastated. The following month, she'd received nightly voicemails pleading for another chance and anguished declarations of love on napkins slipped into her work locker. It was too much and had died down only when Taylor told her there was absolutely no chance she'd ever date Sylvie again.

She was just so *intense*. What was it that Sylvie said on their first date? She was *hungry for a forever love*. Taylor had dated plenty of U-Haul lesbians before, but no one like her.

Taylor's shift ended at five a.m. It was still pitch-black out when she emerged into the empty parking lot. In the dark, the wooden Western-themed structures looked more like a ghost town. She clasped her pepper spray close as she passed the vintage show wagon propped up in the lot's center. She always hated this part of the night—holding her purse close, turning constantly for any sign of an assailant. Her friends mocked her for being paranoid, but Hollywood was the ugliest part of the city. She couldn't take any chances.

As Taylor neared her Honda Civic, she heard tires screech to a stop behind her. She hardly had time to turn around before a figure in a black mask was yanking her into an open van. "No, no," Taylor gasped.

What had those college self-defense classes taught her? Aim for the eyes. Before the figure could pull her in, Taylor reached out, ripped its mask off, and jabbed her finger into its eyes—"Sylvie?"

Sylvie's navy eyes blinked back at her before she jerked away at the pain of the jab. Taylor sprayed the pepper spray in her face and ran as fast as she could in the opposite direction.

She was ten paces away when she realized Sylvie had her purse and, with it, her keys and phone. The van was blocking the path to

Denny's, so she was forced to sprint down El Centro Avenue. She could hear another woman yelling, *"Shit, shit, fuck, Sylvie!"* but didn't dare turn around.

El Centro was run-down and mostly comprised construction sites and parking lots. There was no one around. *"Help!"* Taylor screamed. *"Someone help me!"* But no one came.

She saw the van's headlights cast on the road before her. It was gaining quickly, and she was out of options. Taylor turned right toward an apartment building, yanking on the doors to the lit entrance inside. But they were locked. *"Help!"* She pounded, jiggling the handle. *"Please help me!"*

There was no more time. Gloved hands seized her by the shoulders, and a wet cloth was shoved over her mouth. Taylor kicked and scratched and fought, and then the grip loosened and she relaxed, because then she was free.

LILA STARED DOWN AT THE DEAD GIRL IN THE BACK OF THE VAN. ONCE THE chloroform had worked enough to get her into the van, Lila had shot her in the head. Sylvie had so fucked this endeavor that she lost the privileges of killing her. Sylvie emerged from the house holding milk-soaked towels to her swollen eyes.

"Do you have her?" Sylvie asked as Lila pulled Taylor Park's body into the chilly morning air.

Lila ignored her, hoisting the girl into her arms bride style. She was in her mid-twenties, probably still on her parents' health insurance.

Sylvie rushed to her side. "I can help."

"Don't touch me," Lila snapped.

"I don't understand." Sylvie dropped her hands. "What's wrong?"

Lila glared. Milk was leaking out of Sylvie's eyes, and she was still choosing to play dumb. "She saw your face. If we had been a second slower, this would be over."

Sylvie laughed uneasily. "Okay, well, we weren't a second slower, and we got her, and everything's fine."

"Everything is not fine," Lila snarled. "Plucking waitresses out of parking lots is not why I started doing this. Just because she dumped you. God, Sylvie, you're a child."

Sylvie's eyes welled up with tears. "If—if you keep talking to me like that, I'll . . ."

"Go to the cops?" Lila asked. "Go ahead."

Sylvie couldn't. She hung her head, tears and snot dripping onto Lila's driveway. "Lila, I'm sorry."

"I'm not taking another chance on you again," Lila said.

"What does that mean?" Sylvie scurried to follow Lila into the house. "Lila . . ."

Lila stopped her in the doorway, holding an arm out. "I need a break."

Sylvie's eyes narrowed. "But I brought her in."

"You've lost your privileges," Lila said. "I need time to myself."

She started to shut the door, but Sylvie wedged it open with her foot. "That's it? You're just *out* after a year of working together?"

"I'm not saying I'm out." Lila sounded exhausted. "I just need a break."

Sylvie's upper lip wobbled. "I love you. I put you before everything."

"You don't love me. You're obsessed with me, like you were obsessed with her." Lila nodded her head toward the dead girl in her arms.

"I open my heart to lots of people because life isn't worth living alone. Maybe if you tried it once in a while, *you* wouldn't be so *obsessed* with murdering people!" Sylvie yelled.

They stared at each other in shock. Lila was rendered speechless. The sky was melting into a light pink color, the sun just poking through the towering oak trees.

"He will never fulfill you," Sylvie whispered.

"What?" Lila said.

"Aidan. You outgrew him."

"Keep his name out of your fucking mouth."

Sylvie shook her head, wiping away the last of her milky tears. "I thought if I gave you time, you could love me too, but I don't think you can. You only had room to care about one person, and once that person was gone, you sewed yourself shut."

She spun around on her heel and walked away.

Twenty-Three

Lila hadn't heard from Aidan in four months. She'd texted, called, desperate for a chance to talk through what had happened, but there was no answer. Coward. After everything they'd been through, he owed her a response at the very least. Every day without an answer, the coil in her stomach grew tighter. The grey thing was angry.

It had nothing to do with Sylvie, of course. Lila and Sylvie coexisted at glob but had otherwise kept their distance since the argument. Lila didn't miss her much. More than anything, she was relieved that the constant frustration and worry of their relationship was gone. The grey thing was apathetic. Now, she could concentrate on getting her family back together.

The filler rejuvenated her, both physically and emotionally. She found it wondrously symmetrical: the people who had destroyed her life gave her a boost when she needed it most. They had lived under her skin for so many years, she hardly felt a difference.

Without Sylvie, she often spent her free time on the floor of the glob store. Nothing compared to the look on their faces as she entered, like they were staring at the sun and had to look away before she'd blind them. She rarely ever spoke to the customers, just a polite smile as she checked in on things. But that was enough for them to decide: *I will buy anything necessary to acquire what she naturally has.*

It was amazing to see the variety of people glob reached. It turned out there was a reason for everyone to want collagen products. An old woman with bright white hair slathered it on her crow's-feet. A multicultural group of twenty-somethings were taking preventative measures. Even a little girl with big grey eyes held her mom's hand while she browsed. Lila's dream had come to fruition; she wondered if they could feel the bits of bone on their skin.

It was only in the middle of the night when she found herself missing Sylvie. When she felt the cold space where Sylvie's body should have been, when she felt the absence of her arm around her chest. But Sylvie had been a temporary convenience. Sylvie wasn't Aidan. Sylvie wasn't home.

The magazine profiles about her boasted that she had built an empire started in her kitchen, and now she felt the familiar pull of all empires—expansion. Total domination. She was scouting the location for the next glob store while fielding pitches for new glob products. With things as busy as they were, she barely remembered Aidan wasn't returning her calls.

Fucking Aidan. Couldn't face what he was really feeling, so he chose to run away. Lila opened her iCloud and scrolled to her 2011–2014 photos. Aidan could pretend Lila and Josie didn't exist, but here was hard proof. He couldn't wash Lila away if he tried.

Josie at the petting zoo. Josie with pudding smeared on her face. Josie dressed as a mouse for Halloween. Josie asleep in Lila's arms. As each photo tugged at her, she found herself struggling to remember the stories behind them. Like she was sifting through the life of an identical stranger.

March 5 came up hard and fast. There was the photo of Josie eating the broccoli with lemon sauce, grinning at the camera. Lila clicked on to the next one, though she knew that was the last photo of Josie she had. She usually never scrolled past that last photo. There was a drunk selfie she'd taken in the bathroom that night with "friends" she'd never see again. Her lipstick was smeared and her nose was red from the beginner's attempt at cocaine. A stupid drunk idea that had seemed brilliant in the moment. She clicked to the next one, willing a new photo of Josie to appear, her tucked safely in bed, but there wasn't.

Only a blurry picture of the ground it looked like Lila had accidentally taken when Aidan had let her in that night—

"What?" Lila murmured to herself. She'd never really looked at this picture before.

She recognized her feet in heels, and at the corner of the frame was one of Aidan's feet in sneakers.

Aidan was wearing shoes.

Aidan never wore shoes.

Why the hell was Aidan wearing shoes at eleven o'clock at night? The man had an aversion to shoes whenever he was within the bounds of his own home. Especially inside the house. And he had told her he'd just put Josie to bed. Why would he put on a pair of sneakers to go into a nursery?

A wave of nausea floated up Lila's throat. She braced her hands on the desk, forcing it back down.

He'd been high that night. She'd forgotten, but Tim Weber had mentioned it in the oral history. Aidan could have easily put Josie to bed and—and dropped her.

No. There was no way. She'd watched him suffer through it for months.

Lila viciously shook her head, pushing the thoughts away. Aidan wasn't a criminal mastermind. That would mean he had staged the entire kidnapping: sent the ransom notes, hired someone to drive the van to the exchange knowing Josie was already dead.

That would mean he dropped her body in the lake.

"*Enough*," Lila told herself. Fox had always called her hysterical; well, this was hysteria. There had to have been a reasonable explanation. Maybe, even, Aidan heard something outside, so he put on his shoes to investigate.

There was a knock on the glass, and Maya came into the office with a large coffee. "I have your latte," she said.

Arthur Allen had killed Josie, and Lila had killed him, and he was gone. No matter what he'd said—no, anyone in his situation would have said anything to be spared. Aidan was a lot of things—spineless, a coward, unwilling to confront the deeper parts of himself—but he would not kill his daughter and frame it on his wife. It just wasn't something he was capable of. He wasn't that good of an actor.

"Lila?"

Lila looked up to see Maya watching her with a faint look of concern, the coffee cup still extended, waiting for Lila to accept it. "Thank you, Maya," she said.

Lila clicked out of the photo album and on her calendar, focusing back on business. She gave it a cursory glance, looking for an item to propel her from the subject of Aidan. "What's this next Monday?" Lila saw a slot for a half hour that just read *Check in with Maya*. "Is there something you want to talk about?"

The tips of Maya's ears reddened. "Oh, it's—we don't have to do that right now. You're busy."

"Hush." Lila waved her off and gestured to the chair across from her desk. "Sit. You know you can talk to me about anything; you don't have to put it in my calendar."

Maya had never been hesitant to approach Lila before. If there was something wrong, if Maya was hurt or in trouble, Lila wanted to know.

Maya perched on the edge of the chair, refusing to settle down. "Really, Lila, if now isn't a good—"

"What's up?" Lila smiled encouragingly. Maya had to learn to command and demand respect. When she showed fear, that was when people would dismiss her.

Maya shifted her feet awkwardly, taking in a shaky breath. "I can't thank you enough for allowing me to learn and grow at glob, but . . . I've decided it's time for me to move on."

"Sorry?" Lila let out a little laugh. It was so canned, so practiced, it sounded like she had memorized verbatim the Google result for *how to quit your job*.

Maya scratched her elbow anxiously. She was so young. She cleared her throat, powering through her little speech. "I'm so grateful for my time here and for you to take this chance on me."

Her face was pasty and anxious. Her gaze flicked back and forth across Lila's face, landing on her nose. She couldn't even look Lila in the eye.

She was serious. A wave of nausea rose up Lila's throat, and she forced it down. Tiny pins pricked her hands; she wiggled them away under the desk.

"I'm afraid I don't understand," Lila said. "Is everything all right?"

Did some fuck-dud executive make a pass at her? Maya was beautiful, no matter how hard she tried to dress down. Was she choosing to bow out gracefully instead of putting glob in jeopardy? Or, God, had someone said something racist? Lila would skin them.

Or even worse—*had another company poached her?*

"Yes, everything's fine," Maya said. Her finger was tugging on the sleeve of her sweater. Why was she nervous? Couldn't she see Lila was the last person who'd want to make her nervous?

"This just seems sudden, given how enthusiastic you've been about being included in my leadership track," Lila said. Then she knew—of course. This was a negotiation tactic. Lila smirked and picked up a pen. "How much are you asking for to reconsider."

"No," Maya said firmly, then exhaled, trying to find the right words. "It's not about money. I've just realized this isn't the right path for me."

The right path. It was adorable to think she had the ability to choose her own path, to stop in the middle of the road and turn back. That life wouldn't shove her down that path anyway with Teflon strength. It was so arrogant, so naive.

Lila licked her lips, forcing herself not to balk at the ingratitude. "I have been up front with you from the start that I see your assistant position as a bridge to an executive—"

"No, I don't mean at glob. I mean just with the beauty industry in general. I want to go back to school," Maya said. "I'm still figuring things out."

Lila stared at her, barely concealing her bafflement. It was like she'd undergone a full personality transplant. What had happened to the ambitious, motivated intern Lila had hired last year? She'd been replaced by a hesitant, unsure impostor. A timid changeling.

"We were going to figure that out together. I was going to mentor you, and you'd learn how to start your own brand," Lila said. Did her voice pitch up? Lila took a sip of coffee.

Maya nodded. "I thought so too. And then, after experiencing it, I realized . . . I don't belong here."

She couldn't have been more wrong. Glob was the *only* place Maya belonged. Lila couldn't fathom a world without Maya seated at her little desk outside.

Lila's hands were getting sweatier. She hid them under her desk, wiping them on the wood. "If anyone has behaved inappropriately to give you that impression . . ."

"I don't want to do beauty," Maya burst out, no longer able to dance around it. "I thought I did, and I could help people doing it, but . . ." She sighed. "It's such an ugly place. It's shallow and it's cruel and it's soul crushing. And frankly, I don't have the stomach for this."

Lila understood exactly what Maya couldn't bring herself to say. She didn't want to work in the golden tower Lila had built by hand; she didn't think it was important enough. She didn't think Lila understood how to tangibly help the world, even though Lila understood it better than anyone.

Somewhere outside the office, a phone rang. Neither of them moved.

"I see." Lila sat back in her chair. "I know it's an awful industry, Maya. But without people like us, who's going to change it? Don't let anyone discourage you from pursuing this. You are worth more than all of them combined. You have no idea how special you are."

"I have a degree in biochemistry," Maya said. "I want to look into marine biology or environmental science. You deserve an assistant who's fully devoted to you. And I will give you plenty of time. Consider this my two months' notice. I will find and train my replacement. It'll be seamless."

This wasn't Maya talking. It couldn't be. Someone had wormed their way into her head and poisoned it. Lila could feel Maya slipping further away as each moment passed. She had to act quickly, before the panic paralyzed her.

"Wherever you end up, I'm not sure they'll be as generous with your salary, especially as an assistant. You'd be starting all over," Lila said.

Maya nodded, standing to leave. "I know."

Shit. Lila struggled to reel her back in. "Maya, with glob or not, I am your number one supporter. I'm just sad to see you go."

Maya relaxed a little, looked less eager to tear out of the room. "Glob has been like a family to me, Lila, really. I'll miss you guys so much."

That was precisely what they were—a family. Families stayed together through storms. They'd weather this one, together. Lila loved Maya; she was precious to her. "I know board members at USC, UCLA. I will help you get into your dream program. Whatever you need," Lila said. She'd even met someone at Stanford at a fundraising gala, but that was too far for her taste.

Maya bowed her head appreciatively. "You have no idea how much that offer means, but I'm not staying in California. I'm moving to New York. Hopefully aiming for Columbia or NYU."

New York? New York was thousands of miles away. New York wasn't an easy car ride or an office check-in. "You're moving?" Lila kept her voice flat, but it was teetering off a cliff.

"Yeah, in April, hopefully. I've been in LA since college, and I'm just ready for something new."

Underneath the desk, Lila's fingers latched on to the loose skin in her nail beds. She began to pick. Pick pick pick.

"My family's still in Mass., so it'll be nice to be closer to them too," Maya said.

The same family that had shunned her? To whom she'd spent years trying to prove herself? Now they were reappearing once she'd gotten on course.

Just moments ago, Maya called glob her family, which seemed the more appropriate definition. She had been taken in, nurtured, championed. Did she not want to be close to glob too? What the hell would she even do as an environmentalist? They'd just about tried everything at this point. Turning off lights and short showers were drops in a bucket compared to a private jet. And they'd never talk the 1 percent out of those. It was a waste of a career, a waste of this young woman bursting with limitless potential.

"Wow." Lila smiled tightly. "That's a big move to make all by yourself."

"Peter's coming with me."

All the pieces clicked together. She was following her thick-skulled boyfriend. Lila had expected Maya to be better than moving cross-country for a boy, but she had been young once too. She had to be gentle.

"You're moving in together?" Lila said lightly. "Sounds serious."

Maya blushed a little. "I guess so."

"Doesn't he have his little . . . thing here?"

"His magic? Yeah, but there are kids' birthday parties nationwide. Luckily." Maya laughed. Lila laughed too, to show they were the same.

She was throwing her life away for a fucking magician. Where were her friends? Why wasn't anyone stepping in for a wellness check?

"He also wants to go back to school," Maya said.

"For what?" Lila was prying, but she didn't care. Someone needed to.

"There's this, like, ninety-year-old French guy, Pierre L'Imbécile, who's opened up this exclusive clowning school he's auditioning for," she said, without irony.

"Clowning school?" Lila said. "Like tying balloons and face paint?"

"No, no, it's like the ancient art. Learning how to 'play.' Peter explains it better than I do." Maya looked down at her shoes, knowing how ridiculous that sounded.

Maybe it was abusive. Peter had been sweet and charming when Lila had first met him, but that meant nothing. The most dangerous ones always seemed hapless.

If Peter loved Maya so much, he would know what was best for her was Lila. Glob. Where she would be secure and safe and protected. It was cruel and deliberate to pluck someone away from where they were flourishing. Under the table, Lila twisted a hangnail and yanked it out.

"I don't want to take any more of your time," Maya said. "You're on that call in five."

Lila nodded. Maya nodded and turned to go. "Maya, even if you're not in the glob family, you're always in my family, okay? Anything you need, I'm here."

Maya's face brightened, her smile earnest. She was a born people pleaser, terrified of disappointing anyone. Just like Lila had been when she was young. "Thank you so much, Lila, for everything."

She shut the door behind her, and Lila removed her hands from under the table. Three fingers were gushing blood. She let out a hiss, wrapping her grey sleeves around them to stop the bleeding. She didn't care if it stained.

Losing Maya would be insurmountable. Her insides knotted just thinking about it. Her father's and Josie's deaths had been sudden and without warning, she didn't even have time to expect them. Maya had given her a timetable of two months, which was almost worse. Instead of a disappearance, Maya would slowly fade away.

She opened Google and searched Peter's name. It was uncommon enough that his personal website came up as the first result, headshot plastered on the welcome page.

Those cornflower-blue eyes watched her with an easy smile; Lila wanted to throw up. He hadn't worked for anything in his life. It was just given to him because of those eyes.

She clicked the drop-down menu. It was divided into magic, acting, and modeling. Lila clicked the magic page and scrolled through videos of Peter performing at birthday parties—nothing particularly impressive, no live animals because he's vegan. Lots of flowers and scarves and making little girls giggle. Exceedingly dull stuff.

She moved to his acting page. There was a reel—bit parts in commercials, but mostly scenes he'd performed in his acting conservatory. Dirk in *Boogie Nights,* Jack from *Titanic.* Every character he played was the same naive, optimistic leading man. Just like he was in real life. And he was good in these scenes, however amateur. Lila bought that he was actually in love with the girl playing Rose.

It made her wonder how much of this was an act with Maya. And he could get away with it as easily as everything else in his life. Lila wiped the blood off her keyboard. She needed to distract herself before she threw her computer across the room.

She opened the list and scrolled until she saw a name.

Twenty-Four

Lydia Novak lived on a farm in the hills above Ojai Valley, about a ninety-minute drive northwest of Los Angeles. Her house was small and weathered, white paint peeling off the exterior in strips. She owned a couple acres of land where she grew fruit and lavender and had two coops for a dozen chickens. She lived in pleasant solitude, a dream since she quit nannying to escape the everyday anxiety of LA, but it never quite lived up to the picture in her head.

Every Tuesday, she drove into the quaint, rustic town tucked snugly in the valley for the weekly farmers market. She would lay out her produce and handmade lavender soaps neatly and watch wealthy tourists examine them with the scrutiny of the most discerning TSA agent. They never bought enough (or anything) to justify her hours of work, yet she thanked them all for their patronage.

Lydia had mellowed with age and distance. Her perpetually pursed lips now slackened with easy smiles. She brushed off snubs from the tourists with no skin off her back. When Lila had known her, she was on permanent alert. Always ready to rush to someone's aid, even when they hadn't asked. It was why Lila had hired Lydia when she was in the deepest pit of postpartum. It was how Lydia had failed her in the end. It was a shame she had opened her mouth and ruined it. But this self-imposed banishment had done Lydia good.

After collecting her meager winnings at the farmers market and receiving a lecture from some blonde about putting soy in her candles, Lydia went to a happy hour at the local watering hole and nursed a beer. She brought a book but looked eager for someone to interrupt. People were friendly, but no one took the time to make conversation.

A couple hours passed before she admitted defeat, jumping in her puttering old truck to drive home. Lila was waiting in the junk van at the end of her drive as the sun set. Once it was dark, she would break into Lydia's house through the screen door on her rotting back porch. People were far more relaxed about security in the country. It seemed strange that Lydia didn't take more precautions, given what she had witnessed eleven years ago. Maybe she thought she was above it. No one was above anything.

After tailing her for a couple of days, Lila didn't think Lydia would be too much trouble. Her nearest neighbors were miles away in much bigger, nicer farms. Lydia was thin, and her body was soft. There would be no fight.

Lila was struck by the blanket of silence that fell over the hills as the sun set. She could never live up here; the quiet made her want to crawl out of her skin. Some people mistook it as peaceful, but Lila knew better. It was the world lying in wait.

Before the sky darkened, the mountains were washed with a soft rose color. It rolled across the sky like watercolors hitting a blank canvas. The townspeople called it "the pink moment." A fraction of a moment when the sun hit the earth exactly right and created something wonderful.

Lila made a note in her phone—it was a good name for a lip gloss. Maybe they'd expand into makeup. She'd float it to Maya.

Before she abandons you. Lila grit her teeth. She couldn't think about Maya right now. This was her self-care time, she deserved to enjoy the break without Maya infecting her thoughts. When Lila looked up at the sky again, the pink moment was already over.

Lila sat still as dusk settled and the mountains turned into hulking shadows, and she sat as the lights turned on in Lydia's house. Lydia cooked pasta by herself and ate it in slow, lonely bites. For a second, Lila felt pity, and then her mouth filled with bile, and she spat the pity out. Lydia had made a choice to talk to the cops, talk to the press, talk to the oral history journalists.

It was dark enough. Lila got out of the car and walked down the dirt road leading to the house. There was a four-foot white fence that ran around the perimeter of the property—a decoration more than anything. It certainly wasn't keeping anything out. Oak trees shrouded the house, towering sentinels. As she neared, Lila could hear the soft clucks of the chickens in their hutch. Through the window, Lydia was washing her plate in the sink.

She didn't have kids of her own. When she died, no one would notice she was gone. Maybe that was why she had fixated on Lila and Josie, why she'd alerted the police and ruined Josie's exchange. She'd become unable to separate them from her actual family. Or maybe she was just a loudmouthed bitch who thought she knew better than everyone.

Lila felt the nylon secured to her waist. Strangulation was cleaner, but she'd brought her handgun as a fail-safe. She crept around the border of the house to face the screen door. Lydia had even propped it open because of the heat. She was less than twenty yards away when a branch snapped.

Lila spun around, but no one was there. She steadied herself. Rural farmland meant animals everywhere. There was no one around for miles, and Lydia lived alone. Maya's impending departure was knocking her off course. She returned her focus on the house.

A low growl echoed from her left. The hair on Lila's neck stood erect. She turned slowly to see a giant, fluffy Labrador, its eggshell-colored coat glowing in the darkness. It was at least 120 pounds—on its hind legs, it was easily as tall as she was. Its porcelain teeth were bared and gleaming in the twilight.

Lydia had a fucking guard dog? Lila laughed a little. She wasn't as dumb as Lila had thought. Still dumb, of course, because a fucking Labrador wasn't going to do shit once it realized she was friendly.

Lila slowly bent to her knees and turned to her side, sticking out a hand for the dog to sniff, careful not to make direct eye contact. It did nothing to soothe it. The dog's hackles went straight up, and it let out a loud, ringing bark.

Lila cast a furtive glance to the house, but Lydia didn't come outside. She took a step back toward the henhouse, and the dog licked its black lips, starting toward her.

Black lips—a memory coasted through her. Her mom's friend had lived out on a farm in Western Mass. that she used to visit as a kid. They had a dog like this one, but it wasn't a Labrador. It was a Great Pyrenees. The Devlins couldn't have a dog in their apartment, so she cherished those visits. He was nocturnal and slept outside to patrol the farm and guard the livestock. They were bred to defend farms against bears.

"Fuck me," Lila whispered, and the dog charged.

She sprinted into the dark woods behind the house, ducking for cover in the oak trees. The dog was right behind her; she could hear its wet, eager pants just at her heels. She crouched under a low-hanging branch, gnarled a few feet above the ground. She'd hoped it would slow the dog's trail, but it soared right over.

And it was gaining on her, running with all four feet lifting in the air. Lila had nowhere to go. Her car was around the perimeter, and she'd have to get past the dog. Up ahead, there was a tree with branches low enough to climb.

She pressed on, seizing the lowest branch and hoisting herself upward. There was no room for thought; her mind was fixated on one bright, blinking word: *LIVE*. She gripped the knotted trunk and threw herself up higher, six feet and climbing.

In a giant leap, the dog grabbed on to her foot. Lila tried to shake it off, but it dragged her to the ground. She didn't even have time to scream as she landed on her back, the wind completely knocked out of her.

She knew she was going to die. She wondered if Josie had known she was dying in her last moments. *Could she have known, so young?*

There was blood on the dog's muzzle, Lila thought dully as it pinned her to the ground. *Oh, it's mine.* It bit her in the gut, and she screamed.

Her hands flailed beside her, brushing against her waist. *The gun.* She still had the gun. Using all her strength, she wrenched it free, and as the dog bent to bite her again, she pressed the barrel to its head and fired.

It let out a startled yelp and swayed backward. Lila fired again until it fell in a heap on top of her, still.

She inhaled a short, sharp breath. The dog's enormous body pressed down on her windpipe, smothering her with its coat. With all her strength, she shoved it off her and rolled to the side, collecting her breath. She used the tree trunk to hoist herself to her feet and looked down at the Great Pyr's body. Its head was completely blown apart, its beautiful coat drenched in maroon blood.

She'd wanted to be a veterinarian once.

Tears spilled from Lila's eyes, and she wiped them away. *Get a hold of yourself.* She'd seen plenty of dead things. She pushed herself off the tree and started toward Lydia's house. Her stomach felt funny, and her left foot dragged a little, but she didn't dare stop. She needed to get this done.

As she neared the edge of the woods, she heard the screen door slam.

"Philip? *Philip?*" Lydia emerged from the house with a shotgun.

Lila ducked behind a tree, pressing herself against the bark, willing her body to fade inside.

Lydia approached the tree line, gun raised. "PHIL—" She let out an awful, garbled sob. She'd seen the body. "No no no no no."

Lila peered out from her hiding place to see Lydia on the ground beside the dead dog. And then she screamed. Lila knew that sound. Pure and total agony. It was the only way to release the grief when it consumed you. *Now she knew how it felt.*

With Lydia's back turned, Lila took a step toward her. But the pain in her stomach was so brutal she nearly doubled over. Lydia turned suddenly, eyes darting around the grove. Lila slid back behind the tree at the sudden movement, but Lydia had seen her. She raised the shotgun and fired lightning fast. "I know you're out there!" she screamed. She reloaded and fired again. It nicked the trunk just above Lila.

Lydia reloaded and started toward her. Lila crept to the safety of the next tree and then the next, her only shield.

"You killed my fucking dog! You're dead, you're fucking dead!"

Lila raised her gun and fired back at her. It wasn't even close. Her hands were shaking too badly to aim properly. Her only option was to run back to the van. She almost giggled, clutching her abdomen. The world had tilted on its side, and they had switched places. A dog had taken a bite out of her stomach, and Lydia Novak was hunting her with a shotgun.

And she was a pretty good shot.

Lila reached the end of the tree line. It was a straight two-hundred-yard stretch down the road to her van. Lydia was swiftly approaching, any trepidation about her dog's death cloaked in pure blind rage. Lila knew she wouldn't stop until she was dead.

She emerged from the safety of the oak tree and ran as fast as she could in sharp zigzagging turns. Every inch of her body was screaming in pain. She felt a piercing pain in her shoulder—the bitch had nicked her. But she kept going. She wasn't going to give Lydia the satisfaction of dying.

She heard the gun click, then click again. Lydia was out of bullets. Lila glanced back as she reached the van. Lydia threw the gun on the ground, running toward her. "I'LL FIND YOU!" she screamed. Lila could hear the blood buzzing in her ears.

Lila yanked the door open and hoisted herself inside. She grabbed the steering wheel with two hands. They looked nearly blue under all the blood. She slammed her foot on the gas pedal and reversed. Lydia Novak fell to her knees in the mud, face streaked with dirt and tears, and wordlessly watched her go.

THERE WAS A LONG SILENCE AS SHE DROVE.

"Do you have something you want to say to me?" Lila finally asked Aidan, who sat pensively in the seat beside her.

He was silent. He had been silent since they left the house, since the paparazzi chased them through Bel Air, all the way to the car exchange in North Hollywood. Now they would reach the 7-Eleven in five minutes to get their child back, and he wouldn't even look her in the eye. He shook his head, running his hands through his hair.

"Aidan," Lila said, though she didn't turn her gaze from the dashboard. "Aidan, please."

"I didn't want to do this," he said quietly, staring at his hands in his lap.

The light in front of them turned red. Lila sped through it without hesitation. "We didn't have a choice."

Aidan just shook his head and stared out the window. She was losing him. "We did. And you made that choice for both of us. And if you're wrong . . ."

"Aidan."

"If you're wrong, our daughter is dead. If she's . . ." He stopped.

Lila's hands were clammy against the wheel. "If she's *what*?"

"Never mind," Aidan said.

"If she's not already?" Lila hissed. Aidan looked away, ashamed of even considering it. Tears gathered in Lila's eyes, but she willed them back. She could not break down, there was too much at stake. They were almost there. Josie needed her to be calm.

"We need the police on our side. They're turning against us," Aidan said.

"They're worthless," Lila said. "It doesn't matter anyway. We'll make the trade-off, and we'll get Josie back, and then all of this will go away. Can you just trust me?"

She took her right hand off the wheel and held it out over the center console, waiting for Aidan to take her hand. After a few seconds, she felt his hand slide into hers, but he did not reply.

And Lila had the terrible feeling that even if this worked, even if they got Josie back, even if Aidan held her hand, it would never be the same between them again.

The 7-Eleven lot was empty when Lila pulled in. Where were the police? There were no unmarked cars, and no cop was that good at hiding. The clock on the dashboard read 9:52 p.m. What? She had missed it—how had she missed it? The drop-off was at 5:00 a.m., which was nearly seventeen hours ago, how did . . .

She heard a faint voice calling her name, and then everything went black.

LILA STOOD BEFORE A DOOR. SHE COULD HEAR A MAN AND A WOMAN ON the other side. She twisted the handle, and it swung open. She was in her childhood duplex in Chelsea. Sitting on a blue couch beside a fire was her mom and dad. He was smoking a cigar, and she was reading a soap magazine, mindlessly scratching the ears of the Great Pyrenees Lila had just shot. They looked up at her pleasantly when she entered.

"Am I dead?" Lila asked.

"Yes," said Denise.

"Oh," Lila said. "Okay."

Denise scooted over on the couch, and Lila sat down beside her. It had been thirty years since she had seen her. Lila realized Denise was younger than her, frozen at thirty-five. Maybe it was in her DNA to die young.

Her dad looked healthy. Not the gaunt shadow of himself that dominated her memory of him. The dog even wagged its tail, nuzzling her hand. Lila ran a hand through its soft fur. "I told you," he said.

"What?" Lila asked.

"The shadow found you. It always does," Mark said.

Before Lila could reply, she noticed someone missing from this picture. "Where's Josie?" Lila stood up.

Denise and Mark looked at her, confused. "What?" Mark said.

"If I'm dead, where's Josie?" Lila looked around the living room. The dog cocked its head. "Why isn't she here?"

The door opened then, and in strolled Nico, or what used to be Nico. His skin was shriveled and rotting, his eyes glassed over. His mouth stretched across his entire face, a giant black hole aiming straight for her. Coming to swallow her whole. Lila backed up against the wall.

Then came Carmichael, the limbs she had dismembered crudely sewn back on. And then Greer Houser with her Hogwarts cookbook. And then Cara Donaldson and Tommy Olsen and Arthur Allen, an endless parade. Their souls long gone now. They stared vacantly right through her. They formed a circle around Lila as they inched closer, their gaping mouths ready to devour her.

LILA'S EYES SNAPPED OPEN. SHE WAS BACK IN HER DISPLAY-CASE HOUSE, snugly tucked in her California king. She was struck with relief and terror of being alive. She couldn't feel anything, but she knew she was in pain.

"Whoa, whoa, easy, girl," Sylvie cooed like she was calming a spooked horse. She had pulled up a chair beside the bed.

"How did I . . ." Lila's throat was dry. Sylvie sensed it and lifted a glass to her lips. She drank greedily until the glass was empty.

"You texted me to meet you at a 7-Eleven in Moorpark. I'm shocked you even made it. You lost a lot of blood," Sylvie said. Panic drowned Lila, but before she could speak, Sylvie cut her off. "No hospital, don't worry. It took me a half hour, but I made it in time. I had my concierge doctor come and fix you up. You got away with some stitches, but you're lucky. It was like *this close* to your liver."

Lila lifted her hand and felt for the bite on her stomach. It was tightly bandaged with multiple layers, but there was a distinct groove where her flesh had been. The dog had even nicked the grey thing too; she could feel it licking its wounds. There was a crater in her gut. "My foot?"

"It's fractured. You'll be on bed rest for a month or so," Sylvie said. "Here, I brought you a fresh pillow."

"But work . . ."

"I sent an email out to let them know you were on leave with a chronic Lyme flare-up."

Lila felt a flame in her stomach. She tore her eyes away from Sylvie's gaze. "Lydia Novak's dog bit me," she said. "I ran, but she's still alive."

Sylvie crossed her arms, then flipped them and crossed them again. "You went without me?"

There was a loose thread on the edge of the duvet. Lila twisted it with her index finger and pulled until it snapped. "I was taking care of it myself."

Sylvie's eyes looked so dark Lila couldn't see her pupils. Just two glittering pools of black. "Seems like that didn't work out so good."

Lila squeezed her eyes shut; she couldn't handle looking at her anymore. She waited for the storm, for Sylvie's righteous anger at being left behind. How arrogant she had been in going. But instead, Lila only heard a small "Are you still mad at me?"

Lila opened her eyes to see Sylvie with her hands on her knees, searching her face anxiously.

"Lila, if something had happened to you. I don't know what I would have done with myself. It would have destroyed me."

Lila looked down at her hands. "I don't understand. After the last time—after everything I said—I don't understand why you'd still come."

Sylvie let out a confused laugh. "I love you; of course I'd come. I'll always come."

This wasn't fair, to string her along. Lila sighed. "But, Sylvie, I don't—"

Sylvie reached out and put a finger to her lips. "I know. I'm not expecting you to say it back. I can wait for you to love me. I'll be here when you realize that you do. But when you were dying, you called *me*. You need me as much as I need you."

Lila wanted to tell Sylvie that she shouldn't wait around. That she didn't understand what inspired Sylvie's unwavering loyalty to her. That she wasn't remarkable like Sylvie and hadn't earned that ferocity of devotion. Maybe the hole in her abdomen had made her soft. But before Lila could respond, sleep overtook her again. Her eyes closed as Sylvie stroked her hair with a warm palm.

"I'm going to take good care of you."

Twenty-Five

It took four weeks before Lila could take a step without wincing. She was confined to her bedroom while Sylvie played nurse and warden outside the door. She slept fitfully during the day, weak and embittered from the bouts of insomnia that plagued her at night. She did not dream, had not dreamed since the night she'd seen her parents. Often, she'd wake to find herself frozen and unable to move, forced to wait until sleep claimed her again.

Slowly, the gap in her stomach healed, and the lacerations turned to scars, which, along with the bruises, faded into traces.

It was difficult to admit at first, but she'd missed Sylvie. Missed her weird outfits and her keen mind and her unflappable presence. Sylvie had saved her life, even after everything she'd said. Sylvie was selfless in a way most people never dreamed of being. They weren't back to the way they had been before their fight the night they killed Sylvie's ex-girlfriend, but they were able to enjoy each other's company.

Just not sexually.

They bonded slowly—first, about whatever crap movie Lila was watching, and then about how she was feeling, and then about how Sylvie was feeling, and then Lila was confiding in her all the fear and anger and pain she'd stifled over the last few months.

"Maya gave notice. She's moving to New York so her boyfriend can attend clown school," Lila sobbed.

Sylvie squeezed her hand. Lila let Sylvie squeeze her hand. "There are plenty of other assistants out there."

"You don't understand." Lila turned around to face her. "I need her."

Sylvie nodded. For all her faults, she was a good listener. "Then we won't let her go."

A MONTH AFTER HER ATTACK, LILA RETURNED TO THE OFFICE. SHE WAS greeted in the lobby by swarms of admirers. Growing up in New England, she'd thought Lyme disease was a one-time thing, but it was apparently a stealthy affliction almost exclusively gripping rich white women. Maya was the only person not smiling. Lila hadn't seen her since she'd announced her leave and had missed her dearly. So much precious time had slipped by, and they had only a month left.

Maya met Lila in the bullpen, far in front of her office. "A detective is waiting by your office. I tried to get him to come back another time, but he knows you're here."

Lila hurried past her to see Fox waiting patiently outside her office. He caught her eye and grinned that giant, corny grin. The LAPD's finest. It had taken him over a year to show up, but better late than never.

Lila strolled over and shook his hand. "Detective Fox. I hope you weren't waiting too long."

Fox shook his head. "Nothing I'm not used to."

Lila led him into her office. His leather shoes tracked dirt on the rug. "Can I have my assistant get you anything? Water, coffee?"

"No thanks." Fox waved her off, making himself comfortable in the chair across from her desk. "I'm glad I finally got a hold of you. I've been trying for a couple weeks, but I was told you had Lyme disease. Didn't know there were many ticks in Southern California."

"It's chronic," Lila said. "I got it in the Hamptons years ago. When it flares, I get very ill."

The smile returned, like this was an inside joke they shared. "That's too bad. You'd never know from looking at you."

And he was looking at her, up and down, delighting in making her squirm. She refused to take the bait; he was on her territory, and she would not let him have the satisfaction of her discomfort.

"That's the most difficult part of invisible illnesses," Lila said. "So, what can I do for you? Do you have any updates on Josie?"

Fox's smile wavered a little, which she appreciated. He could go on a wild-goose chase all he wanted, but she would never stop reminding him that he'd failed at the most important job he'd ever had.

"Unfortunately, not today," Fox said, fidgeting with his notepad. "Ms. Devlin, are you aware that an oral history detailing your daughter's abduction was released last year?"

He had nothing. Even if he managed to link the disappearances, nothing was tying her to them, especially not without the bodies.

Lila folded her hands together. "Of course. It's difficult to miss," she said. "I even heard you were a part of it."

"I gave an interview about my thoughts on the case," Fox replied, nodding.

Lila wanted to reach across the desk and rip that smile off his face. The only thing keeping him alive was the number of red flags that would be raised if he was gone. He didn't realize how lucky he was. She couldn't believe she had ever tried to forgive him, that he'd deserved forgiveness.

"Are you here to apologize?" Lila asked.

Fox could barely contain his annoyance, shifting in his chair. "There's been a series of disappearances over the last year—Nico DeLuca, Greer Houser, John Carmichael, Cara Donaldson, Tommy Olsen. All of them quoted in the oral history. Lydia Novak suffered a home invasion last month that may also be connected."

He didn't know about Arthur. Carmichael had been the only one who'd found him. Lila watched his eyes scan her face for any sign of recognition. "That's horrible," Lila said, face blank. "Is Lydia all right?"

"She's fine. You two don't talk?" Fox asked. She hated the way he watched her, like he was enjoying this.

"I don't tend to respect the kind of person who'd talk about my personal life in an oral history," Lila said. "Are you saying someone is stalking and killing those involved in the case? Should I be worried?"

Fox nodded. "Probably a safe bet to watch your back. My guys talked to you about Nico, didn't they? You two met the day he disappeared?"

"That afternoon, yes," Lila said. "But 'your guys' dismissed me because he was out that night."

"It's just your luck to be tied up in a missing person case for the second time," Fox said, holding eye contact.

She was losing control. Lila changed the subject. "Have you been keeping tabs on Arthur Allen?"

Fox cleared his throat, crossed his legs. "We're in the process of—"

"You let him get away once. Maybe he's behind the disappearances. Maybe he's mad that this is all getting dredged up again. Should I be worried for my safety?" Lila's voice wobbled.

Fox's jaw tightened, sending a thrill of pleasure up Lila's spine. She gorged herself on his frustration. "Arthur Allen is not a threat."

"He stalked me," Lila said. "Just because you couldn't make an arrest doesn't mean he was innocent."

"If I were you, I'd be more concerned about myself than Arthur Allen."

"I'll be sure to tell my lawyer."

He was just a bully. He could only attempt to intimidate her into a confession because he wasn't smart enough to get one any other way.

"If you're truly worried about an attack, I'm sure we could arrange some kind of LAPD protection."

"Well, you did a hell of a job the last time."

Fox scowled, deciding he'd asked enough questions. Lila led him back out into the larger glob office. The underlings tried not to stare.

"If there's anything else you need, you know how to find me," Lila said.

Fox nodded, studying the walls of glob, smirking at the neon "Manifestation Works!" sign.

Lila wanted to shake him. Couldn't he *see*? Manifestation *did* work. He had believed she was a killer with every ounce of his will, and she'd become one. He'd made his own mental vision board, decorated it in glitter, glued "BLUE LIVES MATTER" patches and a detective's badge and Lila's mug shot. She wanted to grab his face and scream, *YOU MANIFESTED THIS!*

Instead, she bid him a polite goodbye and ensured the receptionist validated his parking. She should frankly be grateful to him. This gave her a perfect excuse to contact Aidan, one that he couldn't ignore.

"Everything all right?" Maya asked when Lila returned to her desk.

Lila smiled at her worried brown eyes and nodded. Fox's attack had made her realize how fragile, how tenuous, everything was. She could waste her time being angry at Maya for leaving, or she could trust that Maya would find her way back. "Can you join me for a coffee?"

They went to the tiny café in the basement of their building. Venturing out to a coffee shop always carried the risk of getting recognized, and then the whole excursion would be wasted. It reminded Lila of the summers when she would meet her mother in the hospital cafeteria, when she got the rare break on a nursing shift. The coffee was burned and the pastries were cardboard, but that time was sacred to her.

She bought Maya her favorite mint tea and sat down beside her.

"I owe you an apology," Lila said.

Maya shook her head. "No, Lila, I sprung that on you—"

Lila held up a hand. "I just didn't want to lose you. You know how much I appreciate your work, but you have every right to pursue your dream. I hope you find exactly what you're looking for."

Maya smiled, tears welling up in her eyes. "That means a lot."

"My . . . Lyme flare put a lot into perspective. Just know I'm always here for whatever you need," Lila said. "Have you heard back from schools?"

Maya shook her head. "Not yet!"

Lila could swear she saw apprehension in her eyes. "Are you getting excited to move?"

Maya took a sip of tea. "Well, yes! Of course! It's just . . ."

Lila gave her an encouraging nod.

"Can you be honest with me, Lila? Like, truly honest?" Maya asked.

"Of course," Lila said.

"I don't feel like I have any idea what the fuck I'm doing with my life. And, I don't know, it's probably cold feet, but am I making a mistake moving cross-country? Am I gonna wake up in a couple months and be like, 'Why the fuck did I give up a job thousands of people would kill for?' If my friend told me she was doing this, I would tell her she was insane." Maya put her head in her hands. "I'd convinced myself that beauty wasn't, I don't know, *righteous* enough. But if this industry is so fucked, shouldn't I be trying to change it from the inside?"

Lila's heart swelled three times its size. She hadn't dared wish for this moment for fear of jinxing it, but she knew if she bided her time, it would come. Maya could stray for a while, but she always knew where she belonged.

She had to be gentle. Featherlight, like when Denise had told her she had cancer. "I'm sorry, that sounds stressful," Lila said. "But it's not my place to make that decision for you."

"No, I know." Maya sighed. "I tried to talk to my mom about it. She was so relieved that I'd come to my senses, and the fact that I even brought it up was horrifying to her. And it's not like I don't get it. I hate a lot of this industry too. But am I just running away? Shouldn't I try to fight back?"

Maya's mother was a moron. Lila was the only person who understood her. She saw herself, after her first movie came out, trapped between the acting career she'd stumbled upon and the split second when she could still return to a normal life. It had taken Lila a long time to understand, but she'd made the right decision. To become an actress, to not turn back. She was meant for far bigger things than Massachusetts could offer. So was Maya.

Lila drummed her fingers on the table, pretending to formulate an answer that had already appeared in blinking letters in her head. "First of all—either way, you will be fine. They're both great opportunities. What I pose to you is: Why did you think beauty wasn't good enough? Did that come from you, or were you comparing yourself to other people's expectations?"

Lila didn't have to mention Maya's parents to know where her mind went.

"I don't know what's me and what's my anxiety trying to torture me." She rubbed her eyes. "I'm sorry, this is a lot."

"Don't ever apologize to me for that," Lila said. "Remember, you're not committing to anything in perpetuity. You could try out New York for a little while and come back if you hate it. You could work here and look into different classes in LA."

Maya brightened at that idea, but then her face fell. "I couldn't do that to Peter now. I pushed him into moving in the first place."

Quel surprise, Peter had reared his giant blond head once again. It was unacceptable that she was so devoted to him, so scared of upsetting him. Lila could see him being domineering in his own soft-spoken way.

"Does he make you happy, Maya?"

"What?" Maya said.

"Does Peter make you happy?"

Maya laughed a little in confusion. For a second, Lila thought she'd come to a shattering realization, that someone had just needed to ask her point-blank and it would occur to her that it was just infatuation, and Peter was just some guy. But her eyes softened, and a faint smile played on her lips. "I didn't always—I didn't always think that I was the type of person meant to be happy. But then I met Peter. He makes me happier than anything."

Lila pushed her features into a supportive smile. She wanted to scream. "I'm so happy for you. You know, you could always do long distance. You're not married," Lila said.

But Maya wasn't acting like the liberated Gen Z feminist Lila knew her to be. Her expression was reluctant, distant. "I want to give it a chance. He was going to do it for me."

Lila knew she wouldn't change her mind. Maya cared about Peter and keeping everyone happy and her own sense of right and wrong too much. That was why, somewhere deep in her subconscious mind, she'd come to Lila. She was trapped and couldn't see the forest for the trees; Lila would save her the way only Lila could.

Peter had to die.

TWENTY-SIX

Every time Peter stepped outside the rent-controlled two-bedroom in Silver Lake he shared with his roommate, he saw someone he knew. Without fail. He made a point of stopping to chat with whoever was walking their dog, or parking their car, or getting their mail. Like a Disney princess, all he had to do was open his front door to be greeted with a chorus of hellos.

Every day, he drove to the office building in Glendale that served as the headquarters for Prestigious Parties Inc. He dressed in a top hat and cape, joining his pirate and princess costume–donning co-workers to the day's parties. When he returned home, it was usually after dark. His roommate worked late shifts at Whole Foods to support their fledgling music career, so Peter was usually on his own. He made grocery runs for his elderly neighbor and fed the resident feral cats. If he wasn't seeing Maya or friends, he would grab his skateboard and cruise the length of the reservoir.

At just past ten p.m., Lila and Sylvie parked at the base of the hill-side that ran along Silver Lake Reservoir. Peter would ride right into their path in a matter of minutes.

"I feel like I'm about to abduct a child," Sylvie muttered.

Peter wore his mask so well that he'd even won Sylvie over, but Lila knew better. He presented as good-natured and dim, so people couldn't reconcile him as anything else. Arthur Allen had done the same thing, cloaked himself in unassumingness, and the cops hadn't realized their mistake until it was too late.

Why him? What did he do? Sylvie had asked when Lila invited her to help.

He's manipulating Maya, Lila said. *We need to protect her.*

He's a magician that goes to clown school. He can't manipulate anyone.

Lila was growing frustrated at Sylvie's obstinance. Did she think Lila wanted to go out of her way to chase this kid? It was a last resort to protect the only family she had. Peter was dangerous. For a flicker of a second, she felt a warm hand on her shoulder and her muscles relaxed. *Josie.* Josie was still looking out for her.

Sylvie had agreed to help, Lila reminded herself. She wouldn't have come if she didn't care. Their relationship was fragile and tenuous, and she did not want to let Lila down just after they'd gotten back on their feet. *You need me as much as I need you.* And after a month without her, Lila didn't want to be apart from her again. They were bonded for the rest of their lives. Even if she had Aidan, she would always cherish Sylvie as her dearest friend. Maybe the only real friend she had ever had.

Peter came barreling down the sidewalk on his skateboard, ripping Lila from her thoughts. He'd completed his loop and was about to head home. "Get the door," Lila told Sylvie. She readied to take her foot off the brake pedal.

Peter looked both ways and started to cross the street. Lila jammed her foot on the gas pedal and aimed to go right through him. For a split second, his gaze met hers and Lila saw the white deer staring back, and she squeezed her eyes shut and braced for impact.

He vanished so quickly that it was like a still frame had been flipped. They felt the crunch of his body under the van, and Sylvie yelped. Lila slammed down on the brakes, and Sylvie grabbed the door handle to steady herself. She looked ill. "Come on." Lila swatted her shoulder, leaping out of the van. "Let's go!"

Peter's body lay in a crumpled heap in the center of the road, unconscious. His fine hair was matted in black gravel. His left leg stuck out underneath him in the wrong direction. "Get his legs," Lila instructed Sylvie. The fresh gash on Peter's forehead dripped blood on her hands. He was the tallest victim they had had to carry; his tangle of limp limbs was like sandbags.

For a second, she looked down at his eyelashes. They were black—unusual with hair so blond. Lila was reminded of the day she'd met him on the plane. It felt like a lifetime ago. He had been reading Joan Didion. He'd been kind to her, she remembered. Lila studied his face. Poreless, smooth. Like porcelain. Had she ever realized how young he was? She wished he would have just left her alone. Everything would have been fine if he'd left her alone.

"Shit, shit—*car!*" Sylvie shrieked, and Lila turned to see headlights in the far distance. Lila snapped back to attention and threw the back doors of the van open. "We gotta move!"

Lila and Sylvie swung Peter's body back and forth, using the momentum to hoist him into the back of the van. He flew through the air, slamming against the rear wall and sliding to the floor. Lila and Sylvie hopped in behind him and shut the door.

Like their hearts were beating in sync, Lila and Sylvie let out a deep exhale. Then Sylvie burst out laughing. Lila grinned at her, giddy with relief. They were safe. They were safe and alive and together; they were impenetrable. Peter lay still on the floor beneath them. Lila was excited to try his collagen—his hair and nails were notably excellent. Beaming with excitement, Lila cupped Sylvie's face in her hand and brought her lips to hers.

"*Lila?*" a groggy voice spoke behind her.

Lila's heart stopped, and she turned to see Peter blinking up at her. He was battered but perfectly conscious. *Like fucking Rasputin.*

"Did you . . . did you run me over?" Peter whispered.

"I did." Sylvie twitched beside her, and Lila put a hand on her knee to stop. She didn't need Sylvie to fight her battles for her.

"Why?" He was so weak he could barely get the word out. It was difficult to make out Peter's magnificent bone structure under the bruises and lacerations. He wasn't much without the good looks he hid behind.

"I can't watch you throw a girl's life away," Lila said, and drove her boot into his stomach.

Peter cried out and curled into himself. It was infantile; he looked like a baby shrimp. "Maya?"

Of course she meant Maya, who the fuck else would she be talking about? Had Peter done this to so many young women that he couldn't keep track? "I know who you are." Lila squatted down to his eye level. His left lid was half closed over his iris.

Peter wobbled around on the floor, coughing blood up in spurts. "I don't understand," he sputtered. He was going to play this little victim game to the grave. "I would never hurt Maya; I love her."

Lila backhanded him across the face so hard it shook the van. He didn't know what love was. Love was knowing what was best for the other person and stepping back to let them flourish, not spiriting them away so you could have a chaperone to goddamn clown school. Peter only crossed his arms over his face in a lame attempt to protect himself. Lila grunted and kicked him in the balls. Peter howled in agony but did not even try to push her away.

"Get up," Lila said.

Peter squeezed his eyes shut, tears spurting down his dimpled cheeks. "Kill me, fine, just please don't hurt Maya."

"*Maya?*" Lila roared. He thought *Lila* dangerous? She'd let the world burn before she touched a hair on Maya's head.

"Please don't hurt her," he sobbed. Ugly, chest-racking sobs.

Lila was infuriated. She grabbed him by his precious golden hair and bashed his head into the wall again and again, until she could see dents forming in his skull. "I'm trying to protect her *from you*! I won't let you take her away from me again!"

And then he was still.

Lila's hands were covered in wet. Blood or brains or a mixture of the two was all over her arms and face like a thick tomato sauce. When she looked down at the violet mess where Peter's head used to be, she couldn't find his eyes. For a moment, Lila thought the earth was quaking beneath her. But when she looked down, she saw her legs shaking so badly she could barely stand.

She collapsed to the floor beside Peter's body, chest heaving, limbs jittering so much it felt like a convulsion. Still, through all of it she smiled. For all the talk she did about inner beauty and self-worth, she still struggled to believe it herself. It was easy enough to encourage other people but impossible to practice on her own. But now? She felt powerful, predatory, a protector of her kin. In this moment, as she stared down at Peter's blood specked across her arms, she felt truly *beautiful*.

She'd done it.

She'd brought Maya home.

"I WANT TO GO HOME," MAYA SOBBED INTO LILA'S CHEST. "I WANT TO BE with my family, but I don't want to leave Peter alone."

The missing person report had been filed three days ago, and Maya was inconsolable. She forced herself to come to work to keep busy, but she was hardly getting anything done by excusing herself to cry in the bathroom every thirty minutes.

That was unfair, Lila chided herself. Maya had every right to mourn him, just as Lila had mourned Josie. Maya deserved to take the time she needed, and then they would rebuild. If Peter had loved her as much as he claimed to, he would want her to enjoy her life—not live according to an effigy to him in her head.

Lila held Maya close to her chest, stroking her thick, silky hair. "It's gonna be okay," Lila whispered.

"We don't know that," Maya said, then paled. "What if it was a hit and run and he's dying somewhere in a ditch waiting for me to find him?"

Maya's nails were covered in dry blood. The anxiety had caused her to pick too. Lila felt like she was watching herself from eleven years ago. She'd wanted to be a mentor to Maya; this was a subject she knew better than anyone. She thought about what wisdom she could impart to Maya that she could have used back then.

"It doesn't do you any good to spiral," Lila said gently. "Going through every scenario in your mind will only drive you crazy. And Peter needs you calm right now."

Maya sniffled and slowly nodded. "I was supposed to see him Tuesday night, he was gonna come over. I should have made him come early. I should have been with him . . ."

They were tied together now, admitted to the cruel, miserable club of people who had lost the person they loved most in the world. If Maya didn't understand how special their bond was before, she would see it now.

"I keep thinking that the universe was listening when I doubted the move to New York. And it's *punishing* me." Her breath came fast and shallow. She desperately tried to keep up, but the air was squeezed out of her lungs before she could reach it. "I can't . . . I can't *breathe*."

"You're okay. You're just having a panic attack," Lila said calmly. "Breathe with me now, slowly."

But Maya couldn't. Her face was bright red, the dam of tears broken and gushing. Lila dropped to her knees beside her, took Maya's hand, and put it over her heart. Maya blinked at her, confused, and Lila squeezed her hand over Maya's. "Feel my heartbeat. Breathe in and out with me."

In and out, in and out. Lila watched as Maya's face slowly relaxed and her eyes fluttered shut. That was how she'd calmed Josie during crying fits—all children were soothed by their mother's heartbeat.

"You need to ground yourself," Lila said. "Find four things you can see and three things you can touch."

Maya pulled her hand away, but Lila could still feel her handprint on her heart. Maya looked around the room, counting to herself, and the panic subsided. She wiped her eyes. "I'm sorry, my brain's going haywire. I haven't slept."

"You still have my spare keys for deliveries?" Lila asked.

Maya nodded, absent-mindedly twisting a little ring on her pointer finger.

"I have a guest room. If you're worried or nervous by yourself, you're welcome to stay with me," Lila said.

"That's so kind Lila, but I don't want to intrude—"

"Come any time. I will always be here for you." Maya would be safer under the same roof.

"Thank you." Maya sniffled, her brown eyes glistening with tears. She was so pretty when she cried.

"You're going to be fine," Lila said.

"How do you know that?" Maya asked.

"Because I am."

TWENTY-SEVEN

"Detective Fox told me people connected to Josie's death are disappearing. I'm terrified Arthur Allen is back. I need to see you."

Aidan was a coward, but he wasn't heartless. He'd just needed an extra nudge in the right direction. After five months of ignored calls, he replied to her text within ten minutes, champing at the bit to be the hero.

They agreed to meet at Lila's house—they needed somewhere private, and Aidan felt uncomfortable inviting Lila into his home while Sonnet was traveling on a shoot. *So concerned about Sonnet's feelings when Sonnet hadn't thought twice about launching herself at another woman's husband.*

Lila had Maya now, tucked snugly under her wing. She had been gifted a chance to have a family again. She thought back to when she was twenty-six and pregnant and terrified, and Aidan had to shoot a movie in Bumfuck, Romania. Or when Aidan couldn't handle a single sleepless night by himself when Lila had postpartum, so he'd brought in Lydia to take care of Josie instead.

All of that was forgiven now.

This was the missing piece of the puzzle, why she'd struggled when she'd first come to LA. She was trying to force-feed forgiveness before she was ready. She'd been attempting to forgive the wrong people. Now, she welcomed Aidan with open arms because she'd let all that resentment and hurt go, all that ugliness.

The shimmering path she had seen when she'd killed Arthur Allen ended here. Her family was nearly whole again, she just needed the last missing piece. For a moment, she thought of Sylvie. She had to know that Lila would choose Aidan before her every time. The part of her that was tethered to Sylvie wept. The idea of losing her was frightening, this person who shared a piece of her soul. But Aidan was her home. He'd been her North Star for over fifteen years. Sylvie would understand.

And Lila wasn't going to walk away from her. Sylvie would be heartbroken for a little while, but she'd move on. She deserved someone as hyperfixated on her as she was on them. Eventually, when Sylvie found them, the two couples would look back on this and laugh.

"I have to pick Talia up from school," Aidan said when Lila greeted him at her front door. "So, I can't stay super long."

It touched her to see him be a hands-on parent. Making up for lost time. How he'd changed, how he'd grown!

Lila led him to the sofa in her living room and sat on the opposite end. Close but not overwhelmingly so. He was like a deer: one misstep, and she'd spook him.

"Thanks for coming," Lila said. "Fox really scared me."

Aidan sighed and scratched the back of his neck. "I know. He came by our house too." Up close, she could see how red and tired his eyes were, how unevenly his stubble was growing. "Every time I think it's over, someone dredges it back up."

He was fighting too hard to escape it, like he was trapped in a riptide. The only way to get through it was to embrace it. Embrace her. Let Josie's spirit cross through him, and the path would open to him too.

"You are the only other person in the world who knows what this is like," Lila said, knee bumping against his like they were twenty-four again and on their first date.

She even looked the same. Arthur and Greer and Cara and Tommy had set the clock ten years back. They swam around inside her; she could feel them smiling at the way things were clicking into place.

Aidan very gently moved his leg away and checked the time.

"I don't want to be alone in this again." A single perfect tear dropped down Lila's cheek.

"You're not alone," Aidan said.

Lila let out a flat laugh. "Aidan, we haven't spoken in five months. Not for my lack of trying."

Aidan was silent, grey eyes inscrutable. Josie's eyes, yet concerned and distant. He wasn't being fair to her.

"I'm sorry," he said finally. "I didn't know what to say."

"So, you hid from me?" Lila said. "After everything we've been through?"

"I love my family," he finally said. But his voice was weak, like the specter of Sonnet was putting a gun to his head.

"Your second family," Lila said quietly.

"Don't." She could hear the pain in his voice.

"Do you think shoving her down and locking her away will make her disappear?" Lila said. "You start over, build a new house on her grave, and you can erase her? She will always be with you, Aidan. Aren't you tired of pretending she doesn't exist?"

Aidan blinked back tears. "It's too painful."

He'd taken care of her when Josie disappeared; she'd leaned all her weight onto him, leaving him no space for himself. Now it was Lila's turn to return the favor. He needed her.

Lila pulled him into a hug, and Aidan wept into her shoulder. "Every time I think it's over and I can start to move on, she comes back."

"But don't you see? She doesn't *want* you to move on," Lila said. "Josie needs us."

Aidan shook his head. "Lila, she's gone."

"When you wake up at two a.m. and feel the spot on your chest where she used to sleep but she's not there, what do you do? Or when you're driving and you look in the rearview and her car seat is missing? Do you tell Sonnet? Do you talk to your wife about her?"

Aidan was silent.

"No. Of course not. She wouldn't understand. None of them would. The only person in the world who knows what you lost is me. You can hide, but I see you. I know you, Aidan."

It was only then that Lila realized how close their faces were. She saw the hunger in his eyes. Grief made you desperate for any spare flicker of connection. She'd been successfully distracting herself from the gaping wound inside for a year.

"Tell me to stop," Lila whispered. "Tell me to go, and you'll never see me again. You won't have to—"

Aidan kissed her.

This time, when they broke apart, it was to pull Aidan's shirt over his head and unbutton the clasp on Lila's blouse until both were naked on her living room couch, tossing pillows to make more room. It was remarkably familiar.

It should have been the culmination of everything she had been working toward since she set foot in Los Angeles. It should have made her feel whole inside, like she had, after eleven years of wandering, finally returned home. But all Lila could think about was Sylvie.

Sylvie liked to say she played Lila's holes like a flute, which Lila found disgusting, but Aidan didn't play at all. He made love to her heavy and gentle, so slow she almost fell asleep. Lila reminded herself as he went that Josie would be happy that her parents were together, where they belonged. Aidan was the man she loved.

Afterward, they lay entangled with each other. Aidan traced loopy patterns on Lila's back, humming to himself. "Is that Bob Dylan?" Lila murmured, flipping over to face him.

Aidan smiled softly, sadly. "I think about the last time I held her that night constantly. I sang 'Farewell, Angelina' to put her to sleep. Remember how important it was to me for her to like good music?"

"You were dead set on her refined palate." Lila chuckled.

His grey eyes brimmed, like a road after a heavy rain. She had resented him for so long because she had to bear the public brunt of their pain, but she had never considered it from his perspective. The Devlin baby would always be hers, not his. You could forget Aidan was Josie's father at all. He hadn't been a perfect father, or even a great one, but he was good. And he was learning.

Lila reached out to take his hand and then her insides hollowed.

"Wait, what do you mean you sang to her? You told me she was asleep when I got home." Something cold knocked at Lila's shoulder.

Aidan smiled, confused. "I meant I sang it to her earlier that day. Before I put her to bed."

"That's not what you said, though. You said that night," Lila said.

He shot her an odd look. She was losing him. "You're right." Aidan shrugged. "I misremembered. It would have been earlier."

"You didn't get home till ten that night. You said Lydia Novak put her to bed and you checked on her and she was asleep," Lila said. She tried to stop herself, to tell herself this line of questioning was ridiculous, to enjoy the moment she had worked so hard for, but the thing inside her pushed to keep going.

They stared at each other. "What's your point, Lila?"

"I'm just trying to understand what you meant."

"All I meant was I miss singing to my child."

"You were wearing shoes that night," Lila said.

For a split second, Aidan opened his mouth and shut it. Faltering. Then he resumed that quizzical look on his face. "Okay? I don't remember."

"You have never in your life worn shoes in the house. Especially not if you were just in our bedroom."

"I don't know, I was drunk."

"*What do you mean you were drunk?*"

He'd told the police he'd driven home sober. Tim Weber had sworn he'd been sober.

"I mean—God, I was just buzzed from Tim's. I wasn't paying attention . . ."

Lila stared up at the ceiling. Willed her mind to stop, to accept what he was saying, to let it go. To be happy. She had been *so close* to happy.

"Do you think Arthur Allen killed Josie?" Lila asked.

"Jesus Christ, Li, what is going on?" Aidan swung a leg onto the ground, running a hand through his hair.

Lila sat up beside him. "I used to. I was positive it was him. I *convinced* myself. But in my heart of hearts, I knew he was too dumb to have gotten away with it."

Aidan stood up. His left hand was shaking, his Rolex bouncing against his wrist. "Lila, calm down—"

"The Mercedes was dented," Lila said. "Do you remember that? I asked you how it got that dent, and you said someone backed into you that night. But that wasn't true, was it? You drove home drunk and you bumped it, didn't you?"

"Tim lived five minutes away from us. I was maybe tipsy and not as careful as I could have been, but that doesn't mean I . . ." He couldn't finish the sentence.

It was him. All this time, it had been him. Those stupid theories of Josie being dropped were right, the culprit had been wrong. Everyone had been so preoccupied with the photos of her doing cocaine that night, they never considered Aidan might not have been sober either. When he'd held her and watched the world rip her to shreds, it had been him.

The breath was sucked out of her lungs and black dots blurred her vision, and she could only just stand there in silence as Aidan collected his things and hurried out of the house.

The path back home had ended with Aidan, but she had gotten the *why* all wrong.

It was so blisteringly simple Lila wanted to scream. He had done the exact thing everyone had accused her of: gotten high and dropped Josie. He'd been so protective of his career that he was willing to see his wife go down for him. Put his extensive theater training to use.

And he'd kept in touch! For over ten years, he'd checked in, assured her that they were still family even as he moved on with his life and settled for cheap replacements. Her skin crawled, pulsing with all the times she'd let him touch her.

"I'm so sorry, Josie," she wept. She even felt sorry for bloody Arthur Allen. He was just like her, a casualty in Aidan's way.

He'd gotten away with everything. The police would never believe her; Aidan had worked hard to make sure she was perceived as unstable, too irrational to be trusted.

She'd underestimated him. It hadn't even occurred to her, even as a worst-case scenario. She didn't think he had the capacity for it. How naive she was. After *everything*. How woefully naive.

All this time, Josie had been screaming at her and she'd misunderstood what she was saying. Willfully ignorant, she'd let her feelings overshadow her judgment, and she'd failed her daughter *again*.

Lila had to make this right.

She didn't want to kill him. That would be too easy and too quick. He needed to suffer for what he had done. Lila thought about the agony he had put her through in those early weeks, like her insides had been ripped out and laid bare. Murder wouldn't do that. Physical pain wouldn't get to his raw core the way he'd gotten to hers. Even to someone like Aidan, there was one thing more precious to him than his own life.

It was time for him to understand what it was like to have the thing he loved most in the world—the little light that guided him—snuffed out.

TWENTY-EIGHT

The world didn't punish men like Aidan. They fell through the cracks, hiding behind meaner, uglier men, and were lauded for it. She had retreated across the world to mourn Josie. Aidan had filmed a Marvel movie.

LILA DROVE TO THE HOUSE AT THE TOP OF THE MOUNTAIN IN REVERENT silence. Sylvie sat beside her in the passenger seat, a ski mask resting at the top of her head, ready to be pulled down at a moment's notice. Her black eyes were alert and piercing, but she knew not to speak. When this was over, Lila would tell her how grateful she was. How grateful Josie would be.

They parked the van a distance from Aidan's gate, just out of view of the camera perched in the tree above. "We can climb over the wall," Lila said.

They slid on gloves, ski masks, and goggles, careful not to leave a trace of anything identifiable.

They shut the doors quietly behind them, carrying the bare minimum of supplies in a backpack on Sylvie's shoulder. Adrenaline flooded Lila when she stood outside, making her heart palpitate so fast she thought, for a moment, she might pass out. She paused, resting her hand against the van to regain her equilibrium. She forgot things like this could affect her.

Sylvie looked at her, concerned. Lila nodded, telling her she was ready to go on. They glanced to ensure no one was around and headed for the wall bordering the property. It was about eight feet high, keeping the gnarled old oak trees on the other side from pouring out.

Sylvie got down on one knee and folded her arms into a ready position. Lila put one foot into Sylvie's hands, and Sylvie boosted her up. Lila pulled herself up to the top and pulled Sylvie after her. One of the many bonuses of being wellness mavens was that they were light on their feet.

They sat atop the wall for a minute, catching their breath. The sky was black and clear and papered with tiny stars, unaffected by LA smog. As untouchable as Aidan.

They climbed down tree branches and landed neatly on the other side. Lila was struck by the ease of it, the fluidity. Like the universe was asking what had taken her so long.

When they emerged from the tree line, Lila motioned for Sylvie to follow her. There was another camera pointed at the front door but none on the side gate leading to the backyard.

They moved across the driveway like phantoms, quickly and in tandem. The night was so quiet that their footsteps on the gravel felt cacophonous. For a split second, Lila's mind leapt to Arthur Allen, wondering how he felt breaking into her house. But that wasn't real; the real villain had been sleeping next to her. And she grew angry all over again.

They scaled the side gate, and Sylvie unlatched it from the other side for an easier exit. The walkway opened onto the backyard, the infinity pool pouring into the canyon beyond it.

Lila tilted her head for Sylvie to follow. They stayed low to the ground as they crept across the lawn. The house was dark. Lila checked for signs of life, even a television on in the master bedroom above them, but all was dark. It was just past midnight now, and Lila knew he'd be long asleep for his early call time.

The girl's room was on the other side of the house, above the veranda that covered the decorative fire pit. When they reached the base, Lila tilted her head upward, and Sylvie understood.

They made their way up slowly, one by one. The pergola was sturdy underneath them, only shaking for a sliver of a moment. They climbed to the top, just at the base of Talia's bay window.

Lila peered inside; Talia was fast asleep. A hand rested on Lila's shoulder, and she jerked back—Sylvie was letting her know she was ready with the lockpick.

Lila stood back in silence as Sylvie worked on the window. She was so quick. Lila had no doubt this wasn't the first lock she had picked, which made her love her even more. When Sylvie was finished, she nudged the window open by a fraction of a hair. There was a magnet censor on the sill for the alarm. Sylvie glanced back at Lila and nodded. It was time.

Sylvie took a credit card from her pocket as Lila moved beside her, readying to open the window. "Count of three," Sylvie said. "One, two, three."

Lila opened the window as Sylvie slid the credit card over the censor to block the magnet. They froze for a second, waiting for the alarm to wail. It didn't. They waited another second to be sure it had worked, and then Lila slid the window open enough to crawl inside.

She hoisted herself over the sill onto Talia's pink-striped window bench. The air conditioner was running, breaking the silence with a faint hum. Lila removed the chloroform from her pocket and sprayed it on a rag.

Lila tiptoed to Talia's bed. She used to do it all the time with Josie, creep into the nursery to watch her, to marvel at her. After months of sleepless nights, Josie had overcome sleeping alone in the dark, a little miracle.

Her shadow hulked over Talia's tiny body, curled in a ball on her side. She murmured something, and Lila froze—no, she was just sleeping. Lila exhaled and raised the chloroform to her mouth. For a moment, her hand shook, but then she felt Josie's over it, guiding it into place.

For a second Talia's eyes blinked, hazy. "Mom?" she murmured. Before Lila could think of a reply, she went limp.

Lila pulled back the covers and lifted Talia out of bed gently. Yes, she could be gentle. Lila would take special care of her. She was so fragile. And the funny thing was the fragility would never go away as she grew up; she would just learn to hide it better. This would be justice for Josie and mercy for Talia. Save her from the darkness waiting just around the corner.

Lila passed Talia to Sylvie out the window and then climbed out after her. Sylvie wordlessly returned Talia to her. Only Lila could carry her; she was a mother, after all. She hoisted Talia's body over her shoulder and down they went, Talia not even slightly stirring.

They crept back across the yard, out the side gate, and into the driveway. Lila kept expecting Aidan to come running out after them, but he never did. This would be his greatest failure in life, not having the psychic bond that parents are supposed to. If only he'd been awake, if only he'd hired security. Lila hoped he was tormented by if onlys.

The climb up the front wall was far easier using the tree as footing. It had become almost like a game—this step, then that one. Nearly to safety now, Lila gave Talia to Sylvie again and returned to the ground, Sylvie following.

They jumped into the van, Sylvie in the driver's seat. Lila slid into the back to cradle Talia from the bumps and jolts of the ride. She was so small in her dachshund pajamas. Lila brushed the hair out of her eyes, and Talia smiled in her sleep. The engine hummed to life, and Sylvie drove off into the night.

IT WAS 12:45 WHEN THEY RETURNED TO THE ENCINO HOUSE. LILA OPENED the garage from her phone, and Sylvie drove the van inside. They could take no chances of a neighbor's Ring camera catching something. When the garage door shut behind them, Sylvie got out of the van and slid the back seat door open.

Talia was curled against Lila's chest like a newborn, eyes blissfully shut. This was probably the best night's sleep she'd ever had in her life.

Would ever have.

"What?" Sylvie said.

Lila blinked up at her. *Had she said that out loud?* "Help her out of the car."

Sylvie gently took Talia out of Lila's arms so Lila could get out of the van. The little girl's head lolled to the right, hanging downward.

"Support her head!" Lila hissed, hurrying to take Talia back.

Then she was safe and snug again in Lila's arms. She saw a world where Josie had a little sister and, despite her preteen protestations, wore beagle pajamas that matched Talia's dachshunds, and they slept in twin beds beside each other. If there ever were an intruder, sister would help sister.

Lila held Talia close enough to feel her heartbeat against the girl's forehead. She wanted Talia to know that she had a heart. That she liked that world and wished it were real, but that wasn't the world they lived in now.

Lila led Sylvie through the kitchen and into the living room, where she sat on the couch. Sylvie watched Lila watch Talia for a moment. "You having second thoughts?" she asked.

Lila smiled down at Talia's peaceful face. She was a beautiful little girl. "I've never been more sure of anything in my life," she said softly.

Sylvie's face flickered for a fraction of a second but returned to placid as soon as Lila met her eye. "I'll get everything ready," she said quickly, heading for the basement.

Lila understood. What they would have to do was not easy, and it was fair that Sylvie would not want to watch. She was a child. And still, Sylvie was going to help her anyway.

Aidan never loved her like that. Sylvie had been here all along, withstood Lila's bitterness and cruelty, and never asked for anything in return. That was true devotion. Persevering for the one you love in the face of terror. Lila's heart grew five sizes larger, overflowing with warmth. She'd always appreciated Sylvie, but she'd never *seen* her before. Now she did.

"Hey, Sylvie?" Lila said behind her.

Sylvie stopped and turned around to look back at her. "Yeah?"

"I love you."

Sylvie froze, her eyes comically wide. Her mouth opened, then shut, then opened again. A year ago, Lila would have said she looked like a fish. Now, Lila grinned.

Sylvie cleared her throat, pink dotting her cheeks. She appeared ten years younger, like a spring maiden in bloom. The most beautiful she had ever been. Lila vowed to spend the rest of her life working to capture the essence of how beautiful Sylvie looked in that moment. "I—I love you too."

"When this is over, we'll take a vacation, just the two of us. Go wherever you want," Lila said.

"*San Diego?!*" Sylvie gasped.

Lila could tell she wanted to stay and bask in their love, but Sylvie knew she had a job to do. They both did. So, she opened the basement door and disappeared down the stairs, and Lila was struck again by her gorgeous, divine commitment.

And then Lila was alone with the task at hand. Talia's chloroform would wear off soon; there was no time left to delay. Lila didn't want to fight; she wasn't cruel. This was about Aidan, not Talia. The girl deserved peace in her final moments.

Lila's hand moved to pick up a throw pillow, but it froze. *She's just a little girl.* Lila tried to grip the pillow, but her hand wouldn't budge. It was like she was paralyzed. Lila had done a lot of ugly things for her daughter, but even this was . . .

The grey thing bit at the walls of her stomach, but still, she didn't move. For a second, she wondered if it was possible to go back, to put Talia back, to resurrect the people she'd killed, to get back on the plane and go back to India and stay there. And maybe this had all been a long, horrible dream, and she'd wake up in the rocking chair in Josie's nursery, and she and Aidan would laugh about it in the morning.

The front door unlatched. Lila froze. Someone was breaking in.

Before she could move, the door opened, and there stood Maya, key in hand, eyes streaked with tears. "I'm sorry, I know it's late. I'm terrified about Peter, and I didn't know where to go."

She stopped speaking when she saw Lila on the ground beside a sleeping child.

Maya blinked. "Oh, I didn't . . ."

"I'm babysitting tonight," Lila said. "She fell asleep."

Maya looked from the little girl to Lila's hand on the pillow. This could be salvaged. Lila could fix this.

"I was just about to sleep on the ground beside her. She has bad nightmares," Lila added.

She sounded too desperate.

Maya smiled, but Lila couldn't read it. She had to believe her. The alternative was too terrible to comprehend. "You're a way better babysitter than I ever was."

"I had some practice," Lila said. Then she laughed, and Maya laughed, and they were laughing together, and everything was fine.

Maya glanced back at Talia, and her brow furrowed. "Isn't that Aidan Reynolds's daughter?"

Lila's mouth was suddenly so dry she couldn't swallow.

Before she could reply, a little hand shot up in the air. "W-where am I?"

Lila and Maya looked at each other and then at Talia. She was rapidly blinking on the couch, trying to get her bearings. Lila's heart sank.

"I should let you get back to, um, bed." Maya smiled, but it was wrong. It wasn't Maya; she wasn't looking at Lila the way she usually did. It was someone else, a body snatcher hiding in her skin.

Maya took careful, slow steps back toward the door, and her hand was fishing in her pocket to remove her phone.

"Drop the phone right now." Lila heard a click and turned to see Sylvie pointing her handgun at Maya's head.

Maya stumbled back, a bit in disbelief.

"*Now!*" Sylvie ordered, and Maya let the phone fall out of her hand. "Kick the phone to me," Sylvie snapped, and Maya realized she had no choice, so she did.

It was moving too fast, the world was starting to spin. "Let's all calm down," Lila started.

"Where's my mom?" Talia started to sit up, still groggy from the chloroform.

"Shit," Sylvie hissed, or maybe it was Lila, or maybe it was both at the same time. Lila couldn't remember; she couldn't remember anything except how dry her fucking throat was. She needed water, or she was going to pass out. *It was moving too fast.*

Tears welled up in Maya's eyes, and Lila could see her legs shaking beneath her jeans. "Maya, darling, it's going to be all right. Everything's going to be okay," Lila assured her. She stood, moving to go to her daughter, to comfort her, but Maya took a step backward.

Talia started to cry. Harsh, wailing cries. "*Where is my mom?*"

"We need to end this now," Sylvie said, pointing the gun at Maya. "Step back, Lila."

"No," Lila snapped. "No," she repeated, quieter now. They could figure this out. They still had time. They had no time. "Maya, take Talia. Pick her up. Everything's going to be fine."

Maya cautiously moved toward the couch and hesitated.

"Do it," Sylvie snarled, gesturing with the gun. Maya picked up the sobbing seven-year-old girl.

"Everything's all right, Maya," Lila told Maya, just like she told Josie after a bad dream. She was a good mom. "Go down into the basement, and we'll get this all sorted out. You're going to be fine."

Sylvie looked annoyed but dutifully shepherded Maya to the basement door. "It locks from the outside," she said as Maya stepped through the doorway. "Don't try anything."

"I promise everything will be fine." Lila nodded so vigorously that her neck cracked. Sylvie slammed the door in Maya's and Talia's teary faces and locked it.

TWENTY-NINE

Even after all the times Maya had come to Lila's house, she had never been down to the basement. She didn't even know Lila had one. She could hear faint arguing that faded off toward the kitchen and knew she couldn't wait by the door for them to come back.

"Where am I?" the little girl asked. She was woozy and disoriented. Lila must have drugged her.

Maya forced a wave of nausea down. Lila fucking drugged her ex-husband's child. Sylvie had pointed a gun in her face. They were arguing about whether to murder her. It was so ludicrous it didn't feel real, like a very bad intrusive thought that plowed into her mind on a shitty workday.

But this was real, and there was a kid in her arms. "Who are you?" the girl asked.

"I'm Maya," Maya forced herself to say. "What's your name?"

"Talia," she said. "Where are we?"

Maya racked her brain to parse out an answer that would convey the gravity of the situation without completely terrifying her. She thought about when adults talked down to her as a kid and how much she hated it. If she wanted Talia to listen to her—and she needed her to listen—she couldn't sugarcoat the truth. "Someone trapped us down here, and we're gonna find a way out."

"Like Nancy Drew."

"What?"

"Bad guys trap her, but she always finds a way," Talia said.

"Exactly," Maya said. "You're going to have to be very quiet, though. Can you do that for me?"

Talia nodded.

"Okay," Maya said, more to herself than to Talia. "Okay."

The stairwell led down to a long hallway with a series of doors. At the very end, there was a light under the door. Probably where Sylvie had come from. Maya felt around her pockets for anything she could use as a weapon in case something was behind the door waiting for her. She was empty-handed except for her car keys, which weren't even keys, just a fob.

"*Fuck me,*" she whispered, then looked at Talia. "Sorry."

She couldn't afford the time to hesitate. Lila liked her, she knew that, beyond even the way the best bosses liked their assistants. But it wasn't enough. And even if she did wait and they did let her go by some miracle, Maya was sure Talia wasn't going to make it out alive.

She thought about Peter and about what he would do in this situation. *It's not about me. You are the most capable person I know,* he would have said.

She rolled her eyes at his imaginary reply because it was so clearly untrue. She was screwed. But Peter believed it, and he was the best person she knew, so she'd have to believe it too.

The first door on her left was dark. Maya opened it before she could hesitate. It was just a home gym: a treadmill, a cycling machine, and some weights in the corner. A golf putter leaned against the wall.

"Can I put you down, Talia? Are you okay to walk?" Maya asked.

"I'm okay," Talia said, and Maya lowered her to the ground. She wobbled for a second but had mostly recovered from the drug's effects.

Maya grabbed the golf club. "Stay close," she told Talia, and headed out down the hall, toward the light.

Maya stopped to listen for any sound, but it was silent. She even waited for typical house sounds, the creaks and the wheezes that her house in New England had. But there was nothing. The house was too new.

"Stay out here until I tell you you can come in. Okay?" she told Talia. Whatever was on the other side, Talia didn't need to be the first to see.

"Okay," Talia said.

Maya gently ushered her to the side and placed her hand on the knob. She readied her golf club as the door swung open to reveal—

Nothing. The room was empty. Maya relaxed, but only slightly. The room looked like a wine cellar, but there was no wine. Rows of labeled jars lined the wine racks and a steel table stood in the center. Maya peered closer—there was medical equipment and . . . a saw?

She shrank back. She did not believe in ghosts, but even she could feel something very dark and very wrong had happened here.

"Stay out there, Talia, I'll be right . . ." Her eyes fell on a jar labeled *GREER HOUSER*. It was a fine beige powder, nearly empty.

Wasn't that the lady with that stupid podcast about Lila's kid? She'd read Lila's Wikipedia entry when she got her job. Her blood ran cold.

But inside the jar was only powder. Maya shook her head: *Just a coincidence.* It wasn't like Lila had dissolved her body and was snorting her—that was absurd.

"Just a coincidence," Maya assured herself, and then wondered why she was giving a woman who had locked her in a basement the benefit of the doubt.

She looked at the jar beside it: *ALLEN*. It was empty. Arthur Allen killed Josie. But Allen was a common enough name; it could easily mean anything.

Maya picked up the one beside it labeled *MAX*—no idea who that was. It was half full of the same fine taupe powder as the others.

What the hell was this powder? So, so fine, a white the color of eggshells. It reminded her of working with Lila on beauty products in the office lab. But that was impossible, with the skin cream she was using—

Maya grabbed the wine rack to steady herself as the world shifted underneath her. It was impossible. She refused to believe it. Putting people's collagen into beauty products? That would be fucking insane. It was unthinkable.

How would anyone be able to tell once it was bleached like bovine collagen is? a voice whispered in her head. Maya shook it off, squeezing her eyes shut, willing it away. *That detective said something about people connected to the case going missing,* the voice reminded her. *But there hadn't been any bodies.*

All those disappearances with no bodies.

Pure dread consumed her. Every fiber in her being wanted to turn around and walk out the door. But instead, Maya sifted through the shelves of jars until she found the name she knew at her core was already there.

PETER.

It was full.

He'd gone missing only a few days ago, after all.

Maya couldn't contain her dread then, or perhaps the dread was actually nausea. Either way, Maya pitched over and vomited.

SYLVIE SHUT THE DOOR ON MAYA AND TALIA, AND THEN IT WAS JUST LILA and Sylvie alone, chests heaving. Out of breath even though they'd hardly moved. "That wasn't necessary," Lila said. "I was handling it."

"The second she recognized Aidan's kid . . . when that girl is reported missing tomorrow, she'll connect the dots. We can't take that chance," Sylvie said.

"I trust her," Lila insisted. Maya had been at her side every step of the way. Maya wouldn't let her down when she needed her most. They were family. Family members could get upset with each other, but they always came back together where they belonged.

"You can't," Sylvie said. "Lila, I'm serious. I know how much you care about her, but you don't know that she won't turn around and go straight to the police."

Lila scoffed, storming away from her.

"Where are you going?"

"To the kitchen, I need water. Is that okay with you?" Lila snapped. Sylvie was impossible to reason with when she decided to be obstinate.

Lila grabbed mineral water from the fridge and chugged, Sylvie practically nipping at her heels. The overwhelming appreciation she'd felt for Sylvie faded with each minute. Why did Sylvie insist on inserting herself where she didn't belong? She needed a goddamn muzzle.

"Lila?" Sylvie said, a little quieter now.

Lila did not respond until she finished the bottle. Her throat was still dry. "You're jealous," she said.

Sylvie scoffed. "I'm not jealous of a twenty-three-year-old."

"I'm not blind, Sylvie. You resent her because, at your core, you are so insecure that no amount of affection can fix you. And the only way you get my undivided attention is to eliminate her," Lila said.

"Lila, no, that's not true. Yes, I love you; that's not a secret. But I love you so much I would never do anything to hurt you. I swear on my life, I'm just trying to protect you." Sylvie eyes welled with tears. She was telling the truth.

Lila gripped her shoulders. She had to shake *sense* into her. "Why can't you see it, Sylvie?"

"See what?" Sylvie raised an eyebrow.

"I know her, Sylvie. She'll help me," Lila said.

Sylvie shook her head, still not understanding. "Lila . . ."

Lila grabbed Sylvie's chin, forcing her to meet her eye. She wasn't listening. "Sylvie, I *know* her. She's my daughter."

Sylvie stilled. "What?"

"I never believed in spiritual stuff. It wasn't because I didn't want to, but I had never experienced it. I was so broken, I couldn't comprehend that pure goodness could actually exist. And then I met Maya. I knew—I knew from the second I met her that she was different. That she was special. Just looking at her, I saw that spark in her. There's a piece of Josie that lives inside of her, Sylvie, I know there is. Josie may be gone, but her spirit lives on in Maya." Lila took Sylvie's hands in hers and squeezed.

Sylvie looked even paler. "But . . . but," she sputtered, "Maya was already a kid when Josie died."

Lila laughed. "I'm not saying she was reincarnated. There's a piece of Josie's soul in Maya, and she found her way back to me. I will protect her with everything I have. We need to let her out and explain the situation to her. Tell her everything. I tried to hide it from her to protect her before, but I understand that was wrong now. She'll help us. The three of us are a family."

A bead of sweat dripped down Sylvie's temple. "She won't, Lila. She might pretend, but we will both be arrested for murder. *Multiple murders.* Do you get that? We'll go to jail for the rest of our lives."

Lila took a step toward her until they were inches apart. Millimeters. Their lips were nearly touching. "If you touch a hair on her fucking head"—Lila reached out and tucked a wisp of black hair behind Sylvie's ear—"I'll kill you."

"She's not Josie," Sylvie insisted. "She can't be."

"You have no idea what you're talking about," Lila said. "I'm going to let her out and get this settled."

She started toward the basement door. Sylvie ran after her. "Lila . . . Lila, please listen to me. I'll never ask you for anything ever again. Please don't do this, please just stay with me. Maya isn't Josie."

Lila ignored her, hand moving to unlock the dead bolt. Sylvie grabbed her and yanked her backward.

"She can't be," Sylvie said. "Because Josie's *still alive.*"

THIRTY

Excerpts taken from THE DEVLIN BABY: AN ORAL HISTORY, PART II, by Lila Devlin's imagination. The following oral history has been compiled and edited over the last five minutes from a primary source (like, the most important one) to piece together a background and timeline of the most infamous crime of the twenty-first century.

SYLVIE LIGHTLY (*kidnapper*): I was broke. I barely made rent with my assistant job on top of dog walking on top of babysitting. I was drowning, Lila. Every day on my lunch break, I'd drive up from the office in Beverly Hills and walk the meanest, most poorly trained dogs I'd ever met. Rich people don't give a fuck about training their dogs because they know somebody else will deal with the worst of them. I didn't mind, though. I always loved your neighborhood. It's my favorite in LA. It was so peaceful. When I was Cara's intern, I used to do errands for her sometimes. Little drop-offs outside your gate. The guy that lived next to you in that mansion that looked exactly like the White House, Bill Thomas? He had these three goldendoodles that were complete nightmares. The scar on my leg? That's from them. I hated those dogs, but I still showed up every day to do a lap with them around the neighborhood, and we would always pass your house. And people like me who worked for the homeowners—we'd chat. I knew Lydia Novak and the gardeners—you look for friendly faces to commiserate when everything around you costs millions of dollars, and you stick out like a sore thumb. One day, I saw you with Josie on your porch through the gate. You were so beautiful, Lila, you always were, and she looked just like you. And I realized I couldn't resent you then because you were so innocent and so perfect that I knew deep down if you knew me, we would be the same.

My boyfriend at the time—well, he wasn't my boyfriend. He was my husband, David. You remember him? When I met him, he was vibrant. He had this curiosity and this love of life, and he sparked it in me too. And then his mom got diagnosed with breast cancer, and he just broke. The cancer took whatever life he had in him away too. And seeing how it hurt him—it broke my heart, Lila. And we couldn't do anything about it; we just had to watch her slowly die. And that meant watching David die too.

So one day, when I was walking the doodles, I passed you and Josie. She was in a stroller, and I didn't want to frighten her, so I moved the dogs off the sidewalk to let you pass. And you looked at me—you looked me right in the eyes—and you said thank you. No one on your street ever bothered to acknowledge that I even existed.

And in that moment, I had an epiphany. Like you did, with glob. If I took Josie, just for a little while, I could make enough ransom money to save David and his mom. I couldn't lose him, Lila. He was everything to me. And I could feel him starting to peel away. And in my soul, I knew you would understand. Because you're just like me. By then, I'd been working for the Thomases for a year and knew your neighborhood, but I needed to know your house. Arthur Allen was new, and he loved his . . . proximity to you. To celebrity. So I struck up a friendship with him, and eventually, one day, when you weren't home, he showed me the outside of the house. The big tree right outside Josie's window.

You know me, Lila. I am diligent. I am careful. I would come and sit outside your gate and watch you come and go. I set up a Google Alert for your and Aidan's names. I got to know your patterns. I didn't know what day I would make my move, but I knew the opportunity would come soon because you were climbing out of your depression. I was so proud of you, Lila, seeing you champion your mental health.

And then, one night, I got a notification that you were out at a bachelorette party. TMZ was posting photos of you doing coke. So I drove to your place and waited for Lydia Novak to drive home, and then I went in. I used a ladder to get to Josie's room, and she was fast asleep; she didn't notice a thing. I carried her down, and she was snug in her car seat—I bought her a car seat, I made sure she was safe—within a few minutes. It was painless, I was very protective of her.

At the time, David and I were living in a one-bedroom in Van Nuys. I hid Josie in the closet. It was ventilated with lots of space. I made sure she ate, and she thought it was an adventure. I wanted to bring her back to you—I tried. I made good on Josie's exchange, but when that cop shot at me, I drove off. It's like when you're on an airplane, and you secure your oxygen mask before helping someone else. I had to put myself first. And then it all got so muddled and messy.

David was staying at his mom's house so often that he didn't even know Josie was staying with me until he came home for a change of clothes. He was furious, but everyone's angry when they don't understand. I tried to explain, but he wouldn't listen. And I realized he would never listen, and he would never understand the sacrifice that I had made for him and his mother, who had never given a shit about me. So, I shot him. I told you, when we killed Nico, I knew what I was doing. I had practice.

I was scared. Everything about your case was blown so hideously out of proportion that I had no other choice. I decided I would wait a few months for the furor to die down. When the body was found in that lake, I had nothing to do with that. I don't know whose body it was. Josie was with me. But once everyone had accepted she was dead, I left her outside a fire station in Riverside. I saw someone bring her inside. I didn't want to retraumatize you by bringing her back. And I had to think of myself—the oxygen mask, remember?

THIRTY-ONE

A low wheezing moan stole the air from Lila's lungs. She stumbled backward, gripping the countertop to stay standing. Sylvie stood wide-eyed and open-mouthed—she had struck herself dumb.

"You knew. From the moment I walked into your office, you knew Josie was alive," Lila whispered.

Sylvie shook her head rapidly, so fast she was a blur. "No, no, Lila, you don't understand. I did it for you. So you could be free, so you could move on."

But Lila wasn't listening. She had crawled inside herself, whispering, "Josie's been alive all this time, and you kept her from me . . ."

"Lila, I have no idea where she is now. She's a needle in a haystack. What if you couldn't find her? I was trying to protect you." Sylvie shook Lila's shoulders rapidly, trying to make her meet her eyes, but Lila was focused solely on a spot just past her on the wall.

"*Protect me?*" Lila spat, almost laughing.

"It's like I told you, the day I first met you, and you had that dirty-brown hair and I told you to go red, remember that? Remember? And then the next time you walked in, and you were so beautiful? And I told you, 'If you think you hate what I did, imagine how I feel.' I meant it. All I could do was make it up to you.

"I will devote my life to making it up to you if you let me. I was in shock when you walked into my office; I couldn't believe the odds. And then I realized it was fate. Fate giving me a second chance to make it up to you. To guide you, follow you, protect you, love you." Sylvie dropped to her knees, holding Lila's feet. "I worship you. You are a goddess to me. Please let me take care of you."

Tears poured down Lila's cheeks, her heart shattering. Sylvie searched Lila's face for a sign of anything, but her eyes were in some distant, far-off place.

"Josie . . ." Lila murmured. "My little girl . . ."

"I love you, Lila, do you understand me? No one will ever love you like I love you. I have killed for you, Lila, who else can say that? And I will do it again. You tell me to jump, I'll ask how high and do it in heels. Please, just tell me how I can make this right. I'm so sorry." Sylvie convulsed with sobs.

"Oh my god!" Lila let out a cry of raw anguish, not even acknowledging Sylvie was there at all. She wasn't *listening*, she never *listened*.

"*I LOVE YOU!*" Sylvie screamed.

"I . . . wasted so much time." Lila staggered away from Sylvie, and her legs started to give out from under her. She grabbed the table to steady herself, chest heaving.

Was it even possible to move past this? Lila wished it were. Lila loved her. After everything they had been through, could she really lose her now?

Lila slowly turned around to face Sylvie, who was waiting on the floor in prayer. Lila extended a hand down to her, pulling Sylvie to her feet.

"I don't want to lose you," Lila said.

Sylvie brightened into a wary, but hopeful, smile. "I will do the work, Lila, I promise. Everything I did, everything I have done, everything I will do, is for you."

Lila took a shaky step toward her. Then another. Sylvie licked her lips; they were slick and cherry red.

"When we have the girls downstairs settled, we'll take a vacation. How's that? Go to San Diego, just like we talked about?" Sylvie said.

Lila wrapped her arms around Sylvie, feeling her heart beat in her chest. They stayed there for years, until their skin weathered and their bones gnarled into each other, petrified. Just holding her was enough for Lila to know everything would be all right.

"What have I always said, Sylvie?" Lila said. Sylvie pressed her cheek into her shoulder. "I find peace in my life; in my life I make peace."

Lila gently removed one of her arms from Sylvie's waist and reached into her back pocket. While Sylvie nuzzled further, Lila wrapped her fingers around the gun's grip and pulled it out. She took a step backward, and before Sylvie could register what was happening, Lila shot her in the stomach.

They stared at each other, stared at the blooming pool of crimson. Sylvie's face turned ashen. Time exhaled, and Sylvie stumbled backward toward the oven and fell to the ground. Her arm jolted upward in a desperate attempt to catch her fall, bumping the knob for the gas stove and igniting it.

A violet flame burst out of the stovetop as Sylvie hit the rug with a moan. Lila stalked toward her and stood over Sylvie's shaking body. Lila's mind was infected with realizations; moments she'd spent with Sylvie she'd been too blind to notice—God, she'd been so blind.

"You didn't come inside the trailer when I killed Arthur Allen," Lila said. "He would have recognized you."

"Lila, please." Sylvie raised her shaking hands to cover herself as Lila raised the gun. "I love you."

"I don't care," Lila said, and fired.

But Sylvie was ready, she grabbed Lila's leg and jerked her to the ground, the gun firing into the ceiling as she fell. Sylvie was on top of her, wrestling for the gun. It fired again and again, bullets ricocheting off the marble countertops, before it ran out of bullets.

Sylvie punched Lila in the throat and grabbed the gun as soon as her grip loosened. "I was trying to protect you," Sylvie cried, slamming the barrel against her face.

Lila tried to wriggle away, but Sylvie was too fast. Her strength was superhuman. She grabbed Lila by the hair and bashed her head into the kitchen island.

"Why couldn't you let me protect you?"

The pain was white hot. Lila jabbed Sylvie in her bullet wound, and she howled. With shaky legs, Lila got to her feet, leaning against the counter for support, stumbling to get as far away from Sylvie as she could. Her hands fumbled for a weapon, anything nearby she could defend herself with. She found a bottle of coconut oil on the countertop and gripped it by the neck, hurling it at Sylvie's head.

But Sylvie was too fast. She ducked down, and the bottle crashed into the stove. A giant flame erupted, consuming the oven and the wall behind it. Lila fell backward, helpless to the rush of scalding heat. When she picked herself off the ground, the fire had spread to the wooden cabinets above the stove and only grew hungrier as it spun outward. She moved to find a blanket, something to stop it, but noticed Sylvie on her hands and knees, attempting to crawl toward the front door.

Lila grabbed a bottle of olive oil but did not make the same mistake. She smashed the bottle against the countertop and brandished the broken neck. Little pieces of glass caught in her skin. She staggered toward Sylvie and yanked her left leg back as hard as she could. Sylvie slid across the floor, pounding against the hardwood like a toddler throwing a tantrum.

Lila rolled her over onto her back and straddled her torso, ignoring Sylvie's petulant slaps and scratches. "Hold *still*," Lila hissed, struggling to keep Sylvie in one place long enough to slit her throat. She was an animal cornered and would fight until her heart stopped.

Her teeth sunk into the flesh of Lila's ear, and Lila screamed. Sylvie pulled as hard as she could, and suddenly the world was muffled, and Lila could feel wetness trickling down the side of her neck. Sylvie spat something large out, her teeth stained with blood.

With the remaining strength she had, Lila dragged the edge of the bottle across Sylvie's velvet throat, leaving a trail of glittering red stars. When she reached the other side, she went back over her work and then back again, digging deeper and deeper. Sylvie coughed and gurgled, her pupils huge black orbs.

And odder still, as the life left her body, Sylvie used her remaining strength to stretch her lips into a wide smile. "What?!" Lila snapped.

Sylvie couldn't speak; she only smiled, eyes drifting down to Lila's chest. Lila followed her line of sight and saw a giant carving knife sticking out of her heart.

"Oh," Lila said softly, and collapsed on the floor beside her.

They lay on the ground for what felt like ages as the fire crawled into view. It was eating the house alive.

Good, Lila thought. She was already dead. She was already dead, and this was a dream. Best for the fire to swallow them whole.

In the last few seconds of her life, Sylvie's hand nudged out to brush Lila's fingers. Pleading to be held. A gaping black hole opened on the floor before them, and Lila knew that wherever they were going, she did not want to go alone. Every synapse in Lila's brain screamed as she used her remaining strength to rest her hand on Sylvie's.

She hoped Maya wouldn't have to see her like this.

Her eyes snapped open.

Maya.

• • •

Maya stood weeping in a pool of her own vomit. Her body gently swayed like the wind was rocking it from side to side. Peter watched her silently from his jar.

She heard Talia's voice in the hallway. "Maya?"

She didn't reply, the words caught in her throat. Every muscle in her body was paralyzed. Peter was dead, and it was her fault. Her hand squeezed around Peter's ring. Lila had been a caring boss, nothing like any boss she'd ever had before. But Maya never imagined she was capable of . . . How could she not have known? She'd missed the signs, and Peter was dead. Because of her.

"Maya, I smell fire," Talia said.

Maya inhaled, and a rope of thick smoke wafted under her nose and hit the back of her throat. She let out a deep hacking cough, hands on her knees to steady herself. "Fuck," she whispered.

Talia was right. She couldn't give up now, not when a little girl was depending on her. It may have been her fault Peter died, but she wouldn't let Talia's death be her fault too. She steeled herself and went out into the hallway.

Smoke was gathering in the air, casting plumed shadows down the corridor. Maya took Talia's hand, clutching the golf club in the other. "Cover your mouth and nose with your shirt. We gotta find a way out."

She ran down the hallway, not daring to cast a glance up at the door to the first floor, where ripples of black smoke were billowing down. Lila and Sylvie had set the house aflame and fled to destroy Maya and all the evidence of what they had done. It filled Maya with rage—all the posturing about making the world a better place and healing her trauma. Everyone had trauma; it didn't give you an excuse to become a psychopath.

Maya kicked each door open, looking for a door, a window, anything leading to the outside, but there was nothing.

"We're stuck," Talia whispered beside her.

The flames were getting louder; she could hear wood cracking above them. Maya knelt to Talia's level. "Focus on me, all right? We'll find a way. I'm okay, you're okay."

Talia wasn't paying attention. Her eyes kept shooting back and forth, tears gathering. Maya gripped her shoulders, forcing her to make eye contact.

"Say it with me. I'm okay, you're okay."

She needed to hear someone else say it.

"I'm okay, you're okay," Talia said quietly.

"Good," Maya said. "Let's get out of here."

Maya opened the door at the very end of the hallway and found a small family room illuminated by a ray of moonlight.

"Look." Talia pointed at a small, slim window at the very top of the high walls. There was no way Maya would be able to fit, but a seven-year-old might be able to squeeze through.

The window had no lock, no way to open it, so Maya motioned for Talia to step aside. "Stand back," she said. As soon as Talia was safely out of the way, she swung the golf club and bashed the window in again and again, until the glass shattered and fell to the floor.

"Help me push this couch under the window," Maya said, and they shoved a blue upholstered couch just under the small window. The air was chalky and rough to breathe; just pushing the couch across the room sent Maya into a coughing spell. The smell was putrid, like burning hair multiplied by a million—Maya recognized it as death. And it was coming for them, fast and hard.

"The second you get up there, you run to the neighbors," Maya told the little girl. "The Browns live next door, they're nice. They'll help you. Knock on their door—pound on it. If they don't come, pick up a rock and throw it through the window, anything to trigger their alarm so the police will come. We need to draw attention, okay?"

Talia nodded, hugging her dachshund pajamas.

"You're gonna be great," Maya said. She stood up on the couch and bent down, making a step with her hands to boost Talia up. But Talia hesitated.

"What about you?" she said, her little forehead furrowed.

"I'll be right behind you," Maya said.

"How?" Talia said.

"Like Nancy Drew, right? I'll find a way." Maya smiled, but it was wobbly. Then she remembered the keys in her pocket. "Here, take my car keys."

She thrust the fob into Talia's hand. Talia looked at her, confused. "You want me to drive?"

"This red button will start the car alarm. As soon as you're out of here, hit the button and let the alarm go off. It'll wake the neighbors,"

Maya said. Maybe if Talia got help fast enough, they could rescue her before she burned. She knew not to get her hopes up.

Talia took a step into Maya's hands, and Maya summoned all the strength she didn't have and hoisted her up to the window. Talia gripped the edge and swung one leg over, then the other, pajamas crunching on the remains of the glass. She was through, she was outside, casting Maya a nervous look back. Knowing, on some level, she was leaving her to die.

"Go," Maya urged her, and Talia disappeared from sight.

As soon as Talia was gone, Maya collapsed to the ground, gasping for air. Her lungs were screaming, shrill and high. The basement was so hot she could feel her skin loosening to drip to the floor. Her mind was growing untethered and blurry.

A part of her wanted to curl into a little ball and let go and hope she'd get to see Peter again. But her life existed before Peter and would go on long after. She had her mom and her dad and her sister and her friends, and she would be okay.

If she could just get out of Lila's burning house.

Maya forced herself back to her feet, covering her mouth and nose with her shirt. There had to be another way. The corridor was even hotter now with dry, baking warmth. She glanced back up at the basement stairs and saw the door was open.

It had been locked just a few minutes ago—had the fire somehow managed to open it? Or worse, was Lila still up there?

"Fuck it." Maya gripped the golf club.

Maya climbed the stairs, getting hotter and hotter. The smoke poured in thick waves, swarming around her. She had to stop and steady herself multiple times, catch what little breath she had. At the top, the fire was so acutely near that her eyes watered. The golf club shook as she walked out into the living room.

She saw no trace of Lila and Sylvie, but then, she could barely see anything. The entire room was aflame, a sea of reds. Maya ducked to her knees, crawling under the banner of smoke that hung above her.

The air caught in her lungs like a thousand tiny needles, but Maya forced herself to keep crawling. Death was creeping up behind her; she saw little spots in her vision. If she hesitated for a second, she'd be lost.

Something groaned beside her. At first, she thought it was the window bench falling to the ground, but then, out from curls of grey, she saw an outline of a figure lying on the ground.

Maya waved the smoke away, and there was Lila. Her face was so revolting that Maya let out a gasp. She was caked in fresh blood like she had been mauled by a bear. Her skin was bubbling and curdling; her brows and lashes were completely singed off. One of her ears was missing, leaving a hollow of gushing blood from one side of her head.

But her eyes were open, and she was alive. Barely. She looked at Maya with pleading brown eyes, and Maya realized Lila had opened the door for her.

She was asking for forgiveness.

It made Maya sad that even in the last moments of Lila Devlin's life, she was still waiting to hear what someone else thought of her.

But Maya didn't owe her anything. She turned away from Lila and sprinted out the door.

THIRTY-TWO

In her final moments, Lila Devlin's life did not flash before her eyes.

Instead, she found herself in a crowded grocery store. A middle-aged woman waited at the checkout counter while a bored thirteen-year-old girl with bright grey eyes browsed magazines on the rack beside her. She paused on some salacious tabloid with Lila's face plastered on the cover. It read "LILA DEVLIN—BEAUTY BUTCHER." The little girl picked it up and started to thumb through the pages.

"Mom, can I get this?" she asked.

"Josie." Lila knew that voice even though she'd never heard it before. She'd waited eleven years to hear that voice. "*Josie!*" She sprinted toward her.

The older woman took the magazine out of her hands. "No, hon, you'll get nightmares."

"Josie." Lila was right beside her now. Her hair was an auburn color tied up in a ponytail, her nose Lila's pert little snub. "Josie, please, you have to listen to me. They're gonna tell you things about me; none of them are true. Everything I have ever done—all of it was for you. Do you hear me?"

Josie didn't. Lila reached for her, but her hands passed through Josie's sweatshirt. The woman put her credit card in her wallet and grabbed the shopping bags off the counter. Time was slipping away.

Tears flowed freely down Lila's cheeks. With every bit of strength she had, would ever have, she reached out and tapped Josie on the shoulder.

And Josie stopped and glanced back at her.

Lila let out a strangled gasp and seized her shoulders. "Lots of people are going to talk about me, I don't care if the whole world talks about me. You're the only one that matters. Don't forget me, Josie. *Please.*"

Josie's brow furrowed, and Lila realized she couldn't see her at all. Josie was only looking at the clock on the wall just behind her. Lila's heart plummeted.

Lila knelt to look Josie in the eye. "I hope I haunt you," she whispered.

"Come on, let's go home." The woman grabbed the shopping cart, and Josie turned to follow her.

"*Please,*" Lila said, trying to keep up with her.

But she was in a tunnel now, and Josie was fading away.

"Please let me haunt you."

ACKNOWLEDGMENTS

I wrote a book!!!! That's so crazy!! I can't really begin to express that two years ago when I wrote the first draft I thought it was impossible, but thanks to a boatload of people you are holding my first novel in your hands.

To Danielle Bukowski, my wonderful lit agent. You championed this book from the beginning; you embraced how weird it is. I say this without hyperbole: Your taking a chance on this manuscript changed the course of my life. I am forever grateful to you for believing in me when I didn't even believe in myself. You were right!

To my amazing editor, Ariana Sinclair, and everyone at William Morrow, thank you for your endless support and passion for this novel. You shaped it into something I am so proud of, and I am eternally grateful for you taking a chance on something that is so off-putting and weird and seeing the gem underneath.

To my team at CAA—Brooke Ehrlich, Will Watkins, Katie Laner, Jacquie Katz, Connie Yan, Pete Stein, and Brian Kend. I am so lucky to have you in my corner. Thank you for your wisdom and guidance on this insane rocket blast my career has been the last year.

To Craig Mazin—I got the idea for this book because we talked *Sweeney Todd* at lunch in the TLOU room and it reignited my love of it. I thanked you once for taking a chance on me, and you said I don't take chances. That meant the world to me. I am so lucky to call you a mentor and a friend.

To Josie Cassens—Thank you for being the most supportive friend I could ask for. I hope you take being the namesake of a dead* child as a compliment. I love you so much.

To Noelle Crochet Guardado—Thank you for always being my first reader. I asked you if the book was insane. You said yes. You also said keep going.

To all my friends and family who supported me throughout this journey. I couldn't have done it without you.

To Jane Smith, my fifth grade English teacher who was the first person who ever called me a good writer. It's been like seventeen years but I hope I made you proud. Please don't read this book.

To Stephen Sondheim—You are one of my greatest influences. I wish I had the chance to tell you while you were still here. But I hope you know, wherever you are, that though I will never write anything a fraction as good as your work, you inspire me every day to try.

To therapeutic ketamine—my doctor didn't believe me when I said I would put this in the acknowledgments. I'm not gonna name names, but thank you to my wonderful therapist! He knows who he is!

Thanks!

About the Author

Caroline Glenn is a screenwriter and novelist from Los Angeles, California. She attended Emerson College and NYU Tisch, where she studied playwriting. Her screenplay, *Don't Borrow Trouble*, was #6 on the 2024 Black List, the industry's top unproduced screenplays. She has worked as a writer's assistant on shows like *The Last of Us*, *The Miniature Wife*, and more. *Cruelty Free* is her debut novel.